Harmony Evans writes sexy, emotional contemporary love stories. She won 'Debut Author of the Year' for the Romance Slam Jam 2013 Emma Awards and was a double finalist for the 2012 *Romantic Times* Reviewers' Choice Awards. She lives in New York City. For more love stories that last a lifetime, follow @harmonyannevans

USA Today bestselling author **Natalie Anderson** writes emotional contemporary romance full of sparkling banter, sizzling heat, and uplifting endings – perfect for readers who love to escape with empowered heroines and arrogant alphas who are too sexy for their own good. When not writing, you'll find her wrangling her four children, three cats, two goldfish and one dog…and snuggled in a heap on the sofa with her husband at the end of the day. Follow her at natalie-anderson.com

USA Today bestselling author **Kat Cantrell** read her first Mills & Boon novel in third grade and has been scribbling in notebooks since she learned to spell. She's a So You Think You Can Write winner and a Romance Writers of America Golden Heart® Award finalist. Kat, her husband, and their two boys live in north Texas.

Sinfully Yours

Sinfully Yours:
The Unexpected Lover

HARMONY EVANS

NATALIE ANDERSON

KAT CANTRELL

MILLS & BOON

First Published in Great Britain 2023
by Mills & Boon, an imprint of HarperCollins*Publishers* Ltd,
1 London Bridge Street, London, SE1 9GF

www.harpercollins.co.uk

HarperCollins*Publishers*
Macken House, 39/40 Mayor Street Upper,
Dublin 1, D01 C9W8, Ireland

ISBN: 978-0-263-31977-4

MIX
Paper | Supporting responsible forestry
FSC™ C007454

This book is produced from independently certified FSC™ paper to ensure responsible forest management.

For more information visit: www.harpercollins.co.uk/green

Printed and Bound in the UK using 100% Renewable Electricity at CPI Group (UK) Ltd, Croydon, CR0 4YY

LESSON IN ROMANCE

HARMONY EVANS

To my beautiful daughter Angelina,
my first and dearest fan.

I'd like to thank Nancy Oakley, Founder,
Project Learn, for her time and patience in
answering my endless questions about tutoring adult
nonreaders and the issues surrounding illiteracy.
Thanks to Mom and Dad, for loving me and teaching
me how to read. Finally, thanks to Michelle
Tackla-Wallace, for believing in me.

Chapter 1

Cara stepped out of the taxi on West 135th Street in Harlem clutching her briefcase like a life preserver, her eyes fixed on the building before her. The growling sounds of a saxophone poured out through an open window belonging to Alex Dovington, a man she'd wanted to meet for nearly thirteen years.

And the same man she had to teach how to read… in three days.

A cramp gripped her stomach like a vise and she bit her lower lip against the hard ridge of pain. For the millionth time, she questioned herself. Could she do this? If Alex found out who she really was, there was no telling how he would react.

The truth was she had no choice.

Her heels crunched through rust-colored leaves as she walked up the stairs of his home, an ornate renovated brownstone. Inhaling the earthy fragrance of the air calmed her nerves.

How she loved autumn! The season was especially beautiful in New York City. But lately, she'd been so busy trying to raise funds for Beacon House, the adult literacy center she'd founded and struggled to keep open, she barely noticed the warm days blending into cool nights.

She'd simply...existed.

She desperately needed the substantial donation she would receive if she succeeded in teaching Alex to read in three days. Failure was unthinkable, and she would do whatever it took to avoid it.

She reached the landing, sucked in another deep breath, pressed the doorbell. Chimes amplified the fresh wave of panic that rippled through her. She spotted a jack-o'-lantern perched on the stoop next door. The ghoulish sentry seemed to mock her with its crooked smile, and she stuck her tongue out at it in defiance.

Just then, the door swung open. Startled, she jerked backward and grabbed hold of the railing to avoid falling off the edge of the stair.

Good Lord.

Her heart scampered into her throat and her eyes widened at the man towering before her.

Album covers and magazine pictures did not do the brother justice. Nearly six feet tall with dark honey-caramel skin and a body that looked like it was made for a woman's most scandalous dreams, Alex was more than fine. He was "now-that-I've-seen-U-I-can-die-now" gorgeous.

A tenor saxophone dangled like an upside-down question mark from a navy blue lariat around his neck.

The large instrument looked like a child's toy nestled against his bare chest and flat, ripped abdomen.

Stop staring! She knew it was rude, yet she found she couldn't help herself.

"Miss Williams?"

Although Cara sensed Alex speaking, her attention focused on a serpent tattoo curled like a vise around the taut muscles of his upper right biceps. The head and forked tongue licked his bent elbow, igniting her curiosity, and she wondered if he had more tattoos and if so, where they were located on his body.

Face flushed, she lifted her eyes to discover he was staring right back. A frown tugged at the corners of his full lips and his fingers gripped the edge of the door, as if to warn her he could slam it shut at any moment.

His voice, a rich baritone that could melt ice, finally reached into her ears, pulled her back to reality. But when she opened her mouth to answer him, nothing came out.

Before she could try again, he shook his head and with an agitated sigh, began to close the door.

Cara leaped forward. "W-wait!" Her voice so loud it echoed in her ears.

He paused, one hand braced against the jamb, the other on the doorknob, brows lifted, waiting. Her heart stopped for a moment and she gulped back her surprise. Met his eyes and forced what she hoped was a confident smile.

"Yes. I'm Cara Williams."

She put her briefcase down, wiped her palm on the side of her skirt and decided against shaking his hand. She didn't want to risk getting the door slammed in her face.

"Sorry if I'm early. I guess I'm eager to get started, given our overall time constraints."

He was silent, choosing instead to let his eyes speak for him. They trailed down and over her body, as if exploring the twists and turns of a melody on his horn, and she fought the urge to look away under his gaze.

Alex reached for her briefcase, his fingers grazing hers, and she tried to ignore the sensations prickling a path from her knuckles to shoulder.

"Come on in," he said, but there was no welcome in his voice.

She thanked him, stepped inside, and her ears twitched as multiple locks clicked into place behind her. He strode past without a glance, leaving her confused and disappointed as he led them down a short hallway to the living room.

Cara's eyes were drawn to a magnificent grand piano that held court in one corner. It seemed to lord over the sheets of manuscript paper scattered on the polished wood floor around it.

But that was nothing compared to the Grammy Award enclosed in glass and the cluster of gold records hanging in an alcove to the right of the piano.

The visual impact of who he was and what he'd accomplished in his career made her knees wobble. She was relieved when Alex placed her briefcase next to a black leather couch and motioned her to sit down.

A bead of sweat trickled down her spine as she watched him unhook the sax from the lariat around his neck, slide the reed off the mouthpiece, wipe the instrument with a cloth and place it in the case.

His gentleness made her feel like she was observing something more intimate than mere ritual, like a father who suddenly reaches out to ruffle his child's hair as he tucks him into bed.

Without a word, he got up and walked over to the piano. Shifting in her seat, she clasped her hands together in her lap for courage she did not feel.

"You don't seem too thrilled that I'm here."

Alex's hand wavered just before he pulled the cord on the music lamp, extinguishing the glow over the black and white keys.

He turned and looked at her. She held her breath, wishing she had insisted the sessions take place at Beacon House. She felt out of her realm here, away from the familiar surroundings of her storefront office.

"You're right." His voice held a hard edge. "I'm not."

He knows. Panic sliced through her and she exhaled in dismay. The knowledge that there were thousands of people with the last name "Williams" in New York City did little to console her.

When she didn't answer, he reached for a stack of papers and started to crumple them with one hand, the sound like kindling popping in a fire. He tossed them into a metal trash can already overflowing with their discarded brethren. There was no anger in the motions, only a touch of resentment.

She found her voice, forced it steady. "I don't understand. I was hired to give you private reading lessons."

"My manager hired you." He stuffed a few survivors into a briefcase she hadn't noticed before and thumbed down the latches. "Not me."

Her secret was still safe.

Relief flooded Cara's body, but she was more confused than ever.

She swallowed the lump in her throat, removed the

contract from her purse. "There must be some mistake." She held it out. "Your signature is right here."

Alex waved away the document. "You don't need to prove it to me, Miss Williams. The fact is Tommy signed the contract in my name. That's what he does when I'm out of town or unavailable."

She peered at the signature. It *was* barely legible, and since it had arrived via fax, she'd just assumed it belonged to Alex. The mistake could cost her.

"Usually he lets me know the nature of the contract before he signs." He lowered the cover on the grand piano with ease. "This time, he did not."

She clutched the contract like a lifeline and watched him walk to the window. He stared outside and Cara could hear the sounds of children playing outside.

"I got back into town late last night. Tommy called me this morning. Dropped the bomb that you'd be coming here. Then he told me why. I called your office right away but there was no answer."

She was afraid to ask the question, but asked anyway. "Why were you trying to reach me?"

He turned, folded his arms and leveled his eyes at hers. "To tell you I have no intention of learning how to read. Not now, not ever."

Her stomach plummeted, and for a moment she couldn't breathe, couldn't think. His tone was indignant, the words decisive and not to be challenged. But he didn't know she never gave up on her students and she wasn't going to start now. Especially when she had so much at stake.

Still, contract aside, he had to want to learn how to read or else there would be little chance for success. She had to convince him to continue with the lessons, to believe he could do this.

A sudden burst of energy rocked her body. She set aside the contract and smoothed her skirt.

"I'm sorry Tommy didn't communicate with you." She kept her voice calm, chose her words more carefully. "You have every right to be upset."

Alex flopped down on the far end of the couch, leaned back and slung his arm over his eyes.

She swiveled her legs to face him. He turned his head and gave her a pointed stare.

"I can tell you this. I don't need a tutor," he retorted, his voice razor-sharp as he jabbed his thumb into his chest. "Even if I did, I should be the one doing the hiring."

Her face burned with anger. Although she knew he was simply blowing off steam, completely understandable in this unusual situation, she had to look away to maintain her composure.

Alex tapped her arm and it pulsated with heat, sending her heart rate to the moon. She turned, hoping her reaction to his touch didn't show in her eyes.

"Look, Miss Williams," he said, his voice several notches softer. Her last name got lost in a yawn. "As you can see, I'm exhausted from my trip. I'm sorry about the inconvenience, but there's no deal. I can't do this."

She unfolded her arms at her sides. "If it's my qualifications you're worried about, I can assure you th—"

"You don't get it, do you?" He leaped from the couch, his voice thundering off the walls. "I should fire Tommy for pulling this stunt, but I can't blame him. He was just trying to protect me."

Her eyes paced with him as he walked in front of the huge marble fireplace until he stopped and leaned his elbow on the mantle.

She got up and took a few tentative steps toward him. "Protect you? From what?"

"My record company! While I was in Europe, they set up a book tour of elementary schools in Harlem. But they..." His voice trailed off and something seemed to deflate within him.

"Don't know you can't read," she finished.

"Bingo."

Their eyes locked, and now that Cara was standing closer to him, she saw his were hazel, the irises speckled with bits of green. She was momentarily mesmerized by their unusual hue and the intense shame color couldn't hide.

So that's why he's so angry. Although he would probably never admit it, she could see in his eyes he was afraid. She had to tread lightly, or she'd lose him to that fear.

Alex parted his lips like he was going to say something else, but instead he stalked away.

She trailed after him. "Well, it is kind of a cool way to introduce your music to a younger audience," she offered. "I know if I was a kid, I'd be excited to see you in person."

A few feet away, he swung around and stared at her like she had two heads. "It's a waste of time! Kids are listening to hip-hop and rap, not jazz. Armstrong, Coltrane, Miles and Ellington—they've never heard of them. If it ain't sampled or doesn't have enough bass to blow their eardrums out, they're not into it."

His eyes shifted to the overflowing wastebasket, then back to her.

"When does the tour start?"

"Week from today," Alex grumbled. "Tommy's trying to get it pushed back."

Cara ran her hand through her curls before walking over to where he stood at the window. "Learning to read is very difficult for anyone, especially for adults. It's not something you want to attempt on your own."

He whirled around and pointed at her. "I told you I'm not interested. I've gotten along fine my whole life and nobody's gonna change that. I'll handle this book tour fiasco in my own way, in my own time, not anyone else's."

He turned and jabbed the windowsill with his knuckles, as if to emphasize that the matter was closed. Still, even his taut arms and the harsh finality of his words rang hollow.

Both of them knew there was no escape from what lay ahead.

He put his forehead against the windowpane. "Tommy is the only one besides my mom who knows about…that I can't…" His voice ebbed away and he shook his head. "He's been with me for years, through everything, almost since the beginning of my career."

She gazed at the muscular expanse of his bare back and a sense of protectiveness winnowed through her. She wanted to wrap her arms around his trim waist and pull him away from his fears. She had to make him believe in himself, and in her.

She approached him, placed her hand on his arm, hating herself for what she was about to say. His skin felt warm and the muscle underneath tensed as he turned to look at her. "It sounds like he really cares about you, and helps you out a lot. But what if, God forbid, something happens to Tommy. What then?"

His shoulders slumped in reply and she knew she'd hit a nerve. Then his eyes, those beautiful hazel eyes filled with pain, bore into hers.

When he finally spoke, his voice was hoarse and splintered her heart. "This can't get out. If it does, it'll destroy my career."

As a high-profile musician and one of the hottest bachelors in Harlem, she knew the media would have a field day if they learned he was illiterate.

"No one will know. I promise," she assured him, keeping her voice light in spite of the emotions churning within her. "I live a very quiet, boring life and I'd like it to stay that way."

"I don't think anything about you would qualify as boring."

She bit her lower lip with pleasure, although she was unsure whether he meant it as a compliment.

"Tommy told me about the big money I'm going to give to you."

She shook her head. "You mean *donate*. None of it is going to me personally. It's going to fund Beacon House."

He gave her a curious stare, then shrugged. "It doesn't matter because you're both nuts. There's no way I can learn how to read in one weekend," he insisted.

She nodded. "You're right. You won't be able to read *War and Peace,* but I promise you'll be able to read a simple children's book by Monday."

Alex shoved his hands into his jeans, revealing a thin line of hair at the base of his abdomen that Cara longed to trace to its final destination.

He sounded doubtful. "I guess I don't have a choice."

She looked him in the eye. "Of course you do," she asserted. "You can quit, but look at your options. If you do the tour, your record company is happy and no one knows a thing. If you don't do the tour, it'll be a PR nightmare. I'm willing to bet they already sent out the press release, right?"

"Yes. My publicist was overjoyed. At least one of us is happy."

"So, what reason could you possibly give for backing out now?"

He smoothed his hand over his perfectly round, bald head and gave a sigh of resignation. "I guess the dog ate my homework wouldn't fly, would it?"

She grinned. "It's going to be okay. I promise," she said, reassuring him. "If you don't want to continue with the reading lessons after the tour, you don't have to. But regardless, your secret will be safe."

And so will mine.

Alex stared at her a moment, and Cara knew he was debating whether to trust her or not. She had to figure out a way to make him feel at ease with her...and soon.

Slipping his hands out of his pockets, he pushed away from the window with his shoulder. "I'm going to take a quick shower and finish packing before my limo arrives."

Panic sluiced through her veins. Tommy had told her Alex's schedule was clear for the weekend. They needed to spend as much time as possible on the lessons and not be disturbed. "Limo? What limo?"

"The one taking us to my home in the Catskill Mountains."

A knot formed in the pit of her stomach. "But I thought I was going to be teaching you here, in Harlem."

He shook his head. "I'd already planned to spend a long weekend in the mountains. I'm supposed to be relaxing, remember? I'm not changing those plans for anybody. Is that a problem?"

The reality of his words hit full force and a shudder of excitement went through her.

Alone with Alex in the Catskills. Where there were no taxis, no takeout and no escape? She was already a hot mess about being with him in his Harlem town house.

She wasn't scared of him, just unused to being alone with a man she was attracted to for an extended period of time. Her dates were few and far between, and most of them never made it as far as her bed. Devoted to her work, the words *sex* and *social life* were missing from her personal dictionary.

There's really no need to worry, she told herself. Alex was her student. She was his teacher. The lines were clearly drawn. Remembering how he'd looked at her at the front door, she, like most women, knew when a man was attracted to her.

And Alex Dovington most certainly was not.

The same could not be said for her.

It was difficult not to stare at him as he stood there, maddeningly out of reach, body cut and chiseled to perfection like a Renaissance statue. The man was off the hook, and off-limits, yet her eyes yearned to do what her lips could not—devour him.

His shoulders moved forward, snapping her back to reality.

"Sorry. I lost my train of thought for a second. That'll be fine. I just need to run home and pack. I should be back in a couple of hours."

He nodded, and she kept her eyes on him as he walked out. After he left, she grabbed her purse and dug for cab fare.

He popped his head in the room and she dropped her bag in surprise. "Oh, I forgot to tell you. I was an absolute terror in school. My teachers hid behind their desks when I walked into the room. Fair warning."

His voice was stern, but she detected a hint of a smile on his lips.

She arched an eyebrow. "I guess I'll just have to get creative to keep you interested."

Where did that come from?

Judging by the odd look on his face, he was just as surprised as she was.

"If you want to grab something to drink before you leave, the kitchen is at the end of the hallway. Help yourself."

Cara waited until he went upstairs, and then drifted over to the little alcove where gold records ornamented the wall. Tucking a curl behind her ear, she gazed at the Grammy Award, but her thoughts were elsewhere.

Had she been flirting with him just now?

She almost laughed out loud. *Absolutely not.* When it came to devising enticing lines to attract the opposite sex, she got a big, fat F.

Passing the piano, her feet kicked something out of the way. Looking down, she saw a balled-up piece of manuscript paper that had somehow escaped burial. She glanced over her shoulder before picking it up.

Smoothing out the wrinkles with the palm of her hand, she hummed the melody. It was the tune he was playing when arrived. Smiling, she refolded the music and stuck it into her purse.

On her way to the kitchen, her smile faded when it suddenly struck her that there were no pictures of Alex's friends or family around, not even of his brother, Michael.

Every small room in her own apartment was filled with pictures, memories frozen in time. She cherished each one, especially the ones of her mother who died when she was nine years old.

Shouldering her purse and briefcase, Cara selected a bottle of juice from the fridge. Her mind wandered to Alex's numerous records, the U.S. and European concert tours, the sold-out performances at jazz clubs across the country and the world. All were trophies to his artistic talent.

But where were the tributes to his personal life?

As she closed the front door, the last thing she heard was the faint sound of water spraying in the shower, re-igniting her nerves. Soon the biggest challenge of her life would begin. She sank down on the stoop, leaned her head against the cold iron railing, and prayed.

Chapter 2

Alex shoved his cell phone into his duffel bag, leaned his head against the window and wished he'd never come back to New York. The gray waters of the Hudson River were dappled in the sunlight as his limo traveled north to the Catskills.

The nasal-knife voice of his publicist still rang in his ears. Word had gotten out about the tour. She was going nuts fielding calls from around the tristate area and as far away as Chicago and Los Angeles. Everyone wanted Alex Dovington to read and perform at their school. Local and national media wanted exclusive coverage and personal interviews.

What a joke.

He eased back into the leather seat and reached for the familiar green bottle. Tipping it back, he enjoyed a long swig. If they knew he couldn't read the label of his favorite beer, or damn near anything else for that matter, they wouldn't want him.

He closed his eyes and tried not to think about what would happen if people discovered his secret. He could almost see the tabloid headline:

Playboy Dummy!
Harlem's Hottest Saxophonist Is Illiterate

The familiar anger rose within him and he gritted his teeth against it. No matter how much he'd already accomplished in his career, in some people's minds, he would be branded as unintelligent. But he wasn't stupid. He just couldn't read.

True, there were some words he recognized by sight. Ones he'd picked up over the years just by living life. *Women. Sex. Money. Music. Jazz. Bar. Liquor. Nightclub. Police. Beer. ATM.* A reluctant grin tugged at his lips. Those were among the most important words in the world. At least in his world.

Everything else was a cloud of letters he could never see through. A jumble of puzzle pieces he could never hope to solve.

The cold beer felt like heaven raining down his throat as he took another long pull. He snuck a glance at Cara. If his teachers had looked like her back when he was in school, he definitely wouldn't have dropped out in the ninth grade.

She sat diagonally from him, reading a newspaper, one slim leg crossed over the other. Her hair billowed out from her head and cascaded down her back in tiny spirals of brown curls spun with gold. He wondered if it felt as silky as it looked.

She lowered the paper for a moment to turn the page and Alex got another glimpse of her face, although the caramel-colored beauty of it had captured his mind the moment he opened his door and found her standing there.

His eyes roamed down the cream blouse and over the navy skirt, all buttoned-up and properly pressed. They curved down her legs, all the way to the peek-a-boo pump dangling from her left foot as it kicked out a sporadic rhythm. No stockings, he noted with pleasure.

Bare legs, one shoe half off, and the wildness of her hair stirred a crazy kind of longing within him. *Hmm,* he thought. Maybe she wasn't all business, all the time.

An image popped into his mind. He pictured her lying beneath him, those gold-brown curls moving like waves over the pillows, her fingers linked with his as he plunged into her. Again and again. Gazing into those soft, almond-shaped brown eyes until they slid shut from pleasure and then—

Her shoe dropped with a soft thud on the carpeted floor. Averting his gaze, he turned his head toward the window and jammed a fist under his chin. He closed his eyes, willed his erection to relax.

Now wasn't the time to be hot for teacher.

He *had* to finish his new tune this weekend. On Tuesday morning he was due in the studio to record his ninth, and hopefully not his last, album for Sharp Five Records.

The muscles in his abdomen tightened with dread. Mo "Money Man" Lowenstein, President and COO, was breathing down his neck. Sales of his last two albums were lower than expected and Mo had threatened to release him from the label.

And now he had to worry about learning the ABC's? His eyes snapped open and he nearly let out a cynical laugh.

Sharp Five Records, one of the largest, most well-respected labels in the music business, specialized in jazz, R&B and world music. Being cut from the artist roster would be a major blow to his career, and there were plenty of cats lined up ready to take his place at a moment's notice.

He lifted the bottle and grimaced as the now-warm remnants of his beer hit his throat. Although Alex dreamed of starting his own label and developing his own pool of talented musicians, he knew it was an impossible goal.

How many business owners couldn't read? He gathered the answer was zero, unless they were as good at hiding it as he was.

He sighed and looked out the window at the blur of trees going by. Life was so much simpler when he was playing for change in the 125th Street subway station. He wondered if he'd known back then that the music business was more about business, and less about music, would he be sitting here today?

He thought about the manuscript paper strewn all over his living room floor. It seemed like he'd rewritten the tune a thousand times, but there was still something missing. He'd hit a wall, and whenever he tried to fix it, it sucked even worse than before.

Could the problem be writer's block? He hoped not. If it were, that would scare him more than losing his recording contract. He knew if he lost the ability to compose music, he just might give up playing forever, because it was the only part of his life where he had complete control.

And if he couldn't play saxophone and compose, what would he do with his life?

He checked his watch and blew out a breath. They'd been on the road for just over an hour, but it felt like an eternity. And they still had about an hour before they reached Cottage Valley Falls, the town where his home was located.

When they'd gotten into the limo, he'd offered Cara a beer, but she'd refused and chose mineral water instead. And that was the last time they had spoken.

The reason why suddenly hit him like a ton of bricks.

Cara was the first woman, the only woman, who knew he couldn't read, and it made him feel like he had been caught by his mother with his hands down his pants.

She knew he couldn't read a menu in a restaurant, the warnings on a bottle of medicine, his royalty statements or countless other things. And that was way too much knowledge for him to be completely comfortable around her.

He frowned and tried not to squirm in his seat, feeling exposed and trapped at the same time. Still he had to find some way to get through this weekend and get back to what was important: making music.

One of the advantages to being a bachelor was he didn't have to justify anything to anyone. The other good things about being single escaped him for the moment and he chalked it up to jet lag, not the fact just being in Cara's presence made him want to forget about a lot of things.

Alex studied her, half wishing she'd put the paper down. What was so interesting she had nothing to say to him? It was almost as if she didn't want to be there, either. Although she'd played down the donation part and seemed excited about teaching him, it could have all been an act.

From the little he'd observed about her so far, she was somewhat aloof but radiated a quiet confidence.

She seemed less like a gold digger and more like the type who wrote letters to the editor or maybe even the President of the United States.

Chicka-bow, chicka-bow, chicka-bow-wow. The Commodores "Brick House" broke through the silence in all its polyphonic glory, courtesy of his cell phone.

Kiki. He swore under his breath and saw Cara jerk the newspaper forward, but she still didn't lower it.

Since he couldn't read the address book, Tommy had programmed a different ringtone for every person in his phone. The man had quite a knack for choosing just the right tone for the individual.

Steeling himself for an argument, he retrieved the phone from his bag and flipped it open.

The first few seconds of the conversation were pleasant, until he broke their date for that evening. When there was a break in Kiki's angry tirade, he gave her his standard line and hung up.

Leaning his head against the seat, Alex exhaled in relief. Out of the corner of his eye, he saw Cara lower the paper, her full lips turned up in a smile.

"What?" he scowled.

"I'll call you, baby," she said in a mock gruff voice, then burst out giggling. "I guess she's pretty upset, huh? I think the tourists in Times Square could hear her yelling."

Alex shrugged. "She'll get over it." *They all do,* he thought as he watched Cara refold the newspaper. When she finished, it looked like she'd never opened it.

"I hadn't heard of her. Kiki, wasn't it? She must be new in your scene."

His forehead crinkled in mild annoyance, although her curiosity pleased him at the same time.

"What do you do, follow my social life?"

She gave a little laugh, stowed the paper in her briefcase, then cocked her head toward him.

"It's not difficult. You're in the press a lot." She curved the index and middle fingers of both hands for emphasis. "The Bad Boy of Jazz, always dating the latest 'it' girl."

It wasn't his fault he was popular with the ladies, but for reasons he didn't understand, he wished Cara wasn't aware of the celebrity gossip that dogged him like a vulture. He shouldn't care what she thought about him, but he did.

"So I like to have a good time," he snapped. "So what?"

She held up a hand. "I'm not hating on your lifestyle. I was just trying to get you to smile. Or at least talk to me. You haven't said a word since we got in here."

Alex arched a brow, surprised and inwardly happy she'd noticed. "You were busy reading, so I figured, you know, that we'd each do our own thing."

Her smile in response lit up the inside of the limo, and his heart. The knot in his stomach loosened a bit, and left him confused and tongue-tied. This woman was riding hard on his emotions and didn't even know it.

His eyes drifted down to the briefcase by her feet, and he managed to clear his throat. "What paper are you reading?"

She hesitated a moment and it was all he could do to keep from tearing his eyes away from her warm gaze.

"The Harlem Gazette."

Alex noted her slender arms as she reached for her water bottle. Her wrists were small and he imagined a pearl bracelet would look nice encircled around them. But other than small silver hoops in her ears, she wore no jewelry.

"It's an independent newspaper that's been around for over fifty years and one of the first black-owned newspapers in the country," she added. "I also read the *New York Times* and the *New York Post*."

His heart sank, for he knew those papers all too well. The reviews of his music hadn't been so glowing lately, but the tabloids were more than willing to publish his picture with a woman hanging off his arm claiming him as her "man."

None of those women understood that he wasn't interested in a serious relationship. He was married to his music and his career. No one got in the way. Until now.

He gripped his beer tighter. "I recognized the word *Harlem* but that's about it."

She clapped her hands together. "Good!" Her face lit up like a thousand stars and she leaned toward him. "What other words do you know?"

He opened his mouth to run down the short list, but for some reason didn't want to risk offending her. She seemed so straitlaced, but not in a nerdy way. On the contrary, the conservative getup was appealing. He wondered if it was real or just for show.

That hair. Those legs. All wrapped up in a very pretty package he didn't dare touch.

He hedged an innocent smile. "Not too many. A little bit of this, a little bit of that."

"I see. That's perfectly normal. It's not uncommon for adult non-readers to be able to recognize some words."

"Adult non-reader? Is that what I'm called now?"

"It's a little awkward-sounding, I know," she acknowledged with a wan smile.

"It's better than some of the things I've been called."

With a grimace, he faced her and memories flowed into words.

"You know, I used to ride the subway to school and I'd see men and women in suits reading the newspaper. They all looked so smart and so important."

He swallowed hard, looked past her at the countryside rolling by. Suddenly aware of what he was about to say, he hoped she would stop him from making a fool of himself. But Cara remained silent, patient, waiting for him to continue.

He met her eyes. "Sometimes I'd sneak a peek at what they were reading, and even though the words always looked jumbled up, I couldn't keep my eyes away. Those letters were like a drug."

A band of dread, mixed with anger, tightened around his chest as he thought about all the times in his life when he tried to make sense of a word, or a group of words, and failed miserably.

"One morning, I was standing next to this man reading the sports section and I couldn't stand it anymore. Before I knew what I was doing, I pointed to the caption underneath the picture and asked him what it said."

Alex felt his spine go rigid and he downed the rest of his beer before continuing.

"He gave me a funny look and said real loud, 'That's the guy from the Yanks who struck out last night and lost the game, bottom of the ninth, you can't read that?'"

Shame hooked its claws and dug into him like it had happened yesterday, and he bowed his head and traced his finger along the top of the beer bottle.

Her voice snuck past the pain. "How old were you?"

"Fourteen," he replied. "A short time later I stopped going to school."

It was the only time he'd ever given up on something.

When she didn't say anything, a knot of embarrassment sank low into his stomach. Avoiding her eyes, he curved his hand around the back of his neck and leaned his elbow against the door.

He felt stupid for confiding in her, a perfect stranger. Yet it was her eyes, caring and warm, that drew him in and caused him to talk about a story he'd never shared with anyone.

Why her? Why now?

He felt a tap on his knee, turned and found Cara sitting right beside him, so close he could smell her perfume, a faint scent of vanilla tinged with rose.

"I want to show you something. May I?"

Before he could respond, she took the empty beer bottle and placed it in a cup holder.

She grabbed his right hand, squeezed it gently. The simple gesture startled him into immediate attention.

"There are twenty-six letters in the alphabet."

He tried to break contact with her before she noticed that his palms were beginning to sweat, but she held firm.

"I know," he said, distracted because he really liked the feel of her hand on his. "Even I watched *Sesame Street*. What's your point?"

At that moment, she tightened her grasp and leaned in close to him, as if she was about to reveal a dark secret.

"Be patient, I'm getting to it."

Drawing back, she turned his hand to reveal his palm. He looked down, relieved to see it didn't look as moist as it felt.

"To start to learn how to read, all you have to remember is that there are five vowels." Slowly she traced each vowel on his palm with her fingertips.

"A-E-I-O-U."

He hitched in a breath as each letter became an invisible imprint, fingernail upon flesh, leaving a trail of indescribable sensations radiating from his palm to his fingertips.

"The rest of the letters are called consonants." She circled her finger in the dip of his palm. "Consonants and vowels work together to form words."

Alex held his breath as she tugged each fingertip down to his palm until his hand was enclosed inside both of hers, warm and gentle.

"The ability to sound each one out individually, then as a whole, is the basis for learning how to read."

Their eyes met and he thought he saw a flicker of desire in hers. But when she dropped his hand right away, he dismissed the notion. Cara had a lust for letters, not him.

"That's it?" his voice doubtful.

"Yes, that's it!"

He pressed a button on the console in front of him and spoke to his driver. "Hey, Frank! Turn this beast around. It's back to Harlem, my man, we're done back here."

Cara giggled. "No! That's not what I meant. Of course there's a lot more to it than that. But at its roots, language is made up of consonants and vowels, kind of like the basic building blocks of music are notes and rhythm."

Leaning forward, he pressed the button again. "False alarm, keep going."

He settled back in the seat, eyed her skeptically. "How do you know so much about music? Are you a musician?"

"No." A shy smile crept across her lips. "Well, maybe. But, I'm just an amateur."

He formed a square with his fingers and looked through them like a camera, appraising her. "Hmm... let me guess. You're a singer."

When she blushed and nodded, he swore. "I knew this was a bad idea."

He reached for the intercom, but Cara swatted his hand away.

"Do you have a problem with singers?"

He crossed his arms. "Yeah. Too much drama."

She drew an imaginary halo around her head and batted her lashes like a movie star. "Me? Drama?"

Enchanted, his lips curved. It seemed there might be a playful little devil ready to bust out of all that innocence.

"So you *can* smile," she teased. "Was that so bad?"

His smile faded, although it struck him funny how a word or two from Cara could turn his mood from happy to sad and everything in between. He moved away and watched the river flow, as wide and vast as the emptiness in his heart.

Sure he had a great career, plenty of money and had dated some of the most desirable women in the world.

But at what cost?

So far, nothing he'd achieved had erased the guilt he lived with every day. Deep down, he feared learning to read would only make it worse.

An hour later, Cara woke with a start to discover she'd fallen asleep on Alex's shoulder. She sat up, her face burning with embarrassment. The driver swerved to avoid a pothole and she yelped in surprise when she crashed back into Alex's side.

"I guess I should get the driveway paved." He grabbed hold of the seat. "But I'm not up here too often and I always forget how bad it is until I come back."

Cara gripped the armrest and righted herself. "I just hope we make it there without cracking our skulls open."

"Don't worry." His thumb jerked up to the ceiling. "It's padded."

Her lips twisted. "But my head isn't."

The limo bucked and Alex caught her in his arms. "Whoops!"

They laughed uncontrollably as the vehicle continued its wild ride up to his house.

By the time they arrived, her stomach hurt. It had been such a long time since she laughed so hard, she'd forgotten how good it felt.

Alex cleared his throat. "We're home."

Her heart did a slow somersault as he held her, the heat from his body enveloping her own. Although his embrace was accidental, it felt purposeful, as if she belonged in his arms.

Her chin tilted up and she saw eyes sparked with interest that went beyond a hearty laugh. He ran a finger down her cheek, dislodging a strand of hair stuck there, stroked it briefly, let it fall against her.

She broke away, trembling, and slid to other side of the limo. Warning bells went off in her head, and she had no one but herself to blame.

What had she been thinking, tracing letters on his palm and fingertips in a way that would have made Big Bird blush?

Excitement darted up her spine remembering the

feel of his hand in hers. His palm, slightly rough around the edges but soft in the middle, the fingertips callused from years of playing the saxophone.

She'd never done anything like that before. But the grace of her touch hadn't lasted long. Almost as quickly as he opened up, he shut her out again. Yet just then he didn't seem to mind having her in his arms.

What was happening between them?

The driver opened up the door and she stepped out, wide-eyed. With its rough-hewn logs, wraparound porch and gabled roof, the quaint little cottage was the perfect mountain hideaway. She fell in love with it at first sight, but her heart raced again at being in such close quarters with Alex.

The air was cooler here than in Harlem. Smelled better, too. Rubbing her arms, her nose twitched as she inhaled the heady evergreen scent of giant fir trees that surrounded the cottage. Somewhere nearby a stream gurgled, completing the Zenlike setting.

Alex appeared at her side, instrument case in hand. "What do you think?"

"It's beautiful."

His hazel eyes brightened. "Thanks. C'mon. I'll show you around."

He guided her by the elbow as they walked. Her heels teetered over the pebbled walkway. Her heart raced anew at his touch.

Was it her imagination or did his hand linger before he released her elbow to unlock and open the front door?

He showed her the gourmet kitchen, the powder room and the laundry room. With an inner frown, she realized there were no pictures of family or friends here, either. Although everything was model-home neat with modern furniture and artwork, it still felt empty. Did Alex feel it, too?

He picked up their bags and they ascended the stairway to the second floor. "This is the guest room." He set her belongings down and pointed down the hallway. "My bedroom is down there and the bathroom is in the middle. There's a linen closet halfway with plenty of towels and soap. I'll leave you to unpack."

Cara nodded and stepped inside the tiny room. Jets of sunlight poured through curtained windows. Besides a dresser and a small nightstand, the bed took up the most space.

It's big enough for two.

Closing her eyes, she indulged in an intimate fantasy of her and Alex on it, doing everything but sleeping.

"Are you okay? You look like you're going to fall asleep standing up."

She whirled around, her left breast grazing his bare arm, and nodded.

"I—I guess I'm still a little tired from the drive."

Stepping back, she crossed her arms, trying to ignore the exquisite tingling radiating through her chest. Time stopped while his eyes scooped and swept over her body like a pleasure bandit, leaving a trail of tight nipples and heat smoldering in her belly. The room seemed to shrink into nothing but unmet need.

Alex cleared his throat. "Ready for lunch? Frank drove up yesterday and stocked the kitchen for the weekend."

"Sounds great," she replied, relieved he broke the silence. "After we eat, we must get started. There's a lot of ground we have to cover."

Alex grunted low and frowned as if to say, "Not *that* again!" and left the room, closing the door behind him.

She changed into jeans and a scoop-necked blouse, then flopped on the bed and stared at the ceiling, shaken and frustrated by the encounter.

What was his deal? He'd start to relax, but when she brought up the reason why they were here, he clammed up. She wanted to believe it was only fear. But what if it wasn't?

She didn't understand him at all, nor did she understand her physical reaction to him. And at this point, she wasn't sure which was worse.

While it was normal for her to care about her students, her feelings for Alex had begun to brew a long time ago. With him, her concern didn't start with paperwork. It started with a plea for justice.

Thirteen years had passed since her father, Crawford Williams, a powerful New York City judge known for his tough rule, had sent Alex's brother Michael to prison.

As always, tears sprang to her eyes whenever she recalled the day she learned her father was responsible for breaking up families across the city.

She had been flipping through the channels, doing her homework and eating dinner, alone as usual, when she caught the tail end of a television news story.

In it, a mother was giving a statement to a reporter on the courthouse steps. Through her tears, the woman told him that she'd written a letter to her father requesting leniency for her son.

"Did the judge even read it?" she said with a shriek that tore at Cara's heart. "I asked him at my son's sentencing. He wouldn't answer and threatened me with contempt of court. If he'd read it, he'd know Michael is innocent!"

She started weeping harder, and a sullen young man

Cara learned later on was her son Alex put his arm around her and led her down the steps.

She remembered the reporter turning to the camera, his voice grim. "There goes another casualty of Judge Williams's notorious crackdown on gangs."

She sat riveted in front of the screen as he continued. "Neighborhoods are safer, but at what price? With sons and daughters, brothers and sisters behind bars, New York families are suffering through harsh jail sentences handed down by Williams that apparently no amount of letter writing or phone calls can take away."

Cara remembered racing up the stairs to her father's office in disbelief, praying that what she heard was all a mistake.

Although aware of her father's stance against gang-related activity, she didn't dwell on it or anything having to do with his job. Whenever he was home and talked about his cases, she feigned interest just to please him. He was under the impression she wanted to be an attorney, when all she really wanted him to do was love her.

She found the letter on his desk and was horrified to see more stacked in a box, some opened, some not.

In it, Alex's mom described how she and her son were devastated by his brother Michael's incarceration. Although no details of the case were given, the purpose of the letter was clear: a desperate plea for leniency that was ultimately ignored.

The anger and pain of Alex's mother so mirrored her own feelings about her father that the next day she told him she wanted to be a teacher. By sharing her love of learning with young people, perhaps she could make a difference. Heal people's hearts, not hurt them, like her dad did so well.

He never forgave her.

Even now, the hollowness she'd felt that day hit her full force, leaving her sick to her stomach.

She wrapped her arms around her pillow and thought about the special bond she'd felt with Alex ever since. In the letter, his mom had mentioned that both Alex and Michael were musicians. For years, she had watched Alex's career blossom, listened to his music and followed his love life, while he didn't even know she existed.

A lump welled in her throat at the irony of it all. A tragedy in *his* life had prompted her to make a positive change in her own that had eventually benefited hundreds of people.

She thought of the challenges many of her students faced. Heart-wrenching, gut-twisting situations most people couldn't imagine were an everyday part of their lives. Homelessness, domestic violence, alcohol and drug abuse, joblessness, not to mention low self-esteem and feelings of inadequacy. Whatever their plight, it was often related to their illiteracy.

Her students came to Beacon House with the hope and desire to change their lives. It was her mission to help them get there. She wanted to do more, needed to do more, but without the necessary funding she was strapped.

Hot tears streamed down her face and she swiped them away, feeling helpless and overwhelmed. Lately her emotions were running higher than ever. But at least now she had a chance to make things right again.

She hugged the pillow and turned toward the window.

Teaching Alex to read was critical to the future of Beacon House, and he wasn't going to make it easy. She had to figure out some way to get past his fear and reach him.

She thought for a moment. He had a job he loved, money and worldwide acclaim. But there had to something he was unable to do. Some dream he'd never achieved because of his illiteracy. She just needed to find out what it was…and fast.

Chapter 3

Thirty minutes later, Cara was eagerly arranging her teaching materials on the coffee table when the sound of glass breaking and a loud curse sent her on a mad dash to the kitchen.

"Is everything okay?" Her heart pounded and her fingers grasped the edge of the doorway.

"Yeah, that's just the way we announce mealtimes around here," he joked and dumped a pile of blue glass into a nearby garbage can.

She giggled, relieved he wasn't hurt.

He retrieved two more glasses from a cupboard and started filling them with ice from the refrigerator.

She moved toward him. "Mmm. So tempting."

Alex looked over his shoulder at her as ice cubes spilled onto the floor. "Excuse me?" he said in a shocked voice.

She laughed and gestured to an island where a

mouth-watering tray of deli meats, assorted cheeses, dill pickles, fresh Italian bread, a tricolor pasta salad and a giant pitcher of iced tea were waiting to be eaten.

The confused look on his face was priceless, then his eyes widened in recognition. "Oh...right. The food."

She pursed her lips. "What did you think I was talking about?"

He flashed a grin, flexing his muscles like a body-builder preening before the judge's table. "My cover-model looks, of course!"

Unable to resist, she picked up an olive. But instead of eating it, she threw it at him.

"Hey!" he shouted when it bopped him on the shoulder.

Alex selected another olive and good-naturedly chucked it at her. "You *do not* want to get in a food fight with me," he warned.

"Oh, yeah?" she taunted, deflecting the green orb with her elbow, before picking up another and tossing it his way. "Why not?"

"Because," he said, reaching up and catching her olive with one hand before dropping it into his mouth. "You'll lose every time."

He grabbed a whole handful and like a pitcher getting ready to throw a fast ball, prepared to attack.

"Okay, okay!" she shrieked, grabbing a napkin off the table and waving it back and forth in surrender. "Truce!"

Alex pumped his fist in the air with a triumphant "yes!" Rich and melodious, the sound of his laughter was like one big hug.

After washing their hands, they loaded up their plates, both a bit cautious of the other, and sat down at the table. As Alex poured the iced tea, Cara admired a bunch of wildflowers stuck into a jelly jar.

"What's the occasion?" she asked, before she bit into her ham and swiss on rye.

"My mom always told me flowers make a table. She said even if you're drinking Kool-Aid and eating macaroni and cheese on paper plates, as we often did, flowers can make it seem like caviar and champagne."

"What types of flowers did you have?"

He looked thoughtful. "When times were good, carnations from the florist down the street. They'd always last real long." He paused, and his shoulders sagged a little. "When times were lean, there were always plenty of dandelions to choose from in Central Park."

She smiled, eager to know more about the woman she'd only met through a letter. "Your mother sounds wonderful."

"She's my rock. I just wish I'd get to see her more often. Now that I'm done touring, I should be able to spend a little more time with her." He bit into his sandwich piled high with roast beef.

"Does she live in Harlem, too?"

Alex swallowed and shook his head. "Not anymore. I bought her a place in Brooklyn a few months back."

Cara felt a pinprick of fear. "Oh? Whereabouts?" she asked, somehow managing to keep her voice steady.

"Park Slope."

Phew, she thought, glad to hear his mother didn't live in Williamsburg, the Brooklyn neighborhood where she lived that was just east of Park Slope. Although it was unlikely she'd ever run into her or Alex, she didn't want to take any chances.

He took one of the wildflowers out of the jar, inhaled its scent, a faint smile upon his lips. "I would have bought her a place near me," he continued, "but she wanted to get out of Harlem. Go somewhere different. I guess memories can do that to a person."

He replaced the flower, and the smile disappeared, eyes clouded over. "Ever since my..." He stopped and took a bite of his sandwich.

"Your what?" she blurted.

The look on his face could have melted concrete. Tension stretched between them and made itself at home.

Way to go, Williams.

When it came to Alex, her natural curiosity went into overdrive. Yet she knew from past experience that sometimes being nosy about someone else's life could lead to more questions about her own. And in this case, that would be a disaster.

Alex looked stricken as he sat there, toying with his pasta salad.

"I'm sorry. It's really none of my business."

She saw something dark flicker in his eyes and vanish.

He waved her apology away, swallowed deep. "My twin brother, Michael. He...left," he swallowed deep. "And my mom hasn't been the same since."

Twins. A lump rose in her throat.

She'd heard that twins shared a strong emotional connection with their other half, even inside the womb, and wondered if Alex and Michael had that type of relationship. They must have.

Then why weren't there any pictures of Michael anywhere?

"I'm sorry," she blurted again. And she was sorry for him, more than he would ever understand.

He pinched the bridge of his nose and then suddenly got up. Cara winced as his chair scraped the floor.

"Would you excuse me?" he said without looking at her.

She bit her lip, remained silent as his plate clattered in the sink and he stalked out, the screen door slamming behind him.

Elbows on the table, she pushed her plate aside and threaded her fingers through her hair, not caring now if she messed it up.

She felt bad about bringing up the past, but unconsciously a part of her wanted to hear Alex talk about her father and what he'd done to his family. She hated keeping secrets, and it could have been an opportunity to tell the truth. Clear the air. Maybe the fact that she was Judge Williams's daughter wouldn't matter to him.

But she was lying to herself, because she knew that it would.

Thirteen years had gone by. Long enough to forget. It was also long enough to remember.

Michael had to be out of jail by now. Unless the crime was so horrible he was still locked up.

She shuddered at the thought, glad Alex wasn't involved. She was a huge fan of his music and respected him as an artist.

She couldn't allow her feelings to go deeper than that. Like any other woman, she knew that falling in love with a musician had extreme heartbreak already built into the package.

Especially someone like Alex, who was all wrapped up in a tight, muscled body that just about knocked her into the next century simply by looking at him.

She had to forget about his past...and his body. The

most important thing was getting the lessons started and they weren't getting anywhere by avoiding each other.

She had to find him.

She washed the dishes and then stepped outside, hoping he wasn't far. The afternoon sun, although filtered by the canopy of leaves overhead, warmed her face.

Moments later, she peered around the edge of the house and spotted Alex on the deck. He was stretched out on a lounge chair, eyes closed, right arm shielding his face. His shirt was off and wedged behind his neck.

She started to walk around the corner, stopped short. Although she never thought herself a voyeur, this was an opportunity she couldn't pass up.

Her eyes traced the hair on his muscular chest all the way down to where it disappeared beneath the waistband of his jeans. A quiver of pleasure swelled deep within her loins and feathered up into her abdomen. She wondered how he could look so sexy doing absolutely nothing.

Normally, she didn't get turned on just by looking at a guy, but Alex was no ordinary man. She'd fantasized about him for years; the sound of his voice, the color of his eyes, the feel of his skin.

Everything.

She leaned against the side of the house, closed her eyes and tried to clear her mind of any thoughts that could get her into trouble.

Alex was within arm's reach, yet still untouchable. It was scary and frustrating at the same time, because even if she had the courage to act on her desires, she couldn't cross the line. It would be very unprofessional. Not only that, she might lose control, and that was something she never did.

To her, losing control meant she needed him. Her

stomach did a little flip. What would she do if she couldn't get enough?

Opening her eyes, she clenched her fists against the warmth pooling low in her belly. *No màs.* The brief contact she'd initiated in the mini-lesson would have to be enough to satisfy her longing.

Just as she was going to announce her presence, her nose did it for her.

"God bless you," he called, after her loud and obnoxious sneeze.

"Thank you," she said in a pinched voice, coming around the corner. "I was just coming to find you." She stood a few feet away from him, covered her mouth and sneezed again.

His eyes opened. "So I heard."

Her heart skittered and for a second she was afraid he knew she'd been watching him. But unless he could see through walls, that was impossible. Until her allergies gave her away, she'd been out of his line of sight the entire time.

She dragged over a lawn chair and sat down. "Ready to—" her body bent over at the waist and she sneezed a third time "—get to work?"

Alex covered his ears. "Good lord, woman. You sound like a foghorn in reverse."

"I do not!" she retorted and sneezed again, hating the sound.

"It's this place." She waved her arms around above her head. "The fresh mountain air. I think I'm allergic to it. You're a New Yorker. You know what I'm talking about."

He laughed. "You got that right. It's why I bought this place. To escape from a lot of things, the air included."

She tapped her fingers on the armrest and wondered what he was trying to escape from. "Are you okay?"

His eyes met hers, crinkled at the edges. "I'm good. It's just been a long time since I talked about my family with anyone."

Relief that he wasn't mad flowed through her. "I'm glad to hear that. I'm far too nosy for my own good."

"You're a teacher. What do you expect?"

She put her hands on her hips and glared at him. "What do you mean by that?"

He sat up and swung his legs over the side. "Chill out. All I meant was the best teachers like to ask questions. They don't accept the status quo. They're always trying to learn new things."

She raised her eyebrows. "It sounds like you hold the profession in high regard."

Her breath hitched in her throat as he pulled the lounger closer to her chair. Her eyes delighted at the hair on his chest, small tight curls, just the way she liked it.

His voiced dropped low. "I'll put it to you this way. I've never met a teacher I haven't been able to, eventually, drive crazy."

The grin on his face would have made a devil proud. Her skin tingled in bewilderment. She wasn't sure if he was flirting with her or just kidding around.

As always, the man was an enigma.

She cleared her throat. "I see. Well, what you don't know about me—I mean, us—is that we can sense when a student is stalling."

She wanted to laugh at his wide-eyed, innocent stare, but held it in as he put a hand over his heart.

"You can't mean me?"

"Yes." She poked him in the chest. "You."

"Ow, woman. There's a law against carrying concealed weapons, you know."

Alex started to lie down again, but Cara stood up, grabbed him by the hand and pulled him to a sitting position. No easy feat.

"Oh, no, you don't. Come on, big boy. Time for school."

He groaned in mock protest as he slid open the patio door and stepped aside, allowing her to go in first.

Cara took her place on the sofa, while Alex sat on the easy chair. She patted the spot next to her.

"Sit here, please," she said, rummaging around in her briefcase for a pencil.

"You don't have a ruler in there, do you?"

Two can play at this game.

"Maybe, maybe not," she bantered.

He moved next to her, pointed at the magnetic letters in front of them and made a face. "You're not planning on teaching me how to read with those, are you?"

"Why not? They're very effective tools for learning."

"Yeah, right." He sniffed, crossing his arms. "Maybe for someone still in diapers."

She sighed in exasperation. "Will you just trust me? I know what I'm doing here."

He linked his hands behind his head, leaned against the pillows and stretched out his legs, lips curved in a sullen yet sexy smile.

"Okay, okay. You're the boss."

She pursed her lips slightly and tried not to stare at the triangular patch of hair at the base of each muscled arm. His nipples budded hard from the cool air. All of that combined with the faint scent of his cologne was slowly driving her crazy.

Oh, my.

"Can you please put your shirt on?"

His smile deepened. "Why?"

"Because I can't teach you when you're half-naked, that's why. Just put it on. Please."

He rolled his eyes and she ignored the urge to give him a playful swat on the behind. He went outside and snatched his shirt from the chaise longue. She had to admit she enjoyed watching his muscled abdomen contort as he pulled it over his head, and she was sorry to see it disappear under his shirt.

He sat down. "Thank you. Now what I'd like you to do is put each one of these in alphabetical order."

Alex cracked his knuckles. "Piece of cake."

He arranged the letters from *A* to *Z,* humming "The Alphabet Song" as he went along. He ended the tune in fake falsetto, holding the last note like an opera diva.

Although she was glad he knew his letters, playtime was over. She had a literacy center to keep open and he had a reputation to maintain. It was as if he'd forgotten the reason they were doing this in the first place.

"Are you always like this?"

"I warned you." He laughed. "I haven't even pulled out my best material yet."

She fought to keep impatience out of her voice. "Let's try to stay focused, okay?"

"I'm sorry." He folded his hands in his lap like a choirboy. "You have my complete attention."

"Next, I'd like you to point to each letter, say it aloud and see if you can think of a word that begins with that sound. I'll write the word on the whiteboard as you say it. I'll go first."

"*C.* Cup." She printed the word neatly. "C-U-P." She put her finger under each letter. "*Cup* begins with the 'kuh' sound." She put the next letter on the board. "Your turn."

Alex glanced at the board, then at her. "This all seems so elementary. Are you sure we just can't—"

"English is a sound-based language," she interrupted. "You'll learn faster if you can hear the sounds at the same time you read them."

She pointed at the letter. "Just take your time."

His brow furrowed in concentration as he looked at the board.

"It looks like the letter *B*."

"That's right, and what sound does the letter *B* make?"

He moved his lips, and she felt bad as he struggled to figure out the sound. But she had to test him a little, to see how much he knew.

He blew out a harsh breath. "I'm sorry. I can't do this."

She put her hand on his knee. "It's okay," she said soothingly. "The sound of the letter *B* is 'buh.'"

"B-Buh." He repeated the sound after her, then several more times. "Beautiful." He turned to face her.

His eyes held hers, and her cheeks flared hot. "Wh-what?"

"You asked me for a word that started with the sound 'buh,' and I'm giving you one. Beautiful."

She stared into his eyes, dumbstruck for a moment, wondering why he would pick that particular word, knowing he couldn't be referring to her, hating herself for wishing that he was.

Alex waved his hand near her face. "Earth to Cara." She jumped and the dry-erase pen rolled onto the floor. "And I thought I was supposed to be the one falling asleep in class."

She ignored his comment and brought out another letter.

"*F.* Hmm..." He rubbed his fingers under his chin as if pondering a theory.

"Keep it clean!" she warned, her insides fluttering.

"I was going to say *Fudge.*" An innocent smile played on his lips. "What did you think I was going to say?"

"Never mind," she murmured, her face warm. "Great job."

"Do I get a gold star?"

She grabbed her magnetic letters. "Perhaps, but there's a lot more to do."

"Wait a minute." He took the letters from her hands and set them on the table.

She looked up at him, a little stunned by the heat that flowed from his fingers as he placed her hand in his.

He paused, like he was trying to find the right words. "I want to apologize for giving you a hard time back in Harlem."

His eyes searched hers, and the sensual feel of his thumb as he rubbed it back and forth over the ridge of her knuckles made it difficult for her to concentrate. She was sure he could hear her heart pounding.

"It's okay," she stammered. "It must have been difficult coming back and finding all that stuff out."

He nodded, not taking his eyes off hers, sucking her in and surprising her with the desire she saw there, making her want to drown in it.

"It was, but I had no right to take it out on you and I want to apologize."

She watched his full lips as he spoke to her, and when her mouth began to water she slipped her hand from his.

"You already have. The thing you have to do is to

keep at this. I know it's hard, but I'll help you. No matter how long it takes.

"And—" she winked "—if you promise to stay on task, I promise…" She quickly racked her mind for ideas and blurted out the first one that popped into her head. "I'll make dinner tonight!"

He leaned back against the pillows with a grin that could light up a city block. "Now that's one offer I can't refuse."

Two hours later, Alex braced his palms against the tile and gritted his teeth as cold water streamed over his body. Arching his back, he shivered more from disbelief than discomfort even though he felt like he was going to explode.

He never would have guessed learning the ABC's would be such an incredible turn-on.

He didn't know what it was about Cara, but he was so attracted to her he could barely concentrate on what he was supposed to be doing. Instead, all he could think about was making love to her.

For him, the afternoon had been a lesson in restraint.

He had to stop himself from tugging on the bun in her hair to release her unruly curls, from caressing her neck and stroking the outside of her thighs when they brushed against his. Her full lips had his complete attention when she spoke, even if the subject matter didn't.

He smiled and wondered whether if he kissed her her caramel skin would glow like it did when he teased her. How would it respond if he were to taste her?

Thinking of her in his arms, he didn't need to look down to know his erection was still at the ready, with no means of release other than by his own hand, and he knew doing that would be wholly unsatisfying. It would just make him want her even more.

His teeth chattered as he sucked in his breath and wished he could make the water colder, even though it was like ice right now.

Alex grabbed the soap and thought about how much he enjoyed flirting with her. Still, it unnerved him that his initial fear of talking to her was starting to disappear. He didn't like the fact he let down his guard a little too easily around her, often without realizing it until it was too late.

First, he'd told her the story of the man who humiliated him on the subway. She didn't have too much of a reaction to that one, or at least one that he noticed. Being an adult literacy teacher, she'd probably heard all sorts of horror stories.

But when he talked about his brother, told her Michael was a twin, he noticed right away the look of shock that came over her face, like she'd seen a ghost or heard some devastating news.

Although he found it odd she would react that way, he supposed many people would be surprised if they knew he had a brother, let alone a twin. He didn't discuss Michael, or any part of his private life, with anybody.

The women he dated were only interested in his money and VIP status, and the press was so busy trying to keep up with his bachelor escapades that they rarely bothered to dig into his past.

That was a good thing.

Pain filled his heart and he squeezed his eyes shut to try to make it go away. But it never did.

His mind reverted back to Cara. If she ever discovered what he'd done in his past, she'd have a different impression of him than she did right now, he realized with a frown.

She probably already thought he was a nut, and he had nobody to blame but himself for his behavior. Happy and joking one minute, storming off the next. But he'd been that way for months, maybe even years. He'd been in a funk so long he'd lost count. It wasn't exactly depression…he just didn't give a damn anymore.

Alex sighed as he twisted his body around to rinse off. So many times during his life he'd been unable to connect with a woman in a personal way.

He spent his days and nights performing, rehearsing, teaching, touring and countless other things that he had to do in order to be able to call himself a professional musician. His hectic schedule didn't leave a whole lot of time for himself or anyone else for that matter.

He stepped out of the shower and toweled off. While he balked at being in a serious relationship with any woman, in the back of his mind, he knew he was missing out.

He stood naked in front of the full-length mirror. In his mind, he saw Cara, her hair spiraling over her shoulders, wearing nothing but desire. The lush curve of her ass, soft breasts tilted up, back arching, hands reaching, and she belonged only to him.

His eyes slid shut, but the image remained and teased.

Go away!

Music was all that mattered in his life. He'd made a conscious choice to be alone, and nothing was going to change that.

Almost against his will, Alex moved closer to the image of Cara in his mind. A few seconds later, his eyes jolted open when he made contact with the mirror. Face contorted in a grimace, he looked down and hoped he'd be able to train his body, and his mind, to stay away from her.

Meanwhile, Cara was downstairs frantically searching for a cookbook. After offering to make dinner, the turnaround in Alex's attention span was downright miraculous. Now she was kicking herself for her kindness.

She knew her way around a take-out menu and could order a meal in several languages. But the kitchen? Foreign territory she didn't dare tread unless there was a powerful yet easy-to-use microwave and a stack of frozen meals in the fridge.

After opening every cupboard, pawing through all the drawers and coming up empty, she blew out a breath and anchored her hands around her hips. She was on her own.

She opened the door of the king-size stainless-steel refrigerator, her eyes widening in amazement. All this food for one man?

Then she remembered Alex was supposed to be entertaining Kiki tonight. Maybe the woman ate as much as he did. *"Chick-a-bow, chick-a-bow, chick-a-bow-wow,"* she mumbled under her breath.

Checking the meat drawer, she found a couple of strip steaks. An avid fan of cooking shows but normally too busy to try any of the recipes herself, she knew she could broil the meat quickly.

After turning the oven on, she found some red potatoes, a package of frozen green beans and a large head of lettuce. She filled two pots with water and set them on the stovetop to boil, made a tossed salad and concocted a simple marinade for the steaks out of olive oil, garlic powder and ground peppercorns.

All without having a nervous breakdown.

She breathed a sigh of relief, then frowned when she realized the only thing missing was some bread, one of her favorite foods and an absolute must-have part of her diet.

She moved toward the pantry and spotted a large, unopened box of biscuit mix.

After a quick glance at the instructions, she opened the package and removed the plastic bag from inside the box. She tried to pull it apart, but used too much force and the bag suddenly exploded, spewing biscuit mix everywhere.

She started to clean up the mess, but stopped when she heard the water going off upstairs. Alex would be down any minute and she wanted to get the biscuits in the oven before he got there.

After pouring what was left of the mix into a bowl, she added milk and frantically began to stir. Just as the dough began to form, she heard the rhythmic hiss and splash of water. She lifted her head and yelped as both pots boiled over.

Spoon clattering to the floor, she sprinted to the stove and turned the gas down under each burner. Whirling around, she leaned against the counter and was fanning herself in relief when Alex walked into the room.

He stopped in his tracks and his eyes grew large.

"Let it snow, let it snow, let it snow!" he hummed. The amused expression on his face made her cheeks tingle.

Flustered, she picked up the spoon and tossed it into the sink. "So I had a little trouble making the biscuits."

She swiped a few loose strands of hair off her face. "And I forgot to put the potatoes on to boil, the steaks on to broil, and well…" Her voice trailed off. "The truth is…I don't know how to cook."

His eyes twinkled. "Well, then, let me help you."

She started to protest, but Alex was already pitching in. He put the steaks in the broiler and added the potatoes and the green beans to their respective pots while she began to roll out the dough.

"Hold up. You're doing it all wrong."

She turned her head to look at him and her breath caught in her throat. He was standing so close that she could see a tiny nick on the edge of his jaw where he had cut himself shaving.

"And I suppose you know the right way?" she countered.

He nodded, a mysterious gleam in his eyes that made Cara's stomach do a one-eighty. "There's a special, yet mostly unknown technique to making biscuits. Now it's time for *you* to get schooled." He winked and gently nudged her aside.

"First you need to prepare your surface, so the dough won't stick." His voice held a tone of grave solemnity and Cara masked a smile as he scattered flour on the counter and spread it with his palm.

He rubbed a little flour on the shaft of the rolling pin and a thousand thoughts went through her mind, none of which had anything to do with making biscuits.

Her pulse quickened as Alex guided her right hand up to grasp the handle of the rolling pin and went into a full gallop when he reached around her waist to do the same with her other hand.

Cara craned her head toward his, eyes full of questions. His only answer was a smile as he laid his hands over hers and laced their fingers together, his hip hovering against her waist.

"Now apply firm, but gentle pressure," instructed Alex, his cheek next to hers, his voice lower than usual.

His warm breath caressed her ear, curled her toes. "Like this."

His chest, wide and hard-muscled, pressed into her shoulder blades, and she inhaled the fresh scent of soap and spicy aftershave. Heat from his hands and fingers penetrated hers and she grasped the handles tighter to keep her hands from slipping.

Together they eased the rolling pin over the dough, his body close enough to tantalize but far enough away to tease. Back and forth. Forward and back. Every so often, her breasts would skim the counter's surface, nipples budding instantly. Lips parted in a trancelike thrill.

Both bending and rolling. Both feeling and desiring.

Eyes half-lidded, her buttocks swished against the silky fabric of his basketball shorts, discovered the hard length beneath. The brief contact left her wet and tight and hungry with need.

Alex abruptly stepped back, their damp fingers stuck together briefly as he loosened his grip.

"Looks like you've got the hang of it now."

She opened her eyes and turned to face him, tingling with desire, already missing the presence of his body near hers.

She inhaled deeply. "What's the next step?" she said eagerly.

He handed her a glass. "You can cut them out with this."

Twenty awkward minutes later, they sat down to eat. When they both reached for a biscuit at the same time, they laughed and the tension was broken.

"Like minds, like biscuits, I guess!" laughed Cara.

He laughed, then gave her a strange look.

Her smile faded. "What's wrong?"

He reached across the table and dabbed her cheek with his napkin. "There's a little bit of biscuit mix here," he murmured, his touch gentle. "There. All better."

She touched her hair and wondered if it too was flecked with biscuit mix. She must look like a mess. "Thanks."

While Alex poured the wine, Cara took the first bite. "Mmm!" she exclaimed.

"I propose a toast." He lifted his glass. "To teachable moments. I think we both learned something today."

She was stunned, and more than a little scared, by the flash of heat that rocketed through her body as their eyes met in silent agreement.

Throughout the delicious meal, Alex entertained her with funny stories about his European tour. But while she was laughing, the headlines detailing his relationships with other women scrolled like tickertape in her head. As Harlem's most eligible bachelor, he'd dated pop stars, reality stars, Broadway stars and even a star forward in the WNBA.

A painful lump rose in her throat, urging her to face the facts. She knew that even if Alex had been flirting with her earlier, and she still didn't want to allow herself to believe that he was, it was only a tool in his repertoire of seduction.

To her, it meant everything. To him, it meant absolutely nothing.

Chapter 4

Alex slowed to a jog, lifting his shirt to wipe the perspiration from his brow. He'd woken at dawn and run ten miles through the dense forest and winding country roads surrounding his property, but it was no use.

He couldn't get Cara out of his mind.

Half walking, half limping along the path, he knew he'd pushed himself too hard. While he was in good shape, his hectic tour schedule had left him little time to hit the hotel gyms. When he reached the garden, he sank down onto the worn wooden bench.

Yawning, he rubbed his eyes and stared ahead in awe. The sun was just beginning to crest over the mountains, tinting the sky in pale hues of pink and orange, inviting the residents in the valley below to rise and shine. It was a scene that demanded to be shared with someone special.

Cara.

Her almond-shaped eyes had pierced his own as they ate dinner last night, seeming to beckon him.

No way, not happening. He'd never shown this place to any woman, and he wasn't going to start now.

With a low grunt, he stretched his sore legs and inhaled the fragrant air. Linking his hands behind his neck, he looked around, and the empty feeling he had inside ebbed away. This was his mecca, a private space he'd created in a small clearing at the edge of the forest, far away from the grit and glamour of New York City.

From the tin-roofed old shed that slanted sideways like a drunk trying to keep his balance, to the trees, the beautiful wildflowers and shade-loving plants. Here he could relax, reflect and rejuvenate. Here he could hide from the pressures of the world, and sometimes (though he didn't want to admit it) from himself.

"Soul Man" burst through the calm. Alex flipped open his phone.

"Hey, if you're planning on stabbing me in the back, could you at least do it while I'm *in* the country?" he growled.

"You're still pissed," said Tommy, his voice raspy from a two-pack-a-day smoking habit he refused to quit.

"Damn straight." Alex stood up, ignoring the pain. "You had no right to—"

"To what? Did you really think I was going to stand by and let you trash your career over pride?" Tommy's voice edged up over the sounds of clanging silverware. Alex knew he was at his favorite diner, eating steak and eggs with a side of oatmeal, and his stomach growled.

"It's not about pride, it's about principle. I'll learn to read when I want to, not because somebody tells me I have to."

"Looks like three months in Europe didn't soften you up one bit. You're still as hardheaded as ever."

Alex could almost see the old man shaking his head from side to side, something he did whenever they didn't agree on something. The gesture was almost fatherly. The fact was, Tommy was the closest thing to a dad Alex had ever known.

He ran his hand down his face, exasperated. Twigs snapped and broke on the forest floor as he paced back and forth. "C'mon, man. You know I wouldn't have signed off on something like this."

"Look, I'm sorry, but we've been over this already. You don't have a choice."

Alex scowled. "I thought you were trying to push back the dates or even cancel this stupid book tour. I don't understand why you—"

"Calm down, Alex." Tommy took a breath. "I talked to Mo late yesterday."

"And?" He stopped pacing, his stomach coiling into a knot.

"No deal."

Frustrated, he bunched up his shirt in his fist. "What did Mo say exactly?"

"He wanted to know why you wanted to cancel the book tour and I told him you were exhausted. That you needed time to recover."

"Man, that's the lamest excuse I've ever heard." Alex snorted, releasing his shirt and wiping his hands on his shorts. "You make me sound like a prima donna or something. No wonder he didn't take you up on it."

"What else could I tell him? The truth? I did my best."

"I know, I know. But can't you—"

"Listen, the bottom line is, you can't afford to make Mo mad right now."

Alex hated to admit it, but Tommy was right. As usual. He sucked in a slow breath.

"Sorry I was so rough on you. I just hate this."

"I know, man. But it'll all be over soon. In the meantime, I'll see if I can think of something else to put you back in Mo's win column."

Tommy didn't sound very convinced, and Alex knew he was just trying to make him feel better.

"By the way, how's everything going with Miss Williams?"

"Great!" Besides the fact that just looking at her lips, her legs and everything in between made him harder than he'd ever thought was possible.

"Good. And what else?" Tommy prodded.

"And," he hedged, "I'm earning gold stars and smiley-face stickers left and right. Happy now?"

"I'm talking about the tune," said Tommy dryly. "The one you were supposed to have done a month ago?"

He toed the ground with his sneaker. "It's coming along." For once, he was glad Tommy wasn't there, so he wouldn't have to lie to his face.

"I hope so, because Mo asked me about the album again. He wants it done Alex—and soon. We can't put this off any longer."

"I know, I know. Tuesday morning, Parkside Studios, 30th and Lex, 10 a.m. sharp. I'll be there," he grumbled.

"Listen, you can do this, man. Just stay focused. I've got another call coming in. Talk to you later."

Alex slapped the phone shut, slumped against a tree and gazed up at the leaves canopied overhead.

Focus. It sounded so easy, but he didn't even know what that word meant anymore.

He knew Tommy was only doing his job by lighting a fire under his butt. He had to finish the tune. *Today.* Forget learning to read. He'd deal with that, and Cara, later.

Right now, he needed to take a shower, grab his horn and get back to the shed. Checking his watch, he headed back toward the house. It was still early. Hopefully, Cara was still in bed and he could sneak back to the garden before she woke up and filled every minute of his time with her tutoring sessions.

If he was lucky, it would only take a few more hours to work out the kinks in his tune and write out the arrangement for the band.

His creativity was more active in the mornings anyway or, his lips curving into a smile, after a couple of rounds of mind-blowing sex. It had been a while, but up until this weekend, he'd been too busy to care.

Although he was trying to disguise his attraction to her, Cara was making it extremely difficult. She triggered long-dormant fantasies within him that were begging to be explored. He felt he was on the brink of unearthing something about himself he never wanted to admit.

His need for a woman in his life.

Her enthusiasm for teaching impressed him. He wished he could bottle it up and drink it down to cure the apathy he was feeling toward his own profession.

Music had been in his life for so long. And now? He didn't care about it or anything else anymore, and he couldn't figure out why.

He just knew he had to do something to get himself, and his mind, back on track where it belonged before it was too late and his career was over.

When he got home, his eyes shifted up to the second floor. The curtains were drawn on both windows of Cara's room.

He exhaled in relief. So far, so good.

He nudged the front door open as slow as he could, frowning when the rusty hinges whined anyway. He took off his shoes and socks and padded barefoot to the laundry room, where he stripped down and threw his running clothes into the washer.

He crept upstairs, wrapping a towel around his waist, praying she wasn't awake yet. But before he even got to the "amen," an unusual sound stopped him dead in his tracks.

Feet sinking into the plush carpet, he pressed his ear to the bathroom door. As he listened to the sounds on the other side, his brow furrowed with anger.

Moments later, his mind churned in disbelief as he took a step back from the door.

Cara *singing*.

The sound of the water masked the lyrics, but Alex recognized the melody immediately.

Hell, he'd written it.

The back of his neck pricked with anger. He felt like he'd been punched, and yet was disturbed by an incredible need to listen to her.

Cara's voice was beautiful. A bluesy alto, meditative and haunting, that wound around his ears and left him wanting more. The melody sprang from her so easily, while he'd been struggling with it for weeks.

But where had she found his music?

His mind snapped to attention, remembering the wastebasket overflowing with discarded manuscript. Cara must have taken a copy of his tune out of the trash. But why?

He wanted to burst through the door and confront her

right then, but hesitated, still mesmerized by her sultry voice that went straight to his gut. His body felt like it was being pulled right into her soul, but his mind was an emotional sandstorm trying to figure out how to handle the situation. He sensed he was hearing something more than raw talent. Much like the woman herself, Cara's voice was a gift yet to be discovered.

Still, she had no right to take his tune and set lyrics to it without his permission.

Regret filled his heart as he realized just how much he was beginning to trust her. He really thought she was different, that perhaps she saw him as more than the means to an end. The heat that burned between them as they rolled out the biscuits, the concern he saw in her eyes, her commitment to teaching him.

And now this?

This didn't feel like caring. It felt like betrayal. His heart rocked in his chest. Everything she'd said and done up until this point must have been an act.

What other secrets could she be hiding?

He tightened the towel around his waist. "Only one way to find out," he muttered.

Arms crossed, he stepped back, leaned against the wall and waited for the door to open.

Cara stepped out of the shower, so jittery with excitement that her towel kept slipping from her fingers as she wrapped it around her body.

Humming merrily, she opened the bathroom door and cried out in shock at the sight of Alex standing there.

His face was like stone, chasing away her happy mood. He too was clad only in a towel. It hung dangerously low around his torso, in stark contrast to the bank of rippled muscles above.

She tore her eyes away from his waist and forced a smile.

"Good morning! I was just on my way to—"

"Steal something else of mine?"

She flinched at his angry tone but managed to square her eyes with his.

"You know, I may not be able to read," he continued, his voice like ice. "But my hearing is fine."

"What are you talking about?"

He took a step forward and she let go of the doorknob.

"I heard you. Singing in the shower. Trouble is, no one but me is supposed to know that tune."

Oh, Lord. Had she been singing that loudly?

Her eyes slid shut as panic swelled. She hated having anyone hear her sing. But worse than that, after last night, she knew she had to put some distance between them. But not like this.

He glared at her. "Why did you do it?"

She knew the answer, but she wasn't ready to admit it, to him or to herself.

She opened her eyes and cringed, feeling exposed and angry, more at herself than him.

She tightened the towel around her breasts. "Excuse me, I need to get dressed."

She tried to walk past him, but he grabbed her arm.

"Not so fast. You're not going anywhere until you tell me why you took my song."

"I didn't take it! I found it on the floor of your living room, okay? You were upstairs getting ready to leave and I just picked it up. Now let me go."

She wrested away from his grasp and looked up. His eyes were blazing like fire.

"You found it?" he said, his tone scornful. "That's a crock. You stole it."

"I—I'm sorry, Alex. I really didn't think anything of it." Cara knew she was telling the truth. Because at the time, she hadn't thought at all.

"You had no right. Why didn't you just pick it up and throw it away in the trash can? You had to open it? You had to keep it? Why?"

Cara opened her mouth to speak, but no words would come out. Alex was right.

"I don't know."

He folded his arms over his chest, as if he didn't believe her. "So you just decided to steal it?"

She clenched her fists. "Stop saying that! I didn't steal it."

"What do you call taking somebody's private property?"

She stepped toward him, shivering from the coldness in his voice. "I can't explain why I did it. All I can say is I'm sor—"

He cut her off with a wave of his hands. "What do you plan to do with it?"

"Nothing, of course! I just liked the melody and then the words just seemed to flow. It's a great tune, Alex."

His lips pursed, emphasizing the doubtful look on his face.

Just then, her towel loosened and she grabbed it just before her nudity was exposed. She looked up and her face got hot, as his eyes raked over her body. Alex might have been angry, but it didn't stop him from checking her out.

"Can we talk about this later? I'm freezing and I want to get dressed."

Without waiting for his answer, she turned and started walking to her bedroom.

"You know, Cara, this changes everything."

A sliver of fear ran through her and she spun around. "What do you mean?"

He walked up to her and stood so close that the tiny hairs on her arm frizzled from the energy between them.

"I can't be around someone who's going to steal from me."

She stepped back and threw up her hands. The towel loosened slightly but she didn't care. She was tired of him making her feel like a criminal.

"Alex, you're making too much of a big deal about this. What do I have to do to make you believe I'm sorry?"

"There's nothing you can do except get dressed and get packed. I'm going to call Frank right now and have him come up here and take you back home to Harlem, where you belong."

Cara's face reddened with anger. "Wait a minute," she exclaimed, turning around and following him as he strode toward his bedroom. "Today I was going to start you on the book I've chosen for you to read on your tour. I know you can do this."

"It doesn't matter anymore."

"Alex, please. I told you I'll give your music back. Then you'll have it and you won't have anything to worry about."

He turned and frowned. "How do I know you didn't or won't take something else?"

She wanted to scream in exasperation, but she

counted to five to calm herself. "Because I said I won't. Isn't that good enough?"

He shook his head. "You should have thought about that before. Look, I don't surround myself with a lot of people." His voice softened. "I was starting to trust you."

She grasped his arm. "Alex, you can trust me," she pleaded. "I promise you can."

His eyes held hers, and for a moment, she thought he believed her.

"I don't think so. Not anymore." Without another word, he stalked into his room and slammed the door.

Fear lodged like a stone in her heart, and she stood there trembling, until finally the chill in the air forced her to move.

Back in her room, she shut the door, collapsed and folded her arms around her knees.

If she didn't teach Alex how to read in three days, she wouldn't receive the money that would help her prevent Beacon House from closing its doors. The domino effect would be swift and negative, extending to the current clients, the community of Harlem and the thousands of unknown individuals whom she would never be able to help.

Taking that music was one of the dumbest things she'd ever done. And now it could cost her everything.

Chapter 5

Within ten minutes, Alex had dressed, grabbed his horn and was running toward the garden. His feet pounded on the hard ground, dodging tree roots fingering across the path. When he reached the shed, he plopped down on a wooden chair, breathing hard.

Maybe now he could finish his tune.

Or what's left of it.

His heart still pounded in anger and disbelief over what had just happened inside.

He shook his head, then picked up his sax and played a flurry of notes, not pausing to take a breath until he felt like his lungs were going to explode.

He wanted to kick himself in the head for being so stupid. For starting to fall for what he thought was strait-laced, sweet innocence. His mother always said he was a bad judge of character.

With an exasperated sigh, he started playing again.

His fingers flew up and down the saxophone, crushing notes and bending pitches along the way.

But all he could hear was Cara's voice. She had taken what was supposed to be an up-tempo bebop tune and flipped it into a ballad. Sweet, sultry, mystifying. Her voice invaded his mind, drowning out any musical ideas he might have had.

He smirked and let his saxophone drop against his chest. *Might* was the operative word. The truth was for the last few months, he'd been having trouble concentrating on composing, or anything else for that matter.

And now he was expected to learn how to read? With a so-called teacher who had pretty much stolen his music?

Yeah, man, like you never did anything wrong in your life.

He pushed the voice inside his head aside, just like he had the past. Or at least he tried to. He had a sinking fear the past was about to catch up with him, and what he was starting to feel for her was only the beginning.

He wasn't sure which was worse.

What he felt couldn't be love. It was too soon for that. Besides, he'd never truly loved a woman, so he wasn't sure he would know how it felt when it came along.

He just knew that despite what she'd done, there was something about her that he found extremely appealing. She piqued his curiosity more than any other woman had in a long time.

But none of that mattered now. She'd be gone in a few hours and he could get back to his so-called wonderful life.

He fingered the saxophone around his neck, the one that he loved so much, that had cost his family so much.

If his fans only knew the truth.

He tipped his head back and stared at the rusty tin roof. His breathing eased and he inhaled the dank smell permeating inside of the shed, even though he'd left the door wide open.

Right now, he felt as old as the shed smelled. Was it because he'd just turned thirty this summer or was it something else?

He inhaled again and his nose twitched at the scent of vanilla, as intoxicating as the woman who wore it.

"I just came to tell you that I'm not going anywhere."

Whirling around, he blasted Cara with a pointed stare. "Yes. You. Are. Frank will be here any minute to pick you up."

With a smug smile, she crossed her slender arms. "No, he won't."

He raised his eyebrows and fought the desire to pull her into his lap. "Oh, yeah? Why not?"

"Because you're not a quitter. You wouldn't have gotten this far in your career if you were."

"Listen, Cara." He got up and stood so close only his saxophone was between them. "You don't know anything about me," he retorted, starting down into her brown eyes. "And if you did, you wouldn't be here right now."

Fire met fire. "And leave this half-finished? No. Way."

He held on to the mouthpiece of his saxophone, never taking his eyes off hers. "Why is this so important to you?"

"I don't like to see anyone giving up on something, and—"

"Oh, c'mon!" he said, his tone mocking. "Do you really expect me to believe your holier-than-thou attitude? You were hired to teach me how to read, not to steal my music."

Her eyes widened with hurt, and he felt guilty for causing her pain. Maybe he was being too hard on her.

Alex took a deep breath, softened his voice. "I'm serious, Cara. I want the truth."

"I know it was stupid," she began, biting her lip. "But when I opened that crumpled-up piece of paper and hummed the melody, I knew it was something special."

She traced a finger down the bumpy surface of his saxophone and he groaned inwardly, wanting her fingers to continue traveling south.

"It sounds dumb, but you create magic every day, and I guess, just for once, I just wanted to be a part of it."

Her eyes bore into his, her need for him to understand so pure his skin tingled. It was then he knew she was telling the truth.

"Magic?" He snorted. "Nah, it's just a lot of hard work."

"True, but it also takes a whole lot of talent and dedication." She placed her hand on his arm, traced his tattoo with her finger, and when his groin quivered, he wished his saxophone wasn't playing referee between their bodies.

"I'm sorry, okay? You have to believe me."

He stared into her brown orbs and his heart dropped when he saw they were brimming with tears.

To his knowledge, he'd never made any woman cry. Remorse tumbled through him. He broke away from her gaze and ran his hand over his head.

"You're good, you know."

She took a step back. "I'm what?" she choked out.

"Good." He cleared his throat. "You have a nice voice."

Her smile was wary, and so sweet to behold. "Thanks. I never thought I could do it. You know, make up words to a song and have them sound like that. So perfect, like they were always meant to be together."

He smiled back, felt something good break within him. "That's what I love about playing jazz. I can get that feeling every day."

"Yeah. I felt like I was high," she confided. "Not that I would know anything about that, you know from a drug perspective that is. I fall out on cold medicine." She giggled.

He laughed. Her sense of humor always caught him off guard.

"It sounds like a dream life, being able to travel the world, play the music you love and get paid doing it."

He shrugged. "I hate to bust your bubble, but the music business isn't all fun and games and VIP parties. Do yourself a favor. Stay an amateur."

"Are you saying I have no talent?" she huffed.

"No, I already told you that you have a great voice, but this is a tough business. If something goes wrong, at least you have something to fall back on."

Unlike me.

He walked over to the bench and plopped down.

"Writing and performing every day, night after night, city after city. For those that really care about the music, for every note you play, you tear away little pieces of your soul until one day there's nothing left."

She sat down, her hair tickling his arm. "And are you one of those people that care?"

He didn't answer, while he wrestled with the part of him that wanted to tell her everything. But there was another part of him that still didn't trust her. Not because she stole his music. It was something else he couldn't quite put his finger on.

"Sometimes I don't think I have the right to care." He gestured toward his home and the forest beyond. "The right to all of this."

She poked him in the arm. "Hello-oo? Who has a Grammy Award sitting on a shelf in his living room? Trust me, I like a guy who's humble, but you need to give yourself a little more credit."

"And here I thought you were into hotheaded jazz musicians," he teased, giving her shoulder a gentle squeeze, loving the glow that lit up her cheeks.

"You know…" she paused, and her smile was shy this time "…I really *am* one of your biggest fans."

He folded his arms. "Oh, really?"

She glanced down at his saxophone. "I've been following your career for a while, and I admire you a lot."

The kindness in her eyes drew him into a place inside himself he wasn't sure he wanted to explore.

"It's got nothing to do with talent. I haven't got a choice. Music is in my blood, it's such a part of me that sometimes I wonder what it's like to be in the real world."

She tilted her head. "The real world?"

"Yeah, the one you and everyone else lives and works in. If I couldn't play music, I'm not sure I could survive."

She shook her head. "That will never happen."

If only she knew.

"Learning to read could open up a whole new world to me, one I'm not sure I'm ready for. I've gotten along this far not knowing how to read, how will I survive actually knowing how to do it? Does that make any sense?"

She nodded. "A lot of my clients feel that way. I realize it might be scary, but you're a long way off from that. Right now, I'm just trying to prepare you for the tour. After that, you can decide how fast or slow you want things to progress. I just need a little more time with you and then you'll never have to see me again."

At the thought of the weekend ending, he felt a twinge of sadness he didn't understand.

"Yeah," he muttered. "I guess we better get cracking, huh?"

He stood, walked over to the shed and shut the door. He'd have to find some way to work on his tune later. Tommy would be calling him for an update tomorrow and he wanted to be able to tell him it was finished.

Although Cara's rendition was beautiful, he would never use it on his album. For some reason, he wanted to keep her voice for his ears only.

She followed him. "Do you actually practice in here?"

"Yeah, when I don't have a beautiful woman trying to teach me the ABC's."

The smile on her face warmed his heart. In fact, her very presence had a calming effect on him, and as they began to walk down the path to the house, he had the strongest urge to take her hand in his and never let go.

When they got back, Cara headed straight for the living room where she had already organized her teaching materials. Her goal for today was to focus on the book he would be reading during the tour.

She glanced at her watch and her eyes widened. Time was definitely not on their side. She had less than forty-eight hours to get Alex to a point where he would feel comfortable reading in front of an audience full of children.

Not an easy task with a man who she'd rather be lying in bed with laughing at Saturday-morning cartoons. Their feet, legs and arms wound around each other like a grapevine.

The fantasy disappeared when a vision of Beacon House, complete with boarded-up windows, graffiti and a padlock on the door, invaded her mind.

Panic crept into her veins at the consequences of failure. All her clients would have to go elsewhere for literacy services. And she would have to face her father, who would only be too glad to comfort the loss of her dream with one of his famous I-told-you-so speeches.

There was no way she was going to allow that to happen. Her stomach grumbled but she ignored it. It was time to get back to work. She glanced around, but while she had been daydreaming, Alex had disappeared. She figured he was in the kitchen, getting lunch.

"Grrr," she grumbled. "That man!"

Just then she heard the floorboards squeak and she raced into the hallway. She gasped when she caught Alex climbing the stairs to the second floor.

"Oh, no, you don't!"

She grabbed his hand, intent on dragging him back to the living room if she had to—all five foot one of her.

"You are *not* getting away this time."

He stopped in his tracks and her heart fluttered when he turned and ran his thumb slowly over hers. When he turned on his heel and walked down the stairs, a look of chagrin on his face, she felt smug satisfaction.

Now we're getting somewhere.

But her victory was short-lived. Her breath whooshed

out of her when Alex suddenly put his arm around her waist and pulled her to him.

"Oh, yeah? Who's gonna stop me?" His eyes had a devilish gleam in them that Cara found hard to resist.

He rested his hands on the small of her back, and she could not help imagining them sliding down to cup her buttocks.

"I am." Her defenses weakened as he drew her even closer, until she had no choice but to place her arms around his neck or have them squished between them.

"Hmm…" She felt his fingers trace a path up her spine until they nestled at the base of her neck. "Care to show me how?"

"I—I," she stammered as he gently massaged her neck with the pad of his thumb.

"I have a variety of methods…um…that I employ for students who are chronic procrastinators."

He smiled innocently. "You can't be referring to me?"

She nodded, as tingles of sensation radiated throughout her spine. Her eyes slid shut as muscle tension melted into desire.

"Who else is in the room distracting me right now?" she murmured.

"I'm not trying to distract you. I'm trying to help you. You seemed so tense back in the garden."

Her eyes snapped open and she tried to step away from his grasp, but he tightened his hold. She wanted to lay her head against his chest, nuzzle the muscles beneath his shirt, feel his heart beating.

But she didn't.

Instead, she lifted her head and looked up into his hazel eyes. His face was unreadable and yet she sensed he was struggling, too.

But with what?

Her lip quivered slightly, but she steadied her voice. "You were so angry at me you told me to hit the road. So yes, I guess I was a little stressed out."

He smiled down at her then and she wanted to shake her head in disbelief. From the intimate way he was embracing her, it didn't seem like he was still angry. His arms, strong and warm, held on to her tightly, almost possessively.

And she didn't mind one bit.

Still, it was hard for her to fathom how he could be so forgiving so soon, when what she'd done was unforgivable. She had yet to hear it from his lips, and feel it with her heart.

"Haven't you ever heard the old saying that everything happens for a reason?" he inquired. "Maybe you taking my music will be the best thing that ever happened to me."

She wanted to ask him how that could be possible, but she was afraid of the answer.

"But I'm still not sure if you've really forgiven me. Have you?" she said, hating the uncertainty in her voice.

"It isn't easy," he admitted with a sigh, his hands heavy on her shoulders. "If you haven't figured it out already, I'm a pretty private person. I was starting to trust you, and that's really hard for me to do, especially with a woman."

"Why is that?"

He shrugged. "I'm not sure. Maybe because I've never been able to be myself with a woman. I like to have a good time, and that's about as far as it goes."

"Except when those good times hit the presses," she added. "*People, US Weekly, Ebony.* It seems like you're never with the same woman twice."

He scowled. "Some of what you read is true, to an extent. But most of it isn't. Being who I am and doing what I do for a living doesn't come without a price. Someone always wants something from you. And if they don't get it, they'll tell anyone they did—for the right amount of money."

She shook her head. "Fame. I think I'll play it safe and just watch the movie."

He laughed out loud. "That's smart. The truth is I don't open up to people very easily. Now whether that's due to being famous or just a part of who I am, I don't know. But despite everything," he said, bringing his hand to her face, "for some reason, I'm starting to feel very comfortable with you."

His words were like a dream, too good to be true, yet wasn't that what she'd wanted to hear all these years? A part of her desperately wanted to believe him. The other part screamed, "Watch out girl, he's a player!"

She pushed both thoughts to the curb as he traced the underline of her jaw with his finger. She closed her eyes, succumbing to the allure of the roughened tip against her soft skin, the feel of his arms around her.

How many times had Cara wished it was her in the glamorous designer gown holding his arm on the red carpet, at the latest club, or dining at the finest restaurants?

But the reality was this: he was a famous musician who made a habit of courting beautiful women, while she made a habit of cozying up with a good book. He was totally out of her league, and if she didn't wake up out of this fantasy, she would lose the only thing she cared about—Beacon House.

She stopped his hand with her own and wriggled out of his grasp.

"I think it's time we got back to business."

At her professional tone, Alex opened his mouth like he wanted to argue, then nodded his head. "Okay, but on one condition."

She cast him a wary glance. "Sure, what is it?"

"Have dinner with me tonight. It'll be fun. We'll eat, then head on over to the club."

She felt giddy and woozy at the same time. "Dinner? Club?"

"Yeah, every time I'm up this way, I sit in with the house band at the Jazz Hideaway, it's a local jazz club in town. Is that okay with you?"

She swallowed hard. "Sounds great! Now that we have all of that out of the way, can we please get to work now?"

"Sure. Let me just make us some quick sandwiches. I'm starving, aren't you?"

She nodded. Her stomach was grumbling. Plus, if they ate now, they could work until it was almost dinnertime.

"That would be wonderful. I have a surprise for you!"

"A surprise?" He raised his eyebrows. "I can't wait."

He reached out a finger and traced the roundness of her cheeks, leaving her knees shaking. "See you in class in fifteen minutes."

She blushed at the sensual undertones in his voice. As he walked down the hall to the kitchen, the heat of his fingers danced on her skin with the undeniable promise of seduction.

Chapter 6

Back in the living room, Cara's encounter with Alex left her dazed and aroused. She could no longer deny her attraction to him. Her body was telling her to go forward, but her negative balance sheet knew better. If there was ever a time to just get the job done, it was now.

But how to resist him, she thought as she sank down into the couch and flopped against the pillows.

Every time she tried to keep their interactions all business and no play, he broke through her professional demeanor with his sexy smile and a masculine vulnerability that was utterly endearing.

She'd realized a long time ago that her heart was her weakest link, and it started and ended with Alex.

He returned with lunch. "I hope you're hungry," he announced. "Turkey sandwiches on rye, pita chips and fresh lemonade."

Plate in hand, he turned to give it to her and suddenly stopped.

"What's that behind your back?"

She gave him a sly smile. "Something that will change your life!"

"Hmm." He set her plate back on the tray. "Let me guess. A baby?"

Cara laughed out loud. "No!"

Alex snapped his fingers. "Darn. Other than marriage, that's the only thing I can think of that would turn my world upside-down. Except if I won the Powerball. Now that would be cool! I'd be a gazillionaire!"

She giggled. "Well, this is kind of like hitting the lottery, at least in my opinion."

"Then what are you waiting for? Let me at it!"

He tried to reach around her waist to grab it, but Cara scooted away to the opposite end of the couch.

"Ta-da!" she shouted with flourish and held the book in the palm of her hands, directly in front of her breasts.

His eyes narrowed. "Is that the one I'm going to be reading?"

She nodded, pointed to the title. "Can you spell out the letters for me?

Her breath hitched as he moved his body closer to hers until their knees were almost touching.

He frowned. "I'll give it a try."

Putting his finger under the words, he traced and spoke each letter.

"T-H-E..."

It was impossible, but she swore she could feel the slow path of his fingertip on her skin through the hardcover of the book.

"J-U-N-G-L-E..."

At his every touch, her loins pulsated with pleasure and she shivered involuntarily. What if there were nothing between his fingers and her skin? For a moment, her imagination ran wild at the thought.

"T-R-U-M-P-E-T-E-E-R."

He stopped talking and looked at her. The fantasy dissolved and left her cheeks tingling with embarrassment.

"The Jungle Trumpeteer," she pronounced. "Very good! I'm proud of you!"

He looked skeptical. "This isn't one of these 'Dick and Jane' books is it? Because if it is, I'm not reading it. Unless—" he flashed a wicked smile "—it's the porn version, of course."

She gasped. "Be serious, okay?" she said, and pretended to smack him lightly on the head with the book. "Don't worry. This book is a simple read that will stimulate your imagination."

He grinned. "I'm going to need a lot more than a book. How are you at massages?"

Heat flared her cheeks at his flirtatious question. What had gotten into this man?

"Uh," she stammered. "That's not part of my lesson plan."

He shrugged. "Oh, well. Can't blame a guy for trying. So what's next? Should I sit on the floor crisscross applesauce?"

She burst out laughing. "One step at a time, okay? Feet on the floor and keep your hands to yourself. Do you think you can do that?"

His eyes penetrated hers and she felt his desire reflecting her own.

"I can. I'm just not sure I want to." His silken voice caressed her with unspoken meaning.

Although it was very difficult to do, she elected to ignore his comment.

"Just let me read the book to you all the way through with no interruptions."

"Okay," he said with a resigned sigh. "You read. I eat."

Satisfied that he was momentarily distracted by food, she cleared her throat and began to read.

The story was about an elephant who believed his trunk was a musical instrument. When he played it, he was able to rid the jungle of poachers and ultimately saved all the animals.

She closed the book. "How's that for a happy ending? Well, what do you think?"

No sooner had the words left her mouth than Cara had a strong feeling his upbeat mood had suddenly soured. He sat there quietly and finished his sandwich, his brow knit together as if he were in deep thought. If she had held her breath in suspense, she would have turned blue.

Finally, he leaned back against the pillows. "Thank you for not torturing me with *See Spot Run*." He turned his head toward hers, and her heart did a little flip. "But I still don't know about all this."

"What do you mean?" she asked, sensing his trepidation.

"Do you really think I can do it?"

"Of course I do, Alex," she said softly, patting his arm, the muscle underneath tight with tension. "You have the basic concepts down. Now it's just a matter of applying what you've already learned. It shouldn't be too hard."

He palmed his head, his voice ragged. "What if I mess everything up? Those kids will see me struggling with the words and—"

"And they'll see someone who's trying to do his best," she replied firmly.

He sat up quickly and she dropped her hand to her side.

"But what kind of man doesn't know how to read?" he said in a disgusted tone. "I'm thirty years old! It's too late."

His negative words didn't surprise her. It was normal for people to feel scared and anxious about learning to do anything they thought they should have learned when they were younger. Whether it was learning to read, playing a musical instrument, riding a bike, or in her case, learning to love and trust someone.

"I have clients ranging from age eighteen all the way up to eighty. It's *never* too late."

When he said nothing in response, she reached out and touched his hand to reassure him.

"Alex, why do you doubt yourself all of a sudden?"

Dropping his elbows on his knees, he shook his head sadly. "You'll never understand."

Her heart squeezed at his comment. "Can I give you some advice?"

"Do I have a choice?"

She shook her head and smiled. "You should focus on all the things you'll be able to read once you become a better reader, rather than the things you're struggling with now."

"Like what for example?"

"What about fan mail?" she suggested. "You do get fan mail, don't you?"

"Of course, I get fan mail, both email and the old-fashioned way."

"Wouldn't you like to be able to actually read them and respond?"

"I have a publicist. That's her job."
Strike one. Think, Cara, think!
"What about love letters?" she blurted.

His eyebrow shot up. Clearly, she was grasping at straws.

"Uh, okay, but I think you're missing one thing. You have to be in love with someone to write or receive a love letter."

Cara's heart pounded. "True. Haven't you ever been in love?"

"You mean a melt-into-your-shoes kind of love?"
She nodded.

"Nope. Is that bad?"

She stared at him in disbelief. "But what about all those ladies I've seen you with on TV and in magazines? Didn't you love any of them?"

He shook his head. "I knew going into those relationships, and I use that term lightly, what most of those women wanted. Eventually, my assumption proved to be correct. They never looked or bothered to see the real me. All they wanted was status and a good time. That's it."

His eyes moved over her face, a touch of curiosity in them. "What about you?"

She shrugged. "Not really. I've been focused on building my career and trying to make Beacon House an integral part of the Harlem community."
But I can easily fall in love with you. Too easily.

"I suppose, that if I was in love, it would be nice to write a love letter and read it to my woman," he conceded, looking straight into her eyes.

Her face warmed, and she glanced at her watch to hide her reaction. It was nearly three o'clock.

"Are you ready to try again?" she inquired.

He nodded and they leaned back against the soft cushions. With the book unfolded across their laps, they began to work again. Although it was still a slow process, Alex was reading the words a little easier now.

While his concentration had improved, she could barely keep her mind on the book. As she watched his full lips form each word, she wondered if his lips would caress her body with the same care.

Not wanting to lose momentum, they stayed at it for a couple of hours, only breaking once to stretch their legs and grab some coffee from the kitchen.

Finally, Alex stood up, and Cara tried not to let her eyes drift south. But she couldn't help but notice how snugly his jeans fit around his long legs. Her breath caught in her throat as she was treated to another glimpse of his muscle-wrapped abdomen as he stretched his arms over his head.

She closed her eyes briefly, and in her mind's eye she saw him standing nude before her and she was doing more than just admiring his well-toned body.

"Cara!" Her eyes opened to the sound of snapping fingers. "Looks like you're as beat as I am. Do you mind if we stop for now? We should rest a little bit before we head out to dinner."

"Not at all." She stifled a yawn. "I think that's a great idea."

They carried the plates and glasses out to the kitchen, rinsed them and put them in the dishwasher. The otherwise mundane task didn't seem so boring doing it with him.

They walked up the stairs and Cara was about to go into her room when Alex grabbed her hand.

"Wait. I have one final question."

And before she could ask what it was, he pulled her

close and drew her into a passionate kiss that went beyond mere lust.

Cara thought she was going to die from the sensation of his lips moving softly upon hers. His tongue teased and probed the core of her mouth, drawing her deeper into him until she felt like she would collapse under the supreme weight of her longing for him.

Crushed against his body, heat was mutually exchanged, stoking an intense need that only increased when she felt the evidence of his desire throbbing against her belly.

Suddenly, he lifted his lips from hers and tilted her chin up with his fingers. She opened her eyes to meet his hazel ones, rimmed with undeniable passion.

"Is that the type of kiss you give to a woman when you are falling in love?"

Rendered speechless, she could only nod her head.

"Just checking." He caressed her lower lip, reddened from his kisses, with the edge of his thumb. "See you downstairs in ninety minutes."

He graced her with a seductive smile and she stood in amazement as he turned and walked down the hallway.

Cara slid into her room, shut the door and leaned against it.

What was that all about?

For the moment, she didn't care. She just wanted to savor the kiss that still sparkled on her lips and not think about the possibility that he might be falling in love with her.

Or that she might be falling in love with him. Both scenarios would be more than she could hope for, and more than she could handle right now.

And although she realized that his offer of dinner

was likely not meant to be a date, his kisses told a different story.

Why not indulge in the fantasy for once?

She decided that for one night, she would pretend that she was Alex Dovington's woman, his confidante, his lover. The only one he desired, needed and loved.

Dreams-come-true always seemed to pass her by. But she had a strong feeling that tonight was the beginning of a whole new adventure.

Back in his own room, Alex stretched out on the bed and closed his eyes, reliving the tenderness of Cara's tawny-pink lips, full and luscious, upon his own. It was a kiss he never wanted to forget.

But what had gotten into him, swooping her off her feet with a kiss that she wasn't likely to forget, either? Although he could play any ballad like his heart had been broken a thousand times, he wasn't the romantic type. He'd even dropped the L word!

He knew the answer. Cara.

This woman, with the wild corkscrew hair and sweet disposition, was making him do things he'd never done before. Feel things he'd never felt before.

He'd never felt so moved by desire for one woman as he was for Cara.

His erection strained against his pants, begging for some kind of release. But he kept his hands at his sides and remained still, content to allow himself to be a prisoner of his passion for her.

His beyond-beautiful, unbelievably sexy reading teacher.

Although she held a certain innocence that was appealing, he was playing with fire and he knew it.

The fact that she stole his music, with no regard to his

feelings or the consequences of her actions, was enough evidence to justify some doubt about her character. He was trying to get past it, and although her reason for doing it seemed plausible, forgiving her was difficult.

He desperately wanted to believe that she wasn't like all the other women he'd come into contact with in his life. Money-hungry, power-seeking, back-stabbing ladies who thought playing with his heart was just part of the "game."

What they didn't know is that love was never a game to him. It was a gift.

Their audacious confidence was all for nothing. Those women never stood a chance.

Cara, on the other hand, was a woman he wanted to know intimately, feel deeply, and make her his own.

She was on the opposite side of his usual spectrum of dating choices. And despite his best efforts to remain cool and detached, she was wriggling her way into his heart.

That was a feat in itself.

Ever since he'd lost his twin brother, his heart had been closed to anyone and everyone. Sure, it had happened years ago, but he could remember it as if it was yesterday. Some hurts never heal, especially when you're the cause.

Slowly, she was breaking through his self-imposed wall of bitterness and hesitation. Her patience with him for the past two days was worthy of sainthood, in his opinion. He knew he could be a real pain in the butt when he felt like it.

He remembered that when he got the news from Tommy that he'd hired Cara to teach him to read, he was angry beyond belief.

But right now, he had the strangest urge to call his aging manager and thank him.

He chuckled low. If it wasn't for Tommy, he wouldn't have experienced one of the most freeing moments in his life. One he definitely wanted to experience again.

The next time he kissed her, he wouldn't be able to stop. By the way she responded to him, he didn't think she would mind at all. She might accept him into her bed, but would she let him into her heart?

He had to admit that Cara was out of his league. She was intelligent and well-read, with an aura of quiet confidence that was evidenced in her demeanor. He loved the way she walked, dressed and spoke. She made him laugh with a sharp sense of humor that always kept him on his toes.

Yes, Cara Williams was class, elegance and playful sexiness all wrapped up in a body that would drive a blind man to distraction.

So what if she couldn't cook?

The most appealing thing about her was how much she cared about him. He could tell that about her almost instantly.

Back at his town house, when he confessed his fear of public humiliation, she acknowledged his concerns with grace. Somehow she knew how important it was to him to maintain his dignity through this ordeal.

And just now, when he was struggling to make sense of the letters and sounds, he'd felt her silently cheering him on. Her smiles of encouragement meant more to him than she would ever know.

Normally, he couldn't be forced into anything and yet here he was, kicking and screaming his way to a world he'd never known. Deep down, he realized that Cara was the key to his success.

But she could also be his downfall.

He ran his hand over his head, suddenly remembering he'd yet to put the final touches on his tune.

He'd never let any woman get in the way of his music, but that was exactly what had happened today—and yesterday for that matter. And he was horrified that a part of him didn't give a damn.

To hell with Mo and Sharp Five Records, he thought for the hundredth time.

His dream to open up his own recording and publishing company was always in the back of his mind. He wanted to be his own boss, chart his own course. Taking orders from someone had never suited him. It angered him that his very future in music hinged on the bottom-line revenue of his next album.

Instead of feeling blessed by his success, he felt trapped.

His goals had felt out of his reach until he'd met Cara, who had inspired a glimmer of hope within him.

It was too soon to tell how well he would read at the book tour, but he was starting to feel more comfortable. His heart swelled with pride, and he was surprised that he was even starting to *like* reading—a little. Words didn't seem like the enemy anymore.

His mood sobered when he remembered that she was only on contract for the weekend. When Monday rolled around and they were back in Harlem, he would never see her again. Although he sensed she was attracted to him, she'd already indicated that her first love was her work. They had that much in common.

He rose and sat on the edge of the bed to prepare for his shower. He slowly removed his pants and boxers, groaning when the hardened length of his penis sprang forth.

Better make this an ice-cold shower.

If not, he knew he wouldn't be able to make it through dinner without stripping her naked and taking her on his own wild ride.

The fantasy alone was tempting enough to make it happen right now, although he feared making love to her one time wouldn't be enough.

He knew without a doubt that he wanted and needed more than just a casual, platonic relationship with Cara. There was so much he didn't know about her that he wanted to discover.

But he cared about her enough to realize that friendship was the only fair and realistic option. She deserved the stability of a husband, not the unpredictable lifestyle of a professional musician.

Had he set her up for a fall by asking her to dinner?

No, he rationalized. She would not take his invite that way. For the past two days, she had tried to maintain a professional relationship. He was the one who had taken it to the next level with a kiss that surpassed even his wildest expectations.

Besides, if she knew what he'd done in the past, she would probably hate him. Or at least lose all respect for him. His heart grieved a little at all the mistakes he had made years ago that were still costing him dearly today.

He sincerely hoped that someday he would have the courage to tell her his story, and more important, upon learning the truth that she would have the courage to stay with him—if only as a friend.

It was all he could hope to be to her.

He heard the water go on in the bathroom, and he swore silently. Cara had beaten him to the shower— again. Knowing her, all the hot water would be gone when she was finished.

He sighed as he plopped back down on the bed to wait his turn. It looked like his wish for a cold shower was about to come true. Too bad his dream of having her in his arms forever would likely remain a fantasy.

Chapter 7

Ninety minutes later, Alex went downstairs, fully expecting Cara to keep him waiting while she did whatever women do to get ready to go out. But she was already there. And she took his breath away.

"Wow." He whistled low. "You look fantastic!"

She blushed in return, pleasing him. He took his time admiring her. His eyes raked over her gray dress with spaghetti straps that was cut low enough to tease and let him imagine the rest.

"Turn around, please."

She gave him a curious look, but then twirled slowly.

He loved the way the knee-length dress shimmered around her bare legs as she turned. It fit her well-toned body beautifully. Her curly mane was down and flowed around her shoulders. High-heeled silver sandals completed the ensemble.

She looked like an angel.

Remembering his vow to use tonight to further cultivate a "friends-only" relationship, he said a silent prayer. He could look, but not touch. Tonight, he would definitely need divine intervention to keep his hands off of her.

He smiled. "Ready to go?"

"Yes. Can't wait!"

When they reached his black Porsche Boxster, he opened the door and waited for her to get in and buckle her seat belt before he entered on the driver's side.

"I hope you don't mind riding in this."

She crossed her legs and he enjoyed watching the smooth and sexy motion.

"Not at all. I've always wanted to ride in a Porsche."

"Great. I keep this just for going into town. My limo will be here tomorrow evening to pick us up and take us back to Harlem."

He thought he detected a shadow cross her face, but quickly dismissed that notion. She was the one who said she was going to recommend another reading teacher to him once they got back to Harlem.

Clearly, she wasn't losing sleep over the fact that their weekend together was almost over.

"Do you hear that?" he said, admiring the low purr of the engine. "It's like music to a man's ears!"

She laughed. "How fast does it go?"

"As fast as you want it to go, baby!" he shot back with a wink.

She cracked up, and he laughed along with her.

"Hmm." Her lips arched into a mischievous smile. "Why don't you show me?" Her throaty voice made his palms sweat.

He grinned. "When you say it like that, your wish is my command."

After looking both ways, he gripped the steering wheel, pressed on the gas and away they went.

Cara whooped with delight as they flew around the mountainous curves at lightning-fast speeds.

It had been a long time since he made a woman so happy with such a simple, albeit somewhat dangerous, show of machismo. Normally, all he'd get was "the eyeball roll" with a bored sigh on the side.

The evening was starting out with a bang, and he hoped it would only get better.

About twenty heart-stopping minutes later, they screeched to a halt in front of Idella's Country Carriage House, spraying gravel all the way.

"Was that fast enough for you?"

"Incredible!" she replied, her eyes dancing with excitement. "Let's do it again!"

The pure joy on her face lit him up on the inside with happiness. "There's more where that came from, but let's eat first. I'm starved."

Just then, the valet opened up the passenger door and Cara got out. Alex dropped the keys into the man's hand and escorted her through the restaurant's foyer.

"Mr. Dovington!" The pretty hostess beamed at the couple. "It's great to see you again! We have everything ready. Right this way, please."

As they walked to their table, there were curious glances from the patrons, a few waves, and a not-so-silent whistle.

Alex pulled out Cara's chair, admiring the delicate roundness of her shoulders as she sat down.

"Alex, this place is beautiful. And the view!"

The semicircular private room they were in overlooked the Hudson River.

"Breathtaking, isn't it?" He sat down and accepted the menus from the server. "Just wait till you taste the food!"

"That's if he doesn't eat it all up first!"

"Auntie Idella!" he exclaimed as he rose, smothering her with a hug.

"Stop your nonsense." Idella sounded stern, but the grin on her face was wide with happiness.

"Aw, you know I can't help giving you some sugar."

"Yeah, and it's always more than I can handle!" Idella guffawed so loudly the sound reverberated throughout the tiny room. "You know I have heart trouble! What are you trying to do? Put me in an early grave?"

He loved making Idella laugh. It brought back happy memories from his childhood, sitting in her kitchen, watching her cook and eating more than a boy should.

"Never!" His smile was as sweet as Idella's disposition. "Who else would make your famous sweet potato pie that folks drive from miles away to eat?"

She shushed him, but Alex could tell she was pleased with the compliment. "Now wipe that million-dollar smile off your face and introduce me to this pretty young lady!"

"She's the reason I've got this crazy grin, Auntie! This is Cara Williams."

"Pleased to meet you. Your restaurant is gorgeous!"

Alex handed Cara a menu. "And only the best Southern cooking you'll find outside of the South. Take a look."

Idella's face beamed. "Soul food with spunk, I like to say."

They ordered seafood muddle soup, smothered pork chops, fried corn and sweet potato biscuits.

"Excellent choices. I'll put your order in myself."

"Thank you. I can't wait!"

Idella poked Alex in the arm. "She's a keeper. Be nice to her," she warned before walking away.

"Ow!" He rubbed his arm. "I'm nice, aren't I?"

"When you want to be," Cara teased.

His eyes were only on Cara as a waiter arrived with a bottle of champagne. He poured two flutes before setting the bottle on ice and leaving.

"I think a toast is in order." Alex raised his glass to meet Cara's. "Here's to private lessons."

They both smiled as they clinked their glasses together.

His face warmed under Cara's gaze as she took a sip. "Hmm…this is delicious. If the food tastes as good as this wine, I'll be in heaven."

He gazed into her eyes. "I already am."

For the first time, he noticed how thick and natural her lashes were, and he wondered how they would feel if he ran his fingertip along them.

"In all seriousness, I'm grateful for what you've done so far. I know I can be a real bear sometimes."

Her brows raised in surprise at his confession. "I'm used to it. Most people go through a range of emotions when they are learning how to read. I just never had to sleep in the same house with them," she added shyly.

"Well, then, in that case, I am honored to have you as my guest."

The waiter set a basket of biscuits on the table. He reached for one, then stopped. "I'm sorry. I always forget my manners around Idella's sweet potato biscuits. Please, you go first."

"Thank you." Cara reached for one of the steaming biscuits, picked it up and immediately dropped it onto the linen cloth. "Ouch! They're hot!"

Alex sprang from his chair and knelt at her side.

"I should have warned you. Idella's biscuits are always pulled straight from the oven.

"Are you okay?" He reached for her hand. "Let me help you."

He blew lightly on each of her fingertips and watched as her eyes slid shut. Then he brushed his lips against each one, loving the feel of her warm fingers against his mouth.

A low ache swelled in his groin when he felt her hand tremble with his every touch. He had the strongest urge to suck on them, but instead he folded her hand in both of his and gave it a gentle squeeze.

Her eyes fluttered open, her voice unsteady. "Th-thank you. That feels much better."

He wasn't surprised when his own legs wobbled when he rose and returned to his side of the table.

"What is it with us and biscuits?"

"I remember the evening quite clearly." She gave him a knowing smile. "Ever think about trying out for *Top Chef?*"

"Not a chance. That was an exclusive lesson reserved for VIPs only."

Right now, the only woman he desired to do and share anything with in the kitchen, or anywhere else, was Cara.

Alex buttered his own biscuit. "Tell me more about yourself, Cara. Inquiring minds want to know."

"There isn't much to tell. I have a degree in elementary education and a master's in adult education from Fordham University. I have a cat named Molly. And I hate broccoli and cauliflower."

He laughed. "Me, too!" He bit into his biscuit and

swallowed, hating his need for an answer to one of the most important questions he would ask her.

"No boyfriend?"

She shook her head and his heart lifted in his chest.

Her face held a trace of sadness. "With my schedule, I don't have time for a serious relationship. I pretty much live at Beacon House."

"I know what you mean. I live in hotels and planes. It's pretty rare when I'm actually home in Harlem."

Like him, working was a means of escape, and he wondered what she was running from in her life.

"I told you about my mother, but what about your family? Do you have any brothers or sisters?"

She took a sip of champagne. "I'm an only child."

"Excuse me, sir." The waiter arrived with their soup. They both inhaled the delicate aroma that swirled between them before digging in with gusto.

He reached for his third biscuit. "What's your father like?"

Cara dropped her spoon and some of the soup splattered on the table, surprising them both.

She mopped up the drops with a napkin. "Ugh. I'm so clumsy sometimes.

"He wasn't around," she said in a smooth tone, honed from answering that difficult question countless times over the years. The people who asked were unaware that those three words were verbal knives to her broken heart.

Alex gave a sympathetic snort. "Sounds like my old man."

"I don't see him too often now."

"Why's that?"

"He and I don't agree on much of anything. So in

order to avoid getting into an argument, we tend to avoid each other."

"I see. What does he do for a living? I can sum up what my dad did in one word—nothing."

Her spoon stopped in midair. "Why all the questions about my dad?"

Her voice had a hard edge and Alex knew he'd pressed too much.

"I just thought deadbeat dads were something we had in common. So I was just curious, that's all. I'm sorry, Cara. I didn't mean to offend you."

"He wasn't a deadbeat, just difficult. I thought I knew him, but it turns out I didn't know him at all. Let's just leave it at that, okay?"

The silence between them made his heart hurt, especially when it was broken only by the low conversation and occasional bursts of laughter from the other diners.

He looked up at Cara and saw that the playful spark had gone out of her eyes. He wanted to bring it back, but all of a sudden he didn't know what to say.

It bugged him that she didn't want to confide in him. Weren't men supposed to be the ones who didn't want to talk?

If she were to ask him, he would admit that she was starting to break down his walls, but hers were evidently stronger. And he wanted to know why.

"Here we are!"

Idella swooped into the room with the rest of their food. She served them and stood back to wait for each of them to take their first bite.

Cara cut and ate a piece of pork chop, so tender it practically melted in her mouth. "Outstanding!"

Alex enthusiastically agreed. "Auntie, you've outdone yourself again!"

"You've always been a charmer, just like Michael."

Oh, God, here she goes again. He felt his body go rigid as Idella turned toward Cara.

"Honey, you should have seen them when they were younger. Like two peas in a pod, and their momma dressed them alike, too. Thicker than thieves those boys were."

Cara smiled at her. "I'd love to hear more." She hesitated and he felt her eyes meet his. "If that's okay with you, Alex?"

His jaw tightened, like it always did when somebody talked about Michael. But he knew it was futile to stop Idella. For one thing, his mother had always taught him it was rude to interrupt his elders. And even if he did ask her to be quiet, she would simply ignore him. That's just the way she was.

"I remember at one family reunion, Alex and Michael entered the potato-sack race. I think they were about ten years old."

She leaned over and nudged Cara with her elbow. "Now you'd think that because they were twins that they'd be able to work together and figure out a way to get across the finish line, right?"

She leaned back, placed her hands on her hips and shook her head. "Oh, no. They decided it was time for them to grow up and be individuals. They each had their own ideas about how to run in that sack. It was hilarious to see them, each trying to do their own thing, and none of it working."

She hooted with laughter. "Those two boys had everybody cracking up until they literally rolled over the finish line."

Alex momentarily forgot his annoyance at Idella and shook his head at the memory. "We were so mad at each other that we started fighting in the sack. Didn't even wait till we got out to throw punches."

"Your daddy had to break it up and then he tore into you," Idella recalled. "Your eyes and your tails were black and blue."

"Yeah," said Alex with a rueful smirk. "He always seemed to know when to put the drink down and show up in time to give us a whipping."

"That day, the whole family realized that the only thing Alex and Michael had in common was getting into trouble," Idella added.

"Michael always blamed me for getting us a whipping from Dad that day. He didn't speak to me for a long time. I don't think he ever forgave me."

"But I bet he's proud of you now!" Cara offered.

The jovial mood in the room deflated into an uncomfortable silence.

"Michael died thirteen years ago," Idella replied.

Cara clasped her hand over her mouth. "Oh, no!"

Alex stared at her. The stricken look on her face had him wondering why she reacted so strongly.

He wiped his mouth with a napkin. "It's nice to reminisce, but some things you don't want to remember."

Idella gave Alex's shoulder a sympathetic squeeze. "Your auntie has too much of a big mouth on this ol' body. I'm sorry, hon."

The couple was silent as she cleared away some of their dishes.

"Both of you better eat up before the rest of your food gets cold. Let me know if you want me to warm anything up," said Idella, then she waddled out of the room.

Cara started to say something, but Alex put up his

hand. As far as he was concerned, the trip down memory lane was over.

"You don't want to talk about your father? Well, I don't want to talk about my brother. End of conversation."

The candlelight flickered, seeming to mock him. The romantic evening he had hoped for had turned into a disaster.

I never should have brought her here.

He loved Idella to death. Telling old stories was how she paid tribute to people that she loved. His aunt had no way of knowing that the mere mention of his brother's name brought every emotion inside him to a screeching halt.

The truth about Michael was known only to him.

But holding the secret inside all these years was getting to be too much to bear. The guilt was eating away at his livelihood, stealing his happiness and making it nearly impossible for him to justify his own existence.

When would it all end?

Tears started to fill his eyes. He pushed his plate away so roughly that Cara jumped in her seat.

"I need some air," he announced and got up from the table. His chair almost fell over, but he caught it just in time and pushed it back in place.

As Cara started to rise, he shook his head. "Please stay and finish your meal." His voice caught in his throat at her worried eyes. "I'll meet you out front in about twenty minutes."

He left the room without another word, but not before he saw the look of hurt and confusion on Cara's face. He hated that he was responsible for putting it there. But he'd never cried in front of a woman, and he wasn't going to start now.

* * *

When Alex left, Cara felt as cold as the ice wrapped around the bottle of champagne.

Michael was dead! How? When?

She'd always assumed he was still in jail, put there by her very own father. The news chilled her to the bone and she rubbed her bare arms in a futile attempt to get warm.

It didn't make sense.

Did her father know? She doubted it. He was so concerned with maintaining his prominence in the New York City judicial system that nothing else mattered.

Not even his daughter, she reflected bitterly.

She walked over to the bay window and tried to focus on the peace and tranquility of the river below.

But it was useless.

All she could think about was Alex and the pain her father had caused his family. Her heart broke anew, especially for his mom and the desperate plea that was never answered.

She walked back to the table, her feet like lead. Pushing the plate of now-cold food aside, she was refilling her champagne when Idella walked into the room.

"Where's my hot-headed nephew?"

Cara shrugged and sipped her champagne. "He stormed out of here about five minutes ago." Her mouth quivered as she spoke. "I don't know what happened."

She turned to Idella and the kindness on her face made her eyes well up. "What did I do wrong?"

Idella patted her arm, before pulling out a chair and sitting down. The wood creaked under her weight.

"You didn't do anything, honey. That boy's been hot-headed for as long as I can remember."

Tears welled up in her eyes because she knew how

it felt to be forced to talk about something you just wanted to forget.

"This is my fault. If only I hadn't been so curious."

Idella shushed her with a wave of her hand. "No, it's mine. You'd think at my age I would know to stop talking before I put my foot in my mouth." She gave a heavy sigh. "But I can't help it. I love telling stories about my family, especially those who have passed on, to keep their memory alive. People forget about you so quickly."

Idella's voice sounded wistful, as if being forgotten hit her a little too close in the heart.

"You wouldn't know it by looking at him, but Alex has been through a lot. The death of his twin brother hit him hard, and as you can see, he's still grieving."

"How did it happen?" She didn't want to deceive Idella but she had to know.

"Michael died in jail from a heart attack soon after he was sentenced for a gang-related crime."

"Isn't it unusual for someone that young to have a heart attack?"

"Yes, his mother had an autopsy done and she found out he had a rare disorder that weakened the ability of his heart to function properly. One day, his heart just gave out and the doctors could not revive him."

Cara gaped at her. "That's awful."

Idella nodded. "When Michael died—" her voice trailed off and she dabbed at the corners of her eyes with a napkin "—Alex was never the same."

Idella's eyes scrutinized her. "You seem like a nice girl. Maybe you can bring some joy back into his life. Money and fame sure haven't done it."

"We're just friends," Cara said firmly, hoping that was still true after tonight's events.

Idella regarded her a moment, shrugged. "You can't

blame an old woman like me for hoping. Alex is very dear to me. He's my only nephew and I want to see him happy."

Cara smiled, got up and walked around the table.

She gave her a warm hug. Idella smelled like talcum powder and barbecue sauce. "He's lucky to have an auntie like you."

Glancing at her watch, she squealed. "Oops, I've got to go. Alex is probably outside in the car. I don't want to keep him waiting."

She opened her purse and dug around for a mirror. "He's taking me to a jazz club. At least, that was the plan before he left." She applied a light-colored lip gloss and powdered her face.

"Sweetie, you're so pretty, you don't even need any makeup."

Cara smiled. "Thanks. It was so nice to meet you. I wish you the best of success with your restaurant."

"Nice to meet you, too, dear. Love to have you back whenever you're in the area."

Cara started to walk out, but then hesitated.

"What's wrong?"

She turned back to Idella. "I don't know what to say to him."

Idella gave her a knowing smile. "Honey, he doesn't need your words. He needs your patience and a whole lot of love."

Cara smiled as she walked over and gave the woman another hug. "Thank you," she whispered.

"Aww." Idella hugged her. "Now get out of here and go meet that stubborn nephew of mine before I get the mind to put you both to work in my kitchen!"

Cara chuckled at the thought and waved goodbye.

When she walked out into the foyer, her breath caught in her throat.

Through the glass doors, she could see Alex outside, leaning against the back of his Porsche, talking with the valet. He was smiling as if nothing was wrong.

But she was beginning to learn the truth about the man hiding behind the façade of fame. She didn't know what would happen between them tonight, but emotionally, she felt closer to him than ever before.

She felt his eyes on her body as she exited the building. Her nipples hardened under his gaze as her mind recalled the incredible kiss they'd shared earlier.

She lifted her chin and sauntered toward him with a confidence she was only beginning to acknowledge within herself.

As she walked, her eyes took in his powerful build, clad in black designer jeans and a black dress shirt that was open at the collar. He was the most beautiful man she'd ever known.

Idella was right.

Sometimes it was the woman who needed to be strong for a man broken by the past. A ray of light through the darkness of memories. An unlikely hero.

Tonight, she would be all those things, and more.

Chapter 8

It was the longest ten minutes of Cara's life. Alex hadn't spoken since they'd left the restaurant, and the silence between them seemed even more overwhelming in the luxurious but cramped Porsche.

She wanted to follow Idella's advice, but how long would he act like she wasn't even there?

Outside it was so dark she could barely make out the trees lining the road. Cara found it hard to believe there was a jazz club out in this desolate area.

Lost in thought, she nearly jumped out of her skin when Alex slammed on the brakes. His elbow dug into her chest as he grabbed her right arm and she cried out in pain.

"Hold on!" he shouted.

The car veered sharply to the left. She screamed and grabbed on to the door handle as they rode over the grassy berm, narrowly missing landing in a ditch.

A few feet later, the car screeched to a halt and Alex slammed on the emergency brake. His hand gripped the steering wheel so tightly his knuckles looked ready to pop out of his skin.

He released her arm, leaned in close. "Are you okay?" His breathing was uneven as he searched her eyes.

Her voice shook. "I think so. What happened?"

He loosened his grip on the steering wheel. "We almost hit a couple of deer! I forgot how much they run around out here."

"City boy," she teased, rubbing her arm in the place where it still hurt from when he'd grasped her.

"Yeah," he muttered, watching her. "I don't belong here."

She shook her head, twisted away and looked out into the darkness. Not even a near-death experience could make things right between them. The silence grew, though she could feel his eyes on her back.

He hissed out a slow breath. "Listen. Are you sure you're not hurt? I know I was a little rough. It's just when I saw those deer, I panicked."

His fingers touched her shoulder. "Look at me."

She did and saw tenderness in his eyes just before he curved his hand around her neck, brought her lips to his and apologized in the sweetest way a man could.

Alex's mouth journeyed over hers, saying what he couldn't say aloud, exploring the need he found there. She captured and held on to the joy as his tongue probed deeper. Both of them reveling in the beauty of wanting, and being wanted.

He broke away, and their eyes found each other in the darkness.

"I guess nothing's broken."

Cara felt her heart soar. *He still cares about me.*

She brought her fingers to her lips. "Yes, it appears that everything is in working order."

And there's nothing like a hot kiss to break the ice, she thought, as he started the car. They pulled back onto the road without a word, yet they both knew the air between them had shifted, like it does just before dawn breaks.

She hesitated only a second before reaching over and placing her hand on his thigh, stroking lightly. His muscles twitched hard in response, and he placed his hand over hers.

She'd always heard that the best part of fighting was making up. As he rubbed his thumb slowly over the ridge of her knuckles, she trembled inside with anticipation. That kiss and this touch hinted at just how pleasurable making up with Alex could be.

A short time later, they arrived at the club. Alex grabbed his saxophone and his eyes were all over Cara as he helped her out of the car. *Now this is more like it,* she thought, warming under his appreciative gaze. Her skin tingled with excitement in anticipation of the rest of the evening.

"You're going to love this place," he whispered in her ear. "It's one of my favorite spots in the world."

He opened the door and the hot sounds of jazz poured out, beckoning them inside.

The place was small and decorated classic cool with bistro tables clad in white tablecloths scattered around the bandstand. There was a bar on her right and red leather booths on the opposite wall. Votive candles were everywhere, adding to the romantic atmosphere. Every seat was taken with people talking and laughing. She noticed more than a few women staring at her with envious eyes.

Alex led her to a reserved booth near the stage. The instruments were all set up but no one was playing, and she realized the music was coming from a sound system.

He slid into the booth next to her and pointed to the walls. "Check out the pictures!"

Cara instantly recognized Thelonious Monk, Miles Davis, Herbie Hancock, Oscar Peterson and two of her favorite singers, Ella Fitzgerald and Billie Holiday. They were some of the greatest jazz musicians that ever lived.

"Which one is your favorite?" he asked.

"I'd have to say Billie, definitely. Her voice has a rawness to it that just makes my heart ache every time I listen to her."

His eyebrow arched at her serious tone, and she blushed as she realized the same thing happened whenever she looked into his eyes, heard his voice or fantasized about being more than just his teacher.

He snapped his fingers. "You see! It's just like I said when we were riding up here from Harlem. You singers are sooo dramatic," he intoned, fanning his hand in front of his face.

She elbowed him in the ribs. "Ow!" he exclaimed, rubbing his side. "Time for a drink. What can I get you?"

"Club soda, please, with a twist of lime."

"Okay, I'll be right back."

As he walked over to the bar, a man carrying a trumpet approached her.

"Hi, you must be Candy. Ol' Alex said you were beautiful, but he didn't say you were drop-dead gorgeous!"

Candy? Who's she?

She smiled politely. "No, my name is Cara."

He laid his hand on his huge belly. "Oh, I'm sorry. I didn't mean to offend. It's just that ol' Alex brings so many beautiful babes up in here, it's hard to keep track of them all."

"No worries," she said, bristling inside. Between this and the daggers being thrown at her from the other women in the club, maybe coming here had been a mistake. She certainly didn't want to be known as one of ol' Alex's babes!

"The name is Mac, and I'm always grateful when Alex takes the time to sit in with us locals."

Cara breathed easier at the sight of Alex returning with their drinks.

"Hey, watch your back, Mac—she's mine."

The two men laughed aloud and exchanged hand slaps.

"Watch out for this man," joked Alex. "He's a monster on the horn, but a kitten with the women."

Both men cut up into a fit of raucous laughter.

"Candy knows the score." Mac guffawed and hooked his thumb toward the stage. "C'mon man, let's hit it."

When he left, she raised an eyebrow at Alex.

He flashed a sheepish grin. "Mac has always been terrible with names."

She sipped her club soda in quiet fascination as he opened up his case and slipped his saxophone around his neck. After adjusting the reed, he tapped each key silently and played a few low notes.

Moments later, the music stopped and the chatter ebbed away as Mac stepped up to the microphone.

"Good evening. Welcome to the Jazz Hideaway. Tonight we have a very special guest with us. Just back in town after a very successful European tour, put your hands together for Sharp Five Records tenor saxophonist Alex Dovington!"

He pecked her on the forehead. "Promise you'll wait for me?" Without waiting for her answer, he strode toward the stage.

"Only forever," she whispered to herself.

Loud hoots of applause resounded throughout the room as Alex counted off the beat.

"Ah-one, ah-two, ah-one-two-three-four."

The band immediately swung into a bebop groove. The bass walked the rhythm of the beat, bolstered by the steady tap of the snare and the hi-hat cymbals. All worked together to support the tune's rapid staccato melody.

Cara sat in rapt attention, watching Alex play so fast that his fingers moved in a blur up and down the keys. Stretching and bending notes at will, he made the saxophone growl, purr and bark.

His improvisation had people in the audience bobbing their heads, as chorus after chorus soared into their ears and their hearts. When he ended on a sinfully low note, they burst into wild applause.

He nodded his head in appreciation, and when he looked over at her, she gave him two thumbs up and the biggest smile she could muster.

When the rest of the quartet was done improvising, Alex picked up the horn again and played the melody out.

"Let's give a big hand to Alex Dovington!" bellowed Mac.

The band played a few more tunes before breaking to rest before the next set.

Her heart skipped a beat when Alex leaned into the

microphone and thanked the band. His baritone voice sounded even sexier reverberating through the small room.

Cara watched in amusement as a small crowd immediately gathered around the stage. Many were women, both young and old, with cameras in their hand, primping and waiting for the perfect photo opportunity. Over the next few minutes, Alex posed for every picture and signed every autograph.

If this is what it's like to be famous, she'd pass. She was glad the only notoriety she'd ever have was the full-page ad in the yellow pages for Beacon House.

Cara straightened as Alex slid into the booth next to her.

"Why didn't you warn me about the groupies? I am seething with jealousy over here."

He draped his arm around the back of the booth and she unconsciously inched closer to him. "There's no competition here." He twisted a lock of her hair around her finger, tugged on it playfully. "You're still my biggest fan, right?"

She lifted her eyes to his and nodded, wishing inside that he knew, that she had the courage to tell him, just how much of a fan she was.

He laid his hand against her cheek, and she felt his warm breath upon her lips. "And I'm yours."

Their lips melted together in quiet intensity, and everything else—their fear, their pasts and their uncertain future—disappeared.

Chapter 9

Alex leaned against the headboard and groaned in frustration. The feel of Cara's sweet lips on his own was still so real in his mind, so alive in his senses, that it was hard to believe she wasn't still in his arms, and in his bed.

Right or wrong, he had wanted to romance her tonight. Make her feel special. A fast car ride, great food and an amazing make-out session in the Porsche after they left the club all added up to an unforgettable night that ended too soon. When they arrived home, she claimed she was "exhausted" and went to her room.

Now, as he sat trying to focus on finishing his tune, he was afraid he'd offended her somehow, and he wondered exactly what she thought about the evening... and about him.

What she didn't know was that his need for her went beyond physical lust. He cared about her, what she felt, thought and needed, more deeply than he could have ever imagined.

He tapped a pencil against his head and stared at the wall, wishing he had X-ray vision, wondering if she was as awake, and as aroused, as he was.

His erection stirred as he remembered the feel of her slender arms around his neck, the luscious dip between her breasts, the small waist that fit perfectly in his hands.

It frightened him that he wanted Cara so much, not only in his bed, but in his life. There was only one day left. It wasn't enough time. What if he lost her forever?

She's already gone, man. You never stood a chance. You really think she wants to be with someone who can't read?

With a sigh of resignation, he shoved the pencil and manuscript paper to the floor and turned off the light.

Cara stared at the ceiling and trembled at the memory of his fingers brushing her hair away from her face like it was crafted of the finest silk. The heat of his gaze tracing her body, penetrating her clothes and making her wet with desire.

She couldn't believe the man who'd kissed her senseless that evening, in the club and in the car, was the same person who'd practically slammed the door in her face barely forty-eight hours earlier.

This evening, she'd learned that Alex was warm, caring and gentle. The kind of man she could fall in love with for a lifetime.

Thin streams of moonlight filtered through the blinds. It was after one o'clock in the morning. He was probably sleeping, and the night that was so magical to her was just a nice memory to him.

Her heart lurched. By this time tomorrow, she'd be back in Brooklyn, alone in her bed as usual. Her time with Alex would be over forever.

The only consolation in the pain was that her identity would be safe. Alex would never know about her father, or what he did for a living, although he'd come close to finding out tonight. Although she never talked about her personal life with her other students, she still felt guilty about not being completely honest.

As long as she kept the survival of Beacon House at the forefront of her mind, she would be okay. But she knew it wasn't going to be easy. When he was kissing and touching her like he couldn't get enough, it was too easy to cross the line, and too hard to go back.

She got out of bed, let her gown puddle to the floor. *Only one more night.*

It was about time that she gave Alex Dovington a personal wake-up call of the most pleasurable kind.

Cara padded barefoot to Alex's room, clad only in a lace thong. His door was ajar and she counted his slow, even breaths as she calmed her own. Thankfully, he was fast asleep.

Moonlight shone through the window and illuminated his body. The sheet, tossed loosely around his waist, made her yearn to rip it off to reveal the rest. But there was no need to rush. She had the rest of the night to enjoy him, and she planned on taking time to savor every inch.

Inhaling deeply, she tiptoed to the edge of his bed, lifted the covers and curved her body to his, her breasts and belly sinking into his warmth.

With the lightest touch she could muster, she traced her finger along the crevice between his shoulder blades, down his spine and back up to the base of his neck. Although he didn't say a word, his involuntary shudder resonated against her stomach and she knew he'd awakened.

She revered his skin, her tongue and lips tasting boldly as the place between her legs began to moisten and throb. She lifted one leg, placed it gently on his thigh. His muscles immediately stiffened, and the hair on his thigh tickled her flesh.

Alex suddenly ripped the sheet off and pulled her on top of him. Wrapping his fingers in her hair, he crushed his mouth to hers.

He tasted of warm spice, and she thirsted for more as his tongue led her in a tribal dance of sensual exploration.

So percussive were their lips upon each other's face and neck, undulating in perfect rhythm, always seeking and finding new skin to taste. Their tongues played and darted, licked and prodded, until they were both breathless.

Skin to skin, Cara's heart pounded with his as Alex cupped her face. No words were spoken, but the question of should they or shouldn't they make love was finally answered in the unadulterated desire they saw in each other's eyes.

The line in the sand had been erased by a tidal wave of passion neither of them understood but both accepted.

His erection, a hard, thick slab against her stomach, tempted her to take a peek. But she didn't, preferring to simply feel his flesh continue to grow and pulse against her skin.

She shivered as his hands slipped down her back, cupped her buttocks. He gripped hard, thrusting her into a gasp, which he smothered with a kiss as he dragged his finger in the narrow gap under the thong, discovering tender flesh. Eager to stroke and coddle, she yelped when he ripped the lacy fabric in half.

Unencumbered, his hands spread her legs a little wider. Sealing her lips to his, his mouth swallowed her moans as his fingers teased, tapping lightly on her sensitive pearl. She threw her head back and panted as his lips traveled over her collarbone.

When his lips found her breasts, she cried out as his mouth fastened on her one tight tip. Wrapping his arms around her waist, he gently rolled her over onto her back while sucking her nipple with immeasurable tenderness.

"You're so beautiful," he whispered, softly anchoring her breasts in his hands. His tongue moved like wildfire over one stiff peak to the other, over and over until she thought she'd go mad. Powerful sensations rushed through her body, and she clamped her legs together. It was too soon.

Her body, tight with desire, strained up toward his mouth when his tongue dipped into her belly button. Laying his cheek upon her abdomen, he released his hands from her breasts and stroked them down her thighs, easing them apart. Cupping her buttocks, he knelt and then gently lifted her to his waiting lips.

Alex kept his eyes on hers as he hovered there, inches away, hot breath on her skin, and she whimpered and twisted with yearning. His tongue flicked like a serpent's and she writhed in response and he tightened his hold. Then lips met flesh and he began to suck and lick her into another dimension.

She leaned up on her elbows. Watching him dip and dive his tongue increased the pleasure and the frenzy for both of them.

"Unh…mhhhh," she cried out, dropping her head back, her hair blanketing the pillows.

Twisting and bucking in his grasp, he brought her close, so close she thought she would pass out. She sank back into the bed, mewing with pleasure, and stretched out her hands to him.

The angles and curves of their bodies melded together in utter need. Alex wove his hand through her hair, brought her lips to his. Penetrated and claimed her as his own.

Oh, how good he felt inside her.

How delicious his mouth tasted.

How perfectly in rhythm they moved together.

He moaned as she wrapped her legs around his waist, urging him to go deeper, rock harder. The primal dance of their bodies thumped flesh upon flesh. Tempo increased, his hands tangled in her curly locks, his mouth never leaving hers. Both seeking, climbing and pleasuring each other without bounds.

"Ahh…lex," she moaned, arching her body into his as he probed her core, thrusting into that secret place that broke her in two.

Her inner flesh held him captive, pulsed and rippled, until soon his entire body stiffened. With a guttural cry, he exploded into her, releasing bright bursts of pleasure that brought tears to her eyes, and she clutched his tight buttocks and rocked to heaven with him.

Their lips, bruised and swollen from their lovemaking, continued to move and explore each other. Both desperately trying to stay in the moment, wishing they could stop time.

As the night ebbed away into morning, neither wanted the pleasure to end and their uncertain future to begin.

Chapter 10

Alex propped himself on one elbow and admired the beautiful creature lying asleep next to him. He loved mornings, but for the first time in his life, he wished the sun wouldn't rise. There was only one word to describe last night: glorious.

Never before had he felt such a sense of oneness with another woman. It was like Cara had been created for him and he was created for her. There was no way he would ever let her go.

In a few minutes, the entire room would brighten. He didn't want the sunlight to wake her before he had a chance to think. He'd never told a woman he was falling in love with her, and he didn't want to screw up.

Speaking his emotions verbally had always been difficult. Words could be rejected, thrown back at his face or used against him.

Words were also so…final.

If only he could play his saxophone, then he could

tell Cara his feelings through his music. That was one reason why he loved playing so much, he could express whatever his feelings were on the spot, through his horn.

He never would have dreamed something positive would come out of his illiteracy. Not only was he learning to read, but because of Cara, he was learning to feel without remorse and love without boundaries. He felt incredibly blessed to know her.

You can't have love without truth.

The thought sucker-punched him, and he lay back upon the pillow and let out a quiet breath.

Would she still care about him if she learned the truth about his past? He didn't think he could bear it if any feelings that she had for him turned into fear.

No, it was too risky, he decided. Things were still too fresh between them. Telling her now would end their relationship before it ever really began.

He turned and propped himself on his elbow again, allowing his eyes to rove her body. Lush, full breasts. A baby-got-back behind. Legs that shouldn't even be legal in the fifty states, much less the U.S. territories.

Her lips were parted slightly, inviting him to bring her home from dreamland. She was a sight to behold. Asleep or awake, he could simply not resist her.

He traced a finger down the tiny crease below her nose. Slowly he lowered his lips to hers and kissed her softly on each corner of mouth before moving to the middle. He nudged her lips open and she moaned as his tongue slipped inside.

Her arms wrapped around his neck, and he deepened the kiss, pleasuring the warmth inside her mouth. He broke their embrace for only a second, noting that her eyes were still closed but her lips curved into a smile.

Slipping under the cool sheets, his lips hungrily sought the underside of her breasts, and it pleased him enormously when her nipples stiffened immediately at the touch of his lips.

His erection was painfully hard and he wanted nothing more than to penetrate her warmth right now. But this wasn't about him, it was about Cara. And this time, when he entered her, he wanted to see her eyes.

He dragged his lips away from her breasts and cupped her face in his hands.

"Good morning," he murmured low into her ear. "How's my little night prowler?"

He kissed her eyelids, and when she opened them his heart dropped. He didn't see desire there. He saw regret.

He took his hands off her face. "What's wrong? Did I hurt you?"

She shook her head and seemed to struggle to form words.

"Cara, what's wrong! Talk to me!" His voice bounced off the walls, louder than he intended, but damn, she was scaring him.

He reached out to stroke her hair, and his heart lurched when she jerked away, her eyes as wide as saucers.

"I shouldn't be here," she whispered. "Oh, my God."

"What are you talking about?" He reached for her hand again just as she was about to leap from the bed. She tried to jerk her hand away, but he held tight. "No, you're not going anywhere until you tell me what's going on."

Her cheeks were flushed, making her even more beautiful. "Last night was a mistake! That's what's wrong," she yelled.

He felt like he'd been slapped.

"What?"

"You heard me. Last night never should have happened, Alex. We...I made a big mistake. Now let me go!"

She wrested away from him and started toward the door, but he leaped out of the bed and slammed it shut before she got there.

He tried not to be distracted by her nude body, but it was difficult.

"Wait a minute. You come into my room and seduce me, and now you're going to walk out just like that?"

She nodded and started to reach for the doorknob.

"Like hell you are!" He grabbed her hand, turned her around and pinned her to the wall as he smothered her lips with a kiss that was meant to pleasure them both and prove to him that the passion he felt from her last night wasn't a dream.

"Kissing you like this is a mistake?" he urged, his voice thick with longing for her.

Her body clung to his as he planted his mouth all over her face and neck before settling back on her lips again, his hard, naked length crushed painfully between them. Their tongues entangled hot and loose with the kind of passion lovers have the freedom to release and the freedom to deny.

She pushed him away again. This time he didn't resist.

"I can't do this. It's the last day we have together to finish the book. I can't teach you under these circumstances."

"Then why did you come into my room last night?" *Why did you make me fall in love with you?*

She wiped her mouth, her eyes blazing. "I—I don't

know. I can't explain it right now. All I know is that it can't…it won't happen ever again."

She covered her breasts with her hands. "Now if you'll excuse me, I want to shower and get dressed. I'll meet you downstairs in an hour so we can wrap this up."

Without another word, Cara opened the door and walked out.

Alex sank down onto the bed. His brain was trying to process a range of emotions—rejection, confusion, anger. But his heart felt only one thing: love.

As far as he was concerned, recess was over. He didn't know what kind of game Cara was playing, but he wasn't going to stop pursuing her until he won her heart.

What have I done?

Cara leaned against the wall sobbing quietly as hot water pelted her body like tiny whips.

For the second time in less than two days, she'd made a colossal mistake that hurt both of them. She wished that the immense ache in her heart could be whisked away down the drain as easily as her tears.

It wasn't supposed to happen this way, and she wasn't supposed to feel like this.

All she'd wanted to do was seduce Alex, to pretend that she was his lover for one night, to do something daring for once in her life.

But her little experiment had blown up in her face. The intended result never involved actually falling in love with him.

Yes, he was the most gorgeous man she'd ever known and yes, he had fulfilled her every fantasy last night. But loving him and desiring him was wrong when she had not been completely truthful with him from the very beginning.

It wasn't like she hadn't had ample opportunity to set the record straight. When Tommy had called her to hire her, she could have said that she couldn't possibly teach Alex for personal reasons.

Or even before she'd stepped over his Harlem threshold, it would have been appropriate to tell him who she really was—and give him the opportunity to tear up the contract in her face if he chose.

But she'd done neither. Instead, she chose deceit over decency, and now she'd destroyed something before it even had a chance to begin.

Alex was the only man who'd ever made her feel like she was the most beautiful woman on earth. To be desired by Alex was a wondrous thing, but to be loved by him, to be his alone, was a dream that could never be fulfilled.

Not if she wanted to keep Beacon House open.

There was no question in her mind that her loyalty to the Harlem community far outweighed her need to be in any romantic relationship. Helping people change their lives was what she lived for. Not love. Not heartbreak.

Even though she cared deeply for him, she couldn't let last night get in the way of her goal. Somehow she had to get them back on track before it was too late.

She only had a few hours to make sure he could read the children's book comfortably and with no errors. After today, if he still needed additional help, she would refer him to one of the other literacy centers in the city.

But how was she going to get through the next few hours and hide the way she felt about him? How would she get through a lifetime without loving him?

She squeezed her eyes shut at the dull ache in her heart, the settling-in-for-winter kind of hurt that wouldn't easily go away with chocolate, ice cream or an afternoon nap. It was the kind of ache and longing that could only be eased by the man you loved, loving you in return.

Did he love her? The answer to that question sparked both hope and fear. She'd always wanted a man like Alex to love, and to love her. He was gorgeous, intelligent and talented beyond measure. He would be a difficult man to forget, let alone her feelings for him.

She turned off the water, wrapped herself in a towel. She rubbed the steam from the glass and when she looked in the mirror, she saw a woman in love. One who could not possibly be with the man she adored, and the tears fell again.

Alex whistled as he expertly flipped pancakes on the griddle, hoping the delicious smell would entice Cara to emerge from her bedroom. No woman could resist his homemade, melt-in-your-mouth, write-home-to-your-momma flapjacks, complete with a side of bacon and fresh-squeezed orange juice.

What better way to discuss their future than over a hot breakfast?

She had to eat, and at some point she had to talk about what happened between them this morning. He deserved to know why she'd walked out, and he wouldn't take "no comment" for an answer. By the time they left for Harlem that evening, he had to have a foolproof plan in place for seeing her again.

"What's all this?"

Alex turned at the sound of Cara's voice and smiled. The sweater she wore was his favorite shade of blue and accentuated her curves in the most distracting way.

Remember. Look, but don't touch.

"Breakfast, of course," he said, sliding the last of the pancakes onto a platter. "It's nearly ready. Why don't you have a seat?"

He couldn't help but notice her eyes, so vibrant and alert last evening, were now puffy and tired. It hurt him to think he was the cause of her tears, and made him all the more eager to make things right again between them.

He walked over to her and cupped her elbow to lead her to the table, but she jerked away.

"I'm not hungry," she mumbled.

He frowned, trying but not succeeding to hide his disappointment from his face. "You haven't eaten since we went to Idella's. And I don't know about you, but hot, steamy sex like we had the pleasure of experiencing last night always makes me hungry the next morning," he added, raising a brow.

She rolled her eyes. "I don't need to be reminded that you've been with other people, Alex."

He bit back a smile at the jealous tone in her voice. She still cared about him. What she didn't know was that none of those women could compete with Cara. They were his past. She was his future.

"I wasn't trying to remind you of anything," he assured her. "I was only stating a fact. Don't you want to get to know me?"

"Of course I do, but like you said yourself, there are some things that should be left unsaid."

"Agreed." He raised his right hand, voice booming. "Thou shalt not speak of past relationships." He could see that she was trying not to grin. "I'm sorry," he said, extending his hand. "Apology accepted?"

Their eyes locked in a battle of egos. She nodded, and when she placed her warm hand in his, it took everything in him not to pull her into his arms.

He released her hand and let out a breath. "Let's eat."

Cara eyed the huge spread of food. "You shouldn't have gone through all this trouble." She sat down, spreading a napkin across her lap. "This is a feast fit for a—"

"Queen," he interrupted, grinning.

Her cheeks reddened and she poured the coffee. "I don't know how you can think about eating, when we have so much to do today."

"Easy." He gulped down some juice. "I'm a guy."

She rolled her eyes. "That old excuse."

He watched, amused, as she stacked three pancakes, followed by four pieces of bacon on her plate.

"Um. For someone who said she wasn't hungry—" He tilted his head toward her plate. "I'm just sayin'!"

"And I'm just leaving," she retorted with a glare, and rose to get up from the table.

Alex burst out laughing and grabbed her hand. "Geez, Cara. It was a joke. Sit down and eat as much as you like."

They ate in silence for a while, and he wondered what she was thinking about, and if her thoughts had anything to do with him.

He was on his second pancake when he couldn't take the quiet any longer. "I made this breakfast special for you," he blurted out. "To thank you for all you've done for me this weekend."

He wiped his mouth, took her hand in his. "Around you, I'm not ashamed that I can't read. I'm not ashamed... to be me."

Her eyes were gentle. "Being illiterate is no reason to be ashamed."

"I know that now," he admitted, feeling the weight of a long-held burden lift off his chest. "And I couldn't have done it without you. I can't do it without you."

He paused, cleared his throat. "I want you to continue to be my teacher, for as long as it takes. What do you think?"

She took her hand from his and turned to look out the window, the sunlight dancing upon her corkscrew curls. He smiled at the memory of playing with her hair last night as she fell asleep in his arms.

Desire rolled through him again and he clenched his fist against it, then realized she hadn't said a word.

"Wow, you're awfully quiet. I hope that means you're thinking about all the wonderful ways you want to say yes to me."

She turned back and shook her head. "It wouldn't work, Alex."

"What are you talking about? We're a great team."

"Yes, but it's not that simple."

"Sure it is. All you have to do is open your mouth and say 'yes.'"

Her lip quivered. "Last night changed everything," she insisted, her tone unfriendly and professional. "We...I crossed a line that never should have been crossed. Severing ties is the only right thing to do."

He couldn't believe what he was hearing. He reached for her hand, and his heart clenched when she moved away and crossed her arms around her chest.

It hurt him to think she wanted to drop out of his life so easily after all they had shared this weekend, both emotionally and physically.

"Severing ties? It sounds like you want to cut off a

limb," he said, half joking. "All I'm asking is to continue the great work we've been doing."

"There are plenty of qualified literacy teachers in the city. As soon as we get home, I'll call Tommy and give him a couple of names to check out."

"So when Monday rolls around, we'll just go back to our lives, huh?"

She nodded, and seemed perfectly fine with the course their conversation was taking. "I'm sorry about last night. I truly don't know what came over me. All I do know is that I don't want it to happen again."

Alex cocked an eyebrow. "From the way you responded to my kisses this morning, I don't believe for a second that you don't want me to make love to you right now."

Cara pushed her chair away from the table and stood. "You're impossible, you know that?" she huffed. "Your ego continues to astound me. You don't know what I want, and if I have anything to say about it, you never will."

Alex gave her a smug grin. *We'll see about that.*

"Oh, my gosh," she gasped with a glance at the clock. "We have to get moving or else we'll never finish what I need to cover today."

At that moment, his phone rang out the melody to Charlie Parker's "Now's the Time."

"Saved by the bell," he said, and she rolled her eyes again.

"What's up, Tommy? Tonight? What time?" He listened for a moment, his eyes locked on Cara's curious gaze. "Yeah, I'll be there. Thanks, man."

He slipped his phone back into his pocket. "Well, I've got to cut the weekend short."

"Why, what happened?"

"I just got a call to play at Lincoln Center this evening. My driver will be here in an hour."

She stared at him, then shrugged. "No problem. We have a couple of hours in the car to study."

He shook his head, hid a smile. "I have to review the charts for the concert tonight. Tommy is sending them to my phone now. I have an app that lets me read them right on the screen."

Her face fell in disappointment, but he was delighted with the turn of events. "The book tour doesn't start till Friday. We have plenty of time between now and then to be sure that I'm ready for it."

"I have other clients who—" she protested.

He cut her off, his voice stern, but his heart was soft. "Teaching me to read in three days is what you were hired to do, wasn't it?"

"Of course, but…" she sputtered.

"But nothing," he insisted. "We both know I'm making great progress, but as you said yourself, I still need a little more work."

He hated what he was about to say, but he had to throw it out there and make his point clear.

"Besides, backing out now would mean that you haven't fulfilled your part of the deal, so obviously neither would I."

His words hung like dynamite in the air. She stared at him in astonishment, and he could tell by the look in her eyes that she was peeved at his threat.

"Of course, Mr. Dovington," she snapped. "I have every intention of completing the assignment to your satisfaction."

He couldn't help but smile, and admire her legs, when with a twirl of her skirt she spun on her heels and left the room.

He whistled as he cleaned up the kitchen. Thanks to fate and a phone call, the day was turning around in his favor.

Chapter 11

A rainy Monday morning, no umbrella, a broken heart and an eviction notice.

I love my life.

Cara stood in front of Beacon House in a virtual stupor. Maybe if she stared long enough at the legal paper of doom, which was already flapping in the wind, it would fly away.

But it didn't budge. Just like her hair, which was now plastered to her face because she'd been standing there so long. Finally, she tore the notice off and unlocked the door.

She walked down the short hallway to her office, slipped off her soppy raincoat, and sat down at her desk, hugging her arms to her body. The building was cold and drafty, but she was hesitant to turn on the heat so early in the season.

Reluctantly, she turned her attention to the eviction

notice. Her hands shook as she carefully read the fine print.

She had thirty days to vacate the premises. Thirty days to find a new location for Beacon House. One that was affordable for her and convenient for her clients.

Cara buried her face in her hands and fought back a fresh wave of tears. She was finished. There were simply no extra funds available. And there wasn't enough time to raise the money she would need to hire movers, let alone rent a place.

Beacon House would cease to exist by Halloween.

Her personal nightmare had begun and she couldn't see a way out. What was she going to do?

Sure, she could call her father, who in turn could make a few phone calls, and all of a sudden, the eviction notice would be retracted by her landlord with profuse apologies.

But she was never the type of daughter to go running to her daddy to solve her problems, and she wasn't going to start now. Even if he was one of the most influential people in New York. Even if it was mighty tempting right now to bow her head and listen to him tell her she should have been an attorney.

She wiped away her tears and yawned. She'd gotten herself into this mess, she'd just have to figure a way out, even though she was so exhausted she could barely move. Alex continued to haunt her thoughts, and last night she had barely slept.

She didn't like that what she'd come to do that weekend was not complete. She'd signed a contract to teach him to read, not fall in love with him. That she would have to see him again didn't make her happy at all. If anything, it made her sad, because it would only prolong what would be an inevitable forever goodbye.

The ride home was as excruciating as she expected. Neither of them spoke much and that was bad enough. The crackle of desire was still there, but there was the undeniable sense that again something had shifted between them.

Alex didn't appear to be affected a great deal one way or another. Once they got in the car, he immediately pulled out his phone and was engrossed in the charts he had to learn. Cara wondered if he even knew she was in the same car with him.

Did he even remember that a few hours before, they were feverishly pleasuring each other in ways she would never forget? Did he even care?

He did seem surprised when she insisted he drop her off in front of Beacon House instead of her apartment. Sometimes her father liked to make unannounced visits to her home. She didn't want to take the chance of running into him.

She'd hoped he would kiss her goodbye, but all she got when she stepped out of the limo was her bags, a polite handshake and a heart filled with pain. It seemed he'd forgotten to pack caring and concern alongside his socks. A classic symptom of the he's-just-not-that-into-you disease.

Then his limo pulled away and she watched it weave through traffic until it was out of sight.

The pain of his rejection seared through her heart anew, and she sighed. It was time to deal with something that could destroy her credit, but not her heart. Accounts Payable.

She was booting up her computer when her office manager popped in the room. "Good morning!"

Cara jumped out of her chair and stretched across

the desk to snatch up the eviction notice she'd left on the corner in plain sight.

"What's that you have there?"

Nancy was in her mid-fifties with the eyes of a hawk, ears of a cat and a heart of gold.

She grasped the document, slid back into her chair. "Oh, nothing."

At Nancy's raised eyebrow, she burst out crying. "Oh, everything!" She handed her the paper. "I don't know what I'm going to do."

Nancy's expression soured and Cara felt even worse. As owner of Beacon House, she was supposed to provide a stable work environment for her employees. Soon they would both be dusting off their resumes.

"I'm sorry. I'm sure you know what this means."

"That you're not giving up?" Nancy pulled up a chair and sat down. "Because I truly hope you are not."

Cara gave her a wan smile. "I don't know if I have anything left to give."

"Hmm. Well, I've learned that sometimes at your lowest point the greatest things can happen."

"I am at my lowest point." Cara looked all around and smirked. "And nope, nothing's happening."

"Give it some time. I bet the answer to your prayers will come walking through the door when you least expect it."

Cara remained silent and fought the urge to roll her eyes. Although she knew she meant well, Nancy was forever waxing philosophical. Like all the world's problems could be solved with a sound byte.

The only thing she'd like to see walking through the door was a gigantic check with Beacon House and tons of zeros written all over it.

Now *that* would be answered prayer.

Nancy rose and stretched. "I better go crank up my own computer and check voice mail. You have back-to-back clients this morning. Mr. Hernandez is your first. Did you remember to bring your smelling salts?"

Cara groaned. Gabe Hernandez was an eighty-year-old man who ate a clove of garlic and drank a shot of whiskey every morning. He claimed they were the secret to his longevity, but they smelled like death to her.

When Nancy closed the door, Cara navigated to the computer file containing all her financial information. She picked up the phone to dial her attorney.

It was going to be a very long and busy day, but time and tasks were exactly what she needed to try to forget Alex Dovington.

Alex squeezed into the A train, jam-packed with folks wishing they were anywhere but on a crowded subway, including him. He was on his way to a friendly showdown with Cara, and he aimed to win.

He probably should have called ahead, but surprising her meant she couldn't run away. That was good, because what he had to ask her could change both of their lives.

He'd just gotten out of a meeting with his public relations manager. Although he made a halfhearted attempt to cancel it, the book tour was a go and it was less than four days away.

His insides quaked with fear, not ready to deal with the publicity and the likelihood that he was going to make a complete fool of himself. He had to do everything in his power to ensure that he and Cara spent as much time together as possible, so that he could prepare for what might be the most embarrassing day of his life.

The entire ride home he had hoped Cara would insist, in her own way, that they continue with the lessons. That she would pull him away from the charts that he already knew backward and forward. But the only time she spoke to him was to decline his invitation to attend his gig at Lincoln Center.

She was a consummate professional and educator, but what did that have to do with their feelings for one another?

While he didn't know the extent of her emotions for him, the sinking feeling that she was hiding something from him was getting stronger. And he didn't like it one bit.

He hoped that tonight he could put his reservations to rest.

At 125th Street, he emerged from the subway with a throng of fellow riders. When he arrived at her office, only a few blocks away, his heart swelled with pride. Located in between two vacant storefronts, Beacon House was literally a diamond in the rough. He admired the gold lettering on the glass and the window boxes filled with yellow and lavender flowers.

He rang the buzzer a couple of times, and when she finally opened the door, her hair and her expression were frazzled.

"What are you doing here, Alex?" Her frustration was palpable, and his heart went out to her.

He smiled. "Is that anyway to talk to your favorite student?"

Her lips were set in a thin line. "I was getting ready to leave."

He pumped his fist. "Perfect timing! You can join me for dinner at my place, and after that, you can continue with the lessons you owe me."

With a sniff, she folded her arms across her chest.

"Is that an order? I guess you're not into asking either, just telling."

She turned and walked away from him, as fast as her tight legs could go. He followed, grinning. At least she was talking to him. He caught up and grabbed her elbow.

Turning her around to face him, he looked into her eyes.

"I'm sorry. That came out wrong. Dinner. Then will you teach me tonight? That is, if you don't have any other plans."

And if you do, it better not be with another man.

She stepped away, but he wrapped his arm around her waist and pulled her close.

His hazel eyes searched her brown ones, saw confusion. She was clearly on the fence about him, but why? Especially when she had so much at stake. He had to find out.

"Please?"

She bit her lip in a way that made his groin tighten. At that moment, he wanted nothing more than to crush her against the wall and taste the place where her teeth made contact with her flesh. But now was not the time.

His grip on her waist loosened and she stepped aside.

"Okay, I'll have dinner with you. But no lesson. Unfortunately, I left the book at home."

"No problem, we can just cab over there and pick it up."

"No!" she exclaimed.

Pain stabbed his heart. This was the second time she refused to let him come to her house. Was there another man in her life?

Cara cleared her throat. "I'll bring in the book tomorrow. Call me in the morning and make an appointment.

Tuesdays are fairly light, so I can probably squeeze you in."

Make an appointment? Squeeze him in? She was really trying his patience.

He shrugged, trying not to show his annoyance. "Sure, whatever you think is best. Ready to head out?"

She nodded. "I just need to gather my things."

He walked into the small waiting room and smiled at the poster featuring Uncle Sam pointing a gnarled finger, declaring "We Want You to Read!"

Minutes later, they stepped outside and she locked the door.

He gestured toward the building with admiration. "You should be proud of yourself, Cara. You're doing great things for the community. I hope you'll be able to continue here for many years to come."

She looked at him, her eyes moist, and he got the feeling she was in trouble, but he didn't want to push her to talk about it.

"Do you mind if we walk?" she asked.

"Not at all, it's only a few blocks."

They fell silent, succumbing to their thoughts and the sounds of rush hour traffic. They arrived at Alex's town house just as it was starting to rain again. He took her coat, hung it in the closet and was escorting her to the kitchen when the doorbell rang.

"I hate to put you to work, but would you mind setting the table while I go see who's at the door?"

Cara agreed and began to search the kitchen for the plates and glasses.

"Dinner is served," announced Alex a few minutes later.

She gaped at the two large paper bags he was carrying, and her face lit up. "You ordered from Sylvia's?"

A soul-food institution, Sylvia's had been serving traditional Southern cuisine in Harlem for over thirty-five years.

"The one and only!" He began unloading plastic containers onto the counter. "I've got chicken, ribs, greens, macaroni and cheese, buttered biscuits, sweet tea and for dessert, pecan pie."

"Why didn't you tell me that in the first place? I wouldn't have hesitated before accepting your invitation."

They laughed as they filled their plates, then sat down to eat in silence.

Later, Cara pushed her plate away. "Delicious, but I'll be paying for it on the scale tomorrow." She sipped her tea. "I read the reviews in the *New York Times*. Sounds like you had a great show last night, congratulations."

Alex swallowed and nodded. "Everything was perfect, except for one thing."

"What's that?"

He pointed his fork at her. "You weren't there."

She looked uncomfortable. "I had to…"

"…pick up your cat, I know," he said dryly. "Anyway, I would have loved to see you in the audience. Don't worry. I'll find a way for you to make it up to me. But first, I want to show you something."

Alex cleared their plates, then went into the living room and carefully took his Grammy Award out of its case. He returned to the kitchen and handed it to Cara.

"Here. I want you to hold it."

Her eyes widened and she gave him a questioning look.

"Seriously, it's okay." He gently placed the award in her cupped hands.

"It's so heavy!" she said in awe.

"That's because of all the blood, sweat and tears that go into winning one of these things," he joked.

He watched her intently. "You know, you're the first person I've ever let touch, let alone hold my Grammy."

"Really? Why me?"

He shrugged. "Because I believe you understand the sacrifices it takes to make your dreams come true."

She nodded in agreement. "You give up a lot, sometimes more than you realize at the time."

"And when you make it, when you achieve what you've wanted since you were a kid, you wonder, that's it? What do I do now?" He paused. "That's where I'm at, Cara."

He took the Grammy back. "I don't know if I want this anymore."

Even as he spoke the words, he couldn't believe he was saying them. But at the same time, an overwhelming sense of relief filled him. It felt good to admit his feelings to someone who cared about him, instead of always hiding behind his public persona.

Her caring about him was one thing he could depend on. It felt great because it was real. He knew that she cared about him, not his money or his status.

She looked at the award, then back at him. "Are you saying you want to get out of the music business?"

He gripped it tighter. "Maybe."

Her voice held no disdain, only curiosity. "Why?"

Alex set the Grammy down on the kitchen counter. How much should he tell her? He wanted to put his trust in her completely, but there was still that nagging feeling that she was hiding something from him.

"There are things you don't know about me, Cara." He sighed. "If I could turn back time I wouldn't even have this Grammy, my town house or anything else for that matter."

"Remember what you said, everything happens for a reason."

"No!" He slammed his fist down on the counter. "Everything doesn't happen for a reason. Things happen as a result of the choices we make. Choices we learn to regret, when it's too late."

He turned away, embarrassed at his outburst. When he felt her presence next to him and her warm hand on his arm, the lump in his throat grew larger.

"Everyone deserves a second chance, Alex. No matter what."

He faced her and she didn't move, their bodies inches away from each other. Lifting one curl of her hair, he spiraled it around his finger, then let go.

"Do you really believe that?" he asked, searching her eyes.

She nodded, her lips quavering. "Yes."

Thank you, Lord.

Her response was music to his ears. It meant that when the day came for him to tell her the truth about his past, she would likely be more open and accepting.

That day was coming soon. He threaded his fingers through her hair. He was falling in love with her, and he knew that keeping secrets would destroy any hope for a future with her.

He closed the gap between them, felt her body tremble when he cupped her chin and gently traced his thumb along the back of her neck. She bent her head back slightly and her long hair tickled his arm.

"If you show me where it is, I'll make us some coffee," she whispered, moving away in an attempt to interrupt his romantic gesture.

Alex blocked her by putting his other hand on the counter, and stepped even closer. When he drew her body to his, he hardened immediately at the sound of her gasp.

A soft moan escaped her lips as he pushed her hair behind her shoulder, then drew a finger along the sensitive folds of the outside of her ear.

"What do you like in your coffee? Cream or sugar?" she said, her breath quickening as he tickled her earlobe.

He placed his hands gently on the sides of her face and looked deeply into her eyes, trying to convey all that he was beginning to feel for her, even though he knew it was impossible.

"Both."

His kiss was light as he pressed into her lips. They tasted of sugar and sweet tea, and he wanted to devour them. But he held back until she slipped her arms around his neck and kissed him back with an urgency that surprised them both.

She parted her lips and accepted his tongue, and he groaned involuntarily. He sunk into the warm cavern of her mouth, drinking in her essence, always wanting more.

His flesh throbbed against her hard abdomen in desperate and painful need as her fingers roved his back, as if on a hunt for buried treasure. His muscles twitched in response to her sensuous touch, and she tore herself away from him, her eyes wide.

"Alex, we need to slow down," she breathed, her face flushed.

He tried to kiss her again, but she scooted away and walked out of the kitchen.

Alex's legs were unsteady as he followed her. "Why does it always seem like you are running away from me?"

Cara grabbed her raincoat from the closet and shoved her arms into it. "I'm not running away. I've had a long day today and I'm tired. I need to go home. Thank you so much for dinner. It was fantastic."

She grabbed the door handle, and Alex put his hand over hers. "We need to talk about this, Cara. And soon."

"We will, I promise," she said, seeming nervous. "Call me tomorrow and we'll set up a time to go over the book once more."

"I'm sorry, I can't. I'll be in the studio all day recording. I guess you're going to have to come to me."

"I have to check my schedule."

Since when did he become just an appointment slot, he thought, his temper flaring, yet his determination and desire for her remained steady.

He kept his voice firm. "Find the time. There's only two more days to the tour. I'll text you the address."

She nodded and they stepped outside. He hailed a cab and before she got in, he kissed her cheek.

"See you tomorrow. And this time, don't forget the book, and your pretty smile."

The cab lurched away and he pumped his fist in the air, happy that Cara agreed to meet him at the studio.

Not that she had much choice.

Before the donation check could be written to Beacon House, she had to fulfill the contract terms and finish teaching him how to read.

His part of the deal was to open her eyes to the fact that she was falling in love with him before she walked out of his life forever.

Chapter 12

The next morning, Cara stepped off the subway platform at 28th Street and Lexington Avenue with one goal: to say goodbye to Alex forever.

She knew it definitely wouldn't be easy to walk away from a man she'd wanted for longer than she cared to remember. But it was the only way to protect both of them from getting hurt.

The October air was crisp and cool as she walked to the recording studio a few blocks away. People hurried by feeding on the upbeat, infectious energy that was the spirit of New York City. Rush hour in New York occurred 24 hours a day, 365 days a week, and normally she found it uplifting, even soothing.

But today, her feet dragged and her mood right along with it. She'd finally found the love of her life and now she had to give him up. All because of her father, and a little thing called fear of commitment.

Put the two together and she was on a one-way trip to perpetual singleness.

The unfairness of it all made her want to do something inane like shake her fist at the sky. But with her luck, she'd probably get struck by lightning.

The kisses they'd shared last night resonated through her mind. His lips, full and warm, were so insistent to claim her again as his own she felt she would drown. He had restored emotions and spine-tingling feelings that she'd thought were long dead. In his arms, she felt amazingly alive.

The studio was located in a nondescript building with no sign. Wary, she pressed a button and someone buzzed her in. She stood in the foyer, clutching her briefcase and purse, not knowing what to do next.

She jumped at the sound of Alex's booming voice. "Cara, we're down in the basement. Come on down and watch your step!"

She walked to the end of the hall, and she and her two-inch heels started to navigate down the stairs.

They almost made it the whole way.

"Whoa!" Alex grabbed her by both elbows just before she fell flat on her face. "Easy there!"

"Special delivery," she joked, as her briefcase and purse flew off her shoulder and thumped to the floor. "You're always in the right place at the time I make a complete fool of myself."

"It's exactly where I want to be." He searched her eyes, and she was touched by the concern in his voice. "Seriously, are you okay?"

Her face heated and she moved out of his grasp as politely as she could. "Yes, although I'm a complete klutz sometimes, if you haven't noticed."

"I think it's kind of cute," he intoned, handing her things to her.

"I think it's kind of dangerous." She smirked, testing her ankle for a sprain.

"Not if I'm always here to save you." He smiled at her as if he wanted a response, but she didn't have one.

Taking her hand, he led her into a room filled with expensive-looking equipment and walled with a gray, spongy material that looked like honeycombs.

"Cara, I'd like you to meet Richie Adams, he's the best sound engineer in the business. He's also the owner, so be nice to him," he joked.

"Don't listen to him," said Richie as he shook hands with Cara. "He's just trying to butter me up so I'll give him more recording time for free."

Everyone laughed. "I hear you're going to be helping us out on the session today," said Richie.

Cara shot Alex a questioning look.

"I'll explain in a minute," he said soothingly, his voice caressing her ear.

Alex turned to Richie. "Hey, man, we'll be ready soon."

"The clock is running right into my bank account," said Richie, tapping his watch. "So take your time. It's all good!"

Alex laughed and the two men high-fived before he led her into another room that could only be described as a "man cave." There was a large flat-screen TV muted to ESPN, a black leather sectional, a small bar and a pool table. The walls were covered with musicians like Jimi Hendrix, John Coltrane and, oddly enough, Liberace.

She set her briefcase and purse on the couch and

pointed at the picture of the deceased eccentric pianist who had dominated Las Vegas in the 1970s.

"That's Ritchie's personal favorite," said Alex. "Don't ask!"

"Trust me, I won't." She put her hands on her hips. "So, what's going on, Alex? I thought you wanted me to come here so we can review the book."

"We'll get to that, but I need you to do me a favor first."

Her eyes narrowed. "What is it?"

"I want you to sing the lyrics you composed for my song."

Her mouth gaped, stunned by what he was asking her. "Why?" she stammered, pulse racing.

"It's for a sound check. Richie got some new equipment in the studio that I've never recorded with before and I want to check levels. I need to make sure everything works properly."

Her voice wavered. "You mean you want me to…"

"Sing," Alex finished for her. "You just need to lay down one track, that's it, okay?"

"Alex, I don't think…" Her voice trailed off.

If she had known Alex would be planning this, she would never have agreed to meet him at the studio. The man was full of surprises.

He gave her shoulders a reassuring squeeze. "Don't worry. Nobody will hear you but me and Richie."

She regarded him thoughtfully, dressed in a cream-colored Cuban-style shirt and black trousers that accentuated his handsome build. It was so hard to say no to him. Especially when he looked off-the-charts sexy.

There was so much of him waiting to be explored. But none of it was possible anymore. She was too busy keeping it real—professional, that is, too afraid to be anything more than his literacy teacher.

"What do you say, Cara? Will you sing?" He lifted her hand and kissed it. His lips felt warm and lush, and the tenderness of his touch spiraled through her body. "For me?"

Blushing from all his attention, she nodded.

His smile lit up her entire world. "Thank you."

Wrapping her hand in his, he led her to the little studio. "Make yourself comfortable."

She sat down on the wooden stool and he adjusted the microphone to her lips. He gave her a set of headphones and placed them over her ears.

She was shocked when he handed her the lyrics she'd sung to his ballad. "But...I—"

He touched his finger to her lips. "Hush. You can do this. Just pretend you're in my shower again."

"I'll let you know when we're ready. Sit tight." He kissed her forehead and left the room.

A few minutes later, she heard Alex's voice through her headphones. "Nod when you hear the instrumental in your right ear." A few seconds later, she heard the piano, bass and drums through her headphones. She nodded.

"Okay. Now just lay down the vocal track right over it. Nice and easy." He smiled at her through the glass. "Ready when you are."

She took a deep breath, closed her eyes and began to sing.

It's tearing me apart
To give you a chance
Still I'd sell
My soul for you

> *And now that you are here*
> *I can't understand*
> *Why you ever*
> *Left me*
> *Now is the time for you and me*
> *To take a chance on love*
> *Don't wait to see*
> *Now is the time for us.*

When she finished, Alex asked her to do it again, then three more times. She was trying hard to be patient, but how long did it take to check levels?

He came in and hugged her. "Great job, thank you. We're done."

"I'm glad I could help, but do you still have time to review the book? I have to leave soon."

"Of course," he said. "That's why I invited you here originally. I appreciate you making time in your schedule."

When they got back to the man cave, Cara headed straight for her briefcase.

"Oh, no!" she cried.

Alex strode over to her in alarm. "What's wrong?"

Cara was so angry at herself she almost burst out crying. "The book. I left it at home," her voice broke. "I can't believe this is happening."

She racked her brain trying to figure out what happened, and then it hit her. She had two briefcases, both black leather, and the one with the book in it was at home, probably being used as a bed by her cat, Molly.

How could she have been so careless?

"It's okay, Cara. Can you drop by my house later tonight?"

She swallowed a frustrated scream, then nodded. What other choice did she have?

She picked up her briefcase and purse. "I have other clients waiting so I better get going."

Alex touched her elbow. "Thanks again."

She gave him a faint smile. "I'll see myself out."

She turned and walked down the hall as fast as her heels could carry her. She didn't want to say goodbye to Alex, but she had no choice. Waiting another day, another moment, would only make it hurt more. By the time she got onto Lexington Avenue, tears of frustration and longing were streaming down her face.

Cara's hands trembled as she pressed Alex's doorbell. She couldn't believe that only five days earlier she'd stood in the very same spot, unsure if she could complete this insane assignment. In a few hours, the task of teaching Alex how to read in time for the book tour would be complete. And her secret would remain hidden.

Both outcomes were what she'd hoped for, prayed for. Then why did she feel so sad?

She slumped against the doorway, knowing the reason, but choosing not to fully accept it. Despite her best efforts, she'd fallen in love with Alex.

The man she'd admired from afar for years had become part of her every thought. His commanding presence remained with her, haunting her dreams, invading her present.

The desire she felt for him was always there, simmering below the surface, ready to erupt at any moment. With him, she was uninhibited, wanton and sensual. And she wanted nothing more than to be with him forever.

But what scared her the most was that he wanted her, too. She could feel it in his touch, the desire in his eyes, the warmth of his arms and his concern for her well-being.

Everything was wonderful now, but how would things be in one month or one year? Would he still feel the same way about her? Was Harlem's most eligible bachelor ready to settle down, too?

She straightened and nervously touched the back of her hair, which she'd wrestled into a neat chignon.

The question of whether he was or was not ready for a relationship with her was moot. He had every reason to hate her father, and when he found out she'd been lying to him, he would hate her, too. And that would be the end of any feelings he had for her.

She wanted to bolt, but she pressed the doorbell again, half hoping he wasn't home.

The door opened and her breath caught in her throat. She'd never known any man who could make her wet with desire just at the mere sight of him. He wore a cream button-down shirt with the sleeves rolled up and gray trousers. Even his bare feet were sexy.

He clasped her hand in his and drew her through the doorway while she discreetly inhaled the spicy scent of his cologne. "I'm glad you were able to make it. Come on in."

He helped her with her coat, his fingers brushing against the back of her bare neck, sending tiny tremors down her spine.

When she faced him again, her face grew hot as his eyes seared her body, clad in a navy wraparound dress that was simple but elegant.

"You look beautiful."

His baritone voice caressed her with admiration, and

she knew she would replay his compliment in her mind over and over.

He took her elbow. "How was the rest of your day?"

"Busy," she replied. "I had a full afternoon of clients, so I didn't get any paperwork done. I brought it home. Hopefully, we'll finish early enough that I can get it done before bed."

He nodded. "I think if we run through the book a few times, I'll be okay. I can't believe the tour starts in less than two days."

"Time flies." *When you're falling in love.*

They entered the kitchen and Cara gasped in surprise. On the counter were votive candles, two glasses, a bottle of wine and a small platter of assorted cheeses and fruits.

"I hope you don't mind. Will you share some with me?"

She bit her lip. "Sure, I'd love a glass of wine. But only one, I do have to work tonight," she warned.

"I understand."

Cara hopped onto the bar stool and crossed her legs. Her dress got caught on the edge, revealing her bare thigh. Swooping it closed, she looked up and caught him watching her. Their eyes met and her throat went dry as he handed her a glass of wine.

He sat across from her and moved his chair closer until their knees almost touched. "I know our time together is about to end, and I just wanted to thank you again for all you've done for me."

The sincerity in his voice wound into her heart, and she blinked back tears. "Alex, I should be the one thanking you. Your donation is going to help so many people overcome illiteracy. I only wish you knew the impact you're going to have on their lives."

Per the contract, she should receive the donation by the end of the week. However, with the eviction pending, it would no longer be enough to save Beacon House from closure. But that was her problem, not his.

He shook his head. "No, I'm only giving money. You give yourself, every day, for your students. You truly are making the world a better place."

"I don't know about all that," she said, humbled. "But I hope I'm making a difference."

"You sure made a difference in my life." He sipped his wine. "I'll admit I was a little resistant at first."

Cara raised an eyebrow and coughed.

"Okay, okay." He laughed, held up a hand. "I was a lot resistant—to you, to learning to read, this whole book tour idea."

"But you came through on the other side. Be proud of yourself!"

"Never would have happened without you," he insisted, clinking his glass to hers. "You're an amazing woman, Cara."

His compliment made her heart glow anew. He held her gaze as they sipped their wine.

Her eyes darted to the digital clock on the stove and she put down her wineglass. "I hate to break up the party, but we better start or time will get away from us again."

His look said "would that be so bad?" but she held her ground and opened up the book on the counter.

"Why don't you read it all the way through first without stopping? Then we'll go back and address any words or phrases that give you trouble."

His voice sounded tentative at first but got stronger as he went along. Her heart swelled with pride as he read. He'd come such a long way, but he had a lot further to go. It saddened her to think that she wouldn't be the one to accompany him on his journey to functional literacy.

When Alex finished, Cara clapped as loudly as she could.

"That was fantastic! Great job!"

He blew out a breath. "I feel like I've benched about 300 pounds. I never knew words could beat a person up like that. No wonder Oscar was always a grouch."

She cracked up. "I never thought about it that way. I thought he was mean because he lived in a garbage can, but maybe he was just trying to escape."

"There is no escape from words," said Alex. "They can hurt, kill spirits and start wars."

She nodded. "They can heal, show love, inspire change, make someone laugh."

He reached over and touched her cheek. "And they can make someone never want to say goodbye."

Fear and choices hung like invisible tightwires between them. However, unlike at the circus, there was no safety net to break their fall. Only pain, uncertainty and secrets. At that moment, neither had the courage to take a step into the unknown.

I don't want to say goodbye, either.

Those were the words she wished she could say. Instead, she cleared her throat and closed the book. "I think you'll be fine on Friday."

"Will you be there?"

She shook her head. "No, I wasn't planning on it, and I have some pretty important meetings that day."

He sat back, an air of defeat surrounding him. "Oh, I was hoping you would be."

Her heart lurched at the disappointment in his voice.

"It's getting late. I'd better head home. I'll email you some names of other literacy teachers."

Alex placed a hand on her knee, his eyes twinkling as he got off the chair. "Wait, I have something I want to give you."

He reached into a cupboard and took out a notebook-size package wrapped in brown paper.

She stood up and went to his side. "What is it?"

"Open it and see, silly!"

She took the package and opened it with care. When she saw what it was, she couldn't believe her eyes.

Framed and mounted was his tune, the one she'd stolen. The song that almost broke them apart now had finally brought them together.

He'd forgiven her.

His gentle eyes caressed her face. "Since you're my biggest fan, I thought you'd like to have it."

"Alex." Her eyes filled with tears and she gazed up at him. "I was so surprised when you asked me to sing it this morning, and now this…gift? I don't know what to say."

"Then let me say it for you." He palmed her face, lowered his lips to hers and treated her to a long and unforgettable kiss.

"Do you have anything else you want to say?" he asked.

Without a second thought, she flattened her hands against his neck, pulled him to her and kissed him long and deep. His mouth was so warm and wonderful, so insistent about her own, that time and the work waiting for her back home were forgotten.

Her body went slack and he linked his arm around her waist, pulling her close. Her fears were wrestled to the ground by his eager mouth and tongue, teasing and taunting her with more pleasure to come.

He leaned her against the table and kissed her nose and her eyelids and grazed her brows with his lips. She loved the feel of his hands clutched around her waist, his hard length imprisoned between them.

Trailing a finger from the bridge of her nose, she bit the tip in mock protest and he smiled.

"Close your eyes," he muttered against her ear, breath ragged. "I have something else to show you."

She laughed. "What do you have up your sleeve now?"

"You'll see. Lights out."

Giggling, she squeezed her eyes shut as he grabbed her hand and led her forward a short distance.

"Okay. You can open up," he said, letting go of her hand.

She blinked in disbelief at the sight before her.

Hundreds of pink and red rose petals blanketed the heavy oak dining table, and right in the center was a Scrabble board.

Cara walked up to it and read the words formed by the little wooden letters:

I LOVE YOU

Tears streamed down her face as Alex stood behind her and wrapped his arms around her waist.

"This is my love letter to you." He twirled her around to face him. "I learned how to read a lot of words over the past few days, but these are the only ones that matter."

He tilted her chin up with the pad of his thumb. "I love you, Cara."

The candles seemed to cheer from every corner of the room as he kissed her tears away. Cara curled into his embrace and succumbed to his kiss fully and completely, drowning in the delicious flavor of his lips, so tempting to bite and lick.

His mouth tasted of wine, and as she stroked her hands up his neck and over the smooth skin of his head, a moan arose from deep within his throat.

The heat of Alex's body invaded her own as her lips parted to take his tongue deeper into her mouth, allowing him to explore her at will.

She murmured low in her throat and he responded by crushing her body against him. Swaying from side to side, she longed to touch and stroke the hard flesh that poked the thin fabric of her dress.

He groaned again, broke the kiss and kept his gaze on hers as he trailed his finger down her chin, the length of her neck.

Slowly he traced the swell of her cleavage, taking a dip into the skin between her breasts as if he only wanted a taste. His fingertips raked lightly across her nipples, and they popped alive from his touch. Her mouth watered remembering the feel of his lips around them.

As if he could read her mind, he traced the curves of her waist and fumbled with the single tie that held her dress together.

Growing impatient, she tried to untie it herself, but he batted her hand away and scolded her by rubbing the pads of his thumbs against her nipples in a circular motion so slow that she felt her knees collapse against him.

Finally, he untied her dress and slid it off her shoulders. He stepped back and she heard him suck in a breath at the sight of her body, now clad in only a lace bra and thong.

With a shy smile on her lips, she reached up and released her hair from the chignon, enjoying seeing his desire for her burn even brighter in his eyes.

She met his gaze and almost laughed aloud when he started unbuttoning his shirt a lot quicker than he'd untied her dress.

She stepped toward him and peppered his neck with slow, sensual kisses as he slid his hands over her buttocks. He squeezed her to him and she cried out when he suddenly lifted her and laid her gently on the table.

The scent of roses wafted around her and provided a velvety texture against the table's hard wood. The square game pieces felt cool against the small of her back, and instead of hurting, they felt amazingly good, heightening her desire.

He leaned over and buried his head in her neck, nuzzling her with tiny kisses. She twisted and moaned when his tongue discovered a sensitive spot and lingered there until she pushed his head away.

He unbuckled his pants and slipped off his boxers. Her mouth watered at the sight of his beautiful body fully exposed to her. He was powerfully built, and there was a sheer layer of sweat contoured over his muscled skin.

At that moment, she wanted him inside her more than anything. Her heart pounded in her chest as she lifted her arms and reached for him, but he caught her wrist in his hand.

"Not yet," he commanded. "I want to look at you."

Slowly he undid the front clasp of her bra, releasing her breasts to his eager eyes and hot tongue. He took his time, kneading and pleasuring and licking until her whimpers became raging gasps. Then he hooked his thumbs in the straps of her thong and planted little kisses all the way down her legs as he eased her underwear off.

He caressed every inch of her body, fire raging in his eyes, leaving her skin tingling with overwhelming physical need. His hands palmed her breasts, barely touching them, before he bent his mouth to each nipple and flicked the stiff tips again with tender abandon.

She threw her head back and his mouth came crushing back down to nuzzle at her neck.

"Cara," he breathed, as he lightly bit, then sucked her earlobe. "You have no idea what you do to me, woman."

She grew even wetter at the sensuality of his words, the natural juice of her need preparing her body to accept him.

Instinctively, she spread her legs and he slid a finger to explore her moist folds and the dark cavern she offered to him freely, lovingly. His tongue played on her flesh, and she squirmed with pleasure, game pieces digging into her back, arms and shoulders.

He stood up and her eyes landed on the hard length of flesh that jutted from his torso. Again, she reached for him. But he stepped back, picked up a handful of roses and let them drift like snowflakes. She closed her eyes as they landed softly on her body. Little petals of soft fire.

"Tell me you want me."

She opened her eyes, and met his. "Let your teacher show you instead," she whispered low.

His flesh was hot and hard as she tenderly stroked him, loved him with the palm of her hand, and when he could take her touch no more, he arched his shoulders back and eased into her lips with a groan. He was exquisite fullness in her mouth, on her tongue, in her grip.

When she broke contact, he pushed her back on the

table and with one swift motion pinned her arms above her head. Lifting her buttocks and pulling her toward him, he plunged his entire length into her body. She cried out and he silenced her by sucking on her bottom lip as he began to master her senses with deliciously slow movements.

She writhed in sensuous agony as his thumbs massaged her taut nipples. Shrieking with pleasure when he completely filled her, she begged him to come back to her when he teased and dragged his hard length against her moist flesh.

The scent of roses wafted in the air as he branded her body as his own, on his own terms. She was barely aware of the table creaking back and forth beneath them as he tugged her closer, delving deeper and deeper into her most private place.

She knew, then and there, that she belonged to him.

"Ohh!" She held her legs sky high as he thrust her into a sensual abyss, and she was falling and screaming out his name when she climbed again, taking him with her now, her lover man, as spasms of pleasure rippled through her body and exploded into his, and he gave her the gift of himself.

Uninhibited release.

Undeniable love.

Their hearts beat together in a rhythmic melody of mutual satisfaction as they lay together, rose petals and game pieces stuck to their bodies.

He brushed the hair from her face. "I love you, Cara. Don't leave," he muttered against her ear, breath ragged. "Stay with me tonight. Stay with me forever."

Tears filled her eyes. His words were so beautiful, but believing them would mean she would have to tell him the ugly truth. Alex would take them back when he found out her father was the judge who sent his brother to jail, where he ultimately died.

No. She didn't belong here, didn't deserve to be with Alex, no matter how much she loved him.

She tried to get up, her body still pulsing with pleasure, but he held on to her arm.

"Wait a minute, what's wrong?"

"I need to go. Right now," she said, wresting her arm away from his grasp and stood up. Scrabble pieces and rose petals littered the floor around her.

"Wait a minute. Why?"

She heard in his voice how hurt he was, and she hated herself for doing this to him…again.

Without looking at him, she pulled her dress around her, walked into the kitchen and grabbed her things.

"Hey!" He jumped off the table after her. "Talk to me."

"There are things about me you don't know, Alex," she cried, as she yanked her coat from the closet. "Things you wouldn't like."

"Nonsense, I know all I need to know. I love you."

He grabbed her arm, but she shook away from his grasp.

"Love is not enough. It never is, don't you realize that?" she shouted. "My job here is done. I can't help you anymore, Alex. It hurts too much."

And with that, she pulled the door open and walked out of his life. The knowledge that she was leaving him broken and hurting because of her own cowardice would haunt her forever.

Chapter 13

The morning after Cara walked out on him, Alex sat in his favorite booth at the Tick Tock Diner, clutching his second cup of coffee. His head pounded like he'd been sucker-punched by a made-for-TV wrestler, but his mind was absolutely clear.

Somehow, someway, he was going to find out where Cara lived and demand that they talk through the problems he hadn't even known they had. He rubbed the heel of his hand against his temple. Why were men always the last to know these things?

She'd mentioned that there were things he didn't know about her. He sucked in a breath. Well, there were some things she didn't know about him either, so they had that in common.

It was time to set the record straight.

But the truth was he didn't want to upset her even more than he already had. Their incredible evening of lovemaking had left him wanting even more of her. The fact that the night had ended so badly made his heart ache. He just hoped he hadn't lost her forever.

Alex was on his third cup when Tommy arrived, wearing his trademark Kangol hat. The waitress came over immediately with a cup of coffee and took their orders. They each had the same meal every time; a tall stack of pancakes with bacon and sausage, and a bowl of grits on the side.

Alex pointed to Tommy's head. "It's a red day, huh?" The man owned Kangol hats in every color of the rainbow, and every morning he chose the color based on his mood.

"Yeah, because I'm hopping mad, that's why!" he grumbled as he stirred sugar into his coffee. "I lost three grand to Big Daddy last night. That boy plays poker like he's on the combat line of a war zone."

"I thought you were going to stop going to Big Daddy's poker nights?"

Tommy gulped his coffee, then pointed a finger at him. "Alex, there are two things I'll never give up. Women and cards."

Alex laughed. "It seems I never have any luck with either, so I better stay away from both."

Just then, the waitress brought their breakfast to the table. The two men dug into their food, wolfing it down in silence. When they had finished, they pushed their plates to the side. Now that their bellies were full, it was time to talk business.

"Speaking of women, how are things with Miss Williams?"

Alex shrugged and idly stirred his coffee. "Why do you ask?"

"Are you ready for the book tour?"

He nodded. "I think so."

Tommy leaned his elbows on the table. "You better be," he warned. "Because I just heard you've been doing more than just reading with her. That's the reason I was late."

Alex stopped stirring. "What are you talking about?"

"Cozying up to the little lady at Idella's. Bringing her to the Hideaway. Plus, to make matters worse, you were seen coming out of Beacon House with her."

He felt his face flush with anger. "Who told you all of this?"

"It doesn't matter." Tommy looked around and lowered his gravelly voice. "You were the one who wanted to keep your illiteracy a secret."

Alex clamped his mouth in a thin line, knowing Tommy was right. His heart thudded in his chest. "How bad is it?"

"Don't be surprised if something pops up in the press in the next few days. They know who she is and what she does for a living. It's only a matter of time before they put two and two together. And even if they don't know for sure, they'll report it anyway," Tommy replied, his face grim. "I'll have to say this, she's about the prettiest one you've had the pleasure of introducing to New York City via the headlines in a long time."

Alex threw his arm over his head and slumped down in the booth. "What am I going to do? I can't let the press get to her. It could destroy her. She's not like the others."

"Are you in love with this woman?"

When Alex looked away and didn't reply, Tommy grinned and slapped his knee. "Hot damn. I never thought I'd see the day when Alex Dovington fell head-over-heels in love."

Alex scowled and gulped down his lukewarm coffee. "Look, even if I am, it doesn't matter. She hates me."

"Why?"

"That's just it. I don't know. There's something she's not telling me."

"A woman always has some kind of secret. That's what makes them so intriguing. Besides, you're no saint, either."

"I know, but why couldn't she just tell me, instead of running away?" *And breaking my heart.*

"Probably because she wasn't sure how you'd react. The question you have to ask yourself is, do you want to know what this secret is, and if so, when you find out, are you willing to stick by her, no matter what?"

Alex steepled his fingers. "I think so."

Tommy tipped his hat back, then leaned in and pointed at him. "Think so?" he snorted. "You gotta *know* so. You gotta be so sure about her that nothing will stand in the way of how you feel about this woman. Otherwise, it's all smoke. You dig?"

Alex nodded and smoothed his hand over his head. He got what Tommy was saying, and it was valuable advice. But it was also extremely risky. He'd told her he loved her, for God's sake. And he did.

But who knew what she was hiding beneath her beautiful face? It must be big for her to run out on him like that. He was never one to take chances. What kind of man would gamble his entire future on a woman?

One who wants to be accepted for who he is, despite his past mistakes.

He was that man, and he realized it was time to come clean with everyone, including Cara.

"Can you get me some time with Mo today?"

"I can give it my best shot, why?"

"I need to tell him about my illiteracy before someone else does."

"Great idea!" Tommy paused while the waitress topped off their cups. "What about Cara?"

Alex rubbed his chin. "I love her, T. I've never felt this strongly about someone in my life. And if she's willing to take a chance on me, I'm willing to do the same."

"Great. Why don't you roll by Beacon House this morning and tell her? Bring her some flowers. Women can't resist them."

Alex's mind flashed back to the evening before. When he made love to Cara, the pink and red rose petals had resembled velvety coins on her nude body. He would never be able to look at those flowers again without thinking about her.

He shook his head. "I can't go there. She wouldn't talk to me anyway. I would visit her at home, but I don't know where she lives."

Tommy laughed. "Why didn't you say so? I know where she lives!"

Alex's eyes opened wide with astonishment. "You do? Where?"

"When we were discussing the contract, she told me she lives in Brooklyn. In fact, she lives right next door to my old pal John Sutton. He takes care of her cat whenever she's away. I think the cat's name starts with an M?"

"Molly."

"That's it." Tommy wrote Cara's address on a napkin and handed it to him. Then he took off his hat and laid it on the table. As if on cue, the waitress came over with the bill.

Outside, the two men pumped hands.

"I'll call you as soon as I set up the meeting with Mo."

"What's going to happen after the book tour? Are you going to continue with reading lessons?"

Alex smiled. "If everything goes well tonight, I have more than reading lessons planned for my future."

Tommy chuckled, waved goodbye and shuffled away.

As Alex headed downtown to Parkside Studios, he knew he'd need more than just luck to get Cara back into his life. Like the cowardly lion, he needed courage.

Cara trudged up the stairs to her Brooklyn town house. Between dealing with insensitive creditors and guilt over the pain she'd caused Alex, this was one of the worst days in her life.

She didn't want to think, didn't want to feel. All she wanted was a hot bath and a very large glass of wine.

With a scowl, she dumped her briefcase and purse on the living room couch.

To top it off, the meeting with her lawyer had not gone well. Her landlord planned on renovating the entire space to attract big-box retailers. The paperwork was in order. Unless a miracle happened and somebody purchased the building, there was nothing he could do to stop the eviction.

She kicked off her shoes and hung up her coat, wishing she could disappear into the depths of her closet. Starting tomorrow, she'd have to hold off on accepting any new students.

It pained her to think of saying no to anyone who wanted to learn how to read. But what choice did she have? She didn't want to accept them, then have to turn around and find them placement in other literacy centers. It was better to cut the cord now, before it was too late.

Her mind troubled, she entered the kitchen and selected a bottle of wine from her collection. As she poured herself a large glass, Molly curled a figure eight around her ankles.

Cara had walked out on the sexiest man alive and was losing the business she'd built from the ground up, but at least she still had her beloved cat.

"You love me, don't you?" she asked optimistically.

But before she could reach down to scratch Molly on the top of her head, her cat walked over to her bowl and meowed.

"Oh, I see how you are," she scolded. "You only love me because I'm the one that feeds you. I get it."

It was pathetic, but her spirits were so low that even her cat's rejection hurt her feelings.

As she fed Molly, her thoughts turned to Alex. After her little drama session last night, she didn't expect to hear from him ever again. She only hoped that it wouldn't affect his performance at the book tour on Friday.

She clapped a hand to her forehead when she realized she might not even receive the donation from him. Even though he was legally bound to pay her, she wasn't sure he would. And she couldn't blame him after the way she acted last night.

Her heart pounded in her chest. She was just an ordinary woman who just happened to love, and be loved by, an extraordinary man. She still could not believe all that had transpired between them.

But by walking out on him last night, she'd missed her only opportunity to express her feelings. Now he would never know how much she loved him, too.

Her eyes swam with tears. The best thing she could do now was to concentrate on saving Beacon House—

on her own. It had been a mistake from the very beginning to count on anyone but herself.

She was on her way upstairs when the doorbell rang.
She peeked through the peephole and frowned. Plas-
tering a cheerful smile on her face, she pulled the door
open.

"Hi, Daddy."

Uh-oh, she thought when he didn't reply as he
shrugged off his coat and hung it up in the closet. She
wondered what the lecture topic would be this time.

"I didn't know you were going to stop by. How are
you?" she inquired as they walked into the living room.

They both sat on the couch with rigid spines and
faces that masked their true feelings.

"Cara, I'm fine. But some pretty disturbing news
about you has come to my attention."

Her heart dropped. "What is it?"

"How could you have allowed yourself to get into a
situation where you're threatened with eviction?"

She sucked in a breath. "How did you find out?"

"I'm a judge. I work in the New York City judicial
system. People tell me things. They know you're my
daughter. Besides it's the only way I ever find out anything about you. You never talk to me."

"I never tell you anything because you never listen,"
she retorted, hating the bitter tone in her voice.

"I'm listening now, and I want to help."

"You want to help?" she snorted and folded her arms.
"Why now? I would think you would *want* me to fail.
You're the one who pressured me to go to law school,
and when I chose to become a teacher, you never let
me forget it."

"I wanted you to become a lawyer because I knew

that the life of a teacher would be difficult, and I didn't want that for you."

She slapped her hands against her thighs in exasperation and rose from her seat.

"But what about what I wanted, Daddy?" Her voice rose. "I wanted a father who was there while I was a kid. Who cared more about me than his political career.

"Did I get it?" she railed. "And now, you have the nerve to come in here and try to rescue me? From something that is absolutely none of your business? If you haven't noticed, I'm an adult now. I. Don't. Need. You!"

Her words hung suspended in the air, but the hurt look on her father's face made her wish she could snatch them back into her mouth.

"I'm not going anywhere until we talk about this," said her father sternly. Then he softened his voice. "I know I wasn't around when you were smaller, especially after your mother passed away. And I'm sorry, but there's nothing I can do to change the past."

He stood and went over to her. "But what I can do is be there now. I've been hearing great things about you, Cara. A lot of the people who've been in my courtroom tell me they've been through your literacy program. And even though they may have temporarily fallen back into crime or drugs, they've told me that you're the one person who really cared about them and gave them hope.

"Beacon House is an important community organization in Harlem, but more than that, it's your brainchild and your dream. You're my daughter, I'm proud of you and I want to help you save it."

This was the first time her father told her he was proud of her. She burst out crying and buried her hands in her face to hide her tears. The moment was bitter-

sweet. Perhaps there was a chance that they could reconcile and she could have the kind of relationship with
her father that she'd always wanted.

"Daddy, I don't know what to do," she cried. "I'm
going to lose Beacon House." The faces of her students
flashed by in her mind. "My clients, where will they
go?" she sobbed. "I've worked so hard…"

His arms closed around her, strong and safe, and she
cried on his shoulder. "Don't worry. We'll find a way."

The doorbell rang again. "Are you expecting anyone?" her father asked.

Cara shook her head, wiping the tears away from
her eyes and nose.

"I'll be back in a minute. Wait here."

When she opened the door, her heart seized with
panic.

Alex.

Oh, God, what if he saw her father? She had to get
him out of here right away.

"Hi, Cara," he said, his voice low and apologetic.
"Mind if I come in?"

Before she could answer, he strode through the
door like he owned the place. She was relieved when
he didn't venture into the hallway but stopped just outside the small foyer.

She closed the door behind them, turned and crossed
her arms. "How did you find me?" she demanded in a
low whisper.

"Tommy gave me your address," he said in an off-
hand manner.

His eyes widened and she felt heat rise to her cheeks.

"You've been crying. What's wrong?" he asked, staring at her tear-stained face.

"Nothing." She wiped the tears away and took a step

forward. Being close to him made her knees tremble, but going to another area of the house was out of the question.

"What are you doing here?"

He winced. He didn't know that her sharp tone wasn't meant to hurt him, but she had to get him out of the house before her father saw them.

"We need to talk about last night."

He tried to embrace her, but she pushed him away and strode back to the foyer. "There's nothing more to talk about, Alex." She placed her hand on the door-knob. "Listen, I'm extremely busy and I'm asking you to leave. Now."

He ran his hand over his head, and she could see on his face that he was struggling to maintain composure.

He gave her a confused look. "What's going on with you, Cara?"

"Nothing's going on," she lied. "I just want to be left alone."

"That's not the impression I got last night when I was making love to you."

She kept her voice calm, and although she knew her next words were a lie, she had to hurt him in order to get him out of her life forever.

"That was a mistake."

He pressed his lips together, his laser-intense gaze boring a hole right into her heart. "You don't mean that."

She lifted her chin, forcing herself to look him straight in the eyes. "Yes, I do, Alex," she insisted. "You're a wonderful, charming man. But it would never work between us. We're too different. I'm too…"

"Afraid?" he cut in, raising an eyebrow. "Isn't that it? Everything we shared at my cottage and last night, my love for you, scares the hell out of you, doesn't it? Why don't you just admit it?"

Her stomach knotted and she winced from the pain. He was right, but she wasn't going to tell him that. It was too late.

She lowered her voice, trying desperately to maintain control over her emotions. "I fulfilled my end of the contract. I taught you to read, enough so you'll be able to complete the book tour. There's no reason for us to see each other ever again."

He nodded, and took a step closer. "Yeah, you taught me how to read, but you forgot one thing."

She narrowed her eyes and pressed her back to the door. "What are you talking about?"

"You weren't supposed to teach me how to fall in love with you and then walk out of my life. I don't think that was part of the deal, was it?"

Oh, Lord, her heart felt like it was being cut into slivers. To know he was hurting, because of her.

It hurt so bad to have this conversation with him, to keep her voice hard and unfeeling and her demeanor tough on the outside. All so he wouldn't think she loved him or needed him, when the opposite was true.

She shrugged. "I can't control how you feel about me."

His shoulders recoiled and he glared at her. "Do you treat all your clients like this?" His voice dripped with sarcasm. "Or just the ones you screw?"

Tears sprang to her eyes. She felt like he'd slapped her and at that moment, she wished she'd never laid eyes on him. Her face burned with anger at this arrogant and self-righteous man. How dare he say something so vile?

"Who do you think you are?" she shouted, her brain so overloaded with pain and despair that she forgot where she was. "You don't know me at all, and you never will."

She abruptly turned her back on him and opened the door. "Get out!" she screamed.

He hung his head, then walked toward her and slammed the door shut so hard the hinges rattled.

He drew in close to her, and placed his palm on the door, and his other hand on the wall. "I'm not going anywhere."

"Yes, you are, young man."

The tone of her father's voice was as powerful as the gavel he wielded on a daily basis, and Cara squeezed her eyes shut against a sudden wave of nausea. How long had he been standing there listening to their shouting match? She'd been so angry at Alex that she'd completely forgotten her father was in the other room.

Alex scowled, dropped his hand from the door, and stepped away from her. She felt invisible as the two men stared each other down like two lions ready to rumble in the jungle.

"Crawford Williams." Her father extended his hand first. "The *Honorable* Crawford Williams. I don't believe we've met."

When Alex ignored the outstretched hand and peered at her father like his face held an answer, she clenched her fists at the panic that rose in her chest.

Alex shook his head, as if trying to jog his memory. "No, we've never met, but haven't I seen you before?"

Her father stared him down, then shrugged. "I don't know. You tell me. And while you're at it, why don't you tell me why you're disrespecting my daughter."

"Your daughter?" Alex whipped around to look at her, and her veins went icy with fear.

"Cara is my daughter. Do you have a problem with

that, young man? Now, you better start talking…or start walking."

"Daddy, please," she begged. "Let us have a moment to ourselves and we'll get this worked out."

Alex looked up at the ceiling. "Wait a minute." He snapped his fingers so loud that the sound echoed off the foyer's plaster walls.

He turned his attention on her father. "You're Judge Williams."

"I believe that's what I already said, young man." He turned to Cara. "He may be rude, but he's smart," he wisecracked.

"You're the one who gave my twin brother that harsh jail sentence."

Her father held up his hand. "Whoa. My sentence always fits the crime."

"Does the name Michael Dovington ring a bell?"

Her father scratched his beard. "No, I'm afraid not. But then again, thousands of cases hit my bench every year. How do you know I was the judge in your brother's case and not someone else?"

"My mother showed me your picture in the newspaper. She wrote you a letter. She asked you to have mercy on my brother. She called and called, but you never responded. Not even once. He died in jail because of you!"

He shook his head. "Listen, son. I don't remember any letter. And why would I? I probably get hundreds of those every year. They're all the same to me. Desperate measures from desperate people," he scoffed.

"Daddy!" Cara cried out. Although she wasn't surprised at his insensitive comment, she hurt for Alex.

He took a step toward the judge, one hand clenched into a tight fist. "You bastard!"

Cara stepped in between the two men. "Alex, Daddy. Please don't do this!"

He turned toward Cara, his forehead creased in anger. "And you knew the entire time, didn't you? How?"

Her chin quivered and her voice was watery. "When I was a teenager, I saw you and your mom on television talking about the letter she wrote. Then I went upstairs to my father's office and I found it. Unopened."

"My mom was right all along. You never read it," he said, more to himself than to them. "I trusted you, Cara." His voice broke. "I trusted you!"

She put her hand on his arm but he shook it off. "Alex, I wanted to tell you, but…"

"But what? You thought I was too dumb to understand? Well, I may not be able to read *War and Peace,* but I can read the writing on the wall. It says you're a liar, just like your father."

He took an envelope out of his coat, tossed it at her feet. "You don't want to see me again? Well, Daddy's little girl's gonna get her wish." Then he pulled open the door and stalked out.

Tears of shock flowed down Cara's face. Her body wouldn't move, her mind only held one horrible, heart-breaking truth.

He's gone.

Her father picked up the envelope and closed the door. He led her into the living room and handed her a box of tissues.

"I don't know who that young man is, but he is obviously in love with you."

She blew her nose and squinted at him, puffy-eyed. "Daddy, that's Alex Dovington. The famous jazz saxophonist. Don't you recognize him?"

Her father made a face. "The guy that's always in the paper with a different woman hanging on his arm like a Christmas ornament?"

Cara giggled, in spite of her sadness. "That's him."

"I don't recall the case."

"His brother was a gang member, and I guess his mom always thought he was innocent of the crime."

Her father rolled his eyes. "All mothers think their sons are innocent, even when the evidence proves that they're not." He sighed. "Maybe that's for the best. Gives these boys some hope, even when they don't stand a chance."

He cast a curious glance at the envelope. "He seems pretty taken with you. What's the nature of your relationship?"

"Alex is illiterate. I was hired to teach him how to read within a very short time frame, in exchange for a donation to Beacon House. I should have told him the truth from the very beginning, but there never seemed to be a right time."

She ran her hands down her face, smearing her makeup even more. "I didn't want to lie to him, but God help me, I didn't want to lose his donation."

"And now you're afraid you won't get it?"

She shrugged. "We have a contract, but I'm not sure if he'll live up to it."

"Well, if he doesn't pay you, let me know. I know a couple of lawyers who'd be glad to take your case."

"That won't be necessary. Besides, it doesn't matter now. Whether he sends it to me or not, it will never be enough to save Beacon House."

"Don't give up yet," he chided gently. "I can't help you with your love life, but at least I can do this." He rose to leave.

"Thanks, Daddy."

After they said goodbye, she took the envelope into the kitchen and eyed it suspiciously. When she opened it, she discovered a CD inside with no label on it, and she popped it into the player. Her mouth dropped open when she heard her own voice through the speakers.

It was a fully produced recording of her singing his ballad. Alex must have mixed in the piano, bass and drums, as well as himself on saxophone, after she'd left the studio.

She began to cry uncontrollably as she listened to her sing words she'd written herself:

> *I can't understand*
> *Why you ever*
> *Left me*
> *Now is the time for you and me*
> *To take a chance on love*

And as the song began to fade and Alex played the last note, she crumpled to the floor and sobbed, "Now is the time to say goodbye."

Chapter 14

Alex propped *The Jungle Trumpeteer* on the music stand and opened it to the first page. He attached his saxophone to his lariat, made sure he was comfortably seated, then played a couple of blues scales to relax. His travel coffee mug was on the floor next to him, plus a cold bottle of Pellégrino.

Everything was in place. There were less than twenty-four hours before the start of the tour and he was ready to review the book. Yet there was one thing missing.

Cara.

His heart was filled with regret over the fight they'd had last night. He wished he could take back all the awful things he'd said to her. He could see on her face how much his words had hurt her, something he never wanted to do.

He hadn't come to her home to fight, but to make

up. To tell her again that he loved her, that he couldn't live without her.

She sure was right about one thing. He really didn't know her at all.

Had he fallen in love with a fantasy?

He clamped his eyes shut and her beautiful face, one he would never tire of adoring, floated through his mind.

Why did she have to lie to him? Why couldn't she have just told him the truth from the very beginning?

If she had, would you have still fallen in love with her?

Alex's eyes flew open, and he hung his head because he knew the answer was no.

If he had found out that the Honorable Crawford Williams was Cara's father, she wouldn't have made it past his doorstep, let alone into his bed. He would have done anything he possibly could to get out of the contract and the book tour. He'd even have risked increasing Mo's displeasure with him.

Instead, he'd been played for a fool. And now his career could be over anyway.

This afternoon, he was scheduled to meet with Mo. He planned to tell the hard-nosed owner of Sharp Five Records about his illiteracy, before he read it in Friday's paper. And if he knew Mo as well as he thought he did, the man would not be happy. When he walked out of Mo's office, he wasn't even sure he'd still be a part of the artist roster.

At this point, he didn't care.

Meeting Cara's father last night was horrible enough. He came face-to-face with his own guilt and he knew he'd never be the same person again. He'd blamed Judge Williams for Michael's death for so long that he'd come to believe it himself.

Yet he was the one responsible.

He ran a hand over his head, remembering the night when his life had changed forever. He'd just gotten off the train from playing a gig uptown, and the leader of the BJD (Brooklyn J-Dawgz), the local gang at the time, was waiting for him with his hand out as usual. He held a knife to his neck when Alex wouldn't give them his gig money. Then he took his saxophone and threw it down onto the tracks, and a few seconds later, the train crushed it.

Alex closed his hand into a fist in anger at the memory. "What are you gonna do now, bro?" the leader had said. "How you gonna earn me some money? I guess you gotta steal one now." The he pressed the tip of his knife into Alex's neck, drawing blood.

Michael was with him that night. He said he would steal the saxophone, and took Alex's place in the gang, so that Alex could continue to make music and money for their family.

Alex hugged the stolen saxophone to his chest and buried his face in his hands. The last time he'd cried was at Michael's funeral. When his brother died, Alex had sealed his heart up so tight no one could get in.

Until he met Cara. Then everything changed. He felt alive when he looked at her sweet face, when he touched her gorgeous body. Her talent, intellect and humor sparked an energy within him that he thought was long dead.

And when they made love, he fit within her deliciously, perfectly. She seemed to be created just for him. He hardened just thinking about their nights together.

God, he missed her.

But there was no way in hell he'd ever try to get her back again.

Since he was a kid, he'd always told himself he'd put his heart on the line only once and if it got tossed back in his face, that was it. He would never take another chance and risk getting hurt again. And he knew in his heart that he would never love another woman like he loved Cara.

But what saddened him the most was that his love for her was only beginning. There were many more feelings and emotions to be explored that would never be experienced.

Alex took a sip of his coffee and gagged. Cold.

He rubbed a hand down his face and took a deep breath. He pulled the music stand closer and began to slowly read aloud. He was on his own now, and he had to make the best of it.

With a sigh, he began to read. Slowly, he spelled and sounded out the letters as Cara had taught him. It was hard, and he had to pause several times and take a breath to quell his frustration.

When the doorbell rang and he jumped up to answer it, hope lodged in his heart.

"It's about time..." His words fell away at the sight of Judge Williams. It took everything in him not to slam the door in his face.

He stared hard at the portly man. "Judge Williams, to what do I owe this unpleasant surprise?"

"May I come in?" His eyes blinked rapidly behind his Malcolm X glasses. "I need to talk to you."

A twinge of fear gripped him. Had something happened to Cara?

With a resigned shrug, he stepped aside so Williams could enter, then shut the door and led the way to the living room.

"Have a seat, *your Honor,*" he said with mock authority.

Judge Williams removed his trench coat, laid it carefully on the arm of the couch and sat down on the leather couch. The cushions whined, but the man didn't seem to notice.

Alex eased into a chair across from him, his face impassive.

Crawford adjusted his glasses. "After you boldly accused me of judicial indiscretion, my curiosity got the best of me. Today, I did a little digging around."

His eyes drifted to his saxophone and Alex felt his stomach plummet. He tightened his grip on the instrument that had been the source of so much joy and pain over the years. How had he let things get this far?

Crawford regarded him a moment. "I may have judged your brother too harshly. The BJD were getting too bold with their criminal activity. They needed to be stopped."

"So what are you trying to say? That you needed my brother to be an example?"

"It wasn't just him, but something like that."

"Michael's dead. He can't be an example to anyone, so, what's your point?"

"You know, Alex, the mind can be the worst jail cell on earth for a brother struggling to forget the mistakes he made in the past. Don't make Cara suffer because you're still struggling to break free."

Alex's heart dropped into his stomach. Everything the judge said made sense. Letter or no letter, although he had no one to blame for Michael's death but himself, maybe it was time to let go of the pain and the guilt that had haunted him for years.

Crawford rose to leave, laying his coat over his arm. "I'm due back in court, not that I'm in any hurry to get there."

Alex escorted him to the door. "Why's that?"

"Son, I've got a double homicide case waiting for me. My fourth this month." Crawford shook his head, blew out a harsh breath. "New York. The city where killers never sleep."

Alex opened the door and the judge walked out without another word.

"Judge Williams," he called out. "Why *did* you come here and tell me all that?"

He turned on his heel and looked at Alex. "Because I love my daughter, and I think you do, too." Then he hailed a cab and sped away.

He's right.

Ever since he'd met Cara, there wasn't a moment when she wasn't on his mind. She was part of his dreams, his very being, and his desire for her had only grown stronger and more powerful the longer he was away from her.

Clearly, she did not feel the same way. So if he could only love her from afar, that's what he would do. He would go on with his own life, but he would love her. No one else. It was as simple as that.

As he gathered up his saxophone and other things he needed for his tell-all meeting with Mo, his mind was formulating a plan. It was a long shot, but if it worked it would fix everything and show his love for Cara at the same time.

Although he wasn't a religious man, his lips moved in a silent prayer for hope, redemption and second chances.

* * *

Cara slammed the phone down and cradled her forehead in her palms, another no clanging in her ears like a church bell. Every moment of the last twenty-four hours had been more miserable than the last. It took everything in her to lift up the phone to plead for help. After a morning of rejections, things were not looking good.

She didn't know how much more of this she could take.

In just under a week, her life had drastically changed. She'd fallen in love, lost her man and was on the verge of losing her business. In the time it took God to create the whole world, she'd managed to nearly destroy everything she'd ever worked for in her own life.

She stretched her hands above her head and yawned, then flopped her head back on her arms like a rag doll. She'd been up half the night crying and listening to the CD he'd given her over and over.

Alex had given her his heart, told her that he loved her. But he probably hated her now. She had betrayed him out of fear, and that was unforgivable.

Her heart wrenched when she thought about him, what she'd lost. She reached up and stroked a single flower in the large arrangement she'd received from Alex yesterday morning. The vase was filled with flowers of many sizes and varieties. She inhaled the scents as she reread the card tied with a red ribbon to a Gerbera daisy.

I didn't know what flower was your favorite, so I bought one of each. I can't wait for our next game of Scrabble. I love you.
Alex

She shook her head. While he was choosing the flowers, he'd probably never imagined that he would discover that she was hiding a secret that would ultimately end any feelings he had for her.

Nancy's voice, patched through the intercom, broke through her thoughts.

"Cara, I'm sorry to disturb you, but you have a visitor."

"What? I thought you canceled all of my appointments for today."

"I did." Nancy's voice dropped to a whisper. "But this man insists on seeing you."

"Who is it?"

"Tommy Jenkins. Do you know him?"

Her heart sank. "Yes, send him in."

A minute later, Cara greeted Tommy warmly at the door. "It's great to finally meet you in person."

His hand felt old and rough on her palm and his smile held the glow of a child on Christmas morning. She felt herself smiling back when she wanted to do nothing but cry.

Tommy hung up his coat and sat down. "Beautiful flowers. Looks like a rainbow exploded. I can appreciate color." He pointed to his bright yellow hat. "I've got one for every mood."

She chuckled. "Oh? What mood are you in today?"

"Thankful. And I think you'll feel the same in due time. How did things go with Alex?"

"You haven't spoken with him?"

"I have, but I want to hear from you."

"Things were difficult at first," she admitted. "Alex put up plenty of roadblocks, but then he relaxed and learned to trust me. After that point, it got much easier to teach him."

"Well, when I spoke to him, he had nothing but compliments about you."

She frowned. "That's surprising."

"Why is that?"

She bit her lip in hesitation. "We didn't part on the best of terms."

"Alex is lucky to have you as a teacher."

"Thank you. Based on the circumstances, I think I've taken him as far as I can. Before you leave, I'll give you a list of other literacy centers he can contact for lessons."

Tommy removed his hat and scratched his head. "Why shouldn't he come here to continue learning to read?"

A lump lodged in her throat. "We've had differences that I believe would impede the learning process. Besides, having a lesson here is not going to be possible—for anyone."

"Why is that?"

She took a deep breath and spoke quietly. "Beacon House will be closing by the end of the month." Even saying the words, she could hardly believe them.

The smile disappeared from Tommy's face. "I'm sorry to hear that. What happened?"

"Too much to talk about, but I am really hoping he'll continue with reading lessons. He's come a long way, but he's got a long way to go."

Tommy pulled an envelope from the front pocket of his shirt. "Maybe this will help?"

Cara accepted and opened the envelope. Her heart leapt, than quickly sank, leaving her dazed. Inside was the donation for her services. It would help maintain payroll and keep the lights on through the end of the month, but not much else.

"Thank you. This is exactly what we agreed to, but I'm afraid it's not enough to keep our doors open."

"I'm sorry to hear that. I'll let Alex know."

"No, don't!"

Tommy raised his eyebrows and she realized she'd spoken a little louder than she intended.

"I'm sorry. It's just that this is a private matter that I wish to handle on my own."

"Birds of a feather," muttered Tommy.

"Excuse me?"

"I don't know you very well, but you're as hard-headed as he is. Both too stubborn to ask for help when you know you really need it, and both too proud to admit you can't live without one another."

"Tommy," she replied. "With all due respect, you don't know me, nor do you know the situation, so you really shouldn't judge me."

He waved her comment away. "I call 'em as I see 'em, just like when I play poker. Only this time, I got a winning hand. I don't even have to look at it to know that you're in love with Alex."

Her eyes welled up with tears as she stared at him in disbelief. Why did her feelings for Alex make sense when they came from someone else's lips, but on her own they only confused her?

"Yes, I am. But that doesn't matter anymore."

"What are you talking about, it doesn't matter—of course it matters. Why, my Dora and I have been married over twenty-five years and you don't think we've had our little spells? But no matter how much she made me angry or hurt me, I still loved her, and she still loved me. Because when a man loves a woman, really loves her, he'll let nothing stand in his way."

Cara snorted. "I guess that answers my question. You don't see Alex around here, do you?"

"There's one thing that marriage has taught me. Sometimes you have to be the one to forgive first. Come to the book reading tomorrow."

"I can't."

"Can't or won't?" countered Tommy.

"He wouldn't want me there. It would only make things worse. This is an important day for him."

Tommy stood up, grabbed his coat and adjusted his hat. "All the more reason for the woman he loves to be there.

"Just think about it."

He shut the door behind him, leaving Cara alone. She squeezed back her tears and accepted the truth.

Alone.

It was exactly what she deserved to be.

Chapter 15

Cara's heels resounded with a confidence she really didn't feel as she walked down the hallway of PS 25. The walls were lined with children's artwork depicting classic elements of the fall season. When she reached the office, Mrs. Esther Dawson, principal of PS 25, greeted her warmly.

"Cara!" she exclaimed, hugging her. "It's so good to see you again."

"It's great to be here, Mrs. Dawson," she replied, hugging her back.

She smiled at the older woman, who stood not much taller than her own five feet and whose moniker was "The Destroyer." But in her case, it wasn't a negative term. She was well-known in New York City for turning some of the worst elementary schools in the system into the best.

"Let's go into my office," she said. "Would you like some coffee?"

Cara declined the offer and had a seat at the little round conference table.

"Did you see the news truck outside?"

Cara nodded and sat up straighter in her chair. "Yes, a crew from NY One."

Mrs. Dawson grinned. "They just arrived. There are other reporters that are supposed to be coming, too. *New York Post*, *New York Daily News*, *New York Times,* even *Entertainment Weekly.*"

"Wow, that's wonderful. Did Mr. Dovington arrange it?"

Mrs. Dawson shook her head. "No, everything was arranged by his record company," she replied. "They shared their media plan with me and everyone that will be present today met my approval. Literacy is a message that everyone in New York and across the country needs to hear. Don't you agree?"

Cara nodded, but her heart went out to Alex, whom she was sure did not want to be the poster child. Was he aware that he was walking into a trap?

"I was surprised and pleased to hear from you yesterday," Mrs. Dawson continued. "The children are so excited about Alex visiting the school, and you being here will make the event that much more special."

Cara smiled. "I always enjoy coming and reading to the kids, especially the younger ones."

"You and Beacon House are a vital part of the Harlem community," agreed Mrs. Dawson. "I don't know what we would do without you! Will you be reading with Mr. Dovington?"

"Oh, no," she interrupted. "In fact, I have a favor to ask."

Mrs. Dawson raised an eyebrow. "What can I do for you?"

"I know this is an unusual request, but I'd rather Alex not know I was here."

"It's none of my business, but can I ask why?"

"My reasons for being here are primarily personal, so I can't really go into it."

"I understand. But the children will be so disappointed. Can't I even announce that you're here?"

"Of course. But I prefer that you do so after you announce Alex. Is that all right?"

"It is unusual, but I'm happy to accommodate you. Can I assume you don't want him to see you, either?"

She nodded. "Is there someplace I can hang out until the event starts?"

Mrs. Dawson nodded and checked her watch. "Alex's publicist said he'd be arriving around 8:30 a.m., so we'd better hurry. Come with me, I have somewhere you can hide."

They exited the office and walked down a sloping hallway to the auditorium. But instead of turning and entering the doors, they went a little farther, and Mrs. Dawson led her backstage.

They stopped in front of a small room lit by a single bulb.

"This is where we keep all the props when we're doing a play. We haven't done one in about a year, so the room is a little dusty, but it will have to do. You should be able to hear me announce your name from the stage."

"This is perfect. Thank you, Mrs. Dawson."

She nodded. "Just remember to turn off the light before you leave."

Mrs. Dawson started to close the door, but then turned to Cara. "I don't know why you're doing all this, but I hope everything turns out the way you want it."

"Me, too," Cara whispered as the door shut.

She backed into the room and jumped when her legs brushed against something rough. As her eyes adjusted to the dim light, she discovered that it was just a stack of old carpeting. She found a wooden chair in a corner, brought it closer to the light and sat down.

She took her phone from her purse and silenced it. A few minutes later, her hand flew to her throat. Alex's rich baritone voice rang through the auditorium as he tested the microphone he really didn't need.

Closing her eyes, she longed to hear his voice against her earlobe, a lover's whisper. Warmth pooled in her belly as she thought about the other evening with Alex in his dining room.

The night he told her he loved her and made love to her with such unforgettable passion.

It was one of the most wonderful nights of her life, and she had ruined it by running away from him. Being with him had been a dream come true, but it was time to wake up to reality. She'd be lucky if he ever spoke to her again.

She opened her eyes and stood. Her hand hovered over the doorknob for a second before she twisted it and cracked open the door.

The stage curtain, a bloodred velvet, partially blocked her view as she peeked through, but there was a tiny opening and she could see that Alex's back was to her.

He was walking back to the podium on the other side of the stage playing a funked-up version of the Rolling Stone's tune "Start Me Up." She could barely tear her eyes away as his body moved ever so slightly in time with the music. She found herself tapping her feet until he suddenly turned and started walking in her direction.

She shut the door and leaned against it, hoping he

hadn't seen her. Her heart was beating so fast that it felt like it was going to thump right out of her chest. He'd stopped playing and she could hear his hard-soled shoes on the wooden floor, walking toward the prop room.

She slowly locked the door a moment before Alex turned the outside knob. Cara held her breath as he jiggled it a few times before giving up. When his footsteps faded away, she exhaled in relief and sat down in the chair.

Maybe hiding in here wasn't such a good idea, she thought, as she realized that until Mrs. Dawson announced him, Alex would probably be waiting backstage, too. She'd have to be extra quiet to avoid being heard. Thankfully, the event would be starting soon.

She jumped in her seat when something hard banged against the door. Tiptoeing toward it, she put her ear against the door.

"Mr. Dovington, is everything okay?" said a voice.

"Everything is fine. I'm just hanging out here until we get started."

"Can I get you some water?"

"Sure, if you could just place it by the podium that would be great."

"No problem, Mr. Dovington, and good luck!"

Her heart wrenched in her chest when he gave no response, just a sigh so deep it rumbled against the door.

He must be so nervous right now, she thought, remembering how terrified he was that his secret would someday be exposed. If only there was something she could do to help him relax.

Carefully, she placed her palms flat against the door, where she thought his shoulders might be leaning. Next, she inched her feet forward until her breasts were grazing the surface. Finally, she pressed her cheek against the door and closed her eyes.

She imagined her arms coming from behind and enclosing him in a surprise hug, her breasts and tummy pressed against the hard muscles of his back. In her mind, she planted a kiss on his shoulder and squeezed him so tight it was like she would never let him go.

When she stepped away from the door a few minutes later, tears were streaming down her face. She twisted a finger around one of her curls, dreading what was to come. For the millionth time, her mind ran through what she would say to Alex.

But there's no easy way to say goodbye.

Although the media coverage was an annoyance, perhaps it wasn't all bad. At least he couldn't throw her out on national TV, she mused sadly.

She was blotting her tears with a tissue, trying to salvage her makeup, when she heard what sounded like hundreds of feet thunder into the auditorium. The children themselves were surprisingly quiet, although she heard the occasional snicker that was quickly followed by multiple rounds of "shhhs."

Even though she was backstage behind closed doors, the hum of excitement in the air was palpable.

"We're ready to get started," announced Mrs. Dawson. "You should all be on voice meter one, which if you are still trying to wake up, means that there should not be one sound coming out of your mouths."

There was a pause while she waited, presumably for everyone to be quiet.

"Students and faculty of PS 25, we have the honor today of being the first school on a city-wide literacy tour conducted by Alex Dovington, world-famous saxophonist."

"Mr. Dovington has nine albums to his credit, one of which won a Grammy Award, the highest honor in the music industry. He is also an alumnus of PS 25 and he had his first jazz performance right on this very stage. Everyone put your hands together now for Mr. Alex Dovington!"

As the auditorium erupted in applause, Cara heard Alex push away from the door and start playing a popular hip-hop tune as he walked onstage. The roar of sound as the kids hooped, hollered and stomped their feet along with the music was amazing to hear.

Cara opened the door and peeked out. After a wailing high note that made the crowd go wild, he walked over to the podium and thanked the audience. A smattering of flashbulbs went off.

"Oh, I nearly forgot," exclaimed Mrs. Dawson, standing at his side. "Excuse me, Alex."

After reclaiming the microphone, she announced, "Children, we have a surprise guest with us this morning. Many of you know her as an educator who has volunteered countless hours in the classroom."

"But you may not know that she is also the author of several books for children and young adults, including the one Alex will be sharing with us today."

"Please welcome to the stage, Miss Cara Williams!"

Even though she was expecting the announcement, her mouth went dry when she heard her name. Her feet felt rooted to the floor. Her hands shook as she opened the door and walked out of the prop room.

She pushed the back of her hand against the red velvet curtain. Her eyes locked with Alex's, and she could see that he was stunned to see her.

The applause made her knees jittery and her heart

beat faster as he started walking toward her from the other end of the stage, his eyes never leaving her face.

And she couldn't take her eyes off him. His navy blue button-down shirt and black dress pants barely contained his sexual magnetism. It lit her body on fire in such a way that made her blush under the hot stage lights.

He was movie-star beautiful, emanating an aura of confidence and self-assuredness that would fool anyone into thinking he was on top of his game.

Only she knew the truth. He was scared. For better or worse, his whole future was about to change.

They met in the middle and her heart leaped in surprise at the grateful smile on his face.

Alex took her gently by the elbow and leaned in close. The scent of his cologne made her mind flash back to the first time he kissed her, and she felt a rush of desire.

Applause encircled them both, but all she heard was his voice whisper low in her ear.

"Thank you for being here."

He linked his arm with hers as he escorted her to the podium as if she were royalty.

He gave her hand a squeeze before he gently let it go. In that moment, she desperately wanted to grab it back, to capture forever the warmth and protectiveness of his flesh on hers.

Alex stepped up to the microphone and Mrs. Dawson motioned to her to sit on one of the folding chairs near the podium.

He unsnapped his saxophone from his lariat and placed it in his instrument stand. He waited patiently until the applause ended before speaking.

"Thank you, everyone, for the warm welcome. It certainly has been a morning of surprises." Her face heated with embarrassment as he turned and glanced at her.

He turned back to the audience. "And I think we may be in for a few more before we're finished here today. But first, I need you guys to answer a couple of questions. Let's say your parents are out of town and you're free to do whatever you want. How many of you would play video games?"

Almost all of the hands in the room shot up.

"How many of you would watch TV or surf the internet?"

Most of the hands were raised.

"Uh-huh, and how many of you would just be hanging with your crew?"

More than a few hands popped up.

"Okay, so how many of you would sit back and read a book?"

Cara counted about seventy-five kids who raised their hands in a crowd of about three hundred. Those who did raise their hands did so tentatively, like they were ashamed.

"Okay, how many would be doing their homework?"

No one raised their hand and everyone laughed, including Alex.

"When you're a kid, you don't realize how important it is to learn how to read," he said, his tone now more serious. "You'd rather be doing anything else in the world because you may think reading is boring, it's hard, or it's just not cool.

"I used to feel the exact same way. School didn't come easily to me. As a matter of fact, I hated it. Eventually I just gave up. I dropped out in the ninth grade and I never graduated from high school. But something much worse happened." He paused for a few beats. "I never learned to read."

There was a murmur of voices and Cara saw several teachers glance at each other at this strange turn of events. The reporters and news crew at the back of the auditorium were perking up and whispering to each other.

"I'm illiterate. Can anyone tell me what the word *illiterate* means?"

Hands shot up and Alex chose a child near the front of the auditorium.

The kid stood up. "It means you can't read or write."

"You got it. I can't read. Not a menu, a grocery list, street signs, the paper, or even my own website.

"I kept it a secret for years. No one knew. Not my record company who set up this tour. Not even my mother."

He took a deep breath. "Let me tell you all something. Not being able to read all these years has been terrible. There's all this knowledge in the world that I couldn't experience because I can't read. It's like being in a prison. And who kept me behind bars?" He pointed his thumb to his chest. "Me. But last Friday, I started reading lessons with Miss Williams."

He walked over and held out his hand to Cara. She looked up at him, confused. He smiled, and enclosing her hand in his led her to the podium.

His eyes locked with hers. "And even though it's only been a week, being able to read, even just a little bit, has changed my life."

Her heart fluttered in her chest; the sincerity in his voice made her want to weep. She gazed at him. The stage lights made his hazel eyes deepen in color, and it was all she could do not to fly into his arms.

The applause and cheers of the children brought her to her senses, and she remembered the second reason why she was here. To say goodbye to him and never look back.

His good looks and charm were meant to be adored by another woman, not her. Someone who had the time and energy for a relationship. Someone who had their life together, instead of falling apart.

"So, when I read to you today, please be patient. I may stumble and fall and make mistakes, but I'm no longer a prisoner.

"Because I can read, now I am free!"

Alex raised both of their hands up in victory, and the electricity she felt between them was incredible.

She was so proud of his courageous act.

"so, would you like to hear Miss Williams read with me?"

"Yeahhh…" the kids screamed.

"Hold up, I gotta ask her first."

He leaned in close to her. "Will you read with me?"

"Yes," she whispered.

"Score! She said yes!"

The kids started cheering again until Principal Dawson raised her hands up like Moses dividing the Red Sea in half.

He put his hand over the mike and whispered into her ear. "We're on fire, and we're not even in bed."

Cara stifled a giggle as they both reached to open the book and their fingers brushed against one another.

He cleared his throat, bent toward the microphone and paused. Alex's hand shook a little as he turned to the first page.

Cara's heart seized in her chest when he looked at

her, raw fear in his eyes. She smiled her encouragement, reached out and gave his hand a gentle squeeze.
He looked away and rolled his shoulders back.

"The Jungle Trumpeteer." He cleared his throat
again. "By Molly Mathers, aka Cara Williams."

Alex turned the page, reached for her hand, and
slowly began to read.

"Sam was a very large elephant who loved to pretend..."

Cara's heart burst with pride as she watched him.
He pronounced each word slowly but clearly and with
much expression.

She looked out at the kids in the audience. Every
eye was on Alex and it seemed in the audience. Every
on his every word, holding their breath and struggling
with him when he got stuck, breathing with relief feeling
he pushed through a difficult passage. when

She jumped in and read some of the other characters
in the book, but only because Alex had asked her to

And when he said "The End," the auditorium erupted
in thunderous applause and cheers.

They both stepped away from the podium and
walked to the middle of the stage.

Cara smiled at Alex, put her arms around him
and hugged him with delight. He took her hand and
squeezed it as they both took a bow.

They both beamed with pleasure from the applause
of the kids. Her hand felt warm in his and she felt so
complete, so wonderful. She'd never imagined things
would go this well.

But in the midst of her joy, sadness dwelled. The
happiness was only temporary because the event was
almost over and so were her dreams of a life with Alex.

Alex walked back to microphone. "Thanks everyone for being so patient and for not throwing stuff at me," he said with a laugh. "I have one other announcement before I play some music and you get to ask me some questions.

"As I mentioned earlier, Miss Williams has been teaching me how to read for the past week. She runs a nonprofit literacy organization called Beacon House, right here in Harlem. She teaches reading to those who cannot read, and gives hope to lives devastated by illiteracy.

"I am profoundly grateful to Cara and have decided to donate fifty percent of the proceeds from my next album to benefit Beacon House."

Cara shrieked and put her hands to her face. His generosity meant that she could purchase the building, and Beacon House could remain open!

Tears stung her eyes as she hugged him, as the kids hooted and clapped and stamped their feet on the floor.

She opened her mouth to speak, but she could not. Instead, she hugged him tighter and cried openly. Tears flowed down her cheeks, for Beacon House and all of her clients, but most of all for Alex.

Lord, how she loved him. How could she possibly say goodbye to him now?

His generosity took care of her problems with Beacon House. She could no longer use that as an excuse to run away from a relationship with him.

But there were still a multitude of issues that made ending her involvement with Alex the right choice. Issues she wasn't sure could be resolved.

Had he truly forgiven her for hiding the truth about her father?

Alex suddenly leaned into her and said, "We need to talk. Will you wait for me backstage?"

She looked up at him and nodded, feeling hope rise from deep within her. Her mind tried to squash it, but her heart knew that right now it was all she had to hold on to, and this time she wasn't letting go.

Cara felt like her whole future was out signing autographs. As she waited backstage for Alex to return, time seemed suspended. She sat in the prop room, her hands trembling so badly they ached, with one thought looping through her mind.

What happens now?

She'd come to support him and then say goodbye. Both were the right thing to do, but Alex changed everything. His generous donation of future album revenues to Beacon House meant she could no longer use her financial difficulties as an excuse to avoid a relationship with him.

In her heart, she knew the one thing that hadn't changed was her love for him. But she still wasn't sure how he felt about her.

There was a knock on the door and she jumped out of her seat.

"Who is it?"

"Your favorite student," replied Alex, his voice low and sexy. Just hearing it calmed her nerves and excited her senses at the same time.

When she closed the door behind him, he set down his instrument case and pulled her into his arms. Relief and happiness flooded through her body at his touch.

She put her arms around his neck and hugged him. "You did it, Alex!" she exclaimed. "I'm so proud of you."

He tightened his hold around her waist. "*We* did it," he emphasized, hugging her back.

When he released her, she looked up and he was smiling ear to ear. "I couldn't have done any of this without you."

She shook her head and played with his collar, her movements shy and tentative. "You did all the work," she insisted.

"Only because I didn't want to end up in the time-out chair," he flirted. "With my face to the wall, how could I have admired your beauty?"

She blushed and waggled her finger at him. "Luckily you were never bad enough."

"Give me another chance, and I'll be the bad boy you've always dreamed of," he joked, but his voice held a seductive note that stirred her desire.

She laughed and hugged him again, feeling blessed that he seemed as happy as she was.

She stepped back. "You were really brave to admit to the kids that you're illiterate. I'm curious. Why did you decide to do it?"

"I was tired of hiding, Cara. You opened my eyes to a world I want to be a part of. When I finally told the truth about myself, I felt like this huge weight that I've carried around for years was lifted from my shoulders. It was amazing."

"What do you think is going to happen now?"

He shrugged his shoulders. "I'm sure the story will be making the newspapers and gossip sites on the internet. Before I came here, I gave a couple of media interviews, and there will be more talk and more questions. I used to be scared of what would happen, but not now."

"Why?"

"Because I have you in my life again. It means a lot to have you here. When I saw you walk across the stage, I was so happy to see you. What changed your mind?"

"It was the right thing to do and—" She paused.

For so long, she'd been afraid to reveal her feelings for Alex, but something inside her, and the courage he'd just displayed in front of everyone, gave her new strength.

"I missed you," she blurted out.

He reached out, ran a finger along the swell of her cheek. "I missed you, too," he replied. "More than you'll ever know."

She trembled inside at his words. They made all the nights lying awake, thinking of him, worth every tear.

"I still can't believe you're going to donate half of the money from your next album to Beacon House."

He smiled at her. "I talked it over with Mo yesterday and surprisingly, he went for the idea. Besides, I'm thinking after this album that I'm going to go out on my own."

She raised an eyebrow. "What do you mean?"

"I'm thinking about starting my own independent record label and music school."

"Oh, Alex, that's wonderful!" she exclaimed, clapping her hands together.

"Thanks! Yes, it's going to be a combination of a music school, recording studio and record label based right here in Harlem. I want to give back to the community like you have, Cara. You inspire me."

"How can I ever thank you?" she whispered, grateful for the kindness she saw in his hazel eyes.

She held her breath as he slowly bent his head toward hers.

"Like this," he said, brushing his lips against hers in a featherlight kiss so sweet and so gentle that tears sprang anew behind her closed eyes.

She leaned into him as his tongue teased her lips open.

"And this." His kiss became more insistent and her body went limp. But at the same time, she felt energy swell within her body that made her feel like she could dance barefoot all the way to the moon.

"And finally this." His hands massaged her back and traveled up to stroke her curls, sending a thousand tingles down her spine.

They held on to each other, arms entangled, mouths moving together in mutual desire as they both lost themselves in one breathless kiss after another.

"Cara," he murmured against her lips. "I need to tell you something."

"Hmm?" she muttered, not wanting to break the kiss.

"About Michael." He stepped back suddenly. "And about me."

Although he kept her only an arm's length away, she shivered from the loss of close contact with his body.

She wanted to tell him that the past didn't matter. But even in the dim light, she could see his eyes were serious. And she sensed in the abrupt change in his demeanor that his mind was made up.

He walked over to the chair, turned it around and straddled it. "I'm a coward."

She rushed to his defense. "No, you're not. You call what you just did out there, placing your reputation on the line, being a coward?"

He held up a hand. "Let me finish. My brother Michael stole my saxophone to protect me from becoming a gang member and living life on the streets. I've carried this saxophone and the weight of guilt over his death for years."

"I'm sorry, Alex," she said, putting her hand on his arm. "That must be so horrible. It wasn't your fault."

"But it was my fault," he insisted. "I should have

never allowed him to take the fall for me. If it wasn't for me, Michael wouldn't have gone to jail, and he wouldn't have died."

Cara looked at him strangely. "But I thought a genetic heart condition was the official cause of death."

"What?" Alex replied in a stunned voice, and he stood up so fast the chair crashed to the floor. "How do you know this?"

"Idella told me at the restaurant. She said your family had an autopsy conducted to find out why Michael died of a heart attack at such a young age. They discovered he had a rare congenital heart condition that went undetected until it was too late."

He ran his hand over his head. "Why didn't my mom or Idella tell me?" he said, pain in his voice.

"I don't know, Alex," she replied, watching him pace back and forth in the tiny room. "Maybe they wanted to protect you from more grief. Idella said his death hit you hard, and even I can see that you're still affected by it."

He turned and leaned against the door. "All these years, I've blamed myself for Michael's death."

"Alex, you didn't know Michael had a heart condition," she said softly, approaching him. "Look at me." She touched his face. "Why continue to punish yourself over something that happened so long ago? It doesn't bring Michael back. Forgive yourself. Let it go."

His eyes were sorrowful as they gazed upon hers, then his voice broke. "I don't know how."

Gently, she laid her hand upon his chest. "You start by looking into your heart. What do you see?"

He glanced down at her hand in silence, eyes questioning.

"I see a caring and generous man who made a mistake. I see someone who needs a second chance," she insisted gently. "A fresh start."

"You're right." He squeezed his eyes shut. "But I still feel like I should do something to somehow make up for everything I did."

"Hmm," Cara said. "Maybe you could purchase some instruments and donate them to PS 25 or other local schools."

He opened his eyes, put his hands on her shoulders and peered at her with amazement. "That's a great idea!"

He frowned again. "What about Michael? Although he didn't know it at the time, his sacrifice allowed me to become who I am today. I need do to something to honor him."

She thought awhile, then took a deep breath. "I think the best way to preserve his memory is to love someone again."

He smiled, his eyes twinkling with surprise at her suggestion. "Miss Williams, are you applying for the position?"

Cara gave him a shy smile. "Maybe, but to be honest, I'm afraid, because I feel like you haven't forgiven me for lying to you about my father. I wanted to tell you so many times during our time together in the Catskills, but I was afraid of losing you."

He tilted her chin up with the tip of his finger. "I have forgiven you, and you will never lose me. Don't ever forget that."

She'd been waiting so long to hear those words that she almost didn't believe him. But when she searched his eyes, her insides quaked when she saw truth there.

He cupped her face gently in his hands. "I love you, Cara. I know I still have a long way to go and a lot to learn. I need a teacher who can handle me, and a wife who will love me forever. Are you up for the task?"

Her heart felt like it was going to explode from joy, and for a moment she was speechless. After thirteen years of hoping and praying, her dream was finally coming true.

Tears of happiness flowed down her face. "Yes, yes, yes!" she exclaimed. "When do you want me to start?"

"How about right now?" he proposed with a passionate kiss, beginning a journey forever filled with books, music and lots of love.

* * * * *

CLAIMING HIS CONVENIENT FIANCÉE

NATALIE ANDERSON

This one is for the nurses – Olivia, Akansha, Gavin, Glenda, Jo (and Arnie!), Karl, Maria, Naomi, Salma, Shannon and Shannon, and all the others who have helped us...you guys are amazing. Thank you so much for everything – not least teaching us Beanie!

CHAPTER ONE

FRENETIC DRUM AND bass reverberated down the dark street. Irritation pulsed along Kitty Parkes-Wilson's veins, keeping time with the relentless beat. It was too much to hope the neighbours would complain; no doubt they were wishing they could be at the party, all desperate to suck up to the rich new blood on the block.

Alejandro Martinez. Former management consultant turned venture capitalist. Millionaire. Promiscuous playboy. Party animal. And, since signing the documents three days ago, proud owner of the beautiful building in the heart of London that had, until said three days ago, been her family home. The home she'd grown up in, the one that had been in the family for more than five generations until her father had seized the wad of cash Alejandro Martinez had waved under his nose and skipped off to his sunny retirement villa in Corsica with his third picture-book-pretty wife. He'd cleared his debts and abandoned his failed business—and floored children.

All of which Kitty could handle. Just. Anyway, as much as she'd have liked to, the fact was she couldn't have bought Parkes House herself. But she hadn't even been told before it had been sold, and something had inadvertently been left in the Edwardian mansion. Something her father didn't own and had no right to sell. And *that* she couldn't cope with. Kitty Parkes-Wilson was on a retrieval mission and nothing and no one was going to stop her.

It wasn't the necklace's material worth that made it so important. Its loss meant her twin, Teddy, was in trouble, and her own *heart* was in trouble.

'You *can't* do this.'

She grinned at the way her brother could sound both aghast and excited.

'You can't stop me—I'm already here,' she answered in a low voice, pressing her phone closer to her ear as she slowed down her pace just before arriving at her former home. 'And you know I can do it.'

'Damn it, Kitty, you're crazy,' Teddy growled. 'You're only just off the train; why do you have to rush into this? Come here and we can talk about it.'

If she stopped to talk about it too much, she'd lose her nerve. 'The sooner I get it back the better. Now's the perfect chance, what with the party and all.'

'But what if you get caught—?'

'I won't,' she impatiently interrupted. 'He'll be too busy partying with his models to notice me.'

Alejandro Martinez only dated supermodels, trading them in with efficient regularity. According to the theatre gossip Teddy had shared when he'd told her that the house was being sold, the current model was Saskia, the number one swimwear model in the North American sports magazine market. Kitty figured that with those legs to distract him, Mr Martinez would never notice the quick in-and-out of an uninvited party guest. Especially one who knew the secrets of the house and how to stay hidden as she snuck her way to the second-floor library.

'It's in the library post, right?' She ignored her stomach's hungry rumble and double-checked with her twin. 'You're sure about that?'

'Positive.' Her brother's tone changed to out-and-out concerned again. 'But Kitty, please, I'm really not sure—'

'I'll call you as soon as I'm clear, okay? Stop worrying.' She ended the call before he could reply.

Adrenalin amped her muscles. She needed to concentrate and keep her confidence high. With a quick glance each way along the street, she quietly braced then hopped the fence. She ditched her small carry-on bag between a couple of shrubs and got to work.

Alejandro Martinez was not getting his hands on her Great-Aunt Margot's diamond choker. He was not putting it on any of his many girlfriends. Kitty would go to prison before she let that happen. It was not a flashy bauble for a temporary lover.

The back door key was still hidden in the same spot of the communal gated garden where she'd first hidden it a decade before. No one but she and Teddy knew it existed or that it was there and so, despite the sale of the property, it hadn't been handed to the new owner. She recovered it in less than ten seconds.

Phase one: complete.

She turned to look at the house. Brightly lit and in beautiful condition on the outside at least, it appeared to be the gleaming jewel in a row of similar styles. But Kitty knew the truth hidden beneath that freshly painted facade.

She made short work of the fence again then crossed to the corner of the street and found her way to the mews laneway behind the mansions. Her heart hammered as she neared the rear of the house. The lights were on, and she could see a catering worker at the sink.

That was when she threw her shoulders back and lifted her chin.

She unlocked the door, stepped in and smiled blithely at the kitchen hand, who looked up and gazed at her in astonishment. She waved the key at him and held her finger to her perfectly reddened lips. 'Don't tell him I'm here—I want to surprise him,' she said as she confidently strolled past him and out into the corridor.

The dishwashing chap didn't stop her. He didn't say anything. He just turned back to the plate he was rinsing.

She'd learned a few things from sitting in on Teddy' drama classes over the years.

Act confident. Fake it till you make it. Act like you own the place and people will believe you do.

People chose to believe the easiest option—the least trouble for them. And with her walking in all smiles, and with a key, who would doubt her right to be there?

Phase two: complete.

All she had to do now was head up the stairs to the private library, retrieve the necklace and get out again as fast as possible.

But curiosity bit. It had been months since she'd been home and now her heart ached with nostalgia for what she'd lost. In the three days since he'd taken over, what changes had Alejandro Martinez made?

Apparently he'd liked the look of the street and knocked on everyone's doors to find someone willing to sell. Her father hadn't been willing—he'd been *desperate*. Alejandro had been the answer to all his prayers. And Alejandro had got a good deal. House. Contents. Even the cars.

Winding up the company was one thing, but for her father to sell this home without saying a word to them beforehand was unforgivable. He'd sold everything *in* the house as well—only stopping to parcel up the few personal papers left in here. There were things she and Teddy might have liked, family treasures that had sentimental value. She didn't care about the monetary side of things; she'd grown up knowing most of it would never be hers. Her father hadn't thought of her—then again, he never had. But for once he'd not thought about Teddy either. Not that Teddy cared—he was glad not to have any reminders of the expectation he could never live up to. Except there was the last legacy from Great-Aunt Margot—the one Kitty had got her hair colour from, the one who'd given Kitty what confidence and fun she had. Great-Aunt Margot was her inspiration.

Kitty ventured down the corridor towards the bubble

of music and chatter and laughter and glanced through the open doorway into the atrium.

The lighting there was much dimmer than in the kitchen. The guests probably thought it was low to set the 'mood' and make everyone look even more attractive, but they really didn't need the help. No, the soft lighting was all about helping hide the aged, peeling paintwork and how much refurbishment and restoration work the house needed. It seemed Alejandro had had no hesitation in stripping the house of all its 'maximalist' decor—all the antique furniture, vases and fine china displays had vanished, and in their place were three dozen nubile, beautiful women. Every last one had to be a model. Kitty's heart puckered. It was weird to have all these other women here, all relaxed and happy and looking as if they belonged, when she no longer did.

Stopping to look had been a mistake.

She skirted the back of the room to confidently—but not too quickly—walk up the stairs. She kept her head high, her shoulders back and sent a glimmer of a smile to the person she saw along the hallway glancing up after her.

Faking it. Making it.

The volume of the music lowered the higher up the stairs she went. By the time she got to the second floor it had become bearable background noise. There was no one in sight up here—the entire house had yet to be taken over by pumped-up party people. She'd timed her arrival just right—enough people were present for her to disappear into, but it wasn't yet wild enough for them to be everywhere.

Despite the disappointment of seeing the stripped out interior below, she couldn't resist pausing by the master bedroom. The door was open—inviting her—but when she peered carefully around it, she found she couldn't step into the room. It was stuffed with boxes and furniture. So th was where everything from downstairs had been shoved. Her heart ached more and she quickly stepped along the hallway. Unfortunately, the library door was closed. She hovered a moment to listen, but heard nothing coming from within the room. Nervously, she turned the handle. To her relief it was dark inside and apparently unoccupied. She knew that if she left the door open, enough light would spill from the corridor for her to find her way. She smiled in anticipation as she lightly tiptoed to the shelves lining the farthest wall. This house had several secrets that the new owner would never know about—her father wouldn't have thought to tell him any of it. Sure, the pleasure she felt at having knowledge over Alejandro Martinez was childish, but the way he'd waltzed in and snatched away her home made her smart.

On the fifth shelf up, behind the fourth book along from the left, there was a small lever. She depressed it and listened to the scratchy whirring sound as a small cavity opened up. She didn't need to take the other books out; it was only a tiny safe—only large enough for a pile of notes written by bored children, or a coil of diamonds in a platinum setting left there by her forgetful, beloved, fool of a brother.

Kitty scooped them up, relief washing through her. She'd half expected them not to be there—Teddy's recollections weren't always accurate. But they were *hers* again and she could get them back to where they belonged. She'd hated the thought of letting Margot down—even though Margot was only alive in memory now.

Swallowing hard, she straightened the chain and put it around her neck, angling her head as she secured the clasp and then ran her finger along her throat to ensure the choker was sitting smoothly. The cold heaviness was familiar and made her heart ache all over again.

These were the only diamonds Margot had ever worn.

She'd bought them for herself, by herself. She'd declared that she needed no man to buy her jewels and had lived her life in defiant independence, refusing to settle into any kind of expectation—ahead of her time and leaving Kitty in awe.

She wished the choker could be hers for good, but it was Teddy's birthright and he'd given up everything else already. Kitty had nothing to lose.

She released her hair from the high topknot she'd coiled it into while on the train. To leave looking different from how she'd arrived was part of the plan and her hair served another purpose now—it mostly hid the gleaming necklace. She pushed the lever again and the compartment slid shut.

Phase three: complete.

Satisfied, she turned, ready to leave.

That was when she saw it—the man's silhouette looming in the doorway. She froze. With the lack of light she couldn't see his face, but she could see he held a phone in his hand. And she could see how tall he was. How broad. How impossible to slip past.

'Hello?' She wished she didn't sound so scared.

She wished he'd answer.

Her heart took two seconds to start pumping again and when it did her pulse thumped loudly in her ears. She hadn't heard him arrive. The floor in the library was wooden and she'd been certain she'd have heard approaching footsteps. But apparently this guy could enable stealth mode. Was he Security? How long had he been watching her? Had he seen what she'd done?

Apprehension fluttered in her belly.

'She wasn't wearing a necklace when she arrived,' he slowly mused. Softly. Dangerously. 'Yet she wears one now.'

She froze at that accented English, at that tone. She was definitely in trouble.

'If you'd get your boss for me, I can explain,' she bluffed haughtily.

'My name is Alejandro Martinez,' he replied, still in those soft, dangerous tones that made her skin prickle. 'I am the boss.'

It was the devil himself. Of course. Kitty's heart thundered.

He reached out a hand, casually closing the door. There was a split second of total darkness before he unerringly turned on the light.

Kitty rapidly blinked at the brightness. By the time the dancing spots cleared from her vision, he was less than a foot from her, his phone gone and his hands free.

She swallowed.

He was very close and *very* tall. She wasn't short yet she had to tip her chin to look into his face. His hair was dark brown and thick and he was so good-looking, he ought to have been outlawed as hazardous to any woman's attention span. Yes, Alejandro Martinez was fiendishly handsome with that olive skin, those chiselled features and those serious, assessing eyes.

Nervously, she flicked her hair in the hopes it would curl around her throat. She wasn't getting past him in a hurry; there was only one exit out of this library and he'd closed the door.

'No, there's no point trying to hide it now,' he mocked softly, but his eyes glittered like polished onyx. He slowly lifted a lock of her hair back with a lazy, arrogant finger. His penetrating gaze lingered on her neck, then raked down her body—her breasts, her waist, her legs. Every inch of her felt grazed.

'A diamond collar for a lithe little cat burglar,' he said. 'How appropriate.'

To her horror, her body reacted to his unabashed sensual assessment of her and to his low accented tone. Her skin tightened. Heat flooded her cheeks, her lower belly and she fought the instinct to take a squirming step back.

Alejandro Martinez was so *not* her cup of tea. Too obvious. Too forceful. Too…everything.

'A ginger she-cat,' he added thoughtfully, his focus lifting to her face. 'Rather rare.'

She bristled. She'd always hated her hair. She'd gone through a phase when she'd dyed it darker, only that had made her almost see-through skin and squillions of freckles look worse. In the end she'd given up and gone back to natural and faced the fact she was never going to be a 'beauty'.

'You know about the bookcase?' she asked, trying to take control of the situation—of herself—and draw attention away from this *awareness*. But her voice sounded husky and uncertain. She had to get herself and the necklace out of here as fast as possible.

'I do now. What other secrets do you know about this house?' His gaze seemed to penetrate right through her. 'What else are you planning to steal?'

A hot streak of stubbornness shot through her. She wasn't going to tell him anything—not about the house, not about herself, not about the necklace.

So she just stared up at him silently, waiting for him to make his next move.

His expression hardened. 'Give me the necklace,' he said firmly.

She shook her head. 'Possession is nine-tenths of the law,' she muttered.

'Possession?' He suddenly looked even more intent, even more predatory as his jaw sharpened and his eyes gleamed as they locked on hers.

Heat unfurled low in her belly. Shocking, utterly unwanted, destructive heat.

'It is very valuable,' he noted, continuing to watch her way too closely for her comfort. Standing too close too. When had he moved closer?

Kitty struggled to keep her brain working. The neckla

was valuable, but not only in the way *he* meant. It was all heart and memory to her.

'You know it's not yours,' she said, determinedly meeting his gaze and refusing to step back and show his intimidation was working.

'I am also willing to bet it's not yours.' His return gaze was ruthless. His stance was implacable.

But all that did was fire Kitty's desire to defy him. This man had taken ownership of everything she loved. He wasn't having this too. But she couldn't halt the telltale guilty heat building in her cheeks.

The diamonds might not belong to her legally, but they were hers in her heart. Damn Teddy's uselessness. 'It's mine to retrieve.'

And hers by love. No one loved this necklace more than her—more than that, she'd loved the woman who'd once owned it.

Alejandro shook his head slowly. 'This building and everything in it belongs to me now.' A small smile hovered at his mouth. 'Seeing as you are so insistent to stay, I guess that includes you too.'

Oh, she did *not* belong to anyone—and most certainly not him. This display of ownership was outrageous and beyond arrogant. 'Actually, I was just leaving,' she snapped coldly.

'No.' That tantalising smile vanished and he firmly grasped her wrist.

Kitty couldn't hide the tremble that rippled through her as she fisted her hand and tried to pull free from him.

'I think that both the necklace and you will remain in my possession until we find the rightful owner.' His eyes glinted. 'Of both.'

Defiance burned, sharpening her senses. Surely he was just being provocative, except she had the feeling he meant

He was clearly used to being in control and having all

the power. She didn't want to tell him the truth about the diamonds. She wouldn't try to appeal to his sensitive side— it was all too obvious he didn't have one. Arrogant jerk.

The pressure on her wrist grew—inexorably he drew her closer.

'What are you doing?' she gasped when he firmly ran his other hand across her stomach.

Alejandro didn't answer as he swept his palm further around her waist. She was a slim thing and had little in the way of curves, most unlike the women he usually spent time with. And yet there was something undeniably attractive about her. Undeniably different. She was clad entirely in black—slim three-quarter-length trousers and a fitted black sweater that emphasised her tall but slender frame. Her eyes screamed outrage and he suppressed a smile at the stiffness of her body as he continued his search. Maybe that was it—she presented resistance, challenge. And for him that was novel.

'You're assaulting me?' she snarled venomously.

'Checking for a concealed weapon,' he answered smoothly, but a grim defensiveness rose within at her accusation. Alejandro Martinez would *never* assault any woman. He was not like—*no*.

He forced his attention to his pretty prisoner, not his past. Her eyes were the weapons here and now, striking like twin daggers and making him smile, a respite from the memory that had flickered. Pleased, he removed the phone from where she'd tucked it into the waistband of her trousers.

He released her to study his prize. The phone wasn't the latest model and had one of those covers that had a pocket for a couple of cards—a bank card and driver's licence tucked inside. Perfect.

'Catriona Parkes-Wilson.' He read the name aloud, glancing to watch her reaction to the identification.

Soft colour bloomed in her pale cheeks again, and her emerald eyes flashed. She really was striking.

'Kitty,' she corrected him quickly.

Catriona—Kitty—Parkes-Wilson was the daughter of the man who'd sold him this house.

Alejandro would have guessed that the diamonds—undoubtedly real—would be hers, but she'd looked so guilty when he'd stopped her that he now wondered. He had to be certain of their provenance before relinquishing them to her just like that.

But finally he understood her presence here tonight. She was on a retrieval mission.

She was also the ultimate in spoilt heiresses—so headstrong and so used to getting her way that she thought she could strut straight into any room and take what she wanted. Why not do the normal polite thing and *ask*? The sleek Catriona seemed only able to take. And no doubt she was used to causing trouble with every step.

He dampened down the rising attraction and told himself it would be fun to teach her a lesson in politeness, and *then* possession.

'Catriona...' he repeated her full name, deliberately ignoring her preference, and couldn't stop his smile when she looked more annoyed '... I'm delighted to have you back in your former residence. Welcome.'

His security detail had informed him of her unorthodox arrival via text but Alejandro had already spotted her from his hidden vantage point upstairs where he'd been having a moment away from his guests. She'd climbed the stairs as though she thought she was invisible. As if hair the sparkling colours of an autumnal bonfire could ever blend into the background. Even when it had been tied in that pile on her head it had caught his attention. Now that it hung loose in a tumble of crazy curls, he was tempted to tangle his fingers into it and draw her close for a kiss...

But he wasn't about to give in to this unexpected burst of desire.

Alejandro enjoyed sex and had no shortage of it, but it had been a while since he'd felt such an instant surge of lust for a woman. It was mildly irritating—he had better control than this and, to prove that to himself, he wasn't about to explore the sexual electricity arcing between them right now. Not yet. It would be more amusing to put this petulant princess in her place. He'd met too many spoilt people who'd never had to do a real day's work in their lives and who had no idea what hardship really was. Catriona Parkes-Wilson needed to learn some genuine manners.

An idea came instantly, as they generally did, but this one made his muscles tighten in a searing burst of anticipation.

'Remain here this evening as my date,' he said bluntly. 'Or I call the police. The choice is yours.'

'Your *date*?' Her eyes widened in surprise.

He knew she felt the sensual awareness the way he did. It seemed she didn't like it all that much either. Inexplicably, that improved his mood. He'd have her apology. And then, if it was good, maybe he'd have her.

'The police?' she suddenly added quickly, almost hopefully.

That threat was the lesser of the two evils to her? He needed to make that option more alarming. 'Your fingerprints are all over—'

'They would be anyway,' she interrupted scornfully. 'I lived here, remember?'

'And I have security camera footage.' He smiled.

That silenced her.

'I can't ignore my guests for hours while I iron out this interruption of yours,' he said. 'So you will remain with me until I have the time to deal with you.'

Her eyes didn't waver from his as he stipulated his rule

'I don't intend to leave your side even for a second,' he informed her quietly, failing to suppress the satisfaction that rose at the thought. 'Slinky cats can be clever escape artists. I'm not having you slip out when I look away for a second.' He read the fire in her gaze and his blood heated. 'And I do expect you to behave.'

Kitty glared at him. The thought of staying as his date should appal her. But what really shocked her was the delicious *anticipation* that shivered down her spine at the thought of such relentless attentiveness from him. What was *wrong* with her?

He bent closer, those full lips twisted ever so slightly into that tantalising smile. Dear Lord, he was too handsome.

'Catriona,' he said softly.

Now he loomed over her. She couldn't tear her gaze away from the bottomless depths of his black eyes. Her mouth parted as she struggled to breathe because her heart was thundering. Anticipation spiralled through every cell. Was he going to kiss her? Was she going to let him? Where had her *will* gone?

He was so close now she could feel his breath on her skin and his eyes were mesmerising and she simply couldn't seem to *move*. Then she felt the warmth of his fingers as he brushed the skin at the nape of her neck. She shivered, drawing in a shocked breath, but it was too late. He'd undone the clasp of the necklace before she'd registered his true intention. Now she could only stare as he stepped back and poured the glittering chain into his inside top pocket—right over the spot where his heart should be. Not that he had one of those.

He'd taken the diamond choker from her and she'd just let him.

She'd stood there like a vacant fool and let him reclaim the necklace. She'd let his good looks and his sexual magnetism render her *brainless*. How stupid could she get?

'I can't be your date,' she snapped, furious with herself.

'Why not?'

'You have a girlfriend already.'

'I do?' He sent her a penetrating look.

'Saskia something.' She straightened and snarled, venting her annoyance on him, 'I'm not helping you cheat on another woman.' She knew how much that sucked. 'Not even pretend cheating. So go ahead and call the police.'

She didn't think for a second he would but, to her apprehension, he pulled his mobile from his pocket again.

Had she misread him? Did he want the police here, interrupting his terribly exclusive party? She'd have to explain all and wear yet more mortification, but that was better than letting this man win. Surely the police would let her off with a warning—as a first time offender, distraught by the loss of her family home and all that... She might even be able to keep Teddy's name out of it.

She watched, breathing rapidly and still feeling too hot, as he held the phone up to his ear.

'Saskia, darling. I wanted to be honest with you and let you know before you heard it from anyone else.' He didn't hesitate. 'I've met someone else.'

Kitty's jaw dropped. He'd phoned the latest model girlfriend? She stared at him in frozen fascination as he kept talking.

'I know it seems sudden, but sometimes that's how life works.'

Had he just broken up with the woman?

OMG. The phone call was swift and to the point and the arrogant bastard smiled at *her* the entire way through.

'You just ended your relationship?' she all but gasped as he ended the call. 'Over the phone?'

'Four dates doesn't really constitute a relationship.' He shrugged and pocketed his mobile.

'And you never go much beyond five dates anyway

Teddy had told her that. Apparently, Alejandro's appetite for a rapid succession of beauties caused frequent comment—celebration by some, such as Teddy, and derision from others. Kitty was firmly in the second camp.

His eyebrows flickered. 'Don't I? I don't tend to keep count.'

Of dates or women? 'You can't just do that.'

'I just did.'

'You don't care?' Was it all *that* meaningless for him? His callousness was repellent, yet there was still that fickle, stupid part of her that was attracted to him.

'No. I don't.' He laughed at her expression. 'She doesn't either. We both knew what we were in for.'

And what was that—a few meaningless hours in bed together? Kitty whipped up her anger on behalf of the woman. 'You're sure about that?'

'Utterly.' He looked bored as he glanced at his watch. 'Now you needn't have any scruples about being my date for the night.'

'No way.' She shook her head, still shocked at his callous phone call. As if she'd ever date someone so ruthless. 'You're heartless.'

'If that's the case—' he reached for his pocket again '—then I will have to phone the police. Naturally, I will push for charges to be laid.' He sent her a mock-apologetic glance. 'It's unacceptable for people to unlawfully enter houses and take whatever they find lying around.'

She narrowed her eyes. He was playing a game. He'd have called the police already if that was what he'd really meant to do. 'You'll do whatever necessary to get what you want, won't you?'

He smiled as if that wasn't something to be ashamed of. 'Always.'

No doubt he'd blackmail, coerce, fight dirty and think nothing of it.

She gazed at him. He was hideously self-assured. Going through women like normal people went through pints of milk—on an almost daily basis and simply discarding the bottle when done. But that someone so shallow could be so attractive-looking? It was so wrong—the guy needed a warning label stamped on his forehead. Yet there was a whole roomful downstairs waiting to step up and be the next one. His looks and charisma had made things— women—far too easy for him.

He sent her that soft, suave smile, totally in control and at ease. 'What's it going to be, Catriona?' he prompted her gently. 'A night with me at your side, or a night in the cells?'

Her body recognised his beauty; her brain recognised he was a calculating bastard. She'd ensure her brain won this battle. She was certain he was not interested in her; he just wanted to teach her a lesson. That was obvious.

But *he* was the one who needed a lesson. The palm of her hand itched, but she'd never resorted to violence, not even in her worst attention-seeking teen tantrums and she wasn't letting this devil get to her in a way no one else ever had.

Nor was she letting him win. She had no idea what he thought he was going to achieve by forcing her to stay with him during his party, but she wasn't letting him have it. She'd make the night as difficult as possible for him. Then she'd tell the truth and demand Margot's diamonds back.

'Don't call the police,' she finally responded, answering demurely. 'I'll be your date.'

His eyes narrowed just the slightest, but his smile was ready and heart-stopping. He pocketed the phone again and then reached out and laced his fingers through hers. 'I never thought for a second that you wouldn't.'

CHAPTER TWO

'YOU'RE VERY SURE of yourself,' Kitty said, counting her breathing in an attempt to slow her speeding heart.

'I'm sure of people,' he answered. 'They are predictable.'

Well, he definitely wasn't predictable. And she *refused* to be—at least to him. 'What is it you want from me?' She tried to extricate her hand from his, but he wouldn't release her.

'What do you think I want from you?' That smile now lurked in his eyes.

Her chin lifted. 'If I knew, I wouldn't be asking.'

His glance sharpened, but he spoke calmly. 'Your time. Your undivided attention. And when every guest has gone tonight, we'll have a reckoning.'

Something flipped in her belly. Half horrified, half intrigued, she couldn't resist asking more. 'What kind of reckoning?'

The smile he flashed was nothing short of wicked. 'I think you've already guessed.'

He couldn't possibly mean *that*. She flushed. 'Never. Happening.'

He laughed then, releasing his grip on her to throw both his hands in the air, surprisingly animated. 'See? Predictable.' That foreign element underlying his American accent had deepened deliciously.

He was teasing her? She shouldn't feel even a hint of disappointment. Yet she did. Alejandro Martinez was too much the practised flirt and too sure of his own attractiveness.

'I'm not in the least interested in you in that way,' she said, determined to make the point as clear as possible.

'Of course you're not,' he soothed, turning to lead the way to the door.

'I mean it. You try anything—'

He sighed theatrically. 'Well, it will be difficult, but I'll try to control my animal urges.'

Okay, so now she felt a fool because of course he wasn't really interested in her like that. He'd be back on the phone to his Saskia soon enough and sorting out the lovers' tiff or he'd be off with another of the models downstairs…

Laughter danced in his eyes as he turned and caught her glaring at his back.

'You are very beautiful when cross,' he said provocatively. 'Does that fiery hair bring a temper with it?'

She refused to answer him. Her hair didn't bring rage so much as rashness. Fool that she was, she should have listened to Teddy and calmed down before deciding to come on this crazy mission. She should at least have eaten something, then she wouldn't be feeling this light-headed.

He paused and waited until she'd looked up into his face again before teasing her further. 'If you are a good date, you might get a reward.'

'All I want is the necklace,' she replied stiffly. And maybe some dinner at some point. Hopefully, there'd be some decent canapés downstairs and not just the tiny, calorie-free stuff that models lived on.

He took her hand firmly in his again and drew her towards the door. He was really serious about her mingling?

'What are you planning on telling your guests about me?' she asked.

A mystified expression crossed his face. 'Nothing.'

Clearly the opinion of others didn't bother him at all. Kitty tried very hard not to be bothered by what others thought, but there was still that soft part of her that ached to please someone. Anyone. Everyone.

She worked hard to fight it and protect her stupidl

vulnerable heart. For too long her self-esteem had been bound up in the opinion of men. First her father. Then her fiancé.

She hesitated at the top of the stairs. Alejandro was already on the first step, but he turned. His eyes were almost at the same level as hers.

'Come on, my reluctant date,' he dared in that divine accent. 'Come down and act the mute martyr.'

Was *that* what he expected her to do?

She went from famished to galvanised in less than a second. She'd act the ultimate party person—something she hardly ever was. With just that one look from him her appetite vanished. It was her twin, Teddy, who usually held centre stage, while she was the quiet foil—always his most appreciative audience. But now? Now she was energised. Now she had a game to win.

'You're obviously very bored with your life.' She placed her hand on his upper arm, leaning close in a parody of an adoring, clinging lover—half hoping he'd pull away.

He didn't. His smile broadened. 'Because I have to coerce a beautiful woman into standing alongside me for the night?'

'Exactly. You must be very jaded,' she murmured, trying not to dwell on the size and hardness of the muscles she could feel under the fabric of his oh-so-perfectly tailored suit. 'Having to spice it up like this.'

He chuckled. 'I haven't the time to deal with you the way I want to right now; I need to spend time with my guests. We'll deal with each other properly later.'

She wasn't sure if that was a promise or a threat. Worse, she wasn't sure what she *wanted* it to be.

'You don't think taking me down there with you is a risk?' She sent him a sideways look. 'Or do you truly think I'm predictable?'

'I'm very good at taking risks,' he said with no trace of

humility. 'And, in my experience, the higher the risk, the greater the reward.'

'So I'm high risk?'

He hesitated, checking his words ever so slightly. 'You're not afraid to put yourself on the line. That makes you interesting.'

She didn't want to be interesting. She didn't want to feel the flush of pleasure that he'd complimented her.

She refused his murmured offer of a drink as they descended the last stairs. As much as she yearned for the Dutch courage, she figured it would be more of a hindrance than a help. She needed all her wits about her to successfully spar with Alejandro Martinez and combat whatever 'reckoning' it was he had in mind.

Maybe she should have confessed all about the diamond necklace when she had the chance upstairs in the library, but he'd been so irritatingly assured, she'd been unable to resist the urge to bait him right back.

She wasn't sure what she'd expected from him once downstairs, but it wasn't the supremely polite courtesy he showed her. He introduced her to everyone as they walked through the atrium to the formal lounge. Many of them were American, like him, and out to enjoy themselves as much as possible. The first few people he introduced her to looked at her with benign disinterest—clearly used to Alejandro appearing every night with a new woman. No wonder he'd looked bemused when she'd asked what he'd say about her to his guests.

'Meet Catriona,' he said to the fourth group of people they stopped beside.

'Kitty,' she sweetly corrected, yet again, and extended her hand to the nearest of the three women. 'I'm his special date for the night.'

Three sets of eyebrows lifted in unison.

'Special?' one rapier-thin woman queried, her gaze equally dagger-like.

'I had to promise her that, or break out the handcuffs,' Alejandro answered smoothly.

The sensuality of his reply rippled through her—and the rest of the group. Eyes widened, then narrowed. But only Kitty knew the truth of his words. Only she knew he didn't mean fur-lined kinky toys, but tight, unbreakable restraints—yet somehow the thought of them wasn't as repellent as it should be. Not when she envisaged Alejandro wielding the cuffs and the key.

As Alejandro turned and led her further into the room, the look he sent *her* was slightly goading as if he knew he was thwarting her prediction of his behaviour. As if he knew the lurching direction of her thoughts. She refused to let the smile slip from her face. She'd 'sparkle' down here even if it killed her.

Except it wasn't that hard at all because he made her laugh too easily. He was extremely charming. In minutes she knew exactly why there were so many women present. He had that charisma, that X-factor, that way of looking at a woman as if she were the only person in the world who mattered to him in that moment. When she was the object of his focus, a woman felt *good*. It was a terrifyingly unfair talent. And he shared it around. He had his fingers laced through hers, but he talked with everyone equally.

Then she noticed people were watching them more attentively. Their gazes rested on the way he remained close to her the entire time. At the way he constantly touched some part of her—a hand on her back, her arm, or clasping her hand. As time passed into the second hour, he placed his arm over her shoulder and drew her closer to his side.

The guests began looking more assessingly at *her*. She heard the ripple of inquiry as they made their way from room to room. She heard the whisper of her name. Surreptitious glances became openly speculative.

If Alejandro noticed he said nothing, but his attentiveness became even more apparent. Until he then led her to a corner and stepped in close to put himself as a wall between her and the rest of his guests.

'You seem to be causing a stir,' he said, his onyx gaze pinning her in place.

'Not me.'

He was the one doing all the touchy-feely stuff that was causing the stares.

'Absolutely you.' He laughed. That amusement danced in his eyes too and she couldn't tear her attention from him.

'You enjoy messing with people's lives?'

'In what way am I messing with your life?' He raised his eyebrows. 'Don't overdramatize having to spend one night alongside me. It's not going to change your world.'

'It's not?' She furrowed her brow in mock-disappointment. 'But I thought any woman who spent a night with the amazing Alejandro had her world *rocked*.'

'Minx.' He laughed again. 'Come on, we'd better keep moving.'

'Must we, darling?' she murmured as she stepped alongside him.

The look he shot her then promised absolute retribution.

Kitty lifted her chin, feeling more game than ever. But, now she could look more freely about the house, she realised there was much gone from the rooms. Her family had had a 'maximalist' rather than a 'minimalist' style of decor but the mantelpieces were bare and shelves barren—the spaces punctuated by used champagne glasses and platters of stupidly tiny delicacies she'd yet to sample. With a pang she wondered what he'd done with all the smaller items of furniture and the trinkets and sculptures that she'd loved all her life—surely they weren't all crammed into those boxes in the bedrooms upstairs.

'Alejandro?' a woman called from almost halfway across the room and walked over with quick, clipping steps. 'I've just had a text from Saskia,' she added, her eyes cold and wide as she locked her gaze on Kitty. 'Bit of a bombshell, actually.'

'Oh?' Alejandro couldn't have sounded less interested but his arm tightened infinitesimally, pressing Kitty closer to his side.

She wished he wouldn't do that; feeling his hard strength was appallingly distracting, but she had the feeling he did it without even realising—so used to having a woman with him.

'She said you've met someone else.'

There was a split-second of awkward silence and Alejandro was utterly still. The woman's confident expression suddenly faltered.

'Oh, that would be me,' Kitty interjected sweetly before Alejandro had a chance to speak. 'When I've had enough of him she's welcome to have him back.'

She heard Alejandro's sharply drawn breath and braced herself. Was he finally going to tell her to go now?

But he drew her closer still. It wasn't an unconscious, almost undetectable gesture now. 'But sweetheart,' he breathed. 'It's my job to ensure you've never had enough.' He turned to the woman. 'If you'll excuse us, I'd like to get Catriona a drink. I think she needs one.'

'How many times do I have to tell you—it's Kitty?' she muttered as he held her hand tightly and drew her through the crowds with him.

He smiled back at her and his hand tightened. 'What will you have?'

She was aware of everyone watching them as he led her through the room. 'Got any cyanide in the champagne?'

'I'll save you some for later, when it's time to face your—how do you say?—fate worse than death.' He looked pleased with himself at that.

'I already told you, that's never happening.'

He stopped in the centre of the room and faced her, apparently uncaring that everyone was staring, and positively *hauled* her right into his arms. 'No? Not even a kiss to say sorry?' Slowly and deliberately he brushed his thumb across her lower lip. 'Methinks the lady doth protest too much.'

'Methinks the asshole doth have an outsize ego.'

He gazed at her, his expression delighted. He couldn't have looked more proprietorial. Or more smitten. But his whispered words were so sarcastic and his awareness of her unbelievably smug. He was enjoying her discomfort hugely. She could tell by the unholy gleam in his eyes, but every touch made her acutely aware of him and his magnetism grew stronger.

She pulled back and made him keep walking.

So. Not. Happening.

It was his reputation that made her so aware of him. All that history, the list of conquests—the world's most beautiful, desired women. But it wasn't only that. There was no denying *his* physical perfection and the supreme assuredness that went with it.

It was impossible to look away from him for long. She'd never met anyone like him and she'd met plenty of wealthy, entitled people in the course of her life. But if you were to strip all those people bare of their designer dresses and jewels and outsize bank balances, many would fade into nothingness. Not Alejandro. Buck-naked in a bull ring he'd still conquer all. And she had the feeling he intended to conquer her. He thought he already had.

He had another think coming.

The awareness of the guests was even more apparent

now. She felt the heat from a zillion hard gazes and fought to keep the polite smile on her face. She wasn't going to lose her confidence. She was going to keep her head high and weather these last couple of hours. But she was quieter as she stood alongside Alejandro, her hand still firmly bound in his, as he talked work with a couple.

That was when she recognised two of the women on the far side of the room. A small British contingent seemed to be standing together. Kitty's heart sank—of course they'd be there. Those two were like pearl hat pins—ultra pretty but with a sharp point they liked to stick into someone given the chance. She hadn't seen Sarah in months, but she didn't imagine she'd had a personality transplant in that time. The woman was a childhood chum of James's—one who'd never approved of his engagement to Kitty and she was with another couple who were also very much 'team James'. And great, they'd spotted her too and were circling closer like a school of sharks honing in for a feeding frenzy.

'Kitty Parkes-Wilson!' the first exclaimed loudly.

'Hi, Sarah.' Kitty smiled, turning to angle herself slightly away from Alejandro. Given he was engrossed in discussing the prospects of another hedge fund, she crossed her fingers he wouldn't hear this conversation—because if anyone here was going to be predictable, it would be this woman.

'Fancy seeing you here this week of all weeks.' Sure enough, Sarah launched her first salvo in a loud chime.

'You mean in my former family home the week we lost possession?' Kitty smiled through her teeth. 'Funny how life works, isn't it?'

'Oh, it is,' Sarah answered as she glanced at Alejandro's hand curling around Kitty's despite the fact he was facing the other couple. 'I never thought you'd be another of Alejandro's notches,' she 'whispered' conspiratorially.

'I'm not!' Kitty flared at the thought and replied swiftly

before thinking better of it. 'I'm only here because he's bullied me into staying.'

Sarah's eyebrows lifted and she laughed a little too loudly. 'Bullied?' Her pointed laugh chimed loudly again. 'Yeah, it really looks like that.'

Was it Kitty's imagination or had Alejandro tensed?

'We haven't seen you in so long,' Sarah added when Kitty didn't elaborate. 'You left London in such a hurry.'

The woman was such a cow to bring that up. Of course she'd left in a hurry. She'd been *hurt*. She'd just found out James hadn't wanted *her* at all. He'd only wanted the wealth he'd assumed came with her. And when he'd found out all the cold hard cash had gone, he hadn't bothered to break up with her before searching the field for her replacement. He'd been trying them all out behind her back. Now, barely six months later, he was engaged to another woman. A beautiful, wealthy one who didn't seem at all bothered about his cheating past.

This time Kitty didn't imagine the sensation. Alejandro's fingers definitely tightened about hers again. But he didn't break his conversation and turn towards her.

'You're finally over James then?' Sarah queried.

She knew it hadn't been her fault, but it still hurt. She'd truly thought he loved her. That he'd got her, and found her attractive. But it was only the money he'd loved. And she'd been so starved for attention, so desperate to believe that a guy finally wanted *her*, she'd not seen through his fickle facade.

She'd been such a fool. And she was a fool now for letting this woman get to her.

Because she was too angry.

She straightened, channelled her inner Great-Aunt Margot and rewrote the rules.

'Oh, yes.' Kitty smiled sunnily at Sarah. 'You know, I didn't want to make things public yet,' she 'whispered'—

every bit as loudly as Sarah had. 'As you've alluded to, it has been a stressful week.'

Sarah's eyes widened and she leaned closer. 'Make what public?' This time her volume really did lower.

'Our relationship,' Kitty answered as if it was obvious.

'Your...' Sarah's jaw slackened in shock, then she almost squeaked. 'You mean with Alejandro? *You're* why he bought this house? He bought it for you?'

It was amazing how the smallest suggestion could snowball into something so out of control so quickly.

'It's a secret, you understand,' Kitty murmured guiltily, not quite correcting Sarah's assumption and hoping Alejandro was still deeply involved with his conversation and not eavesdropping.

'The two of you are that...*serious*?' Sarah's voice rose.

She was so obviously thunderstruck at the notion that Kitty was suddenly irate. Why was it so shocking that an attractive man might want *her*? Just for once she wanted to knock the superior smirk from this woman's face—and every other person who'd looked at her as if she were a loser freak. 'We're—'

Sarah's eyes narrowed on the way Alejandro was holding Kitty's left hand so firmly. 'You're *never* engaged,' she breathed.

'We're...er...' Kitty suddenly realised a metaphorical crevasse had opened at her feet. She was in real trouble.

That was when Alejandro turned.

If only the earth really would open up and swallow her whole.

'Kitty's just told me the news.' Sarah reached out and put a hand on his wrist and shot Kitty a sharp look before Kitty could even draw breath. 'Congratulations.'

Kitty couldn't bring herself to look at him.

And then Sarah did it. She asked so loudly that several heads turned. 'Are you two really engaged, Alejandro?'

CHAPTER THREE

ALEJANDRO'S FINGERS TIGHTENED again on Kitty's—extremely firmly.

But Kitty didn't wince. She held her breath, waiting for the ultimate in public humiliation. It was suddenly so quiet, it was as if the rest of the world was holding its breath with her. This would actually be worse than when she'd finally found out about James's infidelity. At least she'd been alone then and not in the centre of a roomful of people.

'Sarah guessed,' Kitty muttered as she finally braved a glance up at him and recklessly killed the silence that had been a fraction too long already. 'She's always been astute.'

His gaze imprisoned hers and for a second everyone in the room faded. His eyes were like banked furnaces, so very black but so very deep and there was a level of emotion in them that she'd not expected and that she couldn't interpret.

Oh, God, she should just run away now.

His fingers tightened even more—to the point of pain—as if he'd read her mind and was physically preventing her escape. But she wanted to run. She *had* to. How could she ever explain?

Sarah—the one who'd never told her that her fiancé was sleeping with someone else. Sarah—who'd never been nice, who'd never welcomed her into the group, who'd never seemed to want her to succeed.

'You've caught her out, Sarah,' Alejandro said quietly.

Kitty started to die inside.

'Catriona was reluctant to announce it so soon…' He trailed off.

Sarah's jaw dropped. So did Kitty's, but she caught herself in time. She licked her lips, her heart thundering as she gazed at Alejandro. He was smiling? He was looking...*satisfied*?

He turned to face her nemesis intently. 'We can trust you, can't we?'

'Of course,' Sarah said weakly. 'But I...er...might have been a bit loud just then.'

'No matter.' Alejandro smiled. 'We're all friends here.'

Did he underline the word 'friends'? He still held Kitty's hand in a vice but he was smiling.

'Congratulations.' Sarah looked stunned.

Alejandro lifted his free hand to place a finger over his lips and winked at her. 'Shh, remember?' Finally he turned to Kitty again. 'Come along, Catriona. I think you need some fresh air.'

He set off at such a pace Kitty almost stumbled. If it weren't for the grip he had on her hand, she might have. Instead he wrapped his other arm around her waist and—under the guise of attentive affection—practically dragged her out through the back room, past that bland dishwashing guy and out into the small private courtyard at the back.

Only once they were alone outside did he release her. Kitty took a quick few steps to the corner of the tiled courtyard. Then turned to face him.

'We're engaged?' He sent her a look.

With the bright lights gleaming from the house, this one was easy to interpret. He was *amused*?

'It's your fault,' she declared, instantly defensive. 'I was trying not to be predictable. You dared me.'

'So it's *my* fault?'

'This entire mess is your fault.' She nodded firmly.

He slowly stepped closer. 'You don't feel any responsibility, given you're the one who broke in and tried to steal from me?'

'I didn't break in; I used a key. And I wasn't stealing anything that belongs to you.'

'No? I wonder.' He was watching her closely, then his smile returned, slow and seductive. 'Catriona, you are going to pay for this, you know.'

'Not in the way you're thinking.'

He laughed and stepped so he was right in her personal space. 'Very much in the way I'm thinking. You think these sparks can be ignored?'

She really wished his accent didn't make his atrocious words sound so damn attractive. His laugh was low and did things to her insides and the cool air did nothing to settle the fever in her bones.

Now she really wished he'd stop looking at her like that. It made her hot and it was even harder to concentrate. And he knew it. He knew he was like catnip to every woman in the world. He loved it. She didn't want to want him at all. But her stupid body recognised the talent and experience in his.

'Is this the bit where you attempt to exert your sexual dominance over me?' she growled as he stepped closer still.

He let out another burst of laughter, but he caught both her hands in his and forced them behind her back in a move of total sexual dominance. 'No, this is the bit where I stop you from saying more stupid things in public.'

'You have no right to censor me.' She had no idea where the wildness came from. She'd never normally speak to anyone like this. Usually she'd duck her head and mind her own business and let Teddy do the talking.

'Not censoring you,' he chided wickedly. 'Kissing you. To leave you speechless.'

'You're...*what*?' Her jaw dropped. 'You're unbelievable.'

'I know. So good.' He mock preened.

But his proximity was getting to her—she could feel his strength and his size and, appallingly, she wanted to lean up against him! She stiffened instead. 'You don't think you're hyping yourself up too much? I'm going to expect something so amazing you're never going to be able to live up to it.'

'I'm willing to take the risk.'

'You're willing to take a lot of risks.'

'Possibly. But this is my home and you will not cause trouble when I have this many guests present.'

'Then let me leave. With my necklace.' She looked up and sent him a brilliant smile, pleased with her comeback. 'It's a very simple solution.'

'No, that can't happen now,' he answered bluntly, his expression intent. 'Stupid talk earns kissing, remember?'

Kitty didn't get the chance to breathe, let alone reply. Because he'd bent his head and brushed his lips over hers. It was the softest, lightest kiss and not at all what she'd have expected. Silenced, stilled, she waited. There was another light, gentle caress—lips on lips. And then another.

That was when she realised he was the kind of lover who would take his time. Infinite time and care, to arouse her. The thing was, she didn't need that much time. Her toes curled in the ends of her shoes as he kissed her again and she couldn't help her slight gasp, the parting of her suddenly needy mouth. But he didn't press closer, harder—instead, he kept the kiss light, almost sweet, and he was utterly in control. There was just that underlying edge as she absorbed the rigidity of his body...and started to realise that the tightness of his grasp on her wrists was no longer to hold her in place, but to hold himself back.

She looked up at him, bemused by his tender, go softly approach. He threw her a small smile, as if he knew exactly how much she'd anticipated a punishing kiss from him— all frantic passion and a duelling race to the finish line.

And she was *not* disappointed it hadn't become that kind of kiss. Nor was she yearning for another.

'That wasn't enough?' he teased knowingly. 'You want a little more?'

'That was more than enough,' she lied with a little shrug. 'I guess this is where you say we English have no passion.'

'I've yet to meet a woman who doesn't feel passion when she's with me—'

'You mean anger? Rage?'

He chuckled and brushed his thumb across her hyper-sensitised lips. 'Too easy.'

Awareness rippled down her spine, a warm tide of liquid desire. It was impossible that she be so drawn to this man. He was a philanderer—a total playboy who'd had more lovers than she had freckles. And she had a *lot* of freckles.

He was just toying with her—too aware of his sensual power and utterly assured of his success.

'I won't be another of your numbers.' She promised herself that.

'No?' He laughed and shook her gently. 'You already are. More than that—you're my fiancée.'

She died of mortification all over again. In the heat of that kiss she'd forgotten that nightmare moment. 'Why didn't you deny it?' She swallowed.

'I don't like seeing anyone ganged up on,' he said simply. 'I dislike bullies. It was evident what was going on.'

What would the supremely successful Alejandro Martinez know about bullies? As she frowned at him another emotion flickered across his face. But he suddenly stepped back, looking as suavely in control as ever. He extended his hand to her and waited. That he was so astute surprised her. Now she knew why he hadn't denied that outrageous engagement story to Sarah. He'd felt *sorry* for her. She felt worse than ever.

She hesitated, looking into his eyes, unable to read him at all now.

'Let's go back inside,' he said quietly.

With a small sigh she put her hand in his and walked back into the house. But they didn't return to the packed ground floor reception rooms; instead he led her up the stairs that she had previously used to get to the private library.

'Stay here awhile, make yourself at home,' he teased wolfishly as he showed her into the room.

She should have known that moment of kindness and humanity wouldn't last in him.

'Where are you going?' She eyed him suspiciously.

He had his phone out and a key in his hand—one of the large old-fashioned keys that fitted the internal doors in this house.

'I'm going to get rid of all my guests. I can do that better if you're not with me.'

'And you're going to lock me in here while you do that?' She folded her arms and called him on it. 'What if there's a fire?'

'I'll play the hero and rescue you.' He simply smiled and looked rakish.

'You're no hero—you're all villain.'

He flashed another smile. 'Women always like the bad boy, isn't that so?'

That was *not* so. She felt like flinging the cushions at him, except she wasn't that childish. Guiltily she remembered her lies downstairs. She'd definitely acted like a proud, childish idiot then.

'Don't fret.' He winked at her just before closing—and locking—the door. 'I won't be long.'

He was an inordinately long time. Eventually she heard voices spilling out into the street and resisted the urge to stand at the window and scream for a saviour. She'd made enough of a fool of herself here tonight. What had she been thinking when she'd led Sarah to think Alejandro had bought the house for her? That they were *engaged*?

Tired defeat permeated her. She'd been up since six, ready to get the train from Cornwall back to London. She'd not eaten on the journey and now she felt queasy. She turned off the main light and switched on the reading lamp, pouring herself a finger of whiskey from the decanter still on the table in the study.

She rarely drank spirits but right now she needed *something* and she trusted her father's old single malt more than the concoctions that had been on offer downstairs. And, anyway, this was for medicinal purposes. The liquid hit her stomach and lit a ball of fire in it. She breathed out and closed her eyes, aching to relax properly. She'd spark up again when Alejandro returned. She just needed a bit of a rest now.

The heat drained from her. That kick of adrenalin vanished, leaving her tired and with a headache threatening. She kicked off her shoes and walked to the deep leather sofa that had been in her father's study all her life, trying not to remember the number of times she'd curled up on it and waited late into the night for him to get home.

She'd spent so long trying to get her father's attention. But he'd been preoccupied lecturing Teddy, the son and heir, and he'd been too busy wooing the glamorous women he'd had affairs with. She'd gifted him her best sculptures as a kid. She'd poured her heart into them, only to see them admired for a half second and then relegated to a bottom shelf to gather dust. They were never properly displayed, never shown off with pride, merely indulged for a brief moment before he turned elsewhere. Which was exactly the way he treated *her*.

All she'd wanted was for him to know her, to love her, to let her *be*... She was such a needy fool.

She'd thought James had understood and that he'd be true to her. But he'd been even worse. At least her father had never hidden his affairs from everyone.

'I was just...I couldn't help myself.' Her father had tried to explain it to her the last time she'd seen him, just after she'd broken up with James, and she'd railed at him for being the same kind of *cheat*.

Impulse. Making that snap decision that was so often wrong. She'd inherited that faulty gene from him. Not when it came to lovers, but in every other aspect of her life for sure.

Her father had made bad business choices; he'd needed to sell property to get a cash injection because he'd known his time as a businessman was up. He'd wanted to retire to his flash estate in Corsica while he still could. And so he had. Leaving Teddy and her alone. But they were almost twenty-four and able to look after themselves.

Now she was exhausted from maintaining smiles in front of all those people. From restraining herself from losing her temper with Alejandro in front of them all. From reining in her reaction to the torment of his touches. From hiding the heartbreak at being back here and knowing she no longer belonged. That she'd never really belonged. There was nothing here for her any more.

She curled her legs under her on the sofa and told herself to shrug it off. She was fine. She'd go and stay with Teddy at one of his friends' places tonight after having it out with Alejandro. She'd go back to Cornwall in the morning and get on with her new life. It was all going to be okay.

But in the meantime she slumped lower in the soft leather.

It took longer than Alejandro desired for his guests to get the idea it was time for them to leave. Admittedly his parties usually went on far later, but he needed to be alone with the vexatious redhead who'd tipped his night upside down. So he smiled, firmly shooting down the teasing pleas for the DJ to play on.

Finally he closed the door on the last couple of guests, who were still shocked and avidly curious. Yeah, that 'friend' of Catriona's hadn't kept her mouth shut. But he'd known she wouldn't. They'd all known that.

Rolling his shoulders to ease the tension mounting in them, he lightly jogged up the stairs. His smile was tight. She was going to be furious with him for taking so long. But when he unlocked the door he wasn't greeted with the instant volley of verbal abuse he'd expected. His breath froze in his lungs at the total silence in the room. Had she escaped somehow? He strode into the library then drew up short—the sight before him rendered him speechless. He simply stared.

She was fast asleep on the sofa, her body a sleek, long shadow of woman. Her skin shone pale in the soft light, but her hair was a riot of flames cascading about her face and shoulders. God, she was beautiful. Different. Sexy as hell.

Desire ripped through him—igniting a fierce animal urge to wake her, kiss her, claim her body with his, here and now. The longing to feel her beneath him was sudden and acute. He clenched his fists at the ferocity of the ache and forced himself to take a calming breath.

No. *No.*

He never wanted any woman as intensely as all that. He never felt *anything* as intensely as all that. He refused. He had reason to.

He breathed deeply again and reminded himself of his rational decisions. He hadn't been going to *make* her stay the night—despite the teasing and the incredibly erotic pleasure of her kiss. He'd been planning to get to the bottom of the necklace situation and then say goodbye to her, hadn't he?

But now here she was with her shoes off, fast asleep on the old sofa. He guessed it wasn't the first time she'd slept on it.

He frowned as he quietly stepped closer to study her. He hadn't seen just how pale she was earlier, or noticed those smudges under her eyes. She looked exhausted.

'Catriona?' he softly called to her. 'Kitty?'

She didn't stir. He'd known she wouldn't. She was in too deep a sleep. Something twisted inside Alejandro as he understood how vulnerable she was in this moment and the degree to which he was entrusted with her *care*. An icy droplet snaked down his spine. This was a complication he hadn't foreseen and didn't particularly want. Maintaining the care and wellbeing of another was not his forte. But he fetched a blanket from his room and covered her to make her more comfortable until she woke of her own accord. He hoped she would soon.

He sat in the large armchair opposite the sofa and pulled the necklace from his pocket to inspect it properly in the lamplight. It was definitely worth serious money and she'd risked a lot to get it back. But it wasn't hers.

Over the years, so many of those wealthy people he'd studied alongside had annoyed him when they'd shown a lack of appreciation of how damn lucky they were. He'd never taken his success or his security for granted. How could he when he'd come from worse than nothing? So he'd worked harder than any of them. Ensured his grades were the best. Swinging from one scholarship to the next, climbing higher and higher out of a life of poverty, misery, desperation. And his 'party lifestyle' that claimed all the headlines was but a tiny fraction of his time. The rest was spent working. Still working. Still achieving. Still ensuring success. And now a spoilt young woman had waltzed in to reclaim—what—her inheritance? The wealth she'd never had to earn for herself.

She'd been brazen and bold in her initial dismissal of him, outrageous in the reckless way she'd back-chatted him, and he'd fully planned to teach her a thing or two. Except he'd then heard the tone in which that other woman had spoken to her and there'd been no mistaking it. He hated bullies—whether they were the kind who used vicious words or the violent fists he'd experienced. So he hadn't shamed her publicly. He'd backed her and there'd been no missing the bright relief in her eyes. But then her nerve in the private courtyard when she'd insisted it was all *his* fault? When he'd given in to that urge to kiss her?

He glanced at his Sleeping Beauty again—remembering the softness of her lips, the stirring in her muscles… the *spark*. He couldn't regret that—no matter the complication that now arose.

But now he was stuck with the story that she and he were engaged. He'd smiled his way through the shocked shouts of congratulations from every one of his guests as he'd ushered them out. He'd explained that Catriona had been overwhelmed by the attention and that they'd have another party soon. It was ridiculous but he hadn't been able to find it within himself to reveal the truth. He'd seen that vulnerability when she'd looked at him. He'd seen that hurt. It echoed within him. Didn't he know what it was like to be that isolated? And afraid.

She was a contrary mix of assertiveness and insecurity, a bit broken but bluffing anyway. He liked that spirit. And he wanted her.

Well, if he was going to have her, he was going to have to play it carefully. She obviously wasn't someone who went from affair to affair.

He felt the vibration again and quietly extracted her phone from his pocket. He didn't want to wake her yet, not when she was so obviously wiped out, but it seemed someone was concerned for her welfare. The name 'Teddy' was written across the screen and the photo beneath the lettering was of the two of them. The resemblance was impossible to miss. The man was blond rather than red-haired, but he shared the same smile, the same shaped eyes. He had to be her brother.

Alejandro didn't answer the call; rather he put the phone on the wide arm of the chair he was sitting in and picked up his own phone. A simple Internet search was all it took to remind himself of the family details. Teddy—Edward—and Kitty—Catriona—Parkes-Wilson were the twin children of the man he'd bought this house from. He entered another search and soon enough came up with a photo of an elderly woman—Margot Parkes—wearing the diamond choker Kitty had come here to collect.

And then there were the pictures of Kitty herself. It seemed she was something of an artist—a sculptor. She'd had a few mentions in the society pages; there was the announcement of an engagement to some man named James that hadn't lasted. Another reason to take care with her. But Alejandro was confident; his affairs always ended easily and well and maybe something light and sexual was exactly what the woman needed. Something fun—he did fun really well.

There were more mentions of her brother. And then there was the item about Alejandro's purchase of Parkes House. Apparently it had been in her family for generations. He didn't feel bad about the transaction. He'd paid more than a fair price and if businesses failed, they failed. He'd needed a London base and he'd got one.

When her phone rang for the tenth time he finally relented, feeling only the smallest sympathy for the man who'd allowed his sister to put herself at such risk for his sake.

He touched the screen to take the call. Teddy spoke before Alejandro had the chance to say hello.

'Kitty? For God's sake, are you okay? Did you get the diamonds?'

'I'm sorry, Teddy,' Alejandro replied calmly. 'Both your sister and the diamonds are with me.'

CHAPTER FOUR

KITTY OPENED HER EYES, blinking at the bright light streaming in through the gap in the heavy brocade curtains. She frowned as she took in the familiar surroundings. She was in the second floor library on her father's sofa—

She froze as it all came flooding back. Alejandro Martinez now owned Parkes House. He'd coerced her into being his date. He'd kissed her. He'd said they'd have a reckoning and here she was, waking the next *day*—

'Good morning.'

She sat up quickly, clutching the soft woollen blanket to her, taking a split second to realise she was still fully clothed. Then she looked up, gaping as he took a seat in the armchair opposite. For a moment all she could do was stare. He looked even more striking in the daylight. So gorgeously striking.

Then she snapped herself together.

'What happened?' Warily she brushed her hair back from her face and shifted so she was sitting up properly, her feet on the floor ready to run.

'You fell asleep while I was getting rid of the other guests,' he said easily. 'You've been out for hours; I was starting to get concerned.'

Kitty's skipping pulse didn't settle. He must've showered not that long ago because his hair was still damp and now he wore jeans and a white tee, but he looked no less wolfish than he had the night before. No less to-die-for.

Half her innards melted. She loathed her reaction to him. How superficial could she get? Wowed by chiselled cheekbones, a fit body and a cockier-than-hell attitude.

In that instant he smiled at her as if he knew exactly what she was thinking.

'I have a proposition for you,' he said.

'I already said no thank you,' she said primly. *Determinedly.*

He gestured to a mug of coffee on the low table beside her. Steam curled in the light. 'I'm guessing you like it strong and unsweetened.'

Clearly she *was* that predictable after all. 'Why do you think that?'

'You're a starving artist who needs to make the most of every drop she gets.'

Silently she reached out for the coffee. He'd been doing some research.

'I made your father an offer he couldn't refuse,' he said. 'I'll make you one too.'

'My father didn't much care for this place anyway,' Kitty muttered and drank the coffee. She needed to kick-start her grey matter. 'He thought it was cold.'

'It is cold,' Alejandro said dryly. 'I've ordered a new heating system.'

Because he had the bajillions required to maintain and upgrade a heritage building like this one. She knew it was petty, but she hated him for that. He had no idea of the history of this house.

'But you like this building.' He smiled when she didn't answer. 'I can tell by the way you look around it. Listen to my offer.'

'I'll refuse anything you offer me,' she said fiercely. She wouldn't be bought as easily as her father had been. She'd never say yes to this man.

Now she remembered the humiliation of Sarah being here last night and seeing her. And the story she'd spun—that they were *engaged*? Oh, hell, the sooner she ran back to Cornwall the better.

'Maybe.' He smiled. 'But you might not want to. Why not hear me out first and then decide?'

He stood and walked over to the desk and returned with a large platter. Kitty looked at the freshly sliced fruit and pastries and swallowed to stop herself drooling. She was *starving*.

'Go ahead and eat,' Alejandro commented lazily. 'It'll make you feel better.'

She restrained herself from sending him a stabbing glance. He might be right, but he didn't need to sound so patronising.

'What's your ever so fabulous offer?' she asked, reaching for the fruit.

He watched as she bit into the pineapple before replying and for a moment Kitty wouldn't have heard or understood a word he said anyway. She was famished—and this fruit was so fresh it was all she could do to stop herself devouring it all in two seconds flat.

She heard his low chuckle and he sat back in the chair and pulled the diamond choker from his pocket.

'Tell me about this,' he said.

She gazed sadly at the coil of glittering stones in his hand but shook her head.

'You think you're protecting someone?' His eyebrows lifted. 'I know it belongs to your brother.'

He *had* been doing his research. 'Yes.'

'But you're the one who loves it.'

She bristled at the hint of censure. Did he think she was a materialistic, do-anything-for-diamonds kind of girl? 'I loved the woman it originally belonged to,' she said haughtily. 'I love what the diamonds symbolise, not what they're worth. They have irreplaceable *sentimental* value.'

His frown hadn't lessened. 'So why do they belong to your brother?'

She sighed. 'Because he's the firstborn and the boy.'

Now a baffled look crossed his face. 'Are we still in the Middle Ages?'

'*You're* the one who forced me to be your date last night, so I'd say I'm currently living in the Neanderthal era. Barbaric caveman,' she muttered beneath her breath.

'Poor baby.' His smile flashed and he leaned back in his seat, oozing sensual confidence. 'So what are you willing to do to get your necklace back?'

'Not that.' She picked up a *pain au chocolat* and chomped on it.

'I'm not that crass. We'll sleep together only when you've grown up enough to admit how much you want to.'

He laughed at her expression. His arrogance knew no bounds.

But then he sobered. 'You didn't think that you could have just contacted my lawyer? Or perhaps knocked on the front door and asked me politely? Explained there was a mix-up?'

Was that a glimpse of hurt in his eyes? Surely not.

'Am I such a monster you had to resort to breaking the law to get what belonged to your family?'

Kitty finally managed to swallow the lump of concrete masquerading as pastry in her mouth. 'You're the one who admitted to doing whatever necessary to get what you want. At the time I thought this was necessary.'

'Fair enough, but you know there are consequences to your actions. All your actions.'

'You're calling the police?'

'You should be so lucky.' His smile this time wasn't so nice. 'No, if you want the necklace back, then you make amends.'

'How do you want me to do that?'

'You fulfil the role you claimed last night. You be my fiancée.'

'*What?*'

Calmly he put the choker back into his pocket and then shot her a look. 'You remain here as my fiancée for a few weeks until we amicably break up and then you leave.'

'Why would you want me to do that?'

'Because it suits me.'

'And it's all about you.'

'Right now, yes, it is.' He shrugged. 'You broke into my house. You spread stories about me to all my friends. I think you owe me.'

She felt guilty enough already; she didn't need him laying it on with a trowel.

'I'm opening up the London office of my company,' he went on. 'It's a big investment and I don't want this sideshow overshadowing or impacting on its success. It doesn't need to be a big deal; interest will fade very quickly once the company set-up is fully underway.'

'I can't just stay here as your fiancée. I have a job.'

'You have a part-time position in a failing art gallery in the south of England where you don't actually get paid; you merely get a roof over your head and use of the small studio out the back.'

Yes, he'd done a *lot* of research. She'd gone to Cornwall on a whim when her engagement to James had ended in that blaze of exposure and humiliation. She'd been there for the last six months. Happy enough, but lonely. She'd been unable to resist Teddy's call for help.

'It's not failing,' she grumbled, just so she could fight with him about something. 'It's a beautiful gallery. The light down there is amazing.'

'I want you to work here and catalogue everything in this mausoleum. There are things in piles of boxes that I haven't the time to open and sift through.'

'So you can auction it off and make money from every little thing?'

'I don't need the money from these trinkets. They'd add less than a drop to my financial ocean.'

Oh, please—bully for him for being so wealthy. 'I could steal from you, you know.'

'I'm willing to take that risk.' He smiled.

'Don't you have ten personal assistants or something?'

'My PA is extremely efficient and I'm sure she'd do a good job, but her talents are better spent on the work she knows best. It's better for this to be done by someone familiar with the content. The place is in a mess and you know it.'

He was right and it wasn't just the boxes; there were years of repairs that had been left undone. Like his business, her father had left the house in a mess.

'It needs an upgrade, and you can make the arrangements, at least for the chattels to begin with. A full restoration programme will take much longer, of course.' Alejandro regarded her steadily. 'So what do you think?'

She thought it was a flimsy excuse to keep her here just because…he simply wanted it. And he always got what he wanted, that was obvious. Yet his plan appealed to the spot where she was most vulnerable. She'd loved this home and she wanted to save some of those things. 'So you're not going to modernise, but restore?'

'The building has many beautiful features that I find attractive and would like to keep.' He nodded. 'Of course I want to see it restored to its glory—not just the shell, but the interior as well.'

She felt her flush of gratitude mounting. It was so stupid, but he'd got her there. And he knew it.

'You have an understanding of the items that are here; you can assess their value and importance. Catalogue them with a sell or keep recommendation and I'll make my decision when I have time.'

She thought about it for a long moment. It was so tempting, but it was also impossible. And insane. She shook her head. 'I can't go from one engagement to another.'

Not even to a fake one.

'It's been about six months, hasn't it?' Alejandro pointed out, lazily selecting one of the grapes she'd left behind on the platter.

'Who have you been talking to?' She was mortified that he knew of her past.

He swallowed the fruit and laughed. 'What does it matter?' He reached forward, his teasing expression back. 'You know a rebound romance is the perfect solution for that bad temper.'

'This will never be a *romance*,' she snarled, shocked at the way she was suddenly burning up.

'No?' He looked amused. 'I was trying to make it sound less...raw.'

'Less tacky, you mean.' He was talking about lust and nothing but.

'You need a system cleanse.' He lifted his hands in that unexpectedly animated way that made her want to smile back at him. 'A little light fun to restore your confidence and independence.'

'And you're offering?' Like the generous, do-good kind of guy he so wasn't. 'A little light fun?'

What, exactly, would that entail? And why was it suddenly so hot in here?

'I'm offering many things. All of them good.' Still leaning forward, he propped his chin in his hand as he watched her. 'You don't have anywhere else to stay in London at the moment. I believe your brother is between apartments as well.'

Oh, hell, he knew it all. And the truth was, the prospect of couch-surfing with Teddy's theatre friends for the next few days was depressing. Her father hadn't thought it necessary to consider whether she'd have a place to stay.

And nor should he. She was twenty-three and perfectly capable of finding her own accommodation. But she hadn't realised how adrift she really was. 'Is there *anything* you don't know?'

'There are many things I don't know about you. Yet.'

The implied intimacy brought more colour to her cheeks.

'It is the organisation of the house that earns you back the diamonds,' he said. 'Our sexual relationship is outside of that bargain.'

'We have no sexual relationship,' she said firmly.

'Yet,' he repeated with a smile. 'It's only a matter of time, Catriona.'

'Not everything is that predictable.'

'This is.'

She drew in a shallow breath. 'And if I refuse to organise the house?'

'No necklace.'

'But it's not yours. It wasn't part of the house sale and you know it.'

'As you said yourself, possession is nine-tenths of the law. I have it, Catriona.' He patted his pocket. 'I'll tell the world about your attempt to break in and steal from me. That initially I covered for you last night to spare your mortification, but that in the end you had to be charged.'

'Wouldn't that bring the "sideshow" you're so keen to avoid?' she asked, delighting in pointing out his own contradiction.

He shrugged. 'I would prefer to avoid that, but I've been through worse. I'm not the villain in this—*you're* the crazy woman.'

She was. She'd be labelled the desperate woman who'd faked a fiancé to save face. Humiliation sucked. This was a way of escaping with some pride intact. And it wasn't all beneficence on his part; she knew what he wanted and frankly she was amazed—and stupidly flattered. She wasn't anything like the beautiful, curvy models he dated.

The sound of a phone ringing startled her. Even more so when she realised it was *her* phone ringing.

Alejandro took her phone from his other pocket and tossed it to her, his gaze alert and speculative. 'You'd better answer this time. He keeps ringing.'

She glanced at the screen. Teddy. He'd be having conniptions.

'Kitty? You're still in his house?' her brother said as soon as she answered.

So Alejandro had spoken to Teddy. No wonder he knew about the diamonds and everything else. Her brother couldn't keep a secret if he tried.

'How did he catch you?' Teddy's astonishment rang down the phone the second she answered. 'You got in and out so many times over the years and *never* got caught.'

Mainly because no one had cared enough to notice if she was missing. 'Well, I did this time.' The guy had to have eyes like a hawk. There'd been so many people present, she never should have been spotted.

'Well, there's the most preposterous story going around. My phone's been ringing flat-out. Everyone thinks you've been seeing him in secret all this time. They're saying you're *engaged*.'

'Oh, hell...' She covered her face with her hand. She'd made the most colossal fool of herself.

She peeked through her fingers and saw Alejandro had sat back more comfortably in his chair and was smiling, as if enjoying her mortification. She realised then that he was waiting for her to decide. That maybe he didn't actually care that much either way.

'So it's not true?'

She heard the disappointment in her brother's voice. And the anxious edge. She didn't want Teddy to worry or try to come charging in here and sorting it out and making it all even more embarrassing. Maybe this situation could be resolved best if the details were kept between her and the devil in front of her. Between *only* them. She'd suffer this mortification in front of Alejandro alone.

'They're saying he stepped in to save Dad's cash flow because he's been in love with you all this time,' Teddy said.

She laughed a little hysterically. 'Oh, Teddy, it's not quite that simple.'

'But you *are* his fiancée?'

She hesitated, glancing up to meet Alejandro's penetrating gaze for a long moment.

'Kitty…' Teddy's voice lowered. 'Are you okay? When I phoned last night he was very short with me.'

'Everything's fine, Teddy.' She tore her gaze from Alejandro's, straightened her shoulders and made herself smile. 'They're more than fine. But things are a little…complicated—'

'I didn't think you even knew him. Last night you were—' He broke off almost as soon as he'd interrupted. 'Shit, is that why you were in such a hurry to get there?'

'Look, I'll come and see you in a couple of days, okay? I'll explain it then. But for now I am staying here.'

'*With* him?' Teddy's excitement barrelled down the phone. 'You're really staying with him?'

'Yes.'

It took almost a full minute after ending the call with Teddy before she could lift her chin and look Alejandro in the face again. She was just waiting for him to gloat with some smart comment. But when she did look at him, she found he was watching her with just the smallest of smiles. It wasn't even a smug one.

'At least here you can have a bed,' he offered blandly.

'My own bed?'

'Of course, until you ask to share mine.'

'Not going to happen.'

He laughed then. 'You're too constricted by your own naivety,' he jeered. 'Believing in some fairy tale version of romance and being in a relationship "happily-ever-after".'

'You don't believe in relationships?' Why wasn't she surprised?

'Not lasting ones.' His smile flashed.

'So not marriage.'

'Definitely not. I will never marry.'

'That's sad,' she said glibly.

'What's sad is the vast number of people who stay in unhappy marriages because they think they have to.' He shrugged carelessly. 'I like indulging—in nice food, pleasant company, good sex. Then a gentle goodbye. What's wrong with that?' He breathed it with utter confidence and arrogance.

'Nothing.' She couldn't fault him for what seemed to be the perfect life. For him. Because she didn't think the goodbye Saskia had got had been all that gentle.

'I work hard. I achieve. I get what I deserve.'

'I hope you do,' she said pointedly.

He didn't look remotely abashed. 'The women I tend to date have worked every bit as hard as I have to achieve their successes.'

'With plastic surgery and liberal use of the casting couch,' she muttered.

'You judge your sisters so harshly?'

She wrinkled her nose, hating that he was right and she'd been bitchy.

'I treat all my lovers with respect and courtesy,' he said meaningfully. 'A little kindness goes a long way.'

'But you have no desire to be faithful?'

His eyes widened. 'I sleep with one woman at a time. I don't date another until I have ensured anyone else I had been seeing is clear that we are no longer an item.'

As he'd done with poor Saskia.

'Is that what you'll do with me if we have an affair? Just flick me a text before jumping into bed with another woman?'

Her cheeks heated. James hadn't done even that. He'd cheated on her.

'We will formally end our engagement. There will be no miscommunication or misunderstanding.'

'And now you think I should just fall into bed with you?'

'I think if you were honest about what you want, that's exactly what you'd do.' He watched her closely. 'There's nothing wrong with lust, Catriona.'

Maybe there wasn't, but she wasn't ready for it. And not for him. 'Okay, here's some honesty for you,' she said, trying to take control of the situation and clarify her intentions. 'You're an attractive man and you know it. But we don't share the same desires. I don't want that kind of empty pleasure. I want something more meaningful and complicated. So I'll do the house. I'll stay until this stupid story blows over. But that's all. And when that's done, then I go.'

He was not winning. He was not getting everything his own way. She'd be his first failure.

'You think you can resist this chemistry?' He grinned, hugely amused. 'Are you one of those women who has to believe she's in love before she'll have sex with a man?'

'Not love necessarily. But something a little warmer than loathing.'

He laughed and stood. 'I will not muddy this affair with false declarations or meaningless promises. When you want me, just let me know.'

'I'll send you a telegram.' She blew him a kiss. 'Now, go to work, darling, so I can steal from you while your back is turned.'

Alejandro knew he could have her far sooner than she pretended. Knew that it would take only a few kisses and she'd be heavy-eyed and restless in his arms, as she'd been for those too brief moments last night. But now he wanted more than that from her. Now he'd seen her defiant rise to his challenge, the determined denial sparking in her eyes. That spirit and courage showed she wasn't so much broken as bruised. He'd help her forget the stupid ex-fiancé.

But he wanted her to hit the ignition on their affair. To be unable to deny this chemistry without his provocation. He didn't know why. Usually he wasn't that bothered— either he took a lover or he didn't. It was straightforward. But Catriona presented a challenge that he couldn't resist engaging with. Maybe some old-fashioned seduction was required, until the electricity was too high a voltage to be ignored and she came to him.

He'd worked like a demon this morning to arrange everything. He'd sent his assistant to stay in a hotel for the week. He'd be at work most of the time, but when he was here he didn't want anyone interrupting him and Catriona. It struck him that things might get fiery at any moment. He was looking forward to that. And, with her unconventional beauty, she fitted in this house. The fact she could help with excavating all the residual stuff that was seemingly cemented inside it was pure bonus.

'I'm happy to have you as my fiancée for the foreseeable future,' he said, pleased with the outcome.

It was the perfect solution. He got someone to sort the house and he'd get to sleep with the most vexingly sexy woman he'd encountered in a while.

'I'm not staying here for long.' She suddenly looked uneasy.

Was she attempting to back out of the deal already? Because she knew she wasn't going to win?

He smothered his smile. 'Why not? The house is big; there's a lot of rubbish to get rid of.'

'It's not rubbish—' Indignation flared in her eyes.

'Well, you'd better do it then—else I'll just dump the lot,' he interrupted dismissively.

She narrowed her gaze at him. 'As if you'd be that reckless with an investment.'

'No, you're the reckless one. I'm on damage control. One month.'

Her mouth opened. Then shut. Then opened again. 'You're not going to get *everything* you want.' She sent him another speaking look. 'No more parties.'

'Pardon?'

'While I'm here as your fiancée there'll be no parties.'

Was she trying to dictate terms to him, to renegotiate when she had zero bargaining power? He stifled another laugh. 'I thought you Bohemian types liked parties.'

'Your definition of a party is very different to mine.'

'How so?' He spread his hands in bewilderment. 'I like parties.'

'You like being surrounded by women who pander to your ego.'

He clamped down another smile. She really didn't want other women around, did she? 'No parties at home,' he conceded, happy to be alone with her for what little time he'd have in the house. 'But we dine out. We dance.'

He liked the ambience of a busy restaurant.

'No dancing.'

'Why not?' He folded his arms, amused by her determined rejection of what he had to offer. 'Don't tell me you can't.'

'Of course I can't,' she declared in total irritation. 'I have no interest in it.'

'I'll teach you,' he said, unbothered. 'Next item?'

'No...' She hesitated. 'No...'

Yes, this was where she really was most vulnerable. 'You don't need to worry.' Hadn't he just told her he only dated one woman at a time?

'I'm not having two fiancés leave me for another woman,' she blurted it out anyway. 'I'm not going through that again. Not even pretend.'

So she had been hurt by the ex-fiancé.

'Fine. You'll break my heart. Unable to get over my rampantly lusty past even though I'll have been nothing but true to you.' He offered the solution softly, watching her closely.

'As if anyone would believe you had.' She rolled her eyes. 'You'll have plenty of women offering to soothe your hurts.'

She was painfully insecure, and breathtakingly insulting, but he didn't blame her. She'd been hurt. 'And you'll have your pride restored.'

A slightly stunned look crossed her face. 'It's not pride.'

'What is it then?'

She shook her head, that expression shutting down. 'You wouldn't understand. You don't seem to have the same kinds of emotions as I do.'

Her words were barbed, and they hit a spot he hadn't realised was exposed. He had emotions all right. It was just that he worked hard to control them. He *had* to. Suddenly raw, he turned and walked towards the door. 'I have to get to work. Be ready for dinner at seven.'

'I don't have any decent clothes with me,' she called after him sulkily.

Drawing in a calming breath, he turned back to face her. 'So buy some more.'

'In case you hadn't noticed, my family has hit the skids. You want to be ashamed by your fiancée when you take her out looking like a bag lady?'

He knew she was deliberately putting obstacles in his way to be as annoying as possible. Too bad, he wasn't going to be bothered. 'You don't look like a bag lady. I like the catsuit thing.' He smiled patronisingly at her. 'But feel free to go out and buy whatever you want for tonight. My treat.'

Her gaze narrowed on his mouth. Awareness arrowed to his groin. He'd known she'd loathe the offer of his money and that her temper would flare. His smile deepened to genuine pleasure in anticipation of her bite.

But she didn't give him a verbal lashing. If anything, she sounded as sultry as a siren. 'What's my budget?'

Only then did she lift her lashes and reveal the fury in her green eyes.

'Will a hundred thousand do to start?' he suggested roughly, unable to resist absorbing her dare and raising the stakes.

She didn't bat an eyelid at that.

He strolled back over to where she still sat on the sofa, enjoying himself immensely. 'We'll have to get you an engagement ring too.' He picked up her hand and studied her long, delicate fingers. 'Just to really set the whole thing off.'

'That's not necessary,' she clipped, tilting her chin so she could keep burning holes in him with her fiery gaze. 'I'm not wearing a ring.'

So she did have a few scruples. Or maybe she was superstitious.

'You've worn one before.' And he felt a twinge of guilt about pointing that out to her so bluntly.

She tried to pull her hand from his but he gripped it harder.

'And it brought me nothing but trouble,' she muttered.

'Poor Catriona.' He couldn't hold back a second longer. He tugged her hand, drawing her into a standing position, and reached out with his other hand to run his fingers down the length of her beautiful hair. 'Go indulge in some retail therapy,' he suggested with a mercilessly condescending tease. 'Spend hard.'

She sent him another foul look. 'You know I could walk out with all this money of yours and skip the country, never to return.'

'You're too polite to do that. And you know that if you did, I would hunt you down.' His gut clenched at the words. It was only a joke; he didn't mean it. Not truly.

'I'm not afraid of you.'

But he was close enough to have felt her shiver and fought his own primal response to pull her closer and keep her. He wasn't going down that possessive route, not when he knew how destructive it could be. How terrifying. He'd rein this in and get it back to nothing more than a seductive, light tease. 'No, but you're afraid of what I can offer.'

'What do you think that you can offer me that I would be afraid of?'

'The kind of passion you think you can't cope with,' he taunted, leaning that last inch into her space.

'Oh, please.' She rolled her eyes, but he'd seen the rise of that pink under her cheeks.

He put his hands on her slender waist. Satisfaction burst within him, desire for more slammed in on its heels. 'I won't deny I want you in my bed, little Cat,' he muttered, his words tumbling, rough and unstoppable now. 'I'm looking forward to hearing you—'

She suddenly stunned him by clamping her hand over his mouth. 'You think I haven't heard those kinds of sleazy lines before? You want to "pet me until I purr"?' She pushed her hand, forcing him to turn his head away for a second. 'If you really want me, you need to try harder.'

Harder? His laugh was harsh as he pulled her flush against him, pressing his lips on hers. For a spilt-second it was pure passion, lip-to-lip, breast-to-chest, hip-to-hip and straining...but then he made himself go gently again.

Slow. Slow right down.

He'd have his control back, thanks. And he'd surprise her into that deliciously unguarded reaction she'd given him last night.

He softened, pressing small kisses on her plump pouting mouth until she opened it with the smallest of sighs. She tasted like fruit and pastry, a little tart, a lot sweet. And hot. So damn hot and vital. She might be slender, but she was strong. He slid his hand up her back, pressing her closer, needing to feel her where he was aching most. Her hands skated up his chest, curling around his shoulders as she arched her back and her neck, pressing her breasts more firmly against him, letting him deepen the kiss even more. And, heaven knew, he did. Slowly and thoroughly, he explored her mouth, caressing her with his tongue because he couldn't get enough of her taste. He widened his stance so he could gather her closer, aching to absorb all her passion. Gentle was all but forgotten. She felt so good pressed up against him.

And, as she kissed him back, his control started to slip again. He wanted more. He wanted it now.

When she breathed so quickly? When she moaned? When her lips were soft and submissive and hungrily seeking, all at the same time? When her hips circled against his in that way that maddened him to the point of *grinding*?

He teetered on the brink of tumbling her to the sofa, tearing clothing and taking her in a frenzy of unfettered, uncontrolled lust—

He pulled back quickly, resisting the urge. It hurt. His breathing sounded loud in his ears.

But so did hers. To his relief—and pleasure—she still felt warm and soft in his arms. Willing. Ready. So close to *his*. Oh, yes, she wanted him too.

Well, she was going to get what they both wanted. When she was ready. When she asked. And when he was in control. He'd keep it light. Always.

Lit up with amusement and arousal and burning-hot satisfaction, he eyed her lazily. 'I don't think I need to try that hard at all.'

CHAPTER FIVE

'SEXUAL ATTRACTION IS easy enough to ignore,' Kitty argued breathlessly, basically hauling herself upright to stop herself leaning on him.

The man packed a serious sexual punch and she'd succumbed again *so* easily. How on earth did she think she could simply ignore the effect he had on her?

'But why would you want to?' He looked mystified.

She pushed out of his arms and walked away from him, needing the space to clear her head. But goodness, her legs felt wobbly. 'You really are bored, aren't you?'

This was just so easy to him—as natural as breathing. But her heart ached for that something *more*. Surely there had to be more?

'And you really are suffering from a lack of self-esteem.'

She shook her head. 'Don't try to flatter me.'

'I'm being honest. Come on.' He flicked his fingers at her. 'Get ready. I've got to go to work and now we have an errand to run first.'

She stiffened. He was used to calling the shots, wasn't he? 'Then fetch my bag from the communal garden, will you?'

'You stashed your bag in the garden?' He sent her an astounded look, ignoring her attempt at a commanding tone to match his. 'You really are a cat burglar.'

'Bet you can't find it.' She smiled at him coyly.

He sent her another look—a lowering one. 'I know what you're doing.' But he left the room anyway.

Amused, Kitty crossed the library, opened the window and leaned out of it to watch him. He glanced back up to the building, somehow knowing she'd do exactly that. She could feel the heat of his glare across the distance, but then he turned his back on her to study the garden for a few minutes and unerringly went to the bush where she'd hidden the bag.

At that point Kitty flounced away from the window.

A few moments later he returned, triumphantly brandishing her bag. 'You don't have much with you.'

'Because I wasn't planning on staying long.' She snatched it from him and stalked from the room.

'You won't need much anyway...' His sensual laughter followed her down the hall.

Kitty locked the bathroom door and showered quickly, briskly soaping herself and ignoring her hyper-sensitised skin and still trembling legs. She was *crazy* to have accepted this arrangement when he could make her want him so easily.

But chemistry *could* be ignored. And a week or so spent here was a chance to say goodbye to her home. A chance to keep her head high the next time she saw those society wenches. And a chance to prove Alejandro wrong— he wasn't going to get everything he wanted. He wasn't going to get her.

As long as she kept her distance from him. No more touching. No more kissing.

She'd been truly hurt by the end of her engagement to James, but she doubted that Alejandro could ever understand the concept. He was total Teflon. Indestructible and impervious to any pain—of feeling any deep emotion, for that matter. As far as she could tell, life was all a party to him. It was all about the next affair while wheeling and dealing the rest of the time. Well, he wasn't having an affair with her, no matter how good he kissed. She refused to be yet another easy conquest.

When she emerged refreshed she found he'd showered again too and changed into a suit. It was navy with a crisp white shirt but he wore no tie with it and his hair was damp; he looked so sharp her eyes hurt. Her resolve wavered. Did she really think she could resist? That unholy smile lurked in his eyes as he watched her walk towards him and she straightened. Of course she could resist. She wasn't an *animal*.

A car was idling for them just outside the house, an enormous, luxurious thing with a suit-and-sunglasses-clad giant sitting behind the steering wheel.

'You might get away with this kind of ostentatiousness in New York, but it's really not the done thing in London, you know,' she offered faux helpfully once they were ensconced in the back seat. 'Better to take a taxi next time.'

'I prefer to rely on my own driver, but thanks for the advice anyway,' he replied blandly.

The car stopped outside a beautiful old building and Alejandro insisted she went inside with him. Only the subtly placed logo near the heavy wooden door clued her in— this wasn't the kind of bank that had tellers behind security grilles and queues of impatient people. This was exclusivity and discretion to the max. The private banker didn't bat an eyelid when Alejandro insisted he issue Kitty a card then and there, preloaded with his wads of cash.

'Show off,' Kitty murmured as they returned to the waiting car less than twenty minutes later.

Alejandro smiled, but she sensed his attention was flicking from her; his expression had become serious and distant—he was entering 'work mode'. A few minutes later the car pulled in again.

'Paolo and the car are at your disposal all day. Get yourself whatever you need,' he said as he looked out of the window at his new office premises. 'Be there when I get home.'

'Or?'

At her tone he turned back to face her and she realised

she'd been wrong about his slipping attention. In this moment, she was the sole object of his searing focus. Her toes curled in her shoes; she was almost melting on the spot.

'Until tonight, sweet fiancée.' He didn't bother replying to her question; he knew he didn't need to.

For a breathless second she wondered if he might take his part too far and kiss her again. But she'd be ready for him this time, right? She'd resist the temptation to slide into his sensuality.

But he didn't lean closer, he didn't kiss her. He just got out of the car.

And that *wasn't* a kernel of disappointment she was feeling. Alejandro waved her off with such a smug, knowing look in his eye that Kitty didn't wave back. The infuriating creature seemed to know everything she was thinking.

'Where would you like to go, Miss Parkes-Wilson?' Paolo asked politely.

Right now? The moon.

'Could you just drive for a bit while I decide?' She pressed a hand to her hot cheeks.

She needed to come up with a decent plan for the next few days—Alejandro was too confident, but she didn't blame him, only herself. She needed something to combat his intensity.

She'd had no intention of spending a penny of his money when she'd made such a drama about her clothes, but now she felt like making him pay in some small way for his intolerable arrogance.

Maybe she should buy the most outrageous couture item she could find? Maybe she should go for something totally off the wall and appalling that she'd never normally be seen dead in. Amused at the thought, she asked Paolo to take her to the flagship store of a high end designer. But, once she was inside, she was almost immediately distracted by a simple black number hanging on a polished rack right near the door. She moved to take a closer look, inwardly grimacing when she saw there was no price tag.

'Would you like to try it on, madam?' A soft-spoken, impossibly groomed man stepped forward to offer assistance.

'Um…maybe?' she mumbled doubtfully, feeling like a fraud.

She was so used to her 'work wardrobe' of black on black—three-quarter-length trousers and long-sleeved sweaters—she was going to feel weird in anything else. She might have long limbs, but there was so much else required to carry off clothing like this.

One summer in her mid-teen years she'd been scouted by a modelling agency. Not to model swimwear, of course, given her pallor and lack of curves, but high-end fashion. At the time she'd been pleased to get the attention and for a few blissful days had actually believed someone thought she was pretty. But then she'd seen the completed booking sheet with her name on it:

Freak chic. Angular, androgynous, tall with red hair, pale skin. Freckles.

She'd filled out a bit since then, but there was no denying she was still the 'freak' and there was no 'chic' about it. After that dose of reality she'd covered up and come up with her own year-in-year-out version of starving artist attire.

'I believe it would suit you, madam.'

He was clearly paid to say that, but she let him lead her to the changing room anyway.

She straightened her shoulders and followed his example of confident posture. She'd never be considered conventionally pretty, but maybe she could wear the damn designer dresses anyway. A dress like this would be like armour, hiding the weaknesses—the imperfections—underneath. Protecting her. She was *so* tempted.

'I need some statement pieces,' she confided to the attendant as he waited at the entrance to the spacious private room. 'Some dresses that scream exclusive.'

'If I may suggest, nothing screams exclusive more than subtlety,' he replied with a quiet courtesy that had her believing him. 'You go ahead and try this on and I'll be back with more in a moment.'

Kitty quickly stripped and then stepped into the dress, blinking as she regarded her reflection in the gleaming mirror. The dress was beautifully cut and sat perfectly on her waist, but it didn't reveal vast quantities of skin. Maybe the man was right about subtlety?

'Madam—?'

She opened the door and saw the saviour of a salesman had returned with an armload of other options for her to try. But now he paused and studied her with a critical eye.

'Yes.' He nodded as she stood in front of the mirror and she felt as if he actually meant it. 'Our dresses never date,' he informed her confidently. 'And they never lose their value.'

Didn't they? She could well believe that, given they were beautifully tailored and had that sleek sort of design that was recognised the world over. And if they didn't lose their value, then perhaps, as soon as these few weeks were over, she could auction any dresses she bought and then give the proceeds to charity?

That would *definitely* work. She'd be making Alejandro pay, but for her own benefit—not ultimately. And if she did that, then she could spend every last penny of his ridiculous 'budget' just to serve him right. She turned to the assistant, inspired and more enthusiastic about shopping than she'd ever been in her life. 'Then let's see what else you have.'

Somehow four hours flew past. After the dress purchases, she succumbed to the temptation of some lacy lingerie. Sure, she couldn't exactly auction those pieces, but the dresses needed the right level of support and discretion—

no visible panty lines or bra straps. It wasn't as if there was any chance of Alejandro seeing her in the lacy smalls...

And then there were shoes—but she chose only a couple of pairs to see her through.

Lastly she ducked into a beauty parlour and spent a little of her own money on a spot of personal grooming. Again, if she was going to look the part, she needed to feel it.

Six and a half hours later she got Paolo to return her to Parkes House, guiltily figuring she'd better get on with her actual 'job'. To be honest, she didn't quite know where to begin. There were so very many boxes, frankly she wouldn't blame Alejandro at all if he decided to just send the lot to the rubbish dump. But she had to start somewhere—and she had to get it *done*.

'You've been busy,' Alejandro called as he stopped by the door of the box-filled room two hours later.

Kitty glared at him from where she stood drowning in boxes, overwhelmed by the enormity of all the stuff she had to process. She'd made the mistake of opening too many too soon.

Alejandro's mouth twitched, as if he was suppressing a laugh at her expense. 'Did you have fun shopping?'

'Oh, yes, I spent all your money,' she lied, turning on a brilliant, totally fake smile.

'Well done.' He nodded approvingly. 'I bet that took some doing.'

She sighed and examined her fingernails in mock boredom. 'Not really—a handful of dresses, a few pairs of shoes...' she shrugged '...and poof, all the money was gone.'

'Wonderful. You can leave the receipts on the desk in the library for me.' He leaned against the doorjamb and frowned at her black trousers. 'Yet you're not ready to go out?'

'We're going out?' She glanced at the mass of boxes

blocking her escape from the room. Her nerves prickled. She was going to have to wear one of those dresses now. She was going to have to live up to the pretence. And she was going to have to look at him across the table… He was too handsome. Too assured. Too damn knowing.

She'd be better off buried in the boxes here.

'Are you not hungry?' Alejandro was feeling extremely hungry and not just for food. She looked beautiful standing there glaring back at him with a raft of emotions flickering across her striking features. 'I believe it's a good restaurant.'

And they needed to get there soon, before he threw all caution to the wind and tried to seduce her here and now.

'Don't you ever just eat at home?' Her glare became less defensive and more curious.

'Why would I?' He didn't enjoy cooking for himself. Usually he went straight to a restaurant from the office. 'I enjoy socialising with lots of people.'

'Oh.' She nodded and seemed to think about it for a moment. 'So you're aware of how boring your own company is.'

He was stunned into silence briefly, but then laughed grudgingly. 'You witch.'

Her smile of acknowledgement lit up her whole face and made him want to step nearer and feel the warmth of it on his skin. But at the same time he felt compelled to get a dig in.

'So you stay home and cook something gourmet for yourself every night?' he challenged her.

Her smile actually deepened. 'I cook instant noodles every night.'

He grimaced and didn't bother commenting.

'I add fresh vegetables,' she added piously.

'As if that makes it any better.'

'I'm a starving artist,' she said loftily. 'What did you expect me to eat?'

'Well, tonight you can eat like a queen. If you'll only hurry up and get ready,' he groaned.

'Okay, darling, I won't be long.'

He watched her navigate the cardboard obstacles with an impressively swift glide, and walk past him and out of the room with a small toss of her head. Shaking his own, he walked down to the library, pulling his phone from his pocket to check on any mail that might have arrived in the thirty minutes since he'd left the office. He might as well do some more work while he waited. But, to his surprise, it was less than fifteen minutes before she cleared her throat.

He looked up to the doorway and promptly forgot his own name, let alone what it was he'd been writing. 'You can spend every last cent of mine if you're going to end up looking like that.'

Her death stare felled him.

'I'm sensing a colour theme.' He noted the black. Again. He'd not seen her in anything else so far. Black clothes that clung, but covered up almost all of her pale, pale skin. *His* skin tightened. He was looking forward to finally getting a proper glimpse of her.

'I'm grieving the loss of my freedom,' she drawled. 'Hence the mourning outfits.'

He laughed appreciatively. 'It's so hard for you, isn't it? Losing the family home.'

'The long goodbye to the family fine china,' she mused. 'It is a burden.'

'Poor baby, the silver spoon's been snatched from you.'

He wasn't going to make it to the damn restaurant if she kept looking at him like that. He was used to dating very beautiful, perfectly proportioned women, but he'd found none as attractive as he found Catriona right now, with her angular defiance and glittering eyes and her chin jutting in the air. He laughed, more to expend some of the energy coiling inside him than from genuine amusement.

In some ways, his reaction to her wasn't funny at all. He'd been so looking forward to seeing what she had in store for him that he'd actually left work a fraction early because he couldn't wait any longer to find out. It was the first time he'd ever done that for a woman. He'd wanted to check she was still there. Catriona Parkes-Wilson wasn't quite as predictable as all that. But, given he'd instructed Paolo to keep his eye on her, he knew she hadn't left the house again since returning from the epic shopping spree. He also knew exactly how much she'd spent and had to admit it had surprised him. But nothing about Catriona was quite as it seemed and he was interested to see how she was going to play this out.

'Shall we go?'

'Where are we going?' she asked.

He named a new restaurant that—according to his PA—had a waiting list of months.

'There'll be celebrities there.' She frowned and glanced down at her dress.

'Are you going to ask for their autographs?'

A giggle burbled out of her.

'You look amazing,' he assured her briefly. 'We need to leave. Now.'

Now or never. Fortunately, Paolo was waiting with the engine running.

'You can't drive yourself anywhere?' she asked pointedly as he held the door for her.

'Why would I when I can hold hands with you in the back seat instead?' he answered, sliding in after her.

He picked up her hand and felt her curl it into a fist. His sensual awareness was stronger now he knew how good she felt pressed against him. Hell, he wanted that again. Now. The energy between them crackled in the air in the confined space. It took all his willpower not to pull her right into his arms and kiss her into saying yes. Instead, he made himself stay a safe distance away. He could stay in control of this. He would always stay in control.

'Sorry we're late,' he said smoothly as he led her to the two vacant seats his colleagues had left in the middle of the large table at the rear of the restaurant. 'I hope you've gone ahead and ordered.'

Catriona's hand tightened on his. 'You promised no parties,' she whispered as she sat in the seat next to him.

'This isn't a party. This is dinner.' He released her to hold her chair out for her.

'It's a dinner party,' she whispered, pausing. 'There are like...' she glanced around the table '...*fifteen* people here.'

Wasn't that the point of dinner? To socialise? He liked being around people, but she didn't seem comfortable. He took a closer look at her face. 'You okay?'

'I'll just fake it till I make it,' she muttered as she glanced again at everyone at the table before sitting down.

He wasn't even sure he was supposed to hear that little quip, but the honesty underlying it smote him. A small surge of protectiveness made him reach out to clasp her hand in his again as they sat side by side. Did she honestly doubt how stunning she was? Was she really intimidated by these others present?

Or was it that she'd wanted to dine alone with him tonight? His pulse struck an irregular beat. He couldn't remember when he'd last dined alone with a woman. Always he had extras with him—work colleagues and acquaintances, or another couple of women, friends of his latest lover. He liked being surrounded by busy, happy people. That was normal, right? And there was safety in numbers.

Too much time alone with a lover might lead to complications he didn't want.

All he really wanted from the women he dated was physical release and fulfilment—the delights of mutual pleasure. If he took a woman home, he encouraged her to leave after they'd had sex. Generally he'd drive her home, then would drive alone for a while, enjoying the late night and the city, the relaxed state of his body. Or if his lover was fast asleep in his bed—as some of them pretended to be—he went into his study and worked through till dawn. When a woman woke up and realised he wasn't there, she soon got the message. Even when he dated a woman for a few weeks, he wanted his own room at the end of each night. He needed his intimate space to himself. Always. And—other than amusement—he needed his emotions minimally engaged.

'Order something to eat—you'll feel better.' He opted to tease Catriona into sparking back at him. Humour was always good.

'I'm starting to think you must be an emotional eater.'

He laughed. 'No, I just recognise "hangry" when I see it. You didn't stop for lunch—you must be starving.'

'And you know this because?'

'Paolo reported in to me.'

'Oh, so my every move is being documented and reported back to you?'

'Naturally. My fiancée's welfare is very much my concern.'

She glowered at the menu and he bit back his smile.

'Something wrong?' He waited, knowing she'd find something. She was never going to make this easy for him.

'I'm vegetarian.' Her glance at him now was positively sugary. 'So this whole French *foie gras* and raw steak thing isn't working for me.'

Of course she was. 'Another whim of yours?'

She lowered the menu and turned to correct him. 'I've been vegetarian since I was seven.'

'You just made that choice one day?'

'Pretty much.'

'Your parents agreed?'

'Of course not. So I went on hunger strike until they did.'

He grinned, imagining the stubbornness of a red-headed wilful child. 'How long did that take?'

'Just over a week.'

'That long?' He'd have given in to her much sooner. 'Why don't you wish to eat meat—for slimming or ethical reasons?'

She sent him a withering look. 'You really have to ask?'

'When you feel strongly about something, you go the whole way with it, don't you?'

'All or nothing.' She nodded blithely. 'Otherwise what's the point?'

'So when you're wrong, you're *really* wrong.'

'No,' she answered haughtily. 'I'm *rarely* wrong.'

'Oh? What about men?' He laughed, enjoying her cutglass perfection. 'Third time lucky, do you think?'

'Once I'm shot of you?' she muttered so the others couldn't hear. 'I'm checking in to a nunnery.'

'Oh, no,' he chided. 'That would never do. You'll always need a release for that passion.'

'That's what my art is for,' she said airily.

He laughed, genuinely amused. Catriona had far too much fire for any kind of life of denial.

'What's so funny, you two?' one of the women across the table called to him.

'Alejandro delights in teasing me,' Catriona answered before he could.

He was going to delight in teasing her. Very much.

He listened as she assumed the role of society fiancée. Most of the guests were over from the States like him, a couple of younger ones for the first time, and Catriona efficiently schooled them in the 'off the beaten track' tourist ideas, getting in a plug for her brother's upcoming play too, he noticed with a wry grin. And, for someone who was 'faking it', she was doing a good job. When the food arrived she quietened, tucking in to the specially ordered vegetarian dish with gusto. All or nothing indeed.

'What are you thinking about?' he asked her gently when he saw the curve of a smile on her mouth.

Her eyebrows shot up. 'Seriously?'

'Yes.' He wanted to know everything that was going on in that head of hers.

'I was thinking how delicious that was.'

'So, despite the initial disappointment of the menu, we've managed to please you?'

'Mm hmmm.' She sat back with a satisfied smile and looked at him.

Her eyes sparkled in the light; her skin was so pale it was almost luminescent. She had such striking colouring and, whether she intended it or not, there was challenge in those emerald eyes. Challenge he could no longer resist.

He pushed his chair back and stood. 'Come with me; there's something you need to see.'

'We're leaving now?' She looked startled and glanced back at the other dinner guests.

'Only for a moment. This way.' He threw a polite smile at the others but firmly took her hand and led her out the back and down the gleaming black corridor. At the very end he paused and turned to face her.

'Why are we here?' She still looked bemused. And beautiful.

'To admire this painting.' He waved a distracted hand at a large modernist painting that was conveniently hung on the wall. 'As an artist, I thought you'd appreciate it.'

'I'm not really that much of an artist. And not the painting kind.' She frowned at the canvas.

'Okay, I brought you here because I wanted to be alone with you.' He wasn't afraid to be honest. He knew she wanted him too. And he wanted her to look at him again, not the stupid painting.

She faced him, that frown replaced by a laughing smile, but it still wasn't enough.

'I thought you liked dinner parties with billions of people,' she teased.

'Shh.' He'd hardly touched her all day and he couldn't resist now. He wanted to taste that smile, to press against the pretty pout of her full lips. He wanted to feel her softness and lithe strength, he wanted to claim her body with his own and see her buck and then break under the pleasure he could push her to—

Her eyes widened as she looked up at him. 'Alejandro—'

He caught her lips with his, groaning as he felt her part for him immediately. Caution and control faded. He tugged her closer, pressing her body against the hard ache of his, wrapping his arms around her waist so he could explore her shape. He couldn't get close enough. He tried to keep it gentle, but the kiss deepened. So did his frustration. He wanted to be alone with her. Warm. Naked. He wanted all the time in the world to explore her—to taste every inch and every secret part of her. But he had to make do with just her mouth. It was good. Too good. And it wasn't enough.

Kitty lost track of time and space and sanity. Never had she been kissed like this. Never had she felt as if she was so close to soaring—so high, so quick. There was only Alejandro, only this warmth, only this surging sense of delight. And need. She wanted to burrow closer, she wanted him to touch her more…there…everywhere. His kisses drugged and ignited desire. Never had she wanted a man like this. The way his tongue teased, the way he nipped the inside of her lip with his teeth, the soothing—then stirring—caress of his lips, the pleasure he promised with every stroke…

She writhed helplessly and recklessly against his firm hold, grinding her hips against his. Her wantonness shocked her. She didn't want this to stop. She didn't want this ever to stop. But—oh, God—that was why it had to. They couldn't. Not here. Not now.

She tore her lips from his, jerking her head back and reminding herself of where they were.

'Alejandro,' she pleaded breathlessly, pushing against his chest. 'There are people.'

They were making out in the restaurant corridor like teen lovers who couldn't go home to their parents' houses for privacy, and she felt out of control.

'We're engaged,' he lifted his head and pointed out with annoying reasonableness. 'Of course we're going to kiss. No one would ever believe I was engaged and not be touching my fiancée any time I could.'

She pushed back a strand of hair and sent him a baleful look, locking her knees to stop her legs from shaking. How could he remain so collected when he kissed like that? 'There's an occasional kiss, and then there's indecent behaviour. I only agreed to this so I *wouldn't* get arrested, remember?'

He looked amused. 'A few kisses aren't going to get you arrested. Or were you about to strip naked and have your way with me up against the wall?'

Oh, if he only knew. She jabbed her finger in his chest. 'Stop provoking me.'

'But it's the most fun I've had in years.' He pulled her close again and brushed another quick kiss on her lips. 'You respond so magnificently. Like lightning, you flare. You must be incandescent when you orgasm.'

A wave of heat almost turned her to cinders on the spot. 'Right now I'm incandescent with rage.' She wished the lighting in the corridor was dimmer so he couldn't see how violently he was making her blush. 'Stop talking like that.'

He bent his head and whispered in her ear, 'But it's turning you on.'

'Everyone is staring,' she hissed. Well, only the couple of people who'd ventured down the corridor, and they'd quickly gone again.

'I don't care.'

'Well, *I* do.' She pushed hard against his chest. If he kept kissing her like that she'd agree to anything he suggested and she refused to let him win so easily. 'It's past my bedtime.'

'You want to go home to bed?' He stepped back and looked wickedly at her.

'Alone,' she lied. 'Yes.'

'Then let's get you there.'

CHAPTER SIX

OFFICIALLY, PARKES HOUSE had eight bedrooms, all of them with private bathrooms. Half were on the second floor, the remainder on the third.

'Which room did you take?' Alejandro asked as they climbed the stairs. 'The one next to mine?'

'Of course not.' It had interested her to see that he'd claimed one of the smaller rooms as his, but maybe that was just because there was so much stuff shoved into all the others.

'So you know which is mine.' He grinned. 'Did you go in and take a good look at my things?'

'Naturally.' She battled her blush and tried to act as if she wasn't embarrassed. 'The more one knows about one's enemy, the better one is equipped to win the battle.'

'Enemy?' He laughed. 'Bit extreme, don't you think?' He took hold of her hand. 'Did you learn anything of use?'

She gently breathed out, trying to slow her pounding pulse. 'You're a show-off. As if you can read all those books at once.' The pile beside his bed had almost exclusively been non-fiction, on a wide and eclectic range of subjects.

'I like reading,' he said. 'You won't find the diamonds, by the way. I keep them with me at all times. They're too precious.' He looked at her curiously as they walked along the corridor of the third floor. 'So which room?'

Her heart still thudded too quickly. She had no idea how she was going to resist him. 'My own.'

His eyes glinted. 'And it's not one of these?' They'd passed all the doors now.

She shook her head.

'Show me.'

'Fine.' She led him to the stairwell again and went first.

'You were up in the attic? Servants' quarters?'

'Don't go thinking I was some kind of Cinderella,' she said gruffly. 'In some ways I was very spoilt.'

'Tell me something I don't know,' he drawled.

She glanced at him but he was smiling. At the top she went a few paces along the much narrower corridor, opened the door, flicked on the light switch and then stood back to let him go in first.

'Oh...' He muttered something under his breath.

'What?' She peeked around the doorway, stopping when she saw he'd halted only a few steps into the room.

He turned to face her. 'It's so light.'

She glanced at the white walls, white furnishings and the myriad small windows that gave the most glorious views to the skies. She couldn't help smiling because he was right—the light was what made this room. Even at night, it had a brilliant quality. She couldn't believe he'd not seen it before.

'Have you not been up here at all?' She was amazed as he shook his head. 'You bought this house and everything in it without even taking a proper look?'

'I liked the location, the convenience to work and the outlook.' He shrugged. 'Anything else I want I can add or rebuild later.'

Didn't he see what was special about the place—its history, its quirks, its sense of *home*?

'I liked the view up here. The light and the space.' She tried to explain it to him as she walked past him. The angles of the ceiling were random because of the roofline. When she'd turned thirteen she'd had the room enlarged to become both her bedroom and her first sculpture studio. Her father hadn't minded paying for the renovation and it had kept her occupied and away from the parade of women he was bringing home. She'd been unable to compete with those beauties who'd turned his attention from his children. She'd spent hours alone up here.

Alejandro was staring grimly at the narrow single bed in the corner with its plain white coverings. Then he turned those penetrating eyes on her. 'Did you sneak boys up here to share this bed?'

'Of course not. What kind of a question is that?' She stuck her hands on her hips and shook her head at him. 'You have such a one-track mind.'

He laughed at her reaction and her heart started its crazy trip-along pace again. 'Oh, come on, all those times using that secret hidden key of yours?' He folded his arms and leaned against the wall, looking utterly roguish.

'Absolutely not.'

Sneaking a lover in was totally the sort of thing *he'd* have done. No doubt he'd been sowing his wild oats since he was a youth.

'I was a good girl,' she added when he kept staring at her with those dangerous eyes.

'You amaze me,' he said dryly. 'Then why the need to sneak in and out if it wasn't to go wild?'

'I was exploring the art scene.' And pushing boundaries to get her father's attention. It hadn't worked.

'So you were the young muse for the Bohemian set?' He waggled his brows at her.

'Actually, my first boyfriend was three months *younger* than me. He was another art student when I was at *university*.'

'Was it sublime?'

Of course it wasn't. She turned her back on his low laughter.

'Poor Catriona. And then there was the dastardly fiancé.'

She hated that he guessed her lack of experience so easily. 'It's not that easy for everyone, you know,' she muttered grimly.

It was a disappointment. She would have liked to have been one of those free spirits who flitted from romance to romance and emerged unscathed, but it wasn't to be. She was nothing like Alejandro. And she didn't want to be with someone who she knew would let her down. Sure, she had his attention now—for whatever reason—but soon enough that attention would turn to someone else and she'd be left in the cold again.

His hands on her shoulders pulled, turning her to face him. 'I'd make it sublime.'

His smile was bewitching, but it was something in his eyes that really had her spellbound.

'You're full of promises,' she muttered gruffly, trying to settle her skipping pulse.

'Ah, so you want proof.'

She didn't know what she wanted any more. But she knew this moment had been building since they'd first set eyes on each other. It was normal for him but so outside her realm of experience she didn't know how to handle it.

'Do you always get what you want?' she asked, genuinely curious.

'When I've decided I want something, I stop at nothing until I have it,' he said, equally honest. Equally serious. 'So, yes, I do.'

'And right now you want me?'

He nodded.

'And you'll stop at nothing?'

He didn't answer. A smile, slow and amused, spread over his face. He tugged her that little bit closer and bent his head to kiss her. And she didn't say no. She didn't step back. She just let him. She stood there and let him pull her into his hot embrace.

And she liked it.

She moaned as he moved her that bit closer, his kiss claiming her. Soft kisses again, teasing ones, tender and tormenting. She pressed closer, seeking more. His hand swept down her back, resting on her hip. It was no longer enough. None of this was enough.

Her legs were shaking. She couldn't stand it any more. Literally couldn't stand.

But she didn't need to say anything. His arms had already tightened about her and somehow the bed was now at the back of her legs. With a smooth movement he eased her onto the narrow little mattress and then came down on top of her. She gasped, trembling at the sensation of finally having him there, so close to her.

He muttered something but she didn't catch it because he'd resumed stroking, trailing those torturously slow fingertips across her waist and up to cup her breast. Her body ached. She longed to burst free of her clothes, even her skin. She was *so* hot. He looked into her eyes for a wordless moment. Passion had darkened his eyes even more and she just drowned in them. His skin was slightly flushed. She didn't think she'd ever seen him look as gorgeous—or as dangerous. Every cell within her tightened in anticipation.

He smiled and she was lost. His hand framed her face, fingers tangling in her hair, and he kept her still so he could savour her lips, plundering her mouth with his tongue. Teasing, touching, until the yearning inside could no longer be contained. Then it wasn't as teasing, wasn't as gentle. Hunger sharpened.

He couldn't seem to get enough of kissing her. Which was good, because she couldn't get enough of kissing him. She arched, aching to get nearer, wanting him everywhere, in every way. Her legs splayed, allowing him the space to press closer, more intimately against her. She groaned as his hard length pressed against her, right there. So good. Uncontrollably she rocked, rubbing against him, trying to ease the need, skating closer and closer to an arousal that could have only one end. Her bra was too tight, her breasts were too full, her nipples too taut. Finally, finally, bless-edly, he moved, kissing down the length of her neck until his hot mouth hit the high line of her dress.

She clenched on her muscles and cried out as need spiked within her as he pressed his open mouth against her jutting nipple, through the fabric and all. He stiffened above her then swiftly returned to kiss her full on the mouth. Not ten-der at all now, but ravenous. She couldn't contain another moan of desire, couldn't stop the ragged, short breaths of desire escaping her lips.

'I want to see you,' he muttered savagely.

His hands dropped to her thighs, to the hem of her dress.

'I want to see every inch of you.'

Kitty opened her eyes, his passion-roughened words shocking her back to reality. The light hurt. It was so light in here. She didn't want to be seen by him in this unforgiv-ing brightness. She didn't want him to see all her imper-fections. In that split second she couldn't help comparing herself to all the other women he'd known—all those beau-tiful women. She gripped his hand, stopping him from lift-ing her dress any higher. There were very, very few people who'd seen her naked. And it would never happen in this bright light. Not with him, not with anyone.

Her emotions spiralled out of control as she realised where she was and what she was doing and with whom and *what was she thinking?* This behaviour was so unlike her. Never had she wanted a man the way she wanted him. It shocked her. It almost scared her.

She froze.

He raised his head and looked down at her, his gaze both astute and tense, his smile rueful. 'You're not ready to let me in, Catriona?'

Dazed, she looked up into his face from where she lay half beneath him. For a fatalistic moment she thought she would *never* be ready to cope with him.

His smile deepened—a little strained, a little tender. 'I think you need to sleep on it.' He levered off the bed.

'You're…leaving?' Even though he was no longer pinning her, she couldn't move, she was stunned. And suddenly desolate.

'Perhaps I have more patience than you give me credit for.' He braced his arms either side of her, leaning over her again only to press a quick, light kiss on her lips. 'I will never do anything you don't absolutely want me to. Let's be very clear on that.'

He straightened and walked away from her before she could think what to say. Kitty sat up, watching him as he left the room. She was hot and cold and confused and part of her was relieved but the other part was nothing short of devastated. As soon as he'd closed the door behind him, she slumped back onto the bed—suddenly sorry that he'd been so restrained. She could have had an experience unlike any other if she'd not been so self-conscious. So insecure. So stupid.

If he'd kissed her for just a few minutes more she'd have been so het-up she'd have agreed to anything. But he wasn't going to let it happen that way. He was too sensitive to her moods. He wanted her commitment to their affair to be made beforehand—not in the heat of the moment. It turned out he was too damn chivalrous to make it easy for her.

She rolled onto her stomach and buried her face in her pillow in a swelter of confusion and desire and contradiction. It was only lust, right? She could get a grip on herself—it shouldn't be that difficult. But the thing was, she did want him and he knew it. He was just going to make her say it so there was no doubt.

Could she take the little he offered? Was it even that little? She'd never had that kind of an affair. Never had the kind of pleasure he'd already made her feel in just those few touches. Maybe she *could* handle it. And maybe, once it was done, it would be over. The desire would die because this driving need would have been filled. All she had to do was swallow her pride and say yes to him.

But she couldn't bring herself to do that either. She didn't want this to be that easy for him. She didn't want to be just another of his notches.

Basically? She was screwed.

She gave up on sleep and rose super early the next morning and grumpily trooped downstairs to the kitchen to find some fruit to freshen her up. But she encountered Alejandro on the second floor landing in shorts and a thin tee, looking hot and sweaty and, when he caught sight of her, grumpy. He'd clearly been out for a run or something. So that was how he did it.

'How I do what?' he asked.

She choked—had she uttered that thought aloud? She must have; he was gazing at her expectantly. But he still wasn't smiling.

Awkwardly, she tried to explain. 'Eat all that rich food but stay so…'

'What?' he prompted when she broke off.

'Fit,' she mumbled.

He didn't smile. If anything, his expression grew even grimmer. 'Is that what you wear to bed?' He gestured at her white pyjamas. 'You wear black during the day and white at night. That's very you.'

They stared at each other across the landing and for a moment neither moved.

'Please be ready to go out when I get home tonight,' he said gruffly. 'Unlike some, I work a long day and when I'm done, I'm hungry.'

Her spine stiffened. 'Certainly, darling. I won't make you wait a second longer than necessary.'

Her gaze clashed with his.

'God,' he muttered hoarsely, 'I hope not.'

* * *

Alejandro threw himself into work, determined to put Catriona out of his mind for the day and concentrate on everything else. But thoughts of her eroded his focus. He'd never met a woman like her—intriguing, contrary. Annoying. She made him laugh. And the feeling of her strong yet soft body arching to meet his? The sound of her breathy moans as her desire escalated?

He puffed out a long-held breath and turned away from his computer in disgust. He was getting nowhere. He fished in his pocket, then laid the diamond choker across the desk. He wanted to see her wearing it again. He wanted to see her wearing the diamonds and nothing else. But that was what had shut her down last night—when he'd said he wanted to see her, she'd stiffened in his arms. She had an insecurity there that he was going to have to sweep clear somehow.

He deliberately worked late because he wanted to prove to himself that he could stay away from her. That he was still in control of himself emotionally and physically. This was nothing, this was easy, this was still *safe*. But when he finally headed home, his pulse started pounding. It was all he could do not to bolt up the stairs and haul her into his arms.

He didn't bolt. He just walked. Still in control.

But his pulse sprinted.

He found her in one of the box-filled upstairs bedrooms. She was in black again—long-sleeved top, slimline trousers and thin black sneakers on her feet. Her hair hung loose down her back, as glorious as ever. His blood fizzed. Just seeing her was a pleasure, but her mouth was downturned as she bent over another enormous cardboard box. She had a clipboard beside her, ready to itemise everything she extracted.

He glanced about the room. He had little sentimentality, but maybe the loss of these things truly made her sad.

'What are these?' He nudged the box she'd been looking into.

'Oh.' She glanced up, startled, and coloured slightly. 'They're the Christmas and birthday presents I gave my father every year since I was about eight. My earliest sculptures. He obviously didn't feel the need to keep them.'

She shrugged.

Alejandro knew there were issues with her father. He'd found him to be somewhat unreliable in his business practice—the amount left behind in the house had been totally downplayed, for one thing, and it seemed Catriona and her father were not close. But Alejandro knew some fathers were worse than others. His father was the worst of all.

Distracting himself, he lifted some of the pottery pieces out. Some had not stood the test of time. Or at least hadn't been kept in a safe place. There were chipped bits and a couple of broken vase tips at the bottom of the box. But a couple—especially one vase and a sculpture that looked like a lion—were very delicate and showed the development of skill. 'Some are—'

'Terrible, I know.' She interrupted him with a brittle laugh. 'I was just a kid. He didn't think I should study art; apparently I needed to get a real job. You know, the kind that earns money. Because that was what mattered most to Dad. The guy who'd married into an old wealthy family and managed to *lose* all the money...' She trailed off and glanced at Alejandro with a wistful smile. 'Your parents must be very proud of you.'

It felt as if a boulder had been lodged in his chest. For a second he gaped before collecting himself. She didn't know about his parents then. She didn't know...

He halted his thoughts. He didn't feel inclined to tell her. He never discussed it and ensured conversation never became personal enough for a woman to ask. Several business colleagues knew, but also knew never to mention it.

He turned away from the box. 'Are you ready for dinner?' he asked bluntly.

'Time sneaked away from me.' Kitty bit her lip, surprised to see icy reserve sweep over him. 'I only need five minutes if we're going out again?'

He'd totally stiffened up, no longer the suave conversationalist and tease.

'Of course.'

She sent him a cautious smile and left the room, quickly moving to change her clothes. Why had he frozen up when she'd referenced his family? It was unlike him to reveal so much; usually he teased to deflect a conversation. A million more questions followed—where did that slight exotic edge to his accent come from? Why was he so driven when he'd had so much success so young? He fascinated her and she wanted to know everything about him.

But at dinner she found that goal impossible to reach. The guests chatted animatedly about topical issues but no one pressed her for any detail about her relationship with Alejandro, no one asked how they'd met or when they'd become engaged. Which was polite. But no one asked him anything intrusive or illuminating either, which was disappointing. They sought his opinion on something to do with work, or debated politics and current affairs. It was all intelligent and interesting, but the only other thing she learned about him was that he was well read, had encyclopaedic general knowledge and would be an extremely useful addition on a pub quiz team.

And as the evening progressed she realised he didn't actually talk that much at all. He smiled and gave a thoughtful insight into something that was business-related or added an occasional witty comment, but, for the most part, his contributions were limited. He seemed happy just to be at the centre of the noise and chatter. Her curiosity deepened.

But she knew she wasn't the only curious one at the

table. The woman sitting opposite her had been avidly watching Alejandro, conversing with him loudly, unsubtle in trying to get his attention. Now she turned to Kitty— her curiosity unveiled as she raked her gaze over her, her eyes narrowing on Kitty's hand.

'Still no ring?' The woman's smile gleamed as she leaned across and spoke in an undertone. 'There's a smidge of hope for the rest of us then.'

The last thing Kitty wanted was to compete for Alejandro—not in any way.

'You're welcome to have him,' she replied directly, but with a smile. 'I keep trying to shake him off, but he's persistent.'

There was a moment of stunned silence around the table. Kitty swallowed; she hadn't realised she'd spoken *that* loudly.

'After Catriona's hurt over her previous engagement, she's decided an engagement ring is bad luck,' Alejandro said with urbane ease. 'I have agreed to surprise her on our wedding day when our vows are taken.' He placed his hand over hers and gave it a squeeze. 'She finds it difficult to trust, but I'm working on it.'

Kitty stared at him, unable to think of a thing to say to that. He met her eyes for a moment, and she saw the humour dancing in his, but there was something else too. Something she couldn't define and couldn't cope with. She turned and caught a stabbing glance at her from the other woman, but she was too floored by Alejandro to bother responding. Her body felt engulfed in flames. She was so embarrassed, but also somehow grateful. It was crazy. She was crazy. And so was he.

'You're a more outrageous liar than I am,' she whispered in his ear in the most provocative way she could manage once normal conversation had resumed, determined to take control of this mad roller coaster ride again. 'That was pretty good. But you know, I've changed my mind. I want a rock. Monstrous huge, please. The gaudiest thing you can drop a few hundred thousand on.'

She sat back and beamed at him.

He cupped her face and inexorably drew her close again so he could whisper in return, 'It's too late; the offer is rescinded. I like my story better about the bad luck engagement ring. It has an air of truth about it.'

He was so near she was lost in the depth of his black-brown eyes. Her heart raced. He was horrendously handsome. She scrambled to stay sane—to stay on top of what was just a game.

'You're heartless. Utterly heartless.'

He laughed delightedly; his warm breath stirred her hair. For a moment it was as if they were in their own bubble of amusement and heat.

'I have no need for a heart,' he muttered.

That hit like a cold wind. Could anyone really be that carefree? She pulled back, wary of the other diners watching them less than surreptitiously. With an effort she maintained her smile and reached for a glass of water.

'Lead me along as far as you dare, Catriona,' he added quietly so only she heard. 'I'll keep step. You won't scare me off.'

'I thought you were out to stop me from saying outrageous things.'

'I've decided I like them. The only person they really cause trouble for is you.'

And wasn't that the truth.

'I am chastened,' she admitted honestly. 'That's it—no more from me.'

He laughed, full bodied and sexy. 'Never. You're too impulsive for that vow to last long.'

The truth was she was trying as hard as she could to hold him off. Because this sparring—this foreplay—was fun. But once she'd given in to him—and to her own de-sire—it would be over. It was all in the thrill of the chase for him. He'd be off on the next hunt once he'd captured this prey. So, back at Parkes House, she didn't let him climb the stairs with her.

'No. No. No. No.' She scampered ahead of him and held up her hands like a metaphorical wall. 'You stay down there.'

He looked up at her, pausing with one foot on the first step. His mouth quirked. 'Not even a kiss goodnight?'

'No. Nothing. Not a thing.'

He leaned back against the railing and his smile broad-ened to positively smug. 'Finding it so hard to resist you can't even risk one kiss?' Amusement danced in his eyes. 'Not long now then.'

His arrogant laughter followed her. He was appalling.

And that was the thing, wasn't it? This wasn't ever going to be for long.

CHAPTER SEVEN

'I'M READY.' KITTY looked up as Alejandro walked in from a frustrating day.

His mouth dried. She was sitting on the sofa in the library with her ankles demurely crossed, clad in another slinky black dress that clung to her curves and suggested total sensuality while keeping her too damn covered up.

Was she ready for him?

He'd let her get away without so much as a kiss yesterday but now he'd had enough. This was the longest amount of time he'd ever invested in a seduction and seeing her sitting there so coolly perfect was the last straw. Hadn't she spent the day thinking of him? Wasn't she being eaten from the inside out by coiling desire the way he was?

'Alejandro?' Her eyes widened as she watched him stalk towards her.

He didn't reply as he pulled her up from the sofa and into his arms. This was what he needed. Her close in his arms, her mouth parting under his, her body softening.

He kissed her the way he'd been fantasising about all day. Long and deep and hungry. His arms tightened as he felt her lean into him. Desire raced as she kissed him back, her energy rising to meet his in a snap. Oh, yes. Ready. So ready.

He lifted his head to look into her eyes for the consent he so badly needed. But she pushed him back breathlessly.

'Stop it,' she panted. 'You're messing up my hair. It took hours to get it this smooth, you know.'

'And it looks lovely.' He reached for her again. He needed to do more than look—he needed to touch. Now. 'Come back here.'

'No—' she stepped further away '—I didn't do it for you.'

'No?' He smirked.

'Of course not!' She rolled her eyes. 'It's for all those wannabe lovers of yours. The troupe of women hanging on your every word. I have to show my cred to them.'

Alejandro paused, dropping his hand. That was ridiculous. She had nothing to prove. 'They think you're my fiancée.'

'Like that matters to them!' She faced him. 'Or to you.' She shook her head. 'If one took your fancy, you'd be gone in a flash.'

He frowned, his irritation building. The last thing he felt like doing was leaving her. And suddenly the last thing he felt like was sharing her with a bunch of other people around the dinner table either. He wanted all her attention on *him*. As his was on her.

'Can you even remember all their names?' she asked.

He stared at her, mystified.

'All your ex-lovers,' she explained grumpily.

It was his turn to roll his eyes. 'Can they remember mine? What does it matter?' They were irrelevant to this. 'What's wrong with living in the moment?'

'It's just so…meaningless.'

And? He really didn't see why she wanted complication, for things to be involved. 'Must you be so deep all the damn time? Must there be meaning in everything?'

'Not everything all of the time. But sometimes. Yes.'

'Work hard, play hard. That's the life I enjoy.' And he didn't see why his past should impact on his affair with her now. He didn't understand why she railed against what they could share in bed together. 'I already told you—I will never marry. I will never have children.'

She hesitated, her fire dropping a fraction. 'You don't like them?'

'It is not something that interests me.' He turned away from her pretty eyes.

'Oh, that's a shame. Who's going to inherit all your billions, then?'

He laughed, relieved to hear her tart tone. She was back to her best with him. 'I'm going to give it away to charity.'

'Nice.' She nodded. 'Just the one charity or are you going to share it around, the way you do your sex skills?'

Ouch. He rubbed his chest with the heel of his hand. 'You're not going to try to convince me to have children? Tell me I'd make a great father?'

'If you don't want them, you don't want them. Who am I to try to convince you otherwise?'

'You want children?' Oddly, his chest felt heavier now. The thought of Catriona cradling a small child made it hard to breathe.

'Possibly.' A wary expression flitted over her features. 'But I'd have to find a decent guy first. In my experience, they're thin on the ground.'

He chuckled, trying to recover his equilibrium. 'Poor princess. You've gone from—how do they say—from the frying pan to the fire.'

'You said it,' she agreed dramatically. 'I escaped the claws of a cad only to fall into the jaws of a shark.'

From one heartbreaking engagement to one fake one. The fake one was more fun, though.

'You'll survive,' he said soothingly. 'You might even have fun.'

Silently, she met his gaze. Her eyes sparkled. She was having fun now and they both knew it.

She drew in a breath and lifted her chin that fraction higher. 'So how many other people are going to be at dinner tonight? Will there be any other men for me to flirt with or will it just be women to fawn over you and stroke your ego?'

Yes, the game was on again. Tension coiled in his muscles at the thought of dinner; he didn't want any distractions now.

'It'll just be the two of us,' he muttered, making that decision then and there. They needed time alone together to get this sorted between them.

'Not the usual entourage?' She turned limpid eyes on him. 'Are you sure you can cope with the depth of conversation that might be required?'

'I think I can keep up with you.'

'So where are we going?' she asked softly.

He didn't know. He quickly texted his assistant to let him know that he and Catriona were not going to be joining the others for dinner then challenged the beautiful woman still standing too far away from him. 'You're the local; you lead the way.'

She skimmed a sharp gaze over his Armani suit and then looked down at her couture dress. 'I'm not familiar with all those super exclusive restaurants you seem to like.'

He shrugged. 'There'll be something nearby.'

He didn't want it to be too far from his bed. As far as he was concerned, tonight she was going to be his.

They ended up in a small Thai takeaway joint. She leaned against the Formica counter, laughing as she ordered a selection for them both.

'You like it spicy?' She sent him a coy look.

'I can't believe you even have to ask.'

'I don't like it too hot,' she said primly.

'I don't believe you.' He flicked her chin. 'I see through you.'

She turned so she faced the other way to see out of the window and watch the passers-by. 'Maybe I see through you too.'

Did she, now? He leaned closer. 'What do you think you see?'

'Someone who sells himself short.'

His eyebrows shot up. Uh, no, he didn't. He knew what he was good at.

'You have much more to offer than good-looks, money-making brains and superb sex skills.'

Both sassy and serious, she stole his breath.

'Oh?' He didn't want to ask. Didn't want it to matter. But suddenly her opinion had value. 'What else do I offer?'

'Humour.' She reached for the carrier bags from the waiter and then glanced at him. 'And you're kind.'

He stilled on his way out of the tiny restaurant. 'You've clearly mistaken me for someone else.'

'Oh, you can have your cruel moments.' She bit her lip ruefully and led him out onto the pavement. 'But you can't hide your underlying tendency towards kindness. You didn't drop me in it in front of all those people at your party. You're letting me sort my family's stuff even though a professional would be much faster, but you know it matters to me.'

He cleared his throat. 'I think you'll find that *kindness* isn't my motivation.'

Her eyes glinted but she shook her head. 'You're fundamentally okay,' she argued. 'I just don't think you realise it. You look after your staff, you go to great lengths to take care of your guests and you actually *do* give money to charity.' She turned and walked snappily along the path. 'Now, we could sit in the garden if you like. As long as you can handle eating with plastic cutlery?'

'I guess,' he muttered dryly, following a pace behind. But the number of times in his youth when he'd eaten with no cutlery… Hell, the number of meals he'd missed because there was no money even to buy bread. She might think she could manage on a bit of a budget now, but she had no idea of his reality. And she had no real idea of him.

Kind? He didn't feel in the least kind regarding her.

He sprawled back on the lawn, recovering from her direct assessment of him, his appetite lost. But he enjoyed watching her, listening to her chattering about her day, about the city, about anything, prompting her with a question when she fell silent. He needed her to distract him from the desire tightening his muscles.

The warm dusk slowly turned into a cool evening. The last of the sunlight made strands of her hair spark. Her vitality glowed. All he wanted to do was reach out and capture it—capture *her*. Yeah, not kind.

'It was good?' he asked as she helped herself to the last spoonful of his curry.

'Mm hmmm,' she mumbled as she finished the mouthful.

'So you do like it hot,' he muttered triumphantly.

She smiled at him and he was felled.

'Let's go home.' The words spilled out. But the second they left his mouth his innards chilled.

Since when did he think of Parkes House as his *home*? Let alone think of *her* as being part of that? And this desire to capture her and hold her close? He froze as his heart slammed his chest. He tried to block the fear trickling in. Catriona was just another woman he was seducing. That was all.

Just another lover who he could take. Or leave.

CHAPTER EIGHT

KITTY WORKED QUICKLY and efficiently, categorising items before re-boxing them neatly, mortified her father had left such a mess for a total stranger to deal with. Much ought to be taken to the rubbish or recycling centre and the sooner the better because she was totally over the blow-hot, blow-cold enigma that was Alejandro Martinez.

He'd fallen silent on the short walk home last night and then vanished to his room without a word—no goodnight call, let alone goodnight kiss. He'd gone to work without speaking to her this morning as well. Which was *fine* and she was *not* disappointed and she should *not* have spent all day trying to work him out. Except he consumed her thoughts. Why did he sometimes seem so unhappy despite all his success? There were moments when she thought an expression of pure pain crossed his face—it had flashed out of the blue when they'd walked home last night. He'd utterly iced up. She didn't understand why—they hadn't been talking anything personal.

She sighed and taped down another box. The mystery of his life was no business of hers; she just needed to get a grip on her own reaction to him. She was not up for a roller coaster ride of his engineering.

The slam of the front door echoed all the way up to the room where she was working. She glanced at the clock. It was only four in the afternoon, way too early for him to have finished work already.

'How's it going?' he asked as he appeared in the library doorway the merest moment later, all tense angles in a navy suit, no tie and no smile.

'I hate my father for letting it get to this state,' she admitted honestly, trying not to stare at him, but failing.

Alejandro's edgy expression softened. 'Another day nearer to your precious necklace. You suffer so for your diamonds.'

'Why are you back so early?' She watched him hovering just inside the room. 'Shouldn't you be running your empire?'

'It's running successfully without me for a few hours.' He looked into the nearest box and poked through the contents. 'It's a test for the new employees.'

'Really?'

He looked back to her. 'No,' he said bluntly.

The atmosphere thickened. Her heart thudded too quickly for comfort. She was too acutely aware of that raw look in his eyes that she didn't understand. He looked as if he hadn't slept well.

Don't get curious. Don't think you're starting to care.

She tried to warn herself—her mother had fallen for a suave, charming swine and so had she in James. She didn't need to make that mistake again. She didn't need him coming home all intense and brooding and pulling her close only to then push away without a minute's notice. But an impulse was rising—she wanted to see his smile again. She wanted him to tease again.

Alejandro's gaze dropped and he sombrely studied the contents of the box nearest him.

'I was thinking you're right,' he said slowly.

Kitty's jaw dropped but before she could speak he flashed the quickest of grins.

'That I should understand more about this house,' he added, walking away from her, the smile gone again. 'And I might as well do that while you're here to explain it to me.'

She was wary of the intense energy emanating from

him. Of this seemingly random request. What did he *really* want?

'Where did you want to start?' she asked as he restlessly prowled round the room, picking up small items and replacing them haphazardly and seeming to avoid looking at her directly.

He fiddled with a small wooden figurine on the table. 'Show me your favourite things.'

She kept watching him steadily but he still didn't meet her gaze.

'I don't have favourite things as much as I have favourite places,' she said.

'Such as the library?'

She wrinkled her nose. 'I used to wait for my father here and it was always a disappointment. That's why Teddy left notes for me in the hidden compartment in the bookcase—to cheer me up.'

He'd left notes because most of the time Teddy was out, supposedly at sports coaching when in fact he was at the local drama club.

'So then it's your bedroom?' Alejandro guessed.

'That came later,' she corrected him. 'My favourite place of all is the secret room.'

He spun towards her, his eyebrows high. 'There's a secret room?'

She laughed, pleased at the flash of interest in his face. 'I know—it's pretty cool.'

'It wasn't on the plans.'

'If it was, it wouldn't be secret!' She rolled her eyes. 'Come on—it's downstairs. It's not huge; it's about the size of a lift compartment.'

'And it exists because…?'

'Because it was an extension of the butler's pantry and its entrance got sealed and hidden because one of my ancestors was a scoundrel and needed to hide from the long arm of the law.'

He stared slack-jawed at her. 'Seriously?'

He laughed as she nodded.

'That sounds like one of your family. Good God!' He walked to the door. 'Show me.'

She overtook him on the stairs, unable to stop her small smile at the thought of sharing the house's secret with him. She'd always loved this little room. 'So, through the kitchen and then out to here.'

'Where every kitchen appliance known to man is stored,' he said dryly.

'That's right,' she acknowledged ruefully. Her father had indulged their old chef back in the day before the money had dried up.

She walked into a corner of the pantry and pushed the old subtle knob that formed part of the decorated skirting board. There was a clunking noise and a part of the wall swung, revealing a narrow gap.

'Oh, my—'

'I know.' She interrupted him. 'Hardly anyone knows it's here.' She squeezed in the gap, her own excitement at being back in the small room rising. 'It's really cute.' She glanced into the far corner where, as a girl, she'd set up a cosy hiding place. Slowly she turned, suddenly remembering. 'But, whatever you do, don't—'

She broke off as he shut the door behind him.

'Don't what?' he asked.

The darkness was complete.

'Oh,' he said, quick to realise. 'We'll have to feel for the door handle?'

'Actually, there's a slight design flaw,' she mumbled in embarrassment. 'No lighting. No interior door handle.'

'Why am I not surprised?' he sighed. 'Are we going to suffocate to death?'

'No, there's a vent.'

'Thank heavens for small mercies. Do I need to break the door open?'

'No, don't damage it,' she said quickly. That old mechanism was too historic and she'd hate its secret to be exposed. 'Can't you call one of your assistants to come and direct them how to open it?'

'I don't have my phone with me.'

Oh. 'I don't either,' she realised. She'd left it on the table upstairs. 'We're stuck.'

Heat flooded her at the realisation. She was locked in, alone and in the dark, with one very sexually magnetic man who was the walking definition of unpredictable.

'There's really no way of opening it from this side?' he asked, a thin vein of irritation in his voice.

'No.' She'd tried hard enough as a girl.

He was silent for a moment and she heard him stepping around, getting the feel for the space. 'Paolo should be here in an hour or so to drive us to dinner. He'll come in through the kitchen entrance; will we hear him arrive?'

'Yes.'

'And will he be able to hear us if we yell?'

'Yes.' She'd yelled when she was a child a few times.

'Then...' He paused. 'I guess we wait.'

For an hour or so. She leaned against the back wall and slid down into her old familiar corner, blocking her mind from sending her images of what they could do to pass the time. She was *not* going to be that easy for Alejandro.

'You know this is dangerous,' he said a bit roughly. 'How did you get out of here when you were a kid?'

She cleared her throat. 'I taped a ribbon over the edge so the door couldn't quite lock into place, but it was almost shut so no one knew I was here.' Or at least that's what she'd pretended. The chef had always known and had always checked on her. Neither of her parents had.

'What did you do in here all by yourself?'

'Drew. Dreamed.' She'd sat with her torch and sketched fanciful creatures—fairies goblins, elves. She smiled self-consciously at the memory—which was stupid, given he couldn't see her. But it was that kind of place for her—secret and a little bit magic.

'You couldn't do that upstairs?'

'When Mother was at home, my father stayed out very late.' Her smile faded. She'd sat in the library and waited for him. 'And when she was away he brought a lot of "guests" home. I preferred to stay out of their way when they were here.'

'Female guests?' Alejandro asked expressionlessly.

'Naturally.'

There was a brief pause. She heard him moving nearer, then felt him sit down next to her.

'Your mother travelled for work?'

She bit back a sad laugh. 'No, she'd go on retreats to "find herself".' She paused. Her mother would routinely just check out of marriage and motherhood. 'After the attic was renovated, I stopped coming down here.' She'd hardly had to come downstairs at all. She could avoid her father's affairs and absence in her own room.

'And what happened to your mother?' That roughness in his voice gave the question an edge.

'Eventually she didn't come back from one of her retreats. Last I heard, she's in Australia. I guess she finally found herself. She gave Dad everything in the divorce—gave up all her material possessions and never came back.' She'd given up her children too.

But Kitty had had the *house* and the things she'd made to decorate it. And she'd had Teddy, when he could bear to be home.

Alejandro didn't say anything in reply to her admission. There wasn't really anything to say and she was glad he didn't bother with platitudes. But of course he wouldn't; he didn't seem to let anything touch him too closely. Or at least that was the appearance he was so determined to convey. But surely there was more than he showed. She saw those quicksilver flashes of emotion. Of depth. How did she push beyond his teasing, suave exterior?

'So your time spent drawing and sculpting led you to study art,' he said, interrupting her thoughts.

'Collection curation in the end.' She hadn't had the true talent to be an artist. 'While you studied...'

'Law, economics, commerce.'

'Oh.' She shivered at the thought of it.

'Very useful degrees.' He nudged her and she heard his short laugh. 'More so than art.'

'It isn't all about making money,' she fired up.

'So speaks someone who has never struggled to make the money to keep a roof over her head, or enough to eat. Would you eat cake when there's no bread left?' he teased.

'I'm not as ignorant or out of touch as all that,' she muttered. 'I just don't see why it all has to be about how much money you can make. I make enough for *me,* whereas you're out to make as much as humanly possible. Self-made guys like you celebrate the downfall of the likes of my father.'

'Not at all.' Alejandro laughed. 'I would never celebrate anyone's failure.'

No, but he was single-minded about success and ruthless in achieving it. He wouldn't give up at a setback; he'd fight back until he'd won in the way he wanted.

'He worked hard, you know,' she tried to explain. 'He just made mistakes. Plenty of them.' She sighed. 'He was trying to groom Teddy to take over the family business but Ted hated it and was hopeless. They fought a lot.'

'And you hung out in the attic.'

Kitty shifted restlessly; somehow she'd ended up talking more about herself and still learned nothing much more about him.

'But you love your father, even though he let you down,' Alejandro said.

'He has his weaknesses,' she replied. 'We all do.'

'I don't.'

She laughed, pleased to hear that amused confidence in him again. 'Yes, you do. You're arrogant and stubborn.'

'What you call weakness, I call strength,' he countered, unabashed as always. 'Stubbornness is determination and it helps me succeed.'

'Bully for you,' she grumbled. 'There's no success that comes with impulsiveness.'

'You think not?' He laughed softly. 'You successfully bring fun. Laughter. The unpredictable.'

'Are you suggesting I'm unpredictable?' she asked archly. 'Coming from you, that's high praise.'

'Are you suggesting that I've finally charmed you?' he teased.

'Oh, no, I still see through you.' Except she couldn't see him at all; she could only hear the warmth in his tone. 'I know you only want one thing.'

Temptation whispered within her. She wanted it too. And she was tired of fighting her attraction to him. Here in the dark, no one would know. Here she could still learn something about him. She could learn the physical. She shivered again. She was too aware of his nearness, of the possibilities.

'It really is pitch-black, isn't it?' she muttered, trying to distract herself.

'Are you scared?' That thread of amusement sounded, warming her.

Honestly, she was always scared when he was around. Not of him but of her reaction to him. She felt him shift beside her. His arm pressed against hers, so did his leg.

'I used to be afraid of the dark,' she confessed distractedly.

'But you got over it?'

'Teddy locked me in here once, not long after we first discovered it. I was terrified. But after a while I got used to it and I refused to let him know how much it bothered me. Then I found it didn't bother me anyway and I didn't have to pretend any more. This became one of my favourite places to hang out.'

'You faked it till you made it?' His chuckle was soft.

'I guess.'

'I like the dark,' he said gently.

'Oh?' She half expected some comment about his liking the dark because he was usually in bed then, but there was a serious note in his voice. 'Why?'

'It's safe—you can't be seen.'

His answer surprised her to silence. What—or who—did he want to hide from? Why didn't he want to be seen? Was he scarred in some way? Her mind raced with questions. She was about to ask but then she heard him—it was almost a whisper.

'You can't be found.'

'You liked to hide?' She never would have guessed that.

He drew in a quick breath. 'Mmm...'

He didn't elaborate. Of course he didn't.

Why had he needed to feel safe?

She reached out, unable to resist any longer—offering the reassurance of touch. His stubble was rough beneath her fingertips. Who was she kidding—this was what *she* wanted. Here, in the dark, no one would know. She couldn't see. He couldn't see. It could be secret, and maybe a little bit magic.

'Catriona?'

'Shh.' She just wanted to explore.

'Do you know what you are doing?'

She smiled in the darkness and leaned closer to press her lips to his jaw. His muscle jerked beneath her lips.

He turned his head towards her and she felt his breath on her face. 'Don't start something that can't be stopped. Not unless you are very, very sure.'

She would never be sure of anything much. Except that right now she liked exploring what she could of him. She liked it here in the dark where she too could hide and neither of them could see. But she could feel.

His hand cupped her chin, he gently traced her lip with the tip of his finger, and she couldn't resist a quick slide of her tongue. His finger paused and she heard his swiftly indrawn breath.

'This isn't a good idea,' he said roughly.

But, before she could reply, he kissed her gently.

'Yes,' she whispered when he drew back.

'Yes, this isn't a good idea or yes this—?'

'Just yes.' She pressed forward blindly, seeking his mouth again.

And it was a good idea. It was a very, very good idea.

Her kiss wasn't gentle. She sank into it, relishing the freedom. Here, in the dark, she relinquished her hold on her desire. It burst free—heating the small space. She wanted to explore him. She ached to touch every part of him, to feel the slide of his skin against her own. She wanted—

He groaned and reached out quickly. Unerringly finding her waist, he lifted her onto his knee, capturing her completely.

'I think you like to take risks, Catriona,' he muttered harshly.

'Alejandro…'

He answered her plea wordlessly, his hot mouth crashing down on hers while his hands explored, lifting under her tee. She moaned as he unclasped her bra and her tight breasts sprang free. He palmed them for a moment and she wriggled on his lap, feeling his hard erection digging into her. Oh, yes, this was what she wanted. This was everything she wanted.

She lifted her arms as he tugged the fabric up, ridding her of both the tee and the dangling bra in the one movement. Then he swept his palms over her naked back, pushing her forward so he could kiss her bared skin, working his way across her body until he sucked her painfully tight nipple into his mouth. She cried out as heat flamed low in her belly.

'I want to taste more,' he said gruffly. 'I want everything.'

He moved, lifting her and placing her on her back beside him. It took nothing for him to slip off her shoes and run his hands up her legs to unsnap the fastening of her jeans and then slide them and her panties down and off.

She was naked now. And hot.

'I want to see you,' he groaned.

But he couldn't and she was pleased because here in the darkness she was free. His hands were warm, his mouth hot as he licked his way up the inside of her thigh. Her legs splayed and he took control, pushing them wider to make room for him between them. He kissed her core, holding her in the most carnally explicit position she'd ever been in in her life. She couldn't control the sobs of pleasure as his tongue caressed her, teasing her most sensitive nub with swirls and licks until she shivered uncontrollably. She was so close.

'*Please,*' she begged him. 'I want you.'

He broke free to brace above her, his body pressing against hers in agonising temptation. 'You had to do this now? When we have nothing here? No bed? No protection?' He swore furiously and at length. 'You madden me.'

'We can just…' She drew in a shuddering breath and writhed under him. She was so close. 'I want to touch you.'

He paused and it gave her enough time to reach up, feeling for the buttons of his shirt. She undid them, sliding her hand beneath the cotton to feel the damp, silken heat of his skin. She tracked her hand through the light dusting of coarse hair and briefly wished she could see him. He shrugged off the shirt completely and she lifted higher, so her tongue could follow the path of her fingertips. His skin was warm and a little salty and she wanted to taste more too.

But he slid his hand between them. She moaned as he parted her, exploring. He swore again. She trembled as he stroked her, drawing her tension out, making it impossible to bear. Because it wasn't enough. His fingers, his tongue weren't enough. She wanted *all* of him.

'I can't take it any more,' she muttered brokenly. *'Please.'*

'Please what?'

In the darkness, in the warmth, in the delirium only he seemed to be able to stir, it was safe to speak. Safe to say exactly what she wanted from him.

'Take me,' she whispered in absolute hedonistic abandonment. 'Take me hard.'

'Oh, hell, Catriona!' he ground out, frantically moving against her. 'I can't resist feeling you—I'll ensure—'

She heard the slide of his zip and melted. 'Yes. Oh, yes.'

'I'm clean...I've never had sex without protection in all my life.'

She was so eager she didn't care. 'Just do it,' she begged. 'I want to feel you.' Inside. Here. Now.

'Just for a moment.' He flexed his powerful body, controlled and slow, but she felt his muscles shaking.

'Yes.' Just this once.

She thought she was going to die if she didn't experience it all with him.

He paused. Then thrust. Hard.

'Alejandro.'

One word shot from his mouth in reply—crude and very much to the point. But she was too far gone, her body rigid and locked on his. She gasped harshly, clutching him closer, her legs parting that bit wider, wanting him closer, closer still, even as he filled her so completely.

'I cannot stop,' he rasped hoarsely. 'I can't...'

'*Yes*,' she cried, trembling and twisting beneath and about him as her orgasm ravaged her body. So, *so* ecstatic.

Suddenly he moved—hard, rough. Pulling back, only to thrust hard again. His hands tightened, holding her in place so he could drive deeper into her, pumping faster and faster.

'Oh, yes,' she gasped, her breath knocked from her. She rocked, meeting every fierce thrust, pushing their pace faster still, her hands greedy on him. It was carnal and hot and wet, and he was big and bossy and she was going to orgasm all over again. '*Oh, yes.*'

She didn't want him to stop. Not ever. Undone at last, they pounded together, frenetic and free. She was hurtling towards another orgasm, her last barely over. Her mouth parted as cries of delight tore from her. It was so good. *So* good. But at that ultimate moment he suddenly pulled out of her. She arched high but it was too late. He was gone.

His seed spurted over her stomach in hot, pulsing bursts as he braced above her, his agonised groan ripped from deep within.

She moaned too, a sound of torn satisfaction, of frustration. She'd wanted to ride through that tornado of bliss with him this time, but he'd wrenched out of her embrace.

'It wasn't supposed to happen like this.' He groaned again and cursed softly. She felt the absence as he lifted right away from her.

She lay still, shocked by how rapidly their passion had escalated into something so out of control. So reckless. So breathtakingly sensational.

'Like how?' Gingerly, she eased up into a sitting position, licking her dried lips as she felt the literal distance between them growing.

'Over so quick. Too quick.'

And it was over. She didn't trust her voice to answer. Her emotions were all over the place and she didn't want to sound tearful. It had been the most sublime experience of her life but all that exquisite joy she'd felt had been snatched away. Suddenly she felt vulnerable. It had happened. They'd had sex. He'd got what he wanted from her. And now it was over.

'Damn it, what time is it?' he muttered roughly. 'We need to get out of here.'

Kitty didn't want to get out of here. She wanted to curl in a ball and stay hidden for ever. She didn't want to look him in the face again. He'd made her feel things no one else ever had. Never had she enjoyed sex like that before. But it meant so little to him—how could it mean so little?

She realised there was suddenly a small light illuminating his face—in that slight glow he looked serious and distant.

Her body chilled as she realised what he was doing. He was tapping the fancy watch on his wrist. He was sending a damn *message*? Eventually he glanced in her direction and now there was a small smile on his face, as if he was pleased with himself.

Oh, she'd just bet he was.

'Did you just use your smart watch to send an email to get us out of here?' She glared at him even as the light went out and she knew he couldn't get the benefit of the full death stare she had on him. 'Only *now*?'

'Only now, because I just remembered that I had it,' he replied calmly. 'Until now, I was somewhat distracted.'

'But you could have sent a message sooner. Before...' She trailed off then cleared her throat determinedly. 'You could have sent a message when we were first stuck in here. But you didn't.'

'Catriona.'

She didn't answer him. She was too busy whipping herself into a fury.

'Catriona.'

Eventually he sighed and she heard his low laugh but she was not finding anything funny right now. She felt around on the floor for her clothes, not bothering with her bra or undies. She tried wriggling awkwardly into her jeans but they were all twisted and she couldn't figure them out in the stupid dark and she hated knowing that he could hear her struggling and was probably laughing inside at her expense. In the end she shoved on her tee and hoped it was the right way round, and who gave a damn about her shoes anyway.

'Alejandro?' a voice called.

Of course Paolo would arrive in less than ten freaking minutes.

'In here!' Alejandro banged on the door. 'The mechanism is down to your right.'

Alejandro had stood but Kitty remained curled on the floor as far in the corner as she could fit.

Light streamed in.

'Thank you,' he said to Paolo, who'd unlocked the door but hadn't stepped in. 'Please leave us now. Immediately.'

Alejandro moved out of the room, leaving the narrow doorway open. He didn't look back at her, but Kitty could see him—still clad in his suit trousers and shoes. But his shirt was off. He was tall and muscular and just that bare back on show made her shiver. She was glad when he disappeared from view, leaving the entranceway empty. But she heard him talking in a low tone, and his brief, infuriating laugh.

Then nothing.

'He's gone,' Alejandro called eventually when she didn't appear, his amusement still evident in his voice. 'You're safe to come out.'

The *last* thing she was, was safe.

But she stood, clutching the rest of her clothes protectively in front of her as she strode out, determined to pack her bags and leave the house this instant. Damn the diamonds, she'd get the lawyer onto it, as she should have right in the beginning.

She stomped past where Alejandro stood in the hallway, heading straight for the stairs. She didn't even glance at him.

'Catriona.'

She ignored that dangerous edge in Alejandro's voice. '*Catriona.*'

'I'm not talking to you.' She turned to face him, tried to ignore how devastatingly gorgeous he looked in just those low-slung, unbelted trousers and no damn shirt on. 'You took advantage of that situation. You manipulated it.'

'How did I do that, exactly?' he asked. 'I wasn't the one pleading. Stop acting like a teenager and creating drama where there is none. You wanted me. I wanted you. We still want each other. What does it matter when I sent the stupid message?'

Because she wouldn't have succumbed to him then and there. She could have held out. Because they hadn't needed to sit there in the darkness together and experience that sense of intimacy build. But it hadn't been real. Not to him.

'It doesn't make any difference, Catriona,' he said. 'Our having sex was as inevitable as the sun rising and you know it as well as I.' He ran his hand through his hair, leaving tufts upright and even more gorgeous. 'Don't try to tell me you regret it.'

Only now could she see those muscles and that delicious olive skin of his and appreciate him truly. He was like a god. And only now did she realise what he was holding in his hand.

'You got Paolo to bring you *condoms*?' she shrieked.

'It seemed like a practical solution.' He shrugged. 'I did not have any.'

She glared at him. He probably did that all the time— sent his assistants out for a coffee and cake and another two dozen condoms because he burned through them so quickly. He was a sex-driven devil. But, heaven help her, hadn't she just benefitted from all that wealth of experience?

'Have you *no* shame?' She turned and took to the stairs, furious with him. She heard his laugh behind her.

'You seem to have enough for the both of us.' He grabbed her arm, stopping her, and turned her to look at him. 'Truly, Catriona,' he said softly. 'There are far worse things to be shamed by.'

His words had that core ring of truth to them. But she didn't want to know the truth. She wanted… She didn't know what she wanted any more.

He waited three steps below her, his eyes just that little bit beneath hers. Beautiful, deep brown eyes. That half smile was so sexy. So assured. And so maddening.

Those hot moments in that small dark space had been the most erotic of her life. That was what she rebelled against. That a man she didn't want to like could bring her to her knees like that. So easily. So carelessly. How was she supposed to protect herself from him when he overwhelmed her so completely? How could she not get hurt in this?

'I don't want to want you like this,' she admitted with a raw edge to her voice. 'I'm leaving.'

His eyes narrowed. 'Do you really think you can walk away right now?'

'Why not?' She shrugged, dropping her gaze. 'We've finally had sex. It's over.'

'It is anything but over.'

'Once was enough.'

He laughed outright at that—but now there was little humour in the sound. 'Was it? Then why are you still fighting me? Why all this heated passion if it doesn't matter?'

'What matters is how you manipulated that to get what you wanted.'

'But it was what you wanted too. I'm not the villain here. I did what you asked me to.'

Heaven help her, she hadn't only asked. She'd begged. And she wanted to beg again.

He wasn't going to give her everything she wanted and needed. But did *that* really matter? She'd thought she'd found that with James and she couldn't have been more wrong. Maybe she did just need a release for once. Something easy and fun and meaningless. Something that wouldn't matter at all in the long run.

'I just hate letting you win,' she confessed.

And she wasn't that much of a prize anyway. Once he'd seen her—once he'd had her again...

'Don't you understand?' He climbed the two steps until he was right in front of her. 'We're both winning.'

'You really want to win this?' She swept off her tee, baring her entire body.

She'd never been as exposed to anyone. Never in the broad daylight like this.

His jaw dropped, his hungry gaze raked down her pale, freckled, angular body. 'Catriona.'

She didn't get the chance to reply or to run. She was in his arms and his kiss was utterly demanding. Utterly dominant.

And she surrendered totally. Her knees buckled and he lowered her exactly where she was, until she was prone on the staircase. He undid his trousers, kicking them off in a fury. That was when she completely forgot about how she looked. All her focus was on him—the expanse of golden skin and the play of powerful muscles just beneath the surface, the masculine whirls of hair on his chest that then arrowed down in a trail of delight to... She swallowed and her womb pulsed at the sight of him. He was physical perfection. She was hurled straight back into that maelstrom of passion and need and unquenched, unbridled lust.

'Please. Please. Please.' Not a plea, a command. She wanted to touch him. Taste. Feel. She was almost in tears with the need to have him.

He left her for a moment, muttering unintelligibly as he struggled to open the box of condoms and sheath himself.

But then he was back just a step below her butt, on his knees between her legs and grasping her hips firmly. He held her high, controlling her position so he could take her as completely, as dominantly as possible. And watch while he was at it—she was sprawled on the staircase before him, so exposed, and he devoured her with raw lust.

For a second he met her gaze; his eyes were dark and intense and so filled with desire. She panted breathlessly, spellbound. Never had she seen passion this raw. Never had she felt it in herself. The strength of it made her shake. Made her hungry. She was more aroused than she'd ever been in her life.

His gaze narrowed. He knew. He saw it in her, felt it in her. His face flushed. She saw his own control slip as his gaze burned down her bared body again—from her jutting breasts to her waist, to her slick, hungry sex.

'I just have to—' He held her firm and bucked his hips, impaling her to the core.

'*Yes.*'

'This time,' he groaned determinedly as he thrust deep inside her again. 'This time we can take our time.'

But there was no taking time for her. Not when he was grinding so hard against her and so deep inside her and all she could see was his powerful body pressing its passionate intent on hers. She was there already. Arched and taut as a bowstring.

'Alejandro!' The orgasm shattered her. She cried in unashamed ecstasy.

'Damn it, Kitty,' he growled as he held her hips more tightly and thrust harder, deeper, his eyes wide and wild as he stared down at her. 'You make me—'

He broke off as a guttural shout burst from him. His veins popped, his skin glistened as he strained, fighting the pleasure that had already consumed him. Because there was no taking time for him either. 'Kitty,' he choked.

She laughed with exultant delight as he thrust that one last time, striving for the ultimate satisfaction with her. She squeezed hard and tight, cresting again as he was ravaged. She rode the rigours rocking his body as his orgasm exploded, and she relished the lack of control he had in that moment.

Serenity and satisfaction flooded her cells as he slumped heavily over her. And then the cold trickle of reality came. She closed her eyes, needing to scrape together some sort of emotional defence. But she was shocked at the uncontrollable, furious chemistry they seemed to share. They'd just acted like wild animals, mating on the staircase in about twenty seconds flat.

Slowly he disengaged and rose to his knees, gazing down at where she still lay, sprawled down the stairs, naked and unable to move. His eyes glinted as he seemed to read her mind. 'You think we're done?' He shook his head as he bent and scooped her into his arms. 'We're very far from done.'

CHAPTER NINE

ALEJANDRO ROLLED ON to his back, appreciating the softness of the mattress beneath him as he pulled Kitty to rest on his shoulder. The bed was better than the hard floor but was too narrow for total comfort. He breathed out, satisfied. Finally he'd managed to have her the way he'd wanted to—taking his time, making her come again and then again before finally letting himself go.

He'd had to make it up to her because in all his life he'd never lost control as quickly as he had when he'd finally first entered her, locked in that little room. Her tight, writhing body had blown his mind, his orgasm impossible to delay. He groaned inwardly at the speed of it. It must have been the lack of condom—the first time in his life he'd taken such a risk. He knew it had been foolishness, but being with her had felt so good, his skin now goosebumped at the recollection. He still didn't know how he'd managed to pull out. It had nearly killed him at the time.

He couldn't take that risk again. He didn't think he'd have the strength to leave her like that a second time anyway.

But he'd had to have her again—especially when she'd started to build walls between them. That second time on the stairwell hadn't been much better, with his pleasure literally coming too soon. Even with a condom his control had not been brilliant. But *seeing* her body then, watching her response and the emotions flashing in her eyes? She was exquisite—her breasts high, her nipples dusky, her waist narrow and at that private heart of her there was a thatch of that fiery-coloured hair... And it turned out that the skin that had been silken and warm beneath his lips in the dark room was moon-pale and luminous, and gently dusted with rose-gold freckles—they covered her shoulders, arms, breasts, thighs…every part of her. He'd traced patterns of them with his tongue, desperate to taste every inch of her, *fascinated*.

She'd not liked being naked in the light. She'd not wanted to admit how much she'd wanted him again. Her anger had flared. But when it had burned off, pure desire remained. She'd become passion incarnate—as voracious and as victorious as he.

He'd carried her up to the shower, then had her again up here in her bed. Yet, even now, despite the residual ache in his muscles, he felt his hunger stirring.

She was stirring too—wriggling away from him. He turned to read her expression but she was studying the ceiling with grim determination.

'You can leave now,' she said quietly. 'It's a bit cramped in here.'

He froze. Was she ordering him from her bed? Seriously? Before he'd even had the chance to catch his breath and cool down? Not if he had anything to do with it. She was not calling time yet.

'It's not that small.' He inched down determinedly.

'I'm hot.'

His body stiffened in instinctive reaction to the dismissive challenge in her voice. 'Then we'll take off the coverings.' He kicked the blanket to the floor and pushed the sheet to her hips. 'You're sleeping naked anyway.'

And just like that he was ready again.

'I'm not planning on going anywhere,' he muttered, rolling to his side to lean over her. 'Except down on you.'

She was forced to look at him then. Her eyes were wide and dozens of emotions flickered through them. He kissed her before she could argue and worked his way down, down, down…

* * *

He woke early in the morning. He blinked at the light streaming in through the windows and saw the clear blue sky. He was cramped and achy all over. In the end he'd slept the night in her stupidly narrow bed. But he'd simply been unable to move—his muscles slammed by total exhaustion.

Now she was snuggled right into his side, her body soft and warm as it encroached on his. Her hair was like a mass of flames across his chest—soft and warming and with a faint fresh scent. He gently lifted a strand to see it glint in the light. His chest tightened and breathing suddenly seemed harder.

He wanted her to wake, yet he also wanted her to rest. He'd woken more than once in the darkness, unused to having someone with him right through the night. But she'd woken too and welcomed him when he'd turned to her, his appetite rapacious again.

Now she opened her eyes with that sense she seemed to have for when he woke. A pair of emeralds glittered at him, filled with accusation. 'You're still here.'

'Yes.' His throat felt raw and his voice sounded gravelly but, given how long and how harshly he'd groaned during the night, he wasn't surprised. 'I'm still here.'

He watched wariness enter her eyes. He tensed in anticipation. Regrets were not allowed. And this wasn't over yet.

She shifted as if to move away from him but he pressed his palm on her back, holding her in place against him. That tight feeling ventured further south—to familiar territory.

'Is that how you greet your fiancé good morning?' He smiled at her and shifted down her body. 'Maybe I should put you in a better mood, hmm?'

To his pleasure, she parted her legs, letting him in. Always he wanted her to let him this close. He adored doing this to her. Teasing her. Arousing her until she thrashed beneath him and begged for it. He didn't think he'd ever tire of hearing her excitement build. Of making her moan for him. Of making her hot and fierce. He smiled as he kissed her slick, sweet core. He didn't take her again, just licked her to orgasm because he imagined she was probably tender today. He'd not been gentle on the stairs. Or when they'd finally made it to the bed. Hell, even he was aching in parts he hadn't realised he could ache in. He blamed that on the cramped little bed.

'Oh… *Yes!*' The cry was wrenched from her as she clenched her hands on his shoulders, shuddering through another orgasm.

He stifled his groan as his need sharpened. He'd hold back this time. He kissed her gently through the aftershocks, feeling laxness grow within her and seeing sleepiness return to her green eyes. He gently stroked her hair until her eyelids fluttered shut. Then he moved. But at the doorway he turned, unable to resist taking in one long, last look before beginning his day. She was beautiful, enthusiastic and generous, and the most gorgeous challenge. He could hardly wait already.

It was mid-morning before Kitty woke again. She'd slept better than she had in months. She stretched languorously. *Oh, hell.* There were aches in places too private to be named. So many aches. And the worst?

In her heart.

Never could she regret what had happened yesterday. He had won. Totally. But it had to be done with. She'd finish sifting through all the family stuff and get out of here before she got too enmeshed in an affair that was only going to end painfully for her. Alejandro, for all his arrogance and immunity to emotional depth, was too easy to like.

She took her time in the shower, hoping the hot water would soothe her muscles and over-sensitised skin. But she was half aroused again already, just *thinking* of him.

It was the most rapacious case of lust ever. Who knew sex could be so addictive, so much fun and so intense? That it could be all those things at once was both mind-blowing and terrifying.

She fought for control over her own damn mind—making herself get dressed and head downstairs and get on with work. Once she was underway with the boxes, she was startled by a repeated knocking on the front door.

'I'm sorry to interrupt you, Miss Parkes-Wilson, but there's a delivery for the top floor.' Paolo didn't look her in the eye as he explained.

She tried to smile but she was mortified. The man had brought condoms when he'd busted them out of that room yesterday! So Kitty looked past him to where a beautifully tailored woman and a couple of brawny delivery men stood in front of a large truck double parked in the street.

'A delivery?' She blinked then stepped aside to let them in. 'Of course.'

Then she saw what it was—a massive, massive bed.

'For the top floor?' she questioned, her voice squeaking. This was going in *her* bedroom?

'Yes, the attic bedroom,' the woman said crisply. 'Mr Martinez requested I dress the bed for him and ensure it's perfect.'

Did he, now? Unable to answer, Kitty stood aside. It was his house now and she had no authority to argue. She went down to the kitchen and hid. A new, massive bed for her bedroom? The guy had serious nerve.

Almost an hour later she heard Paolo calling for her.

'All done?' She stepped out into the hallway, glad when he nodded.

'You don't wish to inspect it?' the woman asked.

'I'm sure it's lovely.' She led them to the front door and opened it. 'Thanks so much.'

She shut the door on them before her blush became visible to the astronauts on the International Space Station and, with a combination of avid curiosity and outrage, ran back up to her bedroom, freezing on the threshold when she saw it.

He'd replaced her ancient little bed with a monstrosity best suited to a whorehouse, with its four posts perfect for tying dominatrix straps to. Except that was her being over-dramatic. It wasn't tacky. It was beautiful. Freshly laundered white linen covered the whole thing so it looked like a soft cloud. The thing that annoyed her the most was that it was *gorgeous* and fitted her room perfectly. And she was turned on just at the sight of it.

She turned on her heel and marched out of the room, determined to get the sorting done even more quickly than she'd planned. The sooner she got away from Alejandro Martinez, the better for her emotional health.

'Darling, I'm back.'

Anticipation rippled through her body. Despite his sarcastic call, she heard the rough edge of desire underneath it.

'What took you so long?' she taunted, knowing full well he was home earlier than usual. Again.

He walked towards her, his gaze penetrating, that cocky smile curving his arrogant mouth. 'I take it the bed arrived? Let's go use it.' He grabbed her hand and led her to the stairs, carrying a plastic bag in the other. 'I walked into the store and chose what I wanted.'

Was this the new routine? *Now* this liaison was exposed as the blistering lust-fest that it was. No dinners out any more—or even in. It was just straight to bed to have sex the second he walked in the door. She ignored her own desire for exactly that—she couldn't let him have it this easily.

'It's too big,' she grumbled as they got to the top floor.

He sent her a sideways look that told her he wasn't

fooled. 'I figured we needed a little more space to be creative.'

She was not hot at the thought of that. She wasn't.

In her bedroom he set another box of condoms on the table. She stared at it, feeling the shifts deep within her treacherous body.

'I suppose the best thing is I'll have the space to be able to sleep without having to actually touch you,' she muttered.

'Yes, because you hated using me as your pillow last night.' He stood his ground as he began to unbutton his shirt. 'Why don't you come closer and try to tell me again how much you don't want me?'

She flung her head back, watching as with each flick of his wrist more of his beautiful skin was exposed. 'What's in the bag—sex toys?'

'Dinner.' He laughed and his muscles flexed in the most distracting fashion. 'I'll get the toys tomorrow now I know you want them.'

'Oh, so I actually get dinner?' she asked tartly. 'But it's takeaway. Disposable. Not the five-star restaurants any more.'

His smile was evil. 'I know what you want more.'

Her skin burned as she watched him strip. His muscles rippled; his body was hard and magnetic.

Two could play at that game.

'And I know what you want.' She lifted her top and whisked it off her head. She wore no bra—her nipples were too sensitive for lace today.

He retaliated by toeing off his shoes, then socks and finally kicking off his trousers and boxers in the one movement. Kitty's mouth dried as she drank in the response of his body; her hands shook as she peeled her jeans and panties off. Naked, trembling, she stared at him from across the room in a wordless but passionate duel.

'Come here,' he breathed his command.

Internally she battled—her pride, her need to deny him when he always got it *all*, versus her own desire for him.

No false declarations or meaningless promises.

This was what it was. The dam had burst and there was no containing it now until the lust had been drained. She needed it to be drained.

She stepped towards him until she was close enough for him to grasp her waist and slam her against him in that last step. She arched her neck, granting him full access even as she stared hard into his eyes and challenged him. 'Do you insist on such total surrender from all your women, the way you demand it from me?'

'No.' Despite gritting his teeth, Alejandro couldn't hold back his honest reply. 'There's just something about you that really ticks me off.'

Something that lit him up. Something he couldn't get enough of. Her, like this, naked and hot and welcoming him. Stripped back to the essentials, this was sexual hunger, unstoppable and fantastic. The sooner it was sated the better and it was killing him trying to hold back from thrusting hard and claiming her with no foreplay whatsoever.

He didn't understand *why* she needed to fight him, but he knew she couldn't help it. Something about him got to her. It was the same for him. He relished sparring with her, anticipated her arguments and ached for the moment she surrendered and welcomed him into her hot, wet body.

'So you want me to submit?' she asked.

And she did that now. Stepping back, she fell backwards onto the big bed, her arms and legs spread-eagled, positioning herself like an offering for him, except her eyes were alight with that challenge. She wasn't giving in to him without extracting something in return.

'Is this what you wanted?' she taunted.

He couldn't get the condom on fast enough. 'This is your fantasy and you know it.' He breathed hard, daring her to deny it but needing to hear something else. Something true. 'You like it when I pin you down and kiss every inch of you.'

He'd known from the second he'd seen her that it would be like this—their physical attraction was combustible. He caressed her until he heard her gasp. Slow. So Slow. Until, hot and wet, she sobbed for her release. Never had pleasuring a woman been so pleasurable for him.

'Yes,' she screamed. *'Oh, yes!'*

He rose in a fury, fired by her raw admission.

'You're obsessed,' she murmured as she spread her legs wider so he could take his place where she wanted him.

'Possibly.'

The words were a warning in his ear. Was this unnatural? Was this constant ache going too far? But he couldn't stop now. With a harsh groan, he buried himself deep inside her, growling at the exquisite torment of her tight silken body. He held fast for a moment, just to prove to himself that he could.

'Please,' she whispered beneath him, her arms holding him tight and close. 'Please.'

And there it was. He couldn't resist that request, couldn't deny her or himself. So, in turn, he too surrendered, driving hard, driving home.

Strong yet soft, she met him thrust for thrust. *'Alejandro.'*

He lay as limp and useless as a rag but despite his exhaustion he couldn't join her in sleep. She was the most sexually compatible lover he'd had. Not that he'd had as many as she seemed to think. It wasn't as if he spent every night with a new woman. Sex was merely a relaxation strategy to combat work hours and stress.

But this was different. This driving resurgence of desire only moments after completion? He felt inhumanly strong and the voracious hunger drove him on. It couldn't last, right? Usually a few days was enough with one woman before he eased off...but he wanted Kitty more than ever. He wanted so much more.

Any kind of obsession was unhealthy, but at least his obsession with work resulted in a productive, safe, outcome. To be obsessed by a woman? That wasn't safe.

And he was obsessed. He was addicted. Not just to sex with her, but to the way she stood up to him, the way she made him laugh, the way she made him feel alive. And he wondered about the wistful expression on her face as she packed up her family's history from this house, but at the same time he knew the connection she felt to this place was something he could never understand, no matter how hard he tried.

And he did demand her surrender. He was obsessed with that.

God, his brain was addled. Never before had he sat at his desk and discovered he'd lost five minutes in a dream-like state, just thinking about a woman. He didn't want to think about anyone like that. He didn't want to lose control of himself in that way. He'd seen what happened when someone became obsessive. Became possessive.

Someone very much like him.

He couldn't let it happen now. Not with sweet, vulnerable Kitty. Not with anyone.

He had to protect her. He had to remember he had too much to do. Work had to take precedence. He breathed out, finally able to relax and sink towards slumber as he realised: work was the answer.

CHAPTER TEN

'I'M GOING TO New York for a week. You'll be all right here on your own?'

Kitty looked up from her checklist and hoped she'd hidden the way her heart had just thudded to the floor. 'Of course. It'll be a nice holiday from you,' she lied. He was home early again, but he wasn't staying. He was going away for *a week*.

'Me and my lecherous demands?' He caught her close and kissed her until she was soft and leaning against him. 'You're not going to miss me at all?' he teased.

'I'm going to catch up on my sleep.' She pushed out of his arms and brushed her hair back from her face.

It was mean of him to invite an admission like that when he'd never admit such a thing himself. She'd be out of sight and out of mind... She frowned.

'I'll call you and—'

'Don't,' she interrupted breathlessly.

A quizzical expression crossed his face. 'Don't call you?'

'Not if you're going to call me like you did Saskia that night. I'd rather you didn't call me at all. I'd rather not know.'

His eyes widened. 'What are you implying?'

'I just mean that when this is over I want you to tell me face-to-face, not a phone call. You think you can hold back from temptation for a week?' She held her head high, even though she hated how shrill she sounded. 'Because I don't think that's too much to ask of my fake fiancé.' She didn't want humiliation in that way.

'Catriona, I'll be working non-stop—'

'You'll have to eat sometime—'

'So I'll eat at my desk.'

She laughed a little bitterly. 'You won't go out to all those fancy restaurants?'

The ones with all those women who'd love nothing more than his attention and for him to take them home for a couple of hours' post-work 'relaxation'.

'I have a lot of work to do; that's all this trip is. For me to *work* hard. I'll play with you when I get back.'

And that was what this was. *Play*. A game that would be over soon enough. It was good to get the reminder.

She nodded and forced a smile, but it was small. 'Okay.'

She wanted to believe him, but past experience told her she was a fool to. Her father. Her real fiancé. And Alejandro himself wasn't one to maintain a relationship. He'd admitted that he didn't ever want to.

'I'll see you soon,' he said.

'You're leaving now?' She bit her lip as she realised how that sounded.

'Yes. I just called by on my way to the airport.'

For a moment she thought he was going to say something more, but he shook his head.

'Okay, then…' She struggled to think. 'Have a good trip.'

He sent her a sombre look, turned and left.

She stared at the empty space in the room that he'd left. That was it? Had he really gone so quickly—with just a few words?

Better get used to it. This was what would happen when they parted for good.

Swallowing back a horribly desolate feeling, she turned back to her checklist. She *wasn't* going to torture herself imagining him with a million women while he was away. She was going to get the work done so she could get away quickly and cleanly once he did return and keep herself from hurting more. And until then, when he was out of sight, *she'd* keep *him* out of her mind.

But she was lonelier than she'd ever been in her life. The house was too empty, that new bed too huge, the ache in her heart too unrelenting. She needed distraction—and plenty of it.

'What the hell is going on with you two?' Teddy's eyebrows were at his hairline as he poured her a coffee in the theatre's green room. 'You've really fallen for him?'

'It's impossible not to fall for him.' Kitty shrugged and forced a smile as she confessed the truth in the safety of a joke. 'Unfortunately. But he's away and I need something to do.'

Her brother eyed her for a moment, then pushed a mug of coffee towards her. 'We need help,' he said. 'We always need help. No one can source cheap props the way you do. Can't pay, though.'

Kitty laughed, grateful for the support. 'Well, duh.'

She enjoyed the theatre scene. Hunting for props was fun, creating them even more so. While Teddy's play was almost due to open, the play next in the schedule needed some items that she was happy to help conjure up. She hadn't done that in an age—not since before she'd had to get a 'real job' as gallery assistant.

True to her request, Alejandro didn't phone her. But that night he did send her a picture. It was of the empty soup container on his desk. His dinner. She sent him a selfie poking her tongue out at him.

The next night it was a pizza box. The night after that, a noodle box.

Less than halfway through his self-imposed respite week Alejandro wondered, for the millionth time, what Kitty was doing. Where she was. Who she was with.

Unease chilled his gut. Would she be out seeing friends? Would she have finished up at the house and left?

She hadn't wanted him to phone. She hadn't been able to meet his eyes when she'd asked him not to and he'd made her explain why. Now he felt embarrassed about that call he'd placed to Saskia in front of her. What an arrogant thing to do. He arranged for a bunch of flowers and a brief, apologetic notecard to be sent to Saskia. He hadn't meant to be cruel, but maybe he had been. Contrary to what he'd told Kitty at the time, he didn't know for sure if all Saskia had wanted was a quick fling. As usual he'd set out his expectations and just assumed she'd accepted them. But too often people hid their true feelings.

He counted down the days but time crawled. The nights were worse. His sleep was disturbed, but not by desire. Twice he woke with sweat filming his brow. That old helpless despair clogged his throat. He stared into the darkness and thought of her to make himself feel better. And worse. Because he couldn't stop thinking of her.

The fourth night away, he couldn't take it any more. He succumbed to the temptation and called Kitty's mobile. But she didn't pick up. The brief message on her answer service wasn't enough to satisfy his need to hear her voice. He tried the landline at Parkes House. She didn't answer that either.

He paced through his Manhattan apartment, his concentration in smithereens. He needed to know where she was. He needed to know *now*. Was she okay? Had she been in an accident? Was she with someone else?

A billion questions swarmed in his mind, stopping him from thinking properly. Slowly, a cold unease seeped into his belly and began to burn. This obsessing over her was becoming a festering wound. Who was he to demand to know the minutiae of her day? Since when was his head so filled with wonderings about a woman? He did not want to be this man. He'd *never* wanted to be this man—not obsessive, not possessive.

His phone rang and he pounced on it. But it wasn't Kitty; it was one of his junior consultants in the London office.

'I've had a question come up—'

'I'll come back early.' Alejandro fell on the excuse gladly.

'You don't need to—'

'I'll be on the first flight.'

It was night-time when he landed.

'Is Kitty at home?' Alejandro asked Paolo the second he saw him waiting for him at the airport.

Paolo looked evasive as he led the way to the car. 'She said she was happy using public transport.'

Grimly, Alejandro said nothing. Paolo was not a gaoler but he was a protector, and Alejandro should have made it clear that he needed to know she was physically safe and secure at all times.

After Paolo dropped him off, he unlocked the door, his anticipation building. But he knew as soon as he crossed the threshold that she wasn't home. He paced though the house, wondering where she was, who she was with, why she still wasn't answering her damn phone.

Finally, almost two stomach-churning hours later, he heard the key in the door.

She was in her usual black trousers, black top ensemble, not one of the designer dresses. Her hair was tied back and hidden under a black wool beanie of all things. She'd not been out to dinner? She was smiling—looking so happy— and she'd not seen him yet.

'Hey.' He couldn't choke out more of a greeting than that. The wave of emotion at seeing her again was too intense.

'Alejandro.' For a moment she looked shocked. But then her brilliant smile broadened. 'You're back early.'

That reaction soothed him, but not completely.

She put her large bag down and unwound the scarf from her neck. 'Did you miss me too much?' She looked sassy.

'I got the work done sooner than I'd expected.' He couldn't relax enough to walk towards her. 'Where've you been?'

She didn't take her gaze from him. 'At Teddy's play,' she said softly. 'It was opening night tonight.'

'You didn't answer your mobile when I called.'

'Because I turned it off. It's polite to do that when you're at a live theatre performance.' Her gaze intensified. 'Before you ask, I've spent the last few days helping out at the theatre with the props.'

'I wasn't going to ask.'

'No?' She chuckled.

He shifted on his feet, not able to bring himself to walk either to her or away from her. He hated the mess of emotion in his gut.

She came nearer.

'You're not a little jealous?' she teased lightly.

'I don't get jealous.' He couldn't even break a smile.

'No?' Her eyes danced. 'Maybe something you ate disagreed with you.'

'I'm not jealous,' he repeated. He hated this feeling. He wanted it to go away. He wanted her to come closer to him.

'You missed me,' he told her. It wasn't a question.

Her mouth tightened and her chin lifted. 'I missed the *sex*.'

Not a good enough answer. 'Not me?'

'And your grumpy mood? Hell, no.'

He reached out to curl his arm around her waist and haul her close so she was pressed against him. Hell, *yes*, that was where he needed her. Close.

'Every step of the way you try to deny this attraction,' he said roughly. 'You deny it even as you dance into my bed.'

'There are moments when I don't like you.' Her eyes

sparkled. 'But as I'm stuck in this situation I might as well use what little you can offer.'

His body tightened at the insult. 'What "little" can I offer?'

'Orgasms,' she answered airily.

'Is that all?'

She chose not to say anything more. Provoking him.

Alejandro gave her a gentle shake. 'Stop trying to annoy me. You won't like it if I retaliate.'

'You're the one being annoying.' She slipped off her beanie, released her hair from its elastic tie and shook it out. 'You're all talk.'

The anger he'd felt suddenly morphed into something else. The desire to control. To prove a point. Deliberately, slowly he lowered his head. Her response to his kiss was instantaneous and made the passion within him flare. But it didn't soothe the need coursing in his veins. He lifted her and carried her up the stairs, kissing her as he climbed. Passion, anger and relief combined, giving him a burst of strength. He couldn't get her naked quickly enough. But he didn't strip himself. Not entirely. He needed to retain some control for what he intended to do.

He forced himself to slow down, to caress—first with fingertips, then lips, then tongue. His blood quickened as he felt her skin warm, as he heard her breathing change. He knew her well now but it still wasn't enough. He couldn't stop touching her, greedy for the feel of her skin against his again. Need spiked. He wanted to kiss her everywhere, touch her everywhere, take her. *Now.*

Too fast again. He growled, pulling back.

She arched, reaching for him.

'Not yet, Kitty,' he said roughly. 'I don't feel like giving you that yet.'

But he was lying to her and to himself. He held her arms pinned above her head with one hand, and with his other he trailed his fingertips over her skin, feeling that silky smoothness and following the pattern of pretty freckles all the way down. She was so gorgeous, she tormented him. It would take nothing for her to come, and he knew it. But he wasn't giving it to her. Which meant he wasn't coming either.

Stalemate.

Kitty looked into his dark eyes, unable to stop herself arching up to him again. He was here, home, with her, but he was so controlled and so grim and so determined to have her total surrender. But she wanted his too. And she saw the flush in his cheeks, the sheen on his skin. She felt the barely leashed energy in his twitching muscles. The rapacious lust in his gaze only turned her on all the more, but no matter how she provoked him, he always had the last laugh. He always won. Suddenly she was angry—with herself for missing him so much, with him for always teasing and never telling the truth—with him for not acknowledging that this thing between them was...*more.*

Impulse burned. Before she thought better of it, she lashed out. 'Do you honestly believe I'm thinking about you?'

The look he gave her then was filthy, fiery fury. He rapidly thrust away from her in a rough motion. She raised up onto her elbows, watching as he stripped out of his pants and jerkily sheathed his straining erection. His lack of finesse proved just how angry she'd made him. She closed her eyes and slumped back in heated agony and anticipation. She'd wanted this. Wanted him to be unleashed. He grabbed her hips and pulled her down until her lower legs dangled over the edge of the bed. She felt him step between her parted knees.

'Open your eyes, Catriona,' he demanded. 'Open your eyes and look at me.'

He kissed the heart of her and she almost came on the

spot. She cried out when he left her just before she could crash over the edge.

'Open your eyes.'

This time she obeyed. Her heart thundered as excitement flooded her veins. He was standing over her, his muscles bunching, his body flushed. She ran her tongue along her dry lips.

'Say my name,' he said as he spread her thighs that little bit more with his broad hands and then bent to brace above her, one fist either side of her head.

'Alejandro,' she whispered, melting in the storm of arousal and need and anger.

'Louder,' he insisted. 'Don't stop saying it, or I'll stop. Don't stop looking at me.'

'Egotistical maniac.' She lifted her chin at the filthy look that flashed in his eyes.

'I just want honesty. Be honest,' he demanded.

He came down hard and thrust into her. One forceful movement.

'Then I expect the same from you!' she cried in his face as the exquisite sensation pushed her past her emotional limits. 'Be honest with me.' She clutched him close, utterly torn between happiness and frustration and the yearning for *more* from him. The need for everything. 'You were *jealous*.'

'I missed this,' he shouted back, his control breaking and he thrust hard and fierce. Uncontrollably, he pumped into her over and over, his passion pushing them both across the bed. 'Missed you,' he corrected brokenly. 'Missed you.' He groaned in tortured surrender. 'God, I missed you.'

'Yes!' she cried, her nails curling into his rigid muscles as she held him tightly.

She'd missed him too. So much. Now she wrapped around him, holding him closer than ever, feeling him there with her. So very *there*. Not just physically but in every way. She gazed into his eyes, swept away on the tide of emotion pouring out of him. Emotion that reflected her own—need, need, *need*.

The orgasm hit too quickly, too intensely. Everything shattered. It was easily the most beautiful experience of her life.

In the end she didn't think she'd ever be able to move again. He was slumped over her, his breathing still ragged, emotion continuing to radiate from him. She stroked his hair back from his forehead. His skin was burning, his face was still flushed from the insane effort he'd unleashed on her. She blinked back the tears that had welled in her eyes then swallowed so she could find her voice.

'I don't know why you make me so mad that I say whatever pops into my head to aggravate you,' she whispered, brushing her fingertips down the side of his face. 'I'm sorry I was such a witch.'

'I was not any better,' he admitted, his voice oddly subdued as he shifted to lie beside her. 'I'm sorry. I was... jealous.'

Peace settled within her as he admitted it and she smiled at him sleepily, her eyes closing.

But he didn't smile back.

Alejandro jolted awake a few hours later. Trying to stay quiet, he mentally counted to regulate his breathing. She was fast asleep, burrowed into his side, and he didn't want her to wake this time, not when his heart was racing, his skin was covered in a cold sweat and nausea roiled in his stomach.

He swallowed hard, his mind whirring as he tried to shut down the nightmare. He breathed slowly, hoping to calm himself. But he couldn't help examining the emotions she'd so easily identified. Emotions he'd never felt before. He'd not let himself feel them before.

He'd turned away from any teen crush, going with the girls who'd wanted something else from him. Something simple. The more he'd had of those, the more there'd been. It had become easy. Just sex. Just pleasure. Nothing deeper.

But now insidious fear crawled just under his skin. Memories scalded, choking him. The malevolence, the neediness, echoed in his head.

'You love him more than me.'

The demands. The obsession.

'You're not leaving. You're never leaving.'

He hadn't had these horror-soaked dreams in years. Hadn't thought about the past in so long. He was fine. Happy. Healthy. Living a great, successful life. But in the last few weeks it had changed. Now it didn't seem as great. Or as successful.

In those days while he'd been in New York, Kitty had been laughing, having fun. She hadn't been missing him at all. Which should be fine. Just as it should be fine for her to spend time with Teddy. How could he be jealous of her *brother*? It wasn't as if he was any kind of threat. Yet here he was, feeling jealous, fighting with her, wanting—what?

His feelings were out of control. *He* was out of control. His worst nightmare had become reality.

CHAPTER ELEVEN

WHEN ALEJANDRO NEXT woke he discovered Kitty had already left the bed. He glanced at the time. It wasn't that he'd slept in; it was that she'd got up appallingly early.

Why?

He pushed back the sheet and tried to swallow down the burn of regret that she wasn't there for him to touch. It wasn't anywhere near as easy. Hell, he was suddenly so *needy*.

He forced himself to shower and dress before going downstairs in search of her. She wasn't in any of the bedrooms on the second floor, but he noticed how much she'd cleared and sorted. She was almost done. That was good. That had to be good.

He finally found her in the kitchen, working at the covered table with a soldering iron in hand, bent over an incredibly weird-looking object. 'What are you doing?'

She glanced up, guilt flashing on her face even as she smiled. 'I hope I didn't wake you.' She looked back at the mass of plastic, metal and wire she was working on. 'I know I should be finishing those last few boxes, but I promised Teddy I'd get this done in time for their rehearsal later.'

He stepped closer to the table. 'What is it?'

'A prototype gamma-ray shield for an intergalactic army.' A self-conscious giggle escaped as she set the soldering iron down. 'The next show at the theatre is a cowboy space opera.'

'Of course it is.' He leaned down to take a better look. 'You made it from scratch?'

She nodded and he was aware of the anxious look in her eyes.

He took a moment to study it. Yet to be painted, she'd constructed it using who knew what and had included details that most likely wouldn't be seen from the stage. It was a miniature work of art. 'It's amazing. Can I pick it up?' When she nodded he lifted it. 'It's so detailed. And exactly what a shield should be like.'

She flushed at his tiny compliment, which both pleased and annoyed him. Why hadn't her family complimented her more?

'But not too heavy?' she checked.

'No.' He carefully tested the weight. 'It's good.'

'Hopefully, if they like it they'll offer me more work. Paid, even.' An excited smile lit up her face. 'I can do it when I've finished here.'

When she left him? He stared, hating the feeling washing through him.

Her cheeks coloured slightly and she looked back to the shield as he carefully put it back down.

'You should come and see Teddy's play.' Her words were rushed. 'He's actually pretty good.'

'You're very loyal to him.' To the point of doing some breaking and entering even.

'Of course. He's my twin—I have to be his number one fan.' She rolled her eyes as she laughed. 'Don't you have any brothers or sisters?'

'No.'

He'd answered too tersely. Now he sensed her biting back follow-up questions. Of course she was curious; he would be too. He walked away so he couldn't see her expressive eyes. He might as well get it over with; she'd have to find out eventually. Obviously she hadn't done the stalker-style Internet search on him that he'd done on her. He shouldn't feel put out by that. He shouldn't feel half of what he was feeling. The nightmares had left a residue of discomfort which left him tired and irritable. Telling her would be good. It would be the beginning of the end.

'My mother is dead,' he said bluntly. 'My father killed her in a jealous rage because she dared try to leave him. The police shot him.'

His blood rushed to his head, making the room spin, and he put his hand out to the wall. He'd not had to say it aloud for a while. He'd forgotten how much it impacted. He tried to count in his head. That numbness that he'd employed for so long came in handy now.

'What?' Her voice was a shocked whisper. 'Alejandro...'

'Everyone knows,' he said brusquely. 'There's no point trying to hide it. It happened. I was a child. I have accepted it and moved on.' He licked his very dry lips. 'I was sent to the States to live. I was very lucky.'

He had been very lucky. After the first two shots, his father had pointed the gun at him. He'd been seconds away from death when the police had killed his father. His mother had been lying just in front of him; she'd stepped forward when she'd seen what his father had in his hand. Nothing could take that image away from him. Nothing could lessen the impact. Nothing could change it.

And he could never be the man his father had been.

'Where were you?' she asked.

'That's why they shot him. He was pointing the gun at me.'

Alejandro turned to look at Kitty in time to see two fat tears rolling down her cheeks. Her simple, heart-rent reaction touched him more than words ever could.

'I'm okay,' he muttered quickly, his breath shortening. 'Better than okay. I was fostered. I focused on school. It was my way out. I got good scholarships. I studied really, really hard.'

Somehow he was standing right in front of her and his arms were around her. She leaned in.

'You're not supposed to comfort me—it's supposed to be the other way round.' Kitty wrapped her arms around him, holding him as tight as she could, wishing she could absorb even some of the pain that was intrinsically bound within him.

He'd told her that truth so baldly, so mechanically.

She wanted to ask so much more. Wanted to know when, how old he'd been, who'd helped him… But it all seemed so inane, those details unnecessary, because they couldn't change the pure horror of what he'd endured. It couldn't make it better. Nothing could make this any better. What about the poor child who'd witnessed that brutality? Who'd lost his mother at the hands of his father?

No wonder he lived his life determined to skate along the superficiality of good times and simple fun. He didn't want complicated. He didn't want emotional.

He didn't want to be hurt again.

'So that's why you don't want marriage or children,' she said when she lifted her face.

'Why would I?' he answered bluntly.

Why, indeed.

'Don't try to change me,' he said softly, his voice a little rough.

'I wouldn't presume to think I could,' she whispered.

'Don't pity me.'

'Don't try to dictate how I'm supposed to feel.' How could she not feel sorry for him, knowing this?

'You only need to feel pleasure.'

His hedonism made total sense now. *He* only wanted pleasure. Only light and easy fun. But life was never like that. Not in the end.

He'd built an impenetrable shell around himself. Always

out, always with people, always having fun. Always that superficial delight. No real emotional intimacy.

'I only want fun,' he warned her one last time.

She gazed at him, then slowly nodded. 'Then let's have fun.'

Alejandro jolted awake. Again he froze so he didn't disturb her, but his heart raced as he blocked the lingering image in his mind. He tried to focus on work instead. But that didn't help much either. Alejandro stifled a groan of despair. He had to go back to New York tomorrow but he was dreading it. He already knew time and distance from her weren't going to help him regain his perspective. He'd thought that if he indulged in her for a couple of days, he'd have had enough. Instead he just wanted more. He liked the way she teased him. He liked listening to her talking about the house, the theatre, the restaurants. He liked her. Maybe telling her about his past had been a mistake—it had broken a barrier within him and she seemed to be able to slip closer than before.

Now he was worried.

He didn't want to feel the gaping loss he'd felt the last time he'd left her—not that massive 'something's missing' sensation. He didn't want that worry, nor the nagging jealousy of nothing. If she was with him, he wouldn't feel that.

Too tired to resist the temptation, he turned and gently roused her. It only took a moment. 'Come with me.'

A twinkle lit her slumberous eyes. 'I did already.'

'No. To New York. Come with me.'

She froze mid-stretch, suddenly looking unsure. He hated that wariness in her, as if she couldn't trust or believe what he was saying.

'I don't want to have another night without you,' he said, her vulnerability forcing him into honesty. Then he smiled. 'Come wear your ridiculous dresses over there. I dare you.'

* * *

He made himself work for a while on the plane—just to prove he could. But the rest of the time he sat comfortably as Kitty curled next to him, engrossed in the movie she'd selected. The limo ride to his apartment took too long and it was dark when he finally led her into his building. It wasn't until he'd flicked the lights on and turned to see her reaction that he realised her pallor.

'Are you okay?' He stepped forward and grabbed her shoulders. She looked as if she was about to fall down at any second.

'I'm just really tired.' She grinned apologetically. 'Like really, really tired. I think the flight got to me more than I thought it would.'

'Then straight to bed.' He led her to the guest bedroom and put her bag just inside the door. 'Come on.'

'I want to explore first.' But she stepped into the room. 'Wow, fancy.'

He glanced around at the sleek interior, with its private bathroom with his-and-hers basins. This wasn't his room; this was the room he used when *entertaining*.

He frowned as he followed her back into the living area. 'You like it?'

'It's very tasteful. Very different to Parkes House.'

'Less full of stuff, you mean.'

'Yeah.' She winked at him and made a beeline for the bookshelf.

But it wasn't the books she was checking out. It was the photo.

'My mother,' he explained, even though he knew it was obvious.

'She looks like you.' She smiled at him shyly. 'Except for your eyes.'

An acrid feeling burned in his throat. 'I have my father's eyes.'

She glanced at the shelf but of course there was no photo there of his father. No other photos at all. For the first time he thought about how boring his apartment must look. The only personal things in it were his books.

'I think you're right,' she said quietly. 'I really need to get some sleep.'

He looked at her; she'd paled again. And suddenly he didn't want her in that bedroom. He didn't want the memory of other women in there with them. He wanted it to be theirs alone.

'Come with me.' He led her up the spiral staircase to his secret space and opened the door to let her past him. 'This is where I usually sleep.'

Her eyes widened as she looked at the small room, her mind processing. 'When you're alone.'

'Yes.' It was small and very simply decorated, safe and quiet, up high on the mezzanine floor. 'You'll sleep better in here.' He cleared his throat. 'It's darker—the curtains are…' He was making excuses. He just didn't want her in that other room.

'Okay,' she said. 'Thanks. I'm sorry I'm so tired.'

So was he, but not because he was desperate to slake his lust. He wanted her to be okay. 'Don't worry, just sleep.'

He climbed in beside her and drew her close so her head rested on his chest. Slowly he relaxed as he felt her sink into sleep in his arms. Warm weariness stole into his bones, and that feeling of anxiety eased until he slept too.

'Alejandro?'

His eyes snapped open; his heart was thundering. Kitty was leaning over him, her eyes wide and worried. He realised the reading light beside her was on and—

'Are you okay?' He sat up and checked his watch. It was only just after two in the morning. 'What's wrong?'

'N-nothing.' She eased back, turning away from studying him so intently. 'I'm fine. I just…'

He waited, rubbing his hand through his hair. His forehead felt damp—had he been dreaming again? He froze.

'I just—I don't know about you, but I'm *starving*.' Kitty suddenly slid out of the bed and sent him a dazzling smile. 'I'm going to go fix something.'

Food? Fantastic. 'I'm not eating noodles,' he muttered.

'Who said I was cooking anything for you?' she said tartly, her spirit snapping. 'Honestly, your arrogance…'

He laughed and rolled out of the bed, inordinately happy that she was back to her best. 'I'll cook. But I can't believe I have to cook vegetarian.'

'You've never used any of this, have you?' She looked around the sterile kitchen while he headed to the pantry, praying he had something edible in there.

He stepped out, brandishing a couple of cans and a bag of rice. The freezer revealed more possibilities.

'Are you sure it'll even work?' she teased as he flicked a switch on the oven. 'I bet you've never turned it on even once before.'

He grinned at her. 'You know I'm very good at turning things on.'

She rolled her eyes.

'Not noodles,' he said pointedly as he placed a steaming dish of rice and vegetables in front of her fifteen minutes later.

'Oh, so good,' she mumbled after the first forkful. Then she glared at him. 'Is there anything you aren't good at?'

'So many things,' he said lightly. 'I won't bore you with the list.'

Only a few hours later, when he got up to go to work, he tried not to disturb her, but she sat up anyway. She still had shadows beneath her eyes. He frowned. He'd been selfish, all these nights of interrupted sleep had taken a toll on her.

He'd been little better than an animal. But she'd wanted it too. She'd pushed him. She'd welcomed him. Even so, she clearly needed a break.

'Lie back down and sleep in,' he told her.

'And miss the chance to explore New York?' she pretty much shrieked. 'Never.'

'Please.' He wanted that pallor to return to a more normal shade. 'Just have a couple more hours' rest then meet me for lunch. I'll send a car.'

'I can find my own way.'

That determined independence annoyed him. It was so unnecessary. But he knew there was no point arguing.

In the end she stood him up for lunch. She sent a text saying she'd meet him back at the apartment before dinner. Apparently she'd got distracted at the shops.

Disappointed, he worked through, but he was glad she must be feeling better. They'd go out tonight, just the two of them. He contacted a friend to find out the city's best vegetarian restaurant and then phoned to secure a table, bribing his way in.

When he finally got home she was ready.

'Where are we going?' she asked before he'd even said hello.

For a moment he didn't answer; he was too busy staring. Now he understood why she'd got distracted. She was in a designer dress, but it wasn't black. It was a beautiful bottle-green and cut to perfectly emphasise her slim waist. The low-scooped neckline showed her delectable freckles. The first time she'd ever worn anything that revealed them. The first time she was in colour. She looked stunning.

He saw the wary hesitancy in her eyes and the way she was holding herself very erect, and knew he was going to need to tread carefully. If he said the wrong thing she'd flare up at him. And for once he didn't want to do that.

Maybe there wasn't a right thing to say. Only a right thing to do. He walked to her and cupped her face in his hands.

'Look at me,' he commanded softly when she avoided his eyes.

Slowly, reluctantly, she met his gaze.

'I can't kiss you or we'll never get out of here tonight,' he muttered hoarsely. 'You've gone to too much trouble to stay home.' For once it hadn't been for anyone else. It had been for him. It touched him more than he could bear. 'You are beautiful.'

She pushed back from him, not meeting his eyes as she blushed. 'You'll sleep with anything.'

'You really know how to insult a man.' He grabbed her hand so she couldn't walk far. 'But you insult yourself the most.'

He had no way to prove how attractive he found her. No way other than sleeping with her—again and again and again.

'I'm not a beast who roots whenever, however, with whatever I can,' he said bluntly. 'I can sleep with none but the world's most beautiful women. A list of models a mile long. Yet I choose to screw you. And only you. Over and over. Why do you think that is?'

'You're going through a phase.'

He laughed and released her hand, giving up on convincing her. 'You wish to burn yourself with insecurity about your appearance, that's your choice.'

Her head whipped as she turned to stare at him, her jaw slack. Suddenly she laughed.

'What?' He queried the change in her demeanour. All of a sudden she was *glowing*.

'You're right.' She giggled again and actually wiped a tear from her eye. 'You're absolutely right. I've been stupid.'

He cupped her face again. 'Not stupid.' He knew she'd

not got the security she needed from her father or her ex-fiancé. 'Sweet.'

She tilted her chin, her eyes glinted, her lips still curved. 'Not that sweet...' she murmured wickedly.

'No,' he muttered hoarsely. 'We need to leave. We're going to the most lauded vegetarian restaurant in the city. You've no idea the hoops I had to jump through to get us a table at such late notice.'

Delight shimmered and she leaned even closer. 'You're going vegetarian for me?'

'Just for tonight,' he drawled. 'So for once you get to choose anything from the menu—you're not limited to one or two same-old, same-old dishes. So let's go.'

But she didn't move; she just smiled up at him and his chest was too tight again and he couldn't seem to move. His heart couldn't pound hard enough. She was sparkling now—her eyes glittering like jewels.

'Kitty—' He pulled the diamond choker from his pocket.

Her soft lips parted as she gazed at them, then back up at him. 'You have it with you?'

'All the time.' He didn't know why. He felt close to her when he had it in his breast pocket. It was stupid, but there it was. 'Please wear it.'

It would look stunning on her.

She shook her head, her smile resolute. 'I can't. It's not mine to wear.'

'You wish it was?' He'd buy them for her if he could.

'It's just not meant to be that way.' She turned away from him.

She deserved more than that. She ought to have her heart's desire. She had such a generous heart.

'You took such a risk for them.' He smiled as he remembered her stealing in to the library that night, all sleek determination and fire.

'Isn't there someone for whom you'd do anything?' she asked lightly. 'No matter the cost or the risk?'

He maintained his smile, but an emptiness gaped in his stomach. She loved in a way he couldn't. The cost of loving like that was too great.

CHAPTER TWELVE

'Kitty?'

It couldn't possibly be morning. It just couldn't. Kitty groaned as she opened her eyes.

Alejandro was already up, dressed in jeans and looking gorgeous as he held a mug towards her. How had she slept through his getting up? She always woke when he did—and not just in the morning, but in the middle of the night when he had those dreams that made his whole body flinch and her heart ache because she didn't know how to help him. The dreams that seemed to be occurring more and more frequently and were more and more frightening for him.

'Coffee?'

'Oh, no, thanks.' She tried to turn her grimace into a smile and rolled over so he couldn't see how bad her attempt was. But the smell was making her gag. She screwed her eyes tight shut and wished she was back in that warm, deep sleep. Yesterday, as the day had worn on she'd felt better, but once again she'd woken feeling so very tired. And queasy as—

Her eyes flashed open and she stared at the white wall of his cosy private bedroom. *Queasy?*

Her mouth filled with bitter spit and she forced herself to swallow it back without moving. Her feminine intuition had kicked in way too late. When was her cycle due? She frowned. She was usually pretty regular and she should have had her period at the end of that first week that Alejandro had been in New York. But she hadn't had it and she'd been so distracted she'd not stopped to think about it at all. Until now.

'I thought I'd take the day off,' Alejandro said huskily

as he sat on the edge of the bed. 'Thought I'd come with you on your sightseeing trip today.'

Her heart would have leapt if it wasn't too busy beating at a billion thuds per second.

'Oh.' *No.*

Not today. Not this. Oh, please, not this.

She shrank into the mattress as her mind scurried. She needed time to figure herself out. Time to reassure herself that she was panicking over nothing and only having an irregular few weeks or something. Her pulse hammered in her ears as she tried to think of an excuse to put him off. 'I'm still feeling tired—I think I need to sleep some more. Maybe later today?'

But he'd offered to take time from work and spend it with her—and she had to turn him down...? She bit her lip, holding the heartbreak and fear inside.

'Are you okay?' He leaned over her and looked at her intently. 'Do you need to see a doctor?'

'No,' she lied and avoided his eyes. 'I'm just tired.' She forced a coy smile. 'I guess I'm not used to the all-night bedroom antics the way you are.'

She felt him withdraw at that flippant comment, but she hardened her heart. She had to have a couple of hours to herself this morning because she was too anxious to maintain a facade of carelessness until later.

'Text me later then.' Alejandro stood. 'I'll see where I'm at.'

'Okay.' She forced herself to snuggle back down in the bed.

He paused on his way out of the room, then turned and walked back to where she was, now almost totally hidden in a tight huddle under the sheets. 'Rest well.'

He pressed his lips to hers. At first she was too scared to be able to relax into the kiss but then that warmth flooded her, overwhelming her as it always did. As *he* always did.

But the moment she heard the door close she sprang out of bed, ignoring the return of the bitter taste in her mouth.

She quickly dressed and then took the elevator down to the ground floor. She smiled confidently at the doorman as he held the door for her to leave the building. She wasn't going to make the mistake of asking him for help finding a pharmacy—that information would be bound to filter back to Alejandro at some point.

She strode along the busy pavement, trying to look as if she knew where she was going. Down two blocks she finally stopped and asked a café worker for assistance.

Five minutes later she handed over the cash for the home pregnancy test. Her fingers were freezing and she almost dropped the change. The chances were so very low, right?

But their first time in that secret room... Surely there'd be only the slightest risk from that? He'd pulled out before he'd orgasmed. How unlucky could they be if a baby had been conceived in that so-brief moment?

Back in his apartment the result flashed almost immediately.

Pregnant.

Kitty stared fixedly at the result, her brain working overtime. She repeated the test. And got the same result.

All kinds of emotions swooped in so quickly she felt faint. She sat down on the floor of the gleaming bathroom. This could *not* be happening.

But it was. Slowly, a feeling of utter certainty and conviction stole over her, giving her an unexpected sense of calm.

She ran her hand over her still-flat belly. There was a tiny life in there. Alejandro's child. Her heart almost burst beneath a wave of unconditional, absolute love. Her muscles flexed in a surge of protectiveness. And suddenly she didn't feel unlucky at all.

But then she thought of Alejandro and how he would

react to this. Her ballooning heart ruptured and she gasped as she realised the hurt they both faced.

This was the very last thing he wanted and it was the very last thing she wanted to do to him.

He didn't want this. He didn't really want her—not for good. Her eyes filled as she realised the happiness she'd felt in the last few days had just been a facade.

She quickly stood. She had no time for tears. She had to leave. She had to think about how she was going to handle everything before telling him. She had to have a sure plan in place before she could even *face* him.

Galvanised into action, she methodically packed her clothing and left the building again with another confident wave at the doorman. She rounded the corner of the block before hailing a cab and heading to the airport. She used the last of the available credit on her card to buy a ticket for the next flight back to London.

She switched her phone off and left it off—from the time she left his apartment, through all the hours during the flight and the time she travelled across London. When she switched it on to phone Teddy, it rang immediately.

Alejandro.

Her heart spasmed. But she didn't answer it yet. She couldn't. Not until she'd figured out a plan that would work. He didn't want marriage, he didn't want children and she knew he wasn't going to change that stance—not for her. But she had that tiny fear that he would try to 'do the right thing'—that he would be as chivalrous and generous as she knew him to be.

So she had to show him that she could handle all of this on her own. That it would make no difference to his life. That he could remain free.

The fact was, he would have lost interest in *her* soon enough anyway. She'd been that temporary aberration, a different kind of fling for him. But her heart sputtered in a last little fight at that thought—she'd started to believe it might be something a little more special than that.

But that wishful thought could never be tested now because she would *never* use this pregnancy to lay *any* kind of claim on him. She had to shut him out for now, until she'd proven her total independence.

'Kitty?' Teddy sounded puffed as he answered her call on only the second ring.

'Yeah—'

'Alejandro has been calling me round the clock wanting to know if I knew where you were and if you're okay. Are you okay?'

She closed her eyes. 'I need your help. Please. Where are you right now?'

Teddy spoke rapidly, his concern audible, but she couldn't tell him anything yet either—only that she needed a safe haven, and quickly. She didn't stop at Parkes House— she went straight to Teddy. And, from him, to a train.

It was another ninety minutes after seeing Teddy before she summoned the strength and courage necessary to phone Alejandro himself. By now she'd been operating on automatic flight mode for so long, it wasn't difficult to sound detached. And that was good. She just had to keep blocking the pain for a few moments longer.

'Where the hell are you?' Alejandro demanded as soon as he heard her voice. 'Kitty, what's happened?'

'Nothing. I just realised I'd made a mistake and wanted to return to London.'

'A mistake?' he queried harshly.

'It's over, Alejandro.' She couldn't get her voice above a whisper.

'What kind of mistake?'

'Coming to New York with you. Us having an affair.'

There was a pause.

'Is there someone else?' he asked, a different tone in his voice. Fear.

Kitty shut her eyes tightly and grasped hold of the excuse he'd just handed her. 'Yes.'

'I don't believe you,' he said bluntly. 'Something's happened. Tell me what's happened.'

She swallowed and repeated her stance, determined to stick to her game plan for forcing him away from her. 'It's very simple. I've met someone else. I wanted to tell you before you found out some other way. It was fun while it lasted.'

Alejandro stopped pacing across the floor of his empty apartment and listened harder, trying to ascertain something—anything—in the resulting silence.

'Kitty?' He couldn't believe she'd just said that.

Now he replayed the cruel words in his head and realised that they echoed those he'd said to Saskia those few short weeks ago. Saskia and every other woman before her. The irony wasn't lost on him. And now his anger began to build.

Had she done all of this deliberately? Was she out to teach him that 'lesson' she'd long ago said he deserved?

'You're back in London?' Now he'd heard from her and could tell that—physically at least—she was safe, he was sure of it. 'I'm on the next flight.'

He walked out of his apartment and locked it as he spoke. He'd been packed and ready for the last twelve hours while he'd been desperately trying to track her down.

'Don't!' she suddenly snapped, her voice rising in pitch and volume. 'You won't find me, Alejandro. Accept it's over and move on.'

She ended the call.

For a moment sheer rage blinded him. He'd find her and find out the goddamn truth or—

What? What would he do?

His blood iced but bile boiled up his throat. Shame burned at how angry he'd felt less than a second ago. And, now, how hurt he felt.

But as he replayed her last desperate words in his mind, he heard the pain evident in her tone. Something was wrong. Very wrong. And when Kitty was hurt or upset she ran away. She'd run to Cornwall when her fiancé had cheated on her. She'd gone to her secret room as a child when her father had let her down.

It was what she always did.

When he called her phone back again she didn't answer. Not the first time. Or the fifteenth.

CHAPTER THIRTEEN

TEDDY PARKES-WILSON STRAIGHTENED up and shook his head. 'I'm never going to tell you where she is,' he said before Alejandro had a chance to speak. 'Say what you like. Do what you like. You'll never get it out of me.'

'Relax. I'm not about to beat it out of you.' Alejandro stared into the younger man's eyes. 'I wouldn't ask you to betray her trust. I wouldn't expect you to and I wouldn't respect you if you did.'

He shoved his hands into his pockets, hiding the way his fingers had curled into fists in frustration. But he meant what he'd said; he wasn't about to bully anyone. That was the whole point. 'I know you're loyal to her,' he said to Teddy, unable to hide his bitter censure. 'Even though you take advantage of her.'

Teddy looked annoyed, but accepting. 'That's why I won't tell you. I owe her and I know it.'

Alejandro had known Teddy wouldn't give his twin up. But he wasn't giving up either. 'I will find her.'

'Even though she doesn't want you to? You'll still hunt her down?'

'Yes.' Alejandro forced himself not to flinch, hating the way Teddy seemed to think he was some kind of monster— what had Kitty said to him? 'Because she and I need to re-solve this face-to-face.'

He needed to see her one last time. If only to under-stand. If only to reassure her that she didn't need to run away from *him*. He didn't understand why she'd run and the least she could give him was that explanation. He re-fused to be someone who was feared. That was his worst nightmare.

'I think this belongs to you.' He pulled the diamond choker from his pocket and held it out.

Teddy's face flooded with colour in that sudden way his sister's did. 'It does, but I don't deserve it.' He took the necklace. 'I'll give it to her.'

Alejandro walked out of the small rehearsal studio none the wiser as to where Kitty actually was. Not Cornwall this time—that would be too obvious. Not Corsica to be with her father. He guessed she'd probably used some of Teddy's resources. But he had resources too. And he'd use every last one of them to track her down.

He hated the darkness of his thoughts, yet he couldn't stop them consuming his mind and time. He couldn't bear the thought of her with another man and refused to believe she actually was. Yet doubts wormed. Jealousy festered. He had to know the truth behind why she'd ended it.

He had to know she was okay.

But it was almost a full month since she'd left New York before his phone buzzed with a profitable call from the private investigator he'd engaged weeks earlier. A month in which Alejandro had worked around the clock. A month in which he'd been unable to sleep, in which he'd not gone out to dinner because he couldn't face the feeling of isolation in crowded places, in which he'd paced the empty rooms of her former family home and wished she was there with him.

A month of hell.

'There's a crofter's cottage on the Highland estate of one of the brother's theatre friends that's sometimes rented out as a holiday home,' the investigator said briskly but with obvious excitement in his tone. 'It's been booked out for the next few months.'

'And she's there?'

'I believe it's her but I'm sending you a picture now for confirmation.'

Alejandro rang off and stared at his phone impatiently,

waiting for the photo to land. When it did he drew in a sharp breath and was glad he was sitting down. His muscles emptied of energy. His heart stopped.

The shot was taken from a distance but with a long lens to get a close-up on her face, which meant it was slightly blurry. But he instantly recognised her. She was wearing a woollen coat—black, of course—and her hair was loose. Her skin was as pale as ever, her freckles as pretty. But there were no sparks in those emerald eyes.

He phoned the investigator back. 'Give me the address.'

'I've texted it to you already.'

Alejandro closed his eyes. 'Is she staying there alone?'

'Yes.'

He cut the call, groaning in bitter relief. He'd go there this instant. He broke into a run, storming out of his office in the early morning, abandoning the meetings scheduled and not giving a damn.

He worked out it was fastest to fly to Glasgow and drive from there. But it still took too long—hours of adrenalin, of a mounting headache that threatened his vision, of a tightening in his chest that made it hard to breathe. Hours of trying to work out what to say to her first.

But when he finally parked up outside the small cottage in the early evening he could see at once that it was empty. The curtains weren't drawn, there were no lights on, no other vehicle on the driveway. He clenched the steering wheel of the plush rental car and bit back his bellow of frustration. Had she somehow heard he was on his way? That was impossible. He'd told no one where he was going.

He got out of the car anyway to peer into the windows of the cottage and see if any of her stuff was visible. In the first window he couldn't see much. There was an open-plan lounge and kitchen with a number of impressive paintings on the wall, a plump armchair placed near the window to catch the sun and the low table next to it had a used teacup and a book on it, but there were no identifiable clothes draped anywhere...

He realised the barking in the distance was growing louder. He stepped back from the window to walk along the small veranda and rounded the corner so he could see behind the cottage.

An Irish red setter bounded towards him ahead of a slim figure walking behind it. She wore a beanie but her fiery hair flowed out from underneath it. And she wore black, of course. Not the cute little tailored trousers; this was an exercise combination—leggings and a sleek merino top that clung to her...*curves*.

She'd been out for a walk. There was colour in her cheeks. That colour drained the second she saw him.

Alejandro's eyes narrowed as he stared hard back at her.

For a heartbeat her pace faltered. Her hand lifted in a barrier across her belly. A small giveaway gesture of protectiveness. That book on the table inside flashed in Alejandro's mind. The title that he'd seen but not really registered.

Pregnancy & Beyond: A Guide to Baby's First Year.

And the expression in Kitty's eyes now?

Guilt.

'How did you find me?' Her voice shook as she neared enough for him to hear her.

He couldn't answer. He couldn't stop staring at the changes in her body—tiny changes, yes, but even in the slimming black attire they were obvious to him. Her breasts were fuller, as was her slender belly. She was pregnant. He was certain of it. And he knew to his bones that it was his.

This was why she'd left him.

He only needed to look into her eyes for a second to know what she was going to do and he'd not expect anything less from her.

She would have the child. She would love the child.

For a second he was blinded and his gut burned. Molten rage scoured his ribs. He had not felt so hurt since—

He shut his eyes. Blocking the memory and the wave of emotion that threatened to overwhelm him.

This was not what he wanted. This was *never* what he'd wanted.

'*That bastard's blood*—' he choked. Unable to move. Unable to utter another word.

He'd never wanted this. Never, ever. He'd wanted the whole sorry mess to die when he did. He'd forced himself to forget it for almost all of his life. It was over. Only now it wasn't.

'Alejandro—'

He threw out his hand to stop her from stepping nearer to him. He was too angry.

'I need time,' he snapped. 'You've had…*weeks* to get used to this. Give me…give me…'

Kitty stopped in her tracks as shame burned. He *knew*. He'd found her and he knew and he was so very angry.

She didn't blame him. She should have told him so much sooner. But the days had slipped by and she'd been focused on finding a quiet place to settle for a while. On keeping well. On *hiding*. She'd been such a coward. But she couldn't be now. She swallowed and made herself speak.

'I'll be in the cottage,' she said quietly. 'Whenever you want to talk.'

She wouldn't blame him if he got back into his car and drove away. He'd hate her for this and maybe he was right to. And wasn't that what she'd wanted? Hadn't she done this deliberately to force this kind of response from him?

Yes, she was that much of a coward.

But she left the door to the small cottage open and stood with her back to the door because she couldn't cope with watching him, waiting to see what he would choose to do. The dog let her know when Alejandro stepped inside. She turned as he barked and saw him run up to Alejandro, his tail wagging crazily as he nuzzled Alejandro's hand, asking for a pat.

Alejandro complied, but he didn't look down at the animal. He was too busy staring at her and so obviously keeping himself in check. Emotion burned in his eyes. The trouble was she didn't know what emotion it was.

'Are you keeping well?' he finally asked.

'I'm fine, Alejandro. I'm okay.' She walked over to him and closed the door.

He didn't take a seat, though; he just stood there—too large for this room. Too big for her heart.

She saw his pallor and the torment in his eyes and her willpower broke. She couldn't help reaching out to cup his jaw. But he flinched and pulled back before she made contact. She curled her fingers into a fist, hurt by his rejection even when she knew she deserved his anger.

She turned away. 'I'll put the kettle on,' she said lamely.

'Don't,' he said shortly. 'This won't take long.'

She hadn't got even halfway across the room. Now she turned back to face him.

'So there is no one else?' he said quietly.

She lifted her chin. 'There's the baby.'

The emotion in his eyes flared as she referred to it. Confirmed it.

'I know you don't want children,' she said quickly. 'That's why I left. I don't expect anything from you. I never will.'

He turned on his heel, strode to the window and stared out of it at the darkening sky. 'You didn't give me a chance. You ran away without talking to me. You have made your decision without me,' he muttered in a low voice. 'I suppose there is nothing more to be said.'

Yes, that was what she'd wanted, right? For him to say nothing. For him not to fight. Not to try to 'step up' and be the husband and father to her child that secretly she so very badly desired. But having him behave as she'd thought she wanted him to hurt.

'You might not want this child, but I do,' she said defensively.

He turned his head and glared at her. 'You want it for the wrong reasons.'

What wrong reasons? 'To trap you into paying money to me?' she guessed wildly. Her hurt morphed into sudden, vicious anger. 'I said I don't want anything from you.'

Which was a lie, but what she truly wanted she could never have.

'You want this baby because you want someone to love you,' he snapped.

Shocked, she just stared open-mouthed at him, feeling as if she'd been ditched—hanging fifty feet up a cliff with no foothold. 'I wasn't the one who didn't bother with the condom. I wasn't the one who—'

'All your life you've wanted someone to adore you and now you think you've got it,' he interrupted coldly.

'I didn't *plan* this—' she fought back.

'But what are you going to do when it gets hard? Are you going to run away and abandon it when times are tough?'

'Of course not.' She flung her head, stung by his attack. 'And you know what? There's nothing wrong with wanting to be loved.' She burned inside—so wounded, so bereft. 'Or with wanting *to* love someone. At least I'm not afraid to put myself out there and *try*.'

His nostrils flared as he whirled to face her, his stance widening as he braced.

But she stepped forward, too hurt to stop.

'You don't let anyone into your life. Not properly. You basically buy their company with your success and your… skills.' She saw him flinch but she carried on anyway. 'It's not the sex that bothers me. It's the *superficiality*. You keep everything shallow so you can't be hurt.'

He paled in front of her and she felt a twinge of remorse. 'I cannot imagine the horror you experienced as a child... But you're stopping yourself feeling anything except shallow pleasure. You use sex as a temporary muscle relaxant. You're worth more than that.'

And so was she.

'You don't understand,' he said gruffly.

'Then help me understand. Talk to me.'

'The way you talked to me?' He stared at her pointedly.

She slumped into a seat. 'I'm sorry, okay? I'm sorry I didn't tell you.' She glanced up at him. 'I'm sorry if I hurt you.'

'It's not about stopping me from getting hurt,' he muttered. 'When I came back from New York that first time I was away from you, I was jealous of your *brother*.' He closed his eyes for a moment and then looked at her bleakly. 'I can't become that obsessed, Catriona. I can't become that monster.'

She straightened, surprised at his bitter words. 'You'd never be a monster.'

He threw her a pitying look and shook his head at her naivety. 'It's started already,' he argued. 'I took you to New York because I couldn't bear the thought of wondering what you were doing. Who you were with. What I was missing out on. Am I going to become so controlling that I can't leave you alone? That's not normal.'

In that moment hope sparked within her. Had he felt that deeply about her? Did he want more than just a temporary fling with her?

He looked tortured. 'I never wanted to spread the poison that's in my veins.'

Now she realised the hell he was putting himself through. She put her hand across her belly. 'This is a totally innocent baby. Just as you were a totally innocent child. You're not him, Alejandro—you'll *never* be him.'

'I have his eyes.'

'You have your own eyes. You're your own person.' She'd had no idea that this was what he feared. Was this what caused his nightmares?

But he shook his head. 'I can't take the risk. I can't get...' he glanced down at her body and then back up to her face '...I can't get involved.'

It hurt to hear him say it so bluntly.

'Are we not worth the attempt?'

He didn't even want to *try*. She understood that he was hurt, but it hurt her too. So much. Why couldn't someone ever love her the way she loved them? What was it that was wrong with her? Why did she have to miss out again?

'You deserve better than this, Kitty. Better than me.'

That wasn't true—she deserved better *from* him.

'Everybody struggles with their emotions sometimes.' She attempted a smile as she tried to reason with him. And to be as honest as she could. 'I've been so jealous of all those women of yours. I've been so insecure.' She still was. 'But I keep on *trying*. You're worth it to me. This is worth it.'

'So worth it, you ran away without giving me any kind of explanation.' His cheeks looked hollow; he was even paler than before.

'I was scared.'

'Of me,' he said heavily.

'Not because I thought you'd hurt me physically. It was just that I wanted more than you wanted to give me.' She drew in her lip and bit down on it hard. But there was no reason to hold back now. 'I want you to love me. Because I love you.'

He shook his head. 'That can't happen.'

'Because you don't want to get hurt again?'

'Because I cannot do to my child what my father did to me,' he corrected her furiously. 'He ripped me apart, Kitty. He destroyed everything I had.'

'Not everything. You're still here. You've rebuilt so much. People get help for all kinds of issues…' She stood up and walked towards him. 'Why let him steal your future? Your happiness?' She reached him, her heart thundering. 'By shutting yourself away you're letting him win.' She gazed into his beautiful troubled eyes. 'He didn't want anyone else to have your mother. No one else to have you. You're letting him win by locking your heart away. You should show him the middle finger and fight to have a full and happy life. You could get some help; I could help—'

'I can't be the man you need me to be,' he snapped. 'I can't be him. I just can't.'

The finality in his tone devastated her. 'Because you don't love me.'

Not enough to want to try. That was what hurt so much. Not her. Not even the tiny baby she carried. Always, she wasn't enough.

'It's because I *do* love you that I can't,' he roared.

'What?' She stared at him fixedly. 'What did you say?'

He looked back at her; that emotion in his deep eyes was nothing but heartbreak. 'Don't,' he whispered. 'Don't, Kitty.'

Don't make him say it again? Don't make it harder? Don't step closer?

Her eyes filled with tears as her heart broke for both of them. Why couldn't he try for her? She framed his face in her hands, feeling the roughness of his evening stubble. His skin was so warm and he was so beautiful to her. Her heart filled to bursting—with disappointment, with desire, with aching love. She reached onto her tiptoes and kissed him.

He was as still as a statue as she kissed him. But he wasn't cold like marble—he was hot and straining as he held back. She didn't want him to hold back any more—not in any of his emotions.

She kissed him more deeply—winding her arms around his neck. She didn't care about anything else in this instant. There was no point in trying to argue any more. In trying to think. In this one moment of life there was only the need to touch and to feel him again. To have him with her.

To love him.

His hands came to her waist and she pressed closer to him, needing to feel his strength against her now more than ever. And she wanted to reassure him somehow. She wanted him to know how she felt. She wanted him to believe that this could work. This strong, gentle man was so scarred that he couldn't see himself as he really was.

He kissed her back now and suddenly turned her so her back was pressed to the wall—his natural inclination to dominate resurging. She welcomed it—helped him, shimmying down her pants as she leaned back against the wall and then fought with the zip of his trousers. She needed him in this way at least. She'd missed this so much—the searing, unstoppable attraction. The need to take and be taken. She sealed his mouth in that hot, deep kiss, silencing any opposition of his or the spilling of more of her secrets. The kiss told him everything anyway.

She wanted him. She needed him. She loved him.

For once it wasn't the culmination of a challenge, or the finale to a playful flirt. This was nothing but pure emotion. A final kiss, a final connection. All the pain of goodbye. All the love that was being lost.

'Please.' She arched in readiness as he angled her hips in that delightfully sure way. He was hard and she was wet and he pushed to his hilt in one powerful thrust. She cried out at the physical pleasure—at the emotional pain. She felt such completion and yet her heart was being torn apart.

'I'm so sorry.' His voice broke as he paused, looking

into her eyes with such torment in his. 'I never wanted to hurt you.'

'It doesn't matter,' she muttered as he gave her the one thing he could.

It was worth it. It would always be worth it.

She rocked her hips, riding him, their coupling hot and wet and as easy as always. But tears coursed down her cheeks as she met him thrust for thrust. He brushed them away but they kept tumbling.

'Kitty,' he pleaded as he pressed deeply into her again and again. His brow was wet, his frown pained. 'I'm sorry.'

Fearlessly, unashamedly she looked into his eyes—she would not hide her feelings from him now. She wrapped her arms more tightly around him and kissed him again and again and again. She loved him. She loved doing this with him. She would never regret any of it. And she never wanted it to end.

But all of the emotions were too big for her to hold—they had to burst free from her. She cried out as the sensations became too exquisite for her body to bear.

He buried his face in her neck. He shuddered violently and his pained, pleasure-soaked groan rang in her ears. She squeezed hard—holding him as deep and as close and for as long as she possibly could. Because it was her last moment with him.

But in the end the intense spasms of pleasure wreaked havoc on her muscles—rendering her limp and weak and leaving her with nothing but words.

He was still. Silent. And, in some ways, stronger than her.

In another heartbeat it would end.

'I love you, Alejandro,' she whispered. 'And I would have loved you no matter what.'

He didn't reply—no word, no look, no action. For one last breath she had him with her. But then she felt his muscles ripple. He flexed and then disengaged—from her body, from her embrace. It took only a moment for him to straighten his clothing and step back from her. His head was bowed so he avoided her eyes. But she wasn't afraid to look at him. There was nothing to be afraid of now. The worst had happened. *Was* happening.

She watched as, without a word, he walked out of her life.

CHAPTER FOURTEEN

KITTY RECEIVED A parcel from Alejandro's lawyer less than a week later. Delivered by courier, the documents explained that a large settlement of money for the child was to be held in trust, together with a monthly allowance that was enough to house, feed and clothe ten children, not just one tiny baby. And he'd gifted her Parkes House and all its contents. No strings. No reversion to the child once he or she was of age. It was hers and hers alone.

There was a note in the letter, penned by the lawyer, informing her that Alejandro was returning to New York and that he planned to stay in a hotel on the occasions he needed to return to London for his work.

She knew he'd avoid it as much as he could. He'd almost never be there.

Her heart solidified. He might be trying to mean well, but she didn't want any of what he was offering her. Not money or physical security.

Time stagnated. The days dragged, but the nights were the worst—she paced, unable to sleep. She missed him. Ached for him. Loved him. And was so angry with him.

A few days later she heard the sound of a car pulling up outside the cottage. Her heart raced for the first time. She opened the door. *Alejandro?*

'Hey, sis! You went quiet—' Teddy broke off from his cheery greeting as he got out of the car and stared at her. His expression morphed to total concern. 'Kit—'

'Don't,' she begged him. 'I know I look... Don't say anything.'

'Jeez, you better get back inside and sit down.' He followed her into the cottage and sat on the sofa opposite her armchair. 'Talk to me.'

'I'm okay, Teddy.'

'Oh, sure you are.' Her twin rolled his eyes. 'You've seen him then?'

She nodded. 'It's finished.'

Teddy frowned then reached into his pocket. 'Alejandro gave it to me.' He handed her Margot's diamond choker. 'But let's face it. It ought to have been yours in the first place.'

Kitty curled her fist around the gleaming coils of platinum and diamonds so she couldn't see it. 'Would you be devastated if I sold it?'

'Why do you want to do that?' Teddy looked shocked.

'Because I need to be independent from him. I can get some capital from this, then sort myself out.' If she was having this baby on her own, she didn't want anyone else to have to pay for it.

'Are you sure the two of you can't work it out?' Teddy leaned forward. 'He looked a wreck. So do you.'

Kitty closed her eyes. 'It's more complicated than… It's just better this way.'

'But you're both miserable. I don't see how that's better than trying to sort it.'

'He doesn't want to try, Teddy,' she said brokenly and the tears finally tumbled. 'That's the point. He doesn't want to *try*.'

Half an hour later, Kitty's tears were dried and she was curled up in the chair watching her brother as he made her a couple of pieces of toast that she didn't feel like eating but knew she had to.

Alejandro wasn't coming back; she accepted that now. No more waiting for a car to arrive. It was over between them. He'd made his decision and she had to move on too.

Maybe Alejandro had been right. Maybe she did run away when times got tough—but not any more.

And maybe part of her wanted this child because she wanted someone to love her. Was that so terrible? But she was the parent here and she was damn determined to ensure that her child felt utterly, *unconditionally* loved. No matter what. Her baby would never feel like he or she wasn't good enough, would never come second to another all the time. Kitty would do everything she could to make her child emotionally whole and secure and happy. The hurts of past generations would not be passed on by her.

And it was beyond time that she pulled herself together and got on with it.

'Can I get a lift back to London with you?' she asked Teddy as he handed her the plate of hot buttered toast.

'Of course.'

New York. The city in which to forget everything. The city where he could get anything, everything and anyone.

Except the one he wanted.

Alejandro stood up from his desk and shrugged on his jacket, ready to go to one of his favourite restaurants. Now was the time to get on with his life. He'd been in a kind of stasis during that month when he'd been unable to find her—he hadn't been able to go back to 'normal' until he'd cleared the air with her. But now he'd done that. More than that, he'd made provision for her and the baby.

His conscience was clear. He'd done all he could.

He'd enjoy his life again. He just needed to get on with it again.

'We haven't seen you here in a while, Alejandro.' The maître d' smiled at him. 'Your guests are already at your usual table.'

'Thank you.'

He'd return to his easy, shallow social whirl.

But it wasn't easy. They welcomed him with bright smiles and barely veiled curiosity that he ignored. He listened to the dinner party chatter. It now seemed inane. Where was the passion? Where was the love for something—anything—other than a party? He glanced around the table, unable to raise a smile. The women were intelligent and beautiful, the men equally talented and all were competitive and driven.

'Are you ready to order, sir?' The waiter interrupted his thoughts.

Alejandro put the menu card down. 'Actually, I've changed my mind. I'm sorry everyone—' he cast a smile around the table '—I won't be dining with you tonight after all.'

He decided to bury himself in work instead. That at least he was passionate about. That at least was productive.

He worked such long hours he lost track of when it was day and when it was night. That was the good thing about having offices in different countries—one was always open. There were always emails to send and markets to watch. Nightmares to avoid. Loneliness to deny.

Who are you going to leave your billions to?

He thought about a tiny baby with hair the colour of a bonfire. Once he'd let that thought whisper in, the rest tumbled behind it in a flood. The memories he'd been blocking for days. The way she'd challenged him. The way she'd laughed with him. The way she'd looked at him. The way she'd held him.

I love you, Alejandro.

She'd felt so good. But then she'd looked so sad. And she was right—he was such a coward. She deserved so much better than him.

So become the man she needs you to be.

He fought against that little voice—the nagging thread of hope. Of possibility. The dream. He was doing the right thing already. She'd get over it. She was better off without him and the risk he bore.

It was almost midnight several days later when the email landed. He stiffened when he saw Teddy Parkes-Wilson's name as the sender. Had something happened? Was she well? Surely Teddy would phone if it was something bad?

He clicked to open it, suddenly fearful of what her brother was emailing about. He'd pulled the investigator off her. Her life was hers; he was not spying on her. He was not becoming that creep.

But there was no message in Teddy's email—only a link to another website. Great, he was being spammed by her brother. He clicked the link anyway.

It took him to an online auction site—specifically to a series of listings from one vendor. His eyes narrowed as he recognised the first few items. All those designer black dresses. Those shoes. Kitty had placed everything she'd bought with his money up for auction. There was a highlighted comment in the blurb on each stating that all the proceeds would be donated to a leading charity for the survivors of domestic violence.

His throat burned. Shame hollowed him out. But he couldn't stop scrolling down. There were so many memories attached to those dresses. Even the ones she'd not had the chance to wear.

He paused when he came to the emerald dress that she'd worn that last night they'd had together in Manhattan. But it was the entry just beneath that which broke his heart.

The antique diamond choker. This time the proceeds were not listed as going to charity. Alejandro knew exactly why.

Teddy had given it to her and she was using it to gain a foothold on her future. He knew the money in the account he'd set up for her had been untouched. She'd save it for the child but not use a cent for herself. Her integrity and pride wouldn't let her. Now she was doing what she thought she had to do, to make her way independently. She was willing to sacrifice something she loved, for the benefit of someone else. She always put others first, even when it wasn't necessary.

Well, not this time. He wasn't letting her.

CHAPTER FIFTEEN

'WHAT DO YOU MEAN, the auction site is down?' Kitty glared at the wall as she tried to understand what the man on the helpline was telling her. 'None of my items are up there any more.'

'I know; we're looking into it. We can phone you back once we've located the issue.'

She didn't want them to phone her back; she just wanted it fixed. But she hung up with a sigh and turned back to her new creation on the dining table. She needed to keep focused, keep working, keep moving forward.

Someone banged on the front door just as she was about to begin sketching a 'laser nozzle' for the interstellar transporter. She wiped her hands and went to the door.

'Alejandro.' She stepped back almost instantly, suddenly self-conscious in her splattered tee and ancient leggings. He might have helped her address her body confidence issues, but she'd still rather not be in her painting rags.

'May I come in?' he asked.

He looked better than the last time she'd seen him—not as pale or angular. His eyes were brighter and vitality radiated from him. That was good, right? He was obviously doing well.

But it ripped her heart all over again.

'Of course.' She brushed her hair behind her ear. 'It's still your house.'

He didn't respond to that as he walked in ahead of her. Nervously, she ran her hands down the sides of her legs and followed him.

'You're making more props?' He turned into the kitchen and noted the clay sticking to her tee with a small grin.

'Yes.' She summoned a smile to match his. 'They liked the shield and commissioned more.'

'I'm not surprised.'

She nodded and then looked at him, her heart thudding. 'How can I help?'

He drew his hand from his pocket. She gasped as she saw what he held—Margot's diamonds.

'Where did you get that?' she asked.

'You're not to sell it, Kitty—it means too much to you.'

'How did you get it?' She'd left it in the safe at the auction house.

'I bought it.' A wry grin crossed his face. 'It and several rather stylish dresses.'

'You *didn't*. From my auction?'

He nodded.

'You bought everything?' That was crazy.

'I know it's stupid, but I couldn't bear to think of anyone else wearing them.'

'But you paid for them all *twice*.'

'I don't care.'

'Oh, Alejandro.' Tears pricked her eyes. He melted her, every time. 'Why did you do that?'

Alejandro turned and walked away from her. There was too much he had to say and he lost track of everything when he looked at her. 'I need to tell you about my father.'

He heard her sharp inhalation.

'You don't have to do that.'

'I do. Please.' He took a seat at the furthest end of the table from her so he wasn't tempted to touch her. He had to get this off his chest. He had to get her to understand. 'I don't like to talk about it much, but there's a lot I remember. There'd been other incidents before that day. He was possessive. Jealous. He hit her. And me.' He dragged in another shuddering breath. Saying this aloud to her was harder than he'd thought it would be. But he'd worked on

it with his new counsellor, and he was determined he'd
get himself sorted. For himself and for Kitty. 'He'd get
jealous of me. He'd say she spent more time with me than
with him. That she loved me more than him. Like it was
a competition.'

Kitty didn't say anything; she just came forward and sat
in the chair next to his.

His father had been wrong. His father had been evil. But
he had his blood in his veins.

'When she took me and left him for good, he flipped
out.' Alejandro avoided looking at Kitty's face as he said
it. 'He tracked us down and came after her. She stepped in
front of me. She died protecting me.' It hurt so much but he
could never forget. And until now he'd never really understood what had driven her. 'That's what mothers do, isn't
it? They fight for their young. They'll do anything for their
children. Fathers should too.' He lifted his head and looked
at her. 'And fathers should love their daughters every bit as
much as they love their sons.'

Her sweet face crumpled. 'Alejandro—'

'I think my father confused love with possession. He
held on to her and refused to let her go because he saw her
as *his*.' He fought back the emotion clogging his throat.
'And I promised myself I was never going to be like that
with any woman. I wasn't going to marry. I wasn't going
to have kids. It was all so clear and so easy for so long.
And then you stole into my new home and I turned into a
demanding creep.'

'No—'

'I locked you in the library,' he growled. 'For heaven's
sake, Kitty, I was awful to you that night.'

But she shook her head. 'You weren't that bad. I was the
one who'd broken in. I was the one in the wrong.'

'But I took advantage of that. I saw you and I wanted
you so I used every chance that came my way to keep you

with me.' He'd taken total advantage of everything to do with her. 'All you wanted was what should always have been yours. The necklace.'

'But I also wanted you,' she said softly with a small shrug. 'I took one look at you and…you fascinated me. Maddened me. But I wanted you the second I saw you. You were more honest about that than me.' She licked her lips. 'And then I got to know you. You didn't bully me into staying there with you. You didn't threaten me with violence. Not once.'

'But you had to stay only because I had something you wanted.'

'What I really wanted was you.' She smiled sadly at him. 'And if I had really wanted to leave, you wouldn't have stopped me. We both know that.'

Did they? Would he have let her walk out? Not with the diamonds, but without. Yes, he would have.

Her smile deepened as she watched him. 'You would have figured out the ownership of the necklace and returned it. You're not dishonest. You're just. And that night with the necklace was the catalyst for the attraction between us. My staying here was convenient for us both. It's just that I couldn't admit it at the time. I never wanted to admit how attracted I was to you because it overwhelmed me. But I stayed and then really got to know you. That's when I was really in trouble.'

Alejandro couldn't dare believe that she truly cared for him. He didn't deserve it when he'd been so arrogant and so damn dismissive. 'I don't want to make you unhappy. I don't want you to feel trapped. I need to be able to let you go. I have to let you go.' He ruffled his hair distractedly, unable to get the words right. 'Because I'm afraid of myself.' He looked up at her. 'But now I'm more afraid of life without you. I'm so sorry I walked away from you that day in Scotland, Kitty. I'm so sorry.'

Kitty was struggling to believe that he was here. That he'd bought all those dresses all over again. That he was gifting her the diamonds.

Most of all that he'd opened up to her about his father and about his fears.

And she was too afraid to really question why. She couldn't bear to have her heart broken twice over.

'There's something I need to tell you,' she said quickly. 'I had my first pregnancy scan yesterday.'

He paled and she saw the fear flare in his eyes.

'It's okay,' she added quickly. 'Everything is okay.' She swallowed. 'Better than okay in some ways.' She breathed out, struggling to stay in control. 'I'm having twins.'

'Twins,' he echoed softly, his eyebrows lifting.

'Two babies. Twins. Yes.' She still couldn't believe it herself. 'That's why I'm showing so much more at this stage.'

'I thought that was just because you're not very...' He trailed off. 'Twins...' He looked dumbfounded.

'Yes. It's in the family.' She half smiled.

But his expression was shuttered.

She kicked herself for the reminder about genetics and the passing on of particular traits. 'Not that we inherit...'

'No, it's okay.' He huffed out a breath. 'It's just that I don't want you to think I'm here because of the baby... Babies.' He rubbed his hand through his hair. 'The pregnancy isn't relevant—it's you I want.'

Her pulse pounded loudly in her ears and she was glad because she was terrified of hearing what he was going to say next.

'Kitty—'

'You know that marriages with multiples are more likely to fail?' she interrupted in a rush. 'Financial pressures. Lack of sleep. Extra stress.'

He smiled at her—a slow, tender, vulnerable smile.

'We won't have financial pressures and we can get help—nannies, cooks, cleaners, whatever it takes. We're in a better position than most. The thing is, I don't know how to be a father,' he said huskily. 'I didn't have a good example.'

She shifted on her seat, moving nearer so she could hear every one of his almost whispered words.

'And I've never had a relationship last much longer than a month.' He leaned closer to her too. 'But I want it all with you, Kitty. I want you. I love you.'

'I don't really know how to be a mother yet, either,' she offered shyly. 'A bit of instinct maybe, some help from the experts, and we'll be okay.'

'More than okay. I know I need help processing everything.' He looked intense. 'I know you know about the nightmares. I hadn't had them in so long, but then with you I guess everything opened up...' He trailed off and cleared his throat. 'I thought I had it all together, but I didn't. I wince at the way I treated those women. I was cavalier. I thought I was doing no harm. But I was.'

She reached out and framed his face with her hands. He needed to stop beating himself up. He needed to believe in himself the way she did. 'You're okay, Alejandro. You're a good guy. And I love you.'

'You've changed my life,' he said simply. 'I love you so much. I want to be the man you need. I'm going to be.'

There was the determination she loved in him.

'You already are,' she promised him. 'You *are*.'

A half smile lit in his eyes and he reached into his pocket. 'I got this for you.'

There was a rushing in her ears as he opened the small box and she saw the diamond ring.

'The jeweller worked round the clock to match the style to the choker, but if you don't like it we can get another.'

'I don't want another.'

'You don't have to wear it.'

She laughed through her tears. 'Stop it. I love it. You didn't have to do that—just coming here was enough. All I wanted was *you*.'

'Oh?' He reached into his pocket again, some of his cocky arrogance returning. 'But I got these too. For, I don't know...next week?'

She stared at the heavy matching wedding bands in his palm.

'Too soon?' There was an edge of anxiety in him now.

'No,' she whispered. 'Oh, Alejandro.' She launched into his arms. 'I need to feel you again,' she confessed. 'So much.'

His laugh was brief but exultant and he stood and quickly turned, flinging the rings to the floor so both his hands were free—to hold her close. Caress her. Claim her.

The kisses were fiery and frantic and the fabric separating their bodies tore. But then, just when he was so nearly hers, he stilled.

'I've missed you.' He trembled as he held back. 'I don't want to hurt you—'

'You won't. It's okay. I want you so much.'

He was gentle anyway, holding her protectively in his arms as they reconnected again in this most intimate, most emotional of ways.

'I love you,' he told her.

Again. Then again. Until her tears flowed and he kissed them away and made her sigh in unbearable pleasure. She'd never imagined it was possible to be *this* happy.

'Two babies,' he breathed hoarsely as he rolled onto his back and lifted her so her head rested on his chest. 'Heaven help me if they have red hair.'

'And freckles.' She mock-shivered. 'The poor kids.'

'They'll be lucky to have them,' he said, idly tracing hers now with a lazy fingertip. 'They're beautiful on you.'

She pushed up and rolled so she was astride him. She

shook her head, letting her hair tumble to tickle him, and delighted in the way he looked at her. Finally, she believed in them both. 'You're crazy.'

He smiled into her eyes, relaxed and free, able to enjoy the tease. 'About you. Absolutely.' He kissed her tenderly. 'Always.'

* * * * *

THE MARRIAGE CONTRACT

KAT CANTRELL

Dayna Hart: this one is for you because *Beauty and the Beast* is your favourite.

One

Despite never having believed in miracles, Desmond Pierce witnessed one at 7:23 p.m. on an otherwise non-descript Tuesday as he glimpsed his son for the first time.

A nurse in navy blue scrubs carried the mewling infant into the small room off the main hospital corridor where Desmond had been instructed to wait. The moment his gaze lit on the baby, he felt a zap of recognition in his gut.

My son.

Awed into speechlessness, Des reached out to touch the future.

Warmth and something totally foreign clogged his throat. Tears. Joy. Vindication.

Amazing. Who knew money really *could* buy happiness?

The kid's face screwed up in a wail of epic proportions as if the nurse had poked him with a pin. Des felt his son's distress with deeper empathy than he'd ever experienced before—and that was saying something. It winnowed through his pores, sensitizing his muscles almost to the point of pain as he held himself back from snatching the boy from the nurse's arms.

Was this terrible combination of wonder, reverence and absolute terror what it was like for all parents? Or had he been gifted with a special bond because his son wouldn't have a mother?

"How are you this evening, Mr. Pierce?" the nurse inquired pleasantly.

"Regretting the sizable donation I made to this establishment," he growled and immediately bemoaned not taking a moment to search for a more acceptable way to communicate. This, after he'd *vowed* not to be his usual gruff self. "Why is my son crying?"

Better. More in the vein of how he'd practiced in the mirror. But the hard cross of his arms over his chest didn't quell the feeling that something was wrong. The baby hadn't been real these last forty weeks, or rather Des hadn't let himself believe that this pregnancy would end differently than Lacey's.

Now that he'd seen the baby, all the stars aligned. And there was no way in hell he'd let anything happen to his son.

"He's hungry," the nurse returned with a cautious half smile. "Would you like to feed him?"

Yes. He would. But he had to nod as emotion gripped his vocal cords.

An explosion of teddy bears climbed the walls behind the rocking chair the nurse guided him to. A vinyl-sided cabinet with a sink occupied the back corner and the counter was strewn with plastic bottles.

Des had done a lot of research into bottle-feeding, as well as all other aspects of parenting: philosophies of child rearing, behavioral books by renowned specialists, websites with tips for new parents. He'd committed a lot of it to memory easily, largely owing to his excitement and interest in the subject, but then, he held two doctorates from Harvard. There were not many academics that he hadn't mastered. He was pretty sure he could handle a small task like sticking the nipple into the baby's mouth.

Carefully she settled the baby into his arms with a gentle smile. "Here you go, Dad. It's important that you hold him as much as possible."

Des zeroed in on the pink wrinkled face and the entire world fell away. His son weighed nothing at all. Less than a ten-pound barbell. Wonder tore a hole through Desmond's chest as he held his son for the first time. Instantly he cataloged everything his senses could soak in. Dark eyes. Dark hair peeking from under the knit cap.

Conner Clark Pierce. His son.

Whatever it took, he'd move heaven and earth to give this new person everything. Private tutors, trips to educational sites like the pyramids at Giza and Machu Picchu, a workshop that rivaled his father's if he wanted to invent things like Des did. The baby would have every advantage and would never want for anything, let alone a mother.

The nurse pulled the hat down more firmly on the baby's head. That's when Conner started yowling again. The baby's anguish bled through Desmond's skin, and he did not like it.

The nurse turned to the back counter. "Let me make you a bottle."

She measured out the formula over the sound of the baby's cries, which grew more upsetting as the seconds ticked by.

Des had always felt other people's pain deeply, which

was one of the many reasons he avoided crowds, but his response to his son was so much worse than general empathy. This little person shared his DNA, and whether the suggestion of it sharpened the quickening under his skin or there really was a genetic bond, the urgency of the situation could not be overstated.

She finally crossed to Des, where he'd settled into the rocking chair, and handed him the bottle. Like he'd watched in countless videos, he held the nipple to the baby's bottom lip and tipped it.

His son's lower lip trembled as he wailed, but he would not take the bottle. Des would never describe himself as patient, but he tried diligently fourteen more times.

"Why is he refusing?" Des asked the nurse as the sense of something being wrong welled up in his chest again.

"I don't know." She banked the concern in her expression but not before Des saw it. "It's not unusual for babies who are taken from their mothers to have difficulty acclimating. We can try with a dropper. A bottle isn't the only way to get the formula into his body."

Desmond nodded and bit his tongue as the nurse crowded into his space.

The dropper worked. For about five minutes. Then Conner started spitting up all over everything. The nurse frowned again and her expression tingled his spine.

Thirty minutes later, all three of them were frustrated.

"It seems he might have an allergy to formula," the nurse finally announced.

"What does that mean? He's going to starve?" Des shut his eyes in pure agony and scrubbed at his beard, which could probably use trimming but, like usual, he'd forgotten. Sometimes Mrs. Elliot, his housekeeper, reminded him, but only if they crossed paths and, lately, he'd been hiding out in his workshop in preparation for today.

For no reason apparently, since none of his prep had covered this scenario.

"No, we're not going to let that happen. We've got some options..." She trailed off. "Never mind that one. I've been made aware of your wishes regarding your son's mother, so—"

"Forget my wishes and tell me your suggestion. The baby has to eat," Des insisted.

The nurse nodded. "The baby might breast-feed. I mean, this is highly unusual. Typically it's the other way around, where we have to supplement a mother's breast milk with formula until a lactation consultant can work with her, but—"

The baby's wails cut her off.

"She's still here? At the hospital?" He'd never met his son's surrogate mother, as they'd agreed, but he was desperate for a solution.

"Well, yes. Of course. Most women take a couple of days to recover from childbirth but—"

"Take me to her." His mind went to work on how he could have said that better, but distress wasn't the best state for a do-over. "Please."

Relief eased the nurse's expression and she nodded. "Just a warning. She might not be willing to breast-feed."

"I'll convince her," he countered as he stood with the baby in his arms.

His agreement with McKenna Moore, his son's surrogate mother, had loopholes for medical necessities. Plus, she was still legally his wife; they'd married by proxy to avoid any legal snarls, but their relationship was strictly professional. Despite the fact that they had never met, hopefully being married would count for something. The baby had to eat—as soon as Desmond convinced Conner's mother that she was his only hope.

Frankly, asking for her help was a last resort. Their agreement limited Ms. Moore's involvement with the baby because Des wanted a family that was all his own. But he was desperate to look after his son's welfare.

Out into the hall they went. At room 247, the nurse stopped and inclined her head. "Give me a second to see if she's accepting visitors."

Des nodded. The baby had quieted during the walk, which was a blessing. The rocking motion had soothed him most likely. Good information to have at his disposal.

Voices from inside the room drifted out into the hall.

"He wants to what?" The feminine lilt that did not belong to the nurse could only be McKenna Moore's. She was awake and likely decent by this time since the nurse was in the room.

The baby stirred, his little face lifting toward the sound. And that decided it. Conner recognized his mother's voice and, despite the absolute conviction that the best way to handle this surrogacy situation was to never be in the same room with the woman who had given birth to his son, Desmond pushed open the door with his foot and entered.

The dark-haired figure in the hospital bed drew his eye like a siren song and when their gazes met a jolt of recognition buzzed through all his senses at once. The same sort as when he'd glimpsed his son for the first time. *Their* son.

This woman was his child's mother. This woman was his *legally wedded wife.*

McKenna Moore's features were delicate and beautiful and he'd never been so ruthlessly stirred by someone in his life. He couldn't speak, couldn't think, and for a man with a genius IQ, lack of brain function was alarming indeed. As was the sudden, irrevocable conviction that he'd made a terrible mistake in the way he'd structured the surrogacy agreement.

He couldn't help but mourn the lost opportunity to woo this woman, to get to know her. To have the option to get her pregnant the old-fashioned way.

How in the hell had he developed such a visceral attraction to his wife in the space of a few moments?

Didn't matter. He hadn't met her first because he hated to navigate social scenarios. He stumbled over the kinds of relationships that seemed easy and normal for others, which was why he lived in a remote area of Oregon, far from Astoria, the nearest city.

Desmond had always been that weird kid at the corner table. Graduating from high school at fifteen hadn't helped him forge a lot of connections. Neither had becoming a billionaire. If he'd tried to have a normal relationship with McKenna Moore, it would have ended in disaster in the same fashion as the one he'd tried with Lacey.

Bonds of blood, like the one he shared with his son, were the only answer for someone like him. This baby would be his family and fulfill Desmond's craving for an heir. Maybe his son would even love him just because.

Regardless, the baby belonged to *him*. Desmond decided what would happen to his kid and there was no one on this entire planet who could trump his wishes.

Except for maybe his wife.

But he'd paid his law firm over a million dollars to ensure the prenuptial agreement protected his fortune and an already-drafted divorce decree granted him full custody. It was ironclad, or rather, would be as soon as he filed for the divorce.

She'd recover from childbirth, take Desmond's divorce settlement money and vanish. Exactly as he'd envisioned when he'd determined the only thing that could fill the gaping hole in his life was a baby to replace the one he'd lost—or rather, the one Lacey had aborted.

Never again would he allow a woman to dictate something as critical as to whether his child would live or die. And never again would he let himself care about a woman who held even a smidgen of power over his happiness. One day, his son would understand.

"Ms. Moore," he finally growled out long past the time when it would have been appropriate to start speaking. "We have a problem. Our son needs you."

Desmond Pierce stood in McKenna's hospital room. With a crying baby.

Her baby.

The one she'd been trying really hard to forget she'd just pushed out of her body in what had to be the world's record for painful, difficult labors…and then given away.

McKenna's eyes widened as she registered what he'd just said and her eye sockets were so dry, even that hurt. Everything hurt. She wanted codeine and to sleep for three days, not a continual spike through her heart with each new cry of the baby. The muscles in her arms tensed to reach for her son so she could touch him.

She wasn't supposed to see the baby. Or hold him. The nurse had told her that when they'd taken him away, even though McKenna had begged for the chance to say goodbye. The cruel people in the delivery room had ignored her. What did they know about sacrifice? About big, gaping holes inside that nothing would ever fill?

For a second she'd thought her son's father had figured that out. That he'd come strictly to grant her wish. The look on his face as he'd come through the door—it had floored her. Their gazes connected and it was as if he could see all her angst and last-minute indecision. And understood.

I've come to fix everything, he seemed to say without a word.

But that was not the reality of why Mr. Pierce was here with the baby. Instead he was here to rip her heart to shreds. Again.

They should leave. Right now. Before she started crying.

"He's not my son," she rasped, her vocal cords still strained from the trauma of birth.

She shouldn't have said that. The phrase—both true and brutal—unfolded inside her with sharp teeth, tearing at her just as deeply as the baby's cries.

He *was* her son. The one she'd signed away because it ticked all the boxes in her head that her parents had lined up. *You should find a man, have lots of babies*, they'd said. *There's no greater joy than children.*

Except she didn't want kids. She wanted to be a doctor, to help people in pain and in need. Desmond had yearned for a baby; she could give him one and experience pregnancy without caving in to her parent's pressure. They didn't approve of western medicine. It was a huge source of conflict, especially after Grandfather had died when homeopathic remedies had failed to cure his cancer.

Being Desmond Pierce's surrogate allowed her a creative way to satisfy her parents and still contribute to society according to what made sense to *her*. That's what she'd repeated to herself over and over for the last hour and she'd almost believed it—until a man had burst into her hospital room with a crying baby in his arms.

And he was looking at her so strangely that she felt compelled to prompt him. "What do you want, Desmond?"

They'd never been formally introduced, but the baby was a dead giveaway. Desmond Pierce didn't look anything like the pictures she'd searched on the internet. Of course she'd had a better-than-average dose of curiosity about the man with such strict ideas about the surrogacy arrangement, the man who would marry her without meeting her.

But this man—he made tall, dark and handsome seem banal. He was *fascinating*, with a scruff of a beard that gave him a dangerous edge, deep brown hair swept back from his face and a wiry build.

Desmond Pierce was the perfect man to be a father or she wouldn't have agreed to his proposal. What she hadn't realized was that he was a perfect man, *period*. Coupled with the baby in his arms, he might well be the most devastatingly handsome male on the planet.

And then she realized. He wasn't just a man. They were married. He was *her husband*. Whom she was never supposed to meet.

"The baby won't eat," he said over the yowls. "You need to try to breast-feed him."

She blinked. Twice. "I need to do what?"

"The nurse said he's allergic to formula. We've tried for an hour." He moved closer to the bed with a purposeful stride that brooked no nonsense and held out the wailing bundle. "He needs you. This is the one thing I cannot give him."

She stared at the wrinkled face of her child, refusing to reach out, refusing to let the wash of emotions beating through her chest take hold. The baby needed her and she was the sole person who could help. But how could she? Breast-feeding was far too nurturing of a thing to do with a baby she wasn't allowed to keep.

How dare Desmond come in here and layer on more impossible emotional turmoil in the middle of her already-chaotic heart?

She'd done her part according to their agreement. The baby was born, healthy and the child was set for life with a billionaire father who wanted him badly enough to seek out an unusual surrogacy agreement and who had the means to take care of him. What more could Desmond Pierce possibly expect from her? Did he want to slice off a piece of her soul when he took her baby away for the second time?

"That's too much to ask," she whispered even as her breasts tingled at the suggestion. They'd grown hard and heavy the moment the baby had entered the room crying. It was simple physiology and she'd known she'd have to let her milk dry up. Had been prepared for it.

What she had not been prepared for was the request to use it to feed her son.

Desmond's brows came together. "You're concerned about your figure?"

That shouldn't have been so funny. "Yeah, I'm entering the Miss USA pageant next week and how I'll look in a bikini is definitely my biggest objection."

"That's sarcasm, right?"

The fact that he had to ask struck her oddly, but before she could comment, he stuck the baby right into her arms. Against her will, her muscles shifted, cradling the baby to her bosom, and she was lost. As he must have known. As the nurse had known.

She shouldn't be holding the baby, but she was, and it

was too late to stop the thunder of her pulse as it pumped awe and love and duty and shock straight to her heart.

My son.

He still cried, his face rooting against her breast, and it was clear what he wanted. She just hadn't realized how deeply her desire to give it to him would ultimately go.

"There's a clause in the custody agreement about the baby's medical needs," Desmond reminded her. "You're on the hook for eighteen years if he needs you for medical reasons."

"Yeah, but I thought that would only be invoked if he needed a kidney or something," she blurted as the baby's little fingers worked blindly against her chest. "Not breast-feeding."

She *couldn't*. Judging by how badly she wanted to, if she did this, it would be so much harder to walk away. It wasn't fair of Desmond to ask. She was supposed to go back to Portland, register for school. Become a doctor like she'd dreamed about for over a decade. That's how she'd help people. This evisceration Desmond Pierce wanted to perform wasn't part of the plan.

"He might still need a kidney, too." Desmond shrugged. "Such is the nature of sharing DNA with another human."

Did he really not get the emotional quandary she was in? All of this must be so easy for him. After all, he was man, and rich besides—all he had to do was snap his fingers to make the world do his bidding. "You know breast-feeding isn't a one-time thing, right? You have to repeat it."

In the tight-knit community her parents belonged to, they raised babies as a village. She'd watched mothers commit to being a baby's sole food source twenty-four hours a day for months. Some women had trouble with breast-feeding. He acted like she could just pop out a breast and everything would be peachy.

"Yes, but once we find an alternative, you can walk away. Until then, our agreement means you have a commitment to his medical needs." He crossed his arms. "There is literally nothing I would not do to help my child. He needs you. Three months, at least. You can live with me, have your own room. Use a breast pump if you like. You want extra compensation added to the settlement? Name your price."

As if she could put a price on the maternal instincts that warred with her conviction that whatever decision she made here would have lasting impacts that neither of them could foresee. "I don't want extra compensation! I want—"

Nothing except what he'd already promised her. A divorce settlement that would pay for medical school and the knowledge that she'd helped him create the family he wanted. It felt so cold all at once. But what was she supposed to do instead? She rarely dated, not after three years with a ho-hum high school boyfriend and a pregnancy scare at nineteen, which was why she refused to go out with one of the men her parents were constantly throwing at her. Dating wasn't worth the possibility of an accidental pregnancy.

She couldn't be a mom and a doctor. Both required commitment, an exhaustive number of hours. So she'd chosen long ago which path worked for her. Because she was selfish, according to her mother, throwing away her parents' teaching about natural remedies as if their beliefs didn't matter.

So here was her chance to be unselfish for once. She could breast-feed for three months, wean the baby as he grew out of his formula allergy and go back to Portland for the spring semester. It was only a small addition to what had already been a year-long delay.

She'd wanted to experience pregnancy to better empathize with her patients. Why not experience breast-feeding for the same reason? She could use a pump if the baby had trouble latching on, just like any new mother. No one had to know that it was going to kill her to give up the baby a second time after she'd fallen the rest of the way in love with him.

She glanced up at Desmond, who was watching her hold the baby with an expression she couldn't interpret. "I'll do it. But you can't stay in the room."

His expression didn't change. "I beg to differ. He's my son."

Great, so now he was going to watch. But she could still dictate her own terms. "Can you at least call the nurse back so I can make sure I'm doing it right?"

Instead of forcing her to push the call button, he nodded and disappeared into the hall, giving her a blessed few moments alone. The hospital gown had slits for exactly this purpose so it was easy to maneuver the baby's face to her aching breast. His cries had quieted to heartbreaking mewls, and his eyes were closed, but his mouth worked the closer she guided him toward her nipple. And then all at once, he popped on like a champ and started sucking.

She was doing it. *He* was doing it.

Entranced, she watched her son take his first meal on this planet and it was almost holy. Her body flooded with a sense of rightness and awe. An eternity passed and a small sound caused her to glance up. Desmond had returned with the nurse, but he was just watching her quietly with far more tenderness than she would have expected.

"Looks like you're a natural, hon," the nurse said encouragingly and smiled. "In a few minutes, you can switch sides. Do you want me to stay?"

"I think I'm okay."

Really, fetching the nurse had been an excuse to get Desmond out of the room. Women had been doing this for centuries, including those of her parents' community who were strong advocates for removing the stigma of public breast-feeding. She wasn't a frail fraidy-cat.

The nurse left. Now that the baby was quiet, she felt Desmond's presence a whole lot more than she had before, like an extra weight had settled around her shoulders. He was so…everything. Intense. Focused. Gorgeous. Unsettling. Every time she glanced at him, it did something funny to her stomach and she'd had enough new sensations for the day, thanks.

Instead she watched the baby eat in silence until she couldn't stand it any longer.

"What did you name him?" Her voice was husky and drew Desmond's attention.

He cocked his head, his gaze traveling over her in a way that made her twitchy. "Conner. His middle name is Clark, after your father."

That speared her right through the heart. She'd had no idea he'd do something to honor his son's maternal heritage, and it struck her as personal in a way that dug under her skin. If all had gone according to plan, she'd never have met Desmond, never have known what he'd called the baby. She wouldn't have looked them up or contacted either of them. Also according to their agreement.

Now it was all backward and upside-down because this was their son. And Desmond Pierce was her husband. She'd just agreed to go home with him. How was that going to work? Would he expect to exercise his husbandly duties?

That thought flittered through her stomach in a way that wasn't difficult to interpret at all. Dear God. She was *attracted* to her husband. And she'd take that secret to the grave.

Mortified, she switched breasts under Desmond's watchful eye, figuring that if she would be living with him, he'd see her feeding the baby plenty of times. Besides, there was nothing shameful about a woman's body in the act of providing nourishment for her son. Somehow, though, Desmond made the whole thing seem intimate and heavy with implication, as if they were a real family and he was there to support his child's mother.

Desmond pursed his lips, still surveying her as if trying to figure something out. "Have we met before?"

Her pulse leaped. "No. Of course not. You wanted everything done through your agent."

Mr. Lively had been anything but. He was about a hundred and twenty years old and spoke slower than a tortoise on Valium. Anytime he'd contacted her about paperwork or medical records, she'd mentally blocked off four hours because that's generally how long the session lasted. Except for when she'd gone with him to the courthouse to complete the marriage by proxy, which had taken all day.

Suddenly she wished they'd done this surrogacy arrangement a different way. But marriage had been the easiest way to avoid legal issues. The divorce settlement, which she'd use to pay for school, was a normal agreement between couples with Desmond's kind of wealth. Otherwise someone could argue Desmond had paid for a baby and no one wanted that legal hassle.

She hadn't minded being technically married when it

was just a piece of paper. Meeting Desmond, being near enough to hear him breathe, changed everything. It felt bigger than a signature on an official document.

"You seem familiar." He shook his head as if clearing it. "It's been a long day."

"You don't say," she said, letting the irony drip from her tone. "I've been here since 3:00 a.m."

"Really?" This seemed to intrigue him.

"Yeah, it's not a drive-through. I was in labor for something like fifteen hours."

"Is that normal?"

She sighed and tried to shift her position without disturbing the baby. "I don't know. This is my first rodeo."

"I'm being insensitive."

Nothing like calling a spade a spade, which McKenna appreciated enough to give him a break. "I'm sure we'll get to know each other soon enough."

Somehow she'd managed to startle him. "Will we?"

"Well, sure, if we're living in the same house."

And she could secretly admit to a curiosity about him that she'd have every right to satisfy if they were in close quarters. There was a certain amount of protection in the fact that her time with him had predefined boundaries. The last thing she needed was additional entanglements that kept her from fulfilling her dreams. "But only for three months, right?"

"We'll do our best to keep it to three months," he said with a sharp nod, but she had the distinct impression he hadn't considered that inviting her to live in his house meant they'd be around each other. What exactly had she signed up for?

It didn't matter. All that mattered was that he'd given her three months with her son that she was pathetically grateful for. It was like a gift, a chance to know him before he grew old enough to remember her, to miss her. A chance to revel in all these newfound maternal instincts and then leave before they grew too strong. She was going to be a doctor, thanks to Desmond Pierce, and she couldn't let his monkey wrench change that.

Two

The house Desmond had lived in for the last ten years was not big enough. Twenty thousand square feet shouldn't feel so closed in. But with McKenna Moore inside his walls, everything shrank.

He'd never brought a woman home to live. Sure, Lacey had stayed over occasionally when they were dating, but her exit was always prearranged. And then she'd forever snuffed out his ability to trust a woman as easily as she'd snuffed out the life of their "accident," as she'd termed it. The baby had been unplanned, definitely, since their relationship hadn't been all that serious, but he'd had no idea how much he'd want the baby until it was too late. He'd always made sure there was a light at the end of the tunnel when it came to his interaction with women after that.

There was no light where his baby's mother was concerned. She'd brought her feminine scent and shiny dark hair into his house and put a stamp of permanence all over everything.

Did she know that he'd made a huge concession when he'd asked her to stay with him? This was his domain, his sanctuary, and he'd let her invade it, sucking up all the space while she was at it. Only for Conner would he have done this.

This, of course, looked an awful lot like he was hiding in his workshop. But he couldn't be in the main part of the house and walk around with the semi-erection McKenna gave him by simply laughing. Or looking at him. Or breathing. It was absurd. He'd been around women before. Gorgeous women who liked his money enough to put up with his idiosyncrasies. None of them had ever invoked such a driving need.

He tried to pretend he was simply working. After all, he often holed up in his workshop for days until Mrs. Elliot reminded him that he couldn't live on the Red Bull and Snickers that he kept in the corner refrigerator.

But there was a difference between hiding and holing up and he wasn't confused about which one he was doing. Apparently he was the only one who was clear on it, though, because the next time he glanced up from the robot hand he was rewiring, there *she* stood.

"Busy?" she called in her husky voice that hit with a solid *thwang* he felt in his gut.

"Ms. Moore," he muttered in acknowledgment. "This is my workshop."

"I know." Her brows quirked as she glanced around with unveiled curiosity. "Mrs. Elliot told me this was where I could find you. Also, we share a child. I think it's okay if you call me McKenna."

But she clearly didn't know "workshop" equaled off-limits, private, no girls allowed. He should post a sign.

"McKenna, then." He shouldn't be talking to her. Encouraging her. But he couldn't stop looking at her. She was gorgeous in a fierce, elemental way that coursed through him every time he got anywhere near her.

And when he stumbled over her breast-feeding? God, that was the worst. Or the best, depending on your viewpoint.

She was at her sexiest when she was nurturing their child. If he'd known he'd suddenly be ten times more drawn to her when she exuded all that maternal radiance, he'd never have invited her to live here.

Of course, he hadn't really had much of a choice there, had he?

Obviously hiding out wasn't the answer. Like always, raw need welled up as he watched her explore his workshop, peering into bins and tracing the lines of the hand-drawn gears posted to a light board near the south wall.

"This is a very impressive setup," she commented as she finished a round of his cavernous workspace.

Her gaze zipped to the two generators housed at the back and then lit on him as he stood behind the enormous workstation spread out over a mobile desk on wheels where he did all of his computation. He'd built the computer himself from components and there wasn't another like it in the world.

"It's where I make stuff," he told her simply because there was no way to explain that this was where he brought to life the contents of his brain. He saw something in his head then he built it. He'd been doing that since he was four. Now he got paid millions and millions of dollars for each and every design, which he only cared about because it enabled him to keep doing it.

"I can see that. It's kind of sexy. Very Dr. Frankenstein."

Had she just called him sexy? In the same breath as comparing him to *Frankenstein*? "Uh...I've always thought of myself as more like Iron Man."

She laughed. "Except Tony Stark is a lot more personable and dresses better."

Desmond glanced down at his slacks. "What's wrong with the way I dress?"

Certainly that was the only part of her assessment he could disagree with—he was by no stretch personable and Iron Man did have a certain flair that Desmond could never claim.

"Nothing," she shot back with a grin. "You just don't look like a billionaire playboy who does weapons deals with shady Middle Eastern figures. Frankenstein, on the other hand, was a doctor like you and all he wanted to do was build something meaningful out of the pieces he had available."

She picked up the robot hand he'd been about to solder for emphasis.

Speechless, he stared at her slender fingers wrapped around his creation-in-progress and tried like hell to figure out how she'd tapped into his psyche so easily. Fascinating. So few people thought of him as a doctor. He didn't even see himself as one, despite the fact that he could stick *PhD* after his name all day long if he wanted to.

What else did she see when she looked at him? That same recognition he'd felt, as if they'd met in a former life and their connection had been so strong it transcended flesh and bone?

Or would that sound as crazy to her as it did in his head?

"I wasn't aware I was so transparent," he said gruffly, a little shocked that he didn't totally hate it. "Did you want something?"

Her dark eyes were so expressive he could practically read her like a book. He rarely bothered to study people anymore. Once, that had been the only way he could connect with others, by surreptitiously observing them until everything was properly cataloged.

All it had ever gotten him was an acute sense of isolation and an understanding that people stayed away from him because they didn't like how his brain worked.

She shrugged. "I was bored. Larissa is putting Conner to bed and it turns out that having a nanny around means that once I feed him, I'm pretty much done. I haven't seen you in, like, a week."

McKenna, apparently, had no such aversion to Desmond. She'd sought him out. So he could entertain her. That was a first.

"I had no idea you'd mark my absence in such a way."

Lame. He was out of practice talking to people, let alone one who tied his brain in a Gordian knot of puzzling reactions.

But he wanted to untangle that knot. Very badly.

"Are you always so formal?" McKenna came around the long table to his side and peered over his shoulder at the monitor where he had a drawing of the robot hand spinning in 3-D. "Wow. That's pretty cool."

"It's just a… No, I'm not—" He sucked in a breath as her torso grazed his back. His pulse roared into overdrive and he experienced a purely primal reaction to her that had no place between two people who shared a son and nothing else. "Formal."

"Hmm? Oh, yeah, you are. You remind me of my statistics professor."

"You took a statistics class?" Okay, they shared that, too. But that was it. They had nothing else in common and he had no reason to be imagining her reaction if he kissed her.

"Have to. It's a requirement for premed."

"Can you not stand there?"

Her scent was bleeding through his senses and it was thoroughly disrupting his brain waves. Of course the real problem was that he liked her exactly where she was.

"Where? Behind you?" She punched him on the shoulder like they were drinking buddies and she'd just told him a joke. "I can't be in front of you. There's a whole lot of electronic equipment in my way."

"You talk a lot."

She laughed. "Only because you're talking back. Isn't that how it works?"

For the second time she'd rendered him speechless. Yeah. He *was* talking back. The two conversations he'd had with her to date, the one at the hospital and this one, marked the longest he'd had with anyone in a while. Probably since Lacey.

He needed someone to draw him out, or he stayed stuck in his head, designing, building, imagining, dreaming. It was a lot safer for everyone that way, so of course that was his default.

McKenna seemed unacquainted with the term *boundaries*. And he didn't hate that.

He should. He should be escorting her out of his workshop and back to the main part of the house. There was an indoor pool that stayed precisely the same temperature year-round. A recreational room that he'd had built the moment Mr. Lively called to say McKenna had conceived during the first round of insemination. Desmond had filled the room with a pool table, darts, video game consoles and whatever else the decorator had recommended. Surely his child's mother could find some amusement there.

"Tell me what you're building," she commanded with a fair enough amount of curiosity that he told her.

"It's a prototype for a robotic humanoid."

"A robot?" Clearly intrigued, she leaned over the hand, oblivious to the way her hair fell in a long, dark sheet over her shoulder. It was so beautiful that he almost reached out to touch it.

He didn't. That would invite intimacies he absolutely wanted with a bone-deep desire but hadn't fully yet analyzed. Until he understood this visceral need, he couldn't act on it. Too dangerous. It gave her too much power.

"No." He cleared his throat and scrubbed at his beard, which he still hadn't trimmed. "A robot is anything mechanical that can be programmed. A robotic humanoid resembles a person both in appearance and function but with a mechanical skeleton and artificial intelligence."

It was a common misconception that he corrected often, especially when he had to give a presentation about his designs to the manufacturers who bought his patents.

"You *are* Dr. Frankenstein," she said with raised eyebrows. "When you get it to work, do you shout 'It's alive!' or just do a little victory dance?"

"I, um…"

She'd turned to face him, crossing her arms under her breasts that he logically knew were engorged from childbirth, though that didn't seem to stop his imagination from calling up what they looked like: expanses of beautiful flesh topped by hard, dusky nipples. McKenna had miles of skin that Des wanted to put his hands on.

What was it about her that called to him so deeply?

"I'm just teasing you." Her eyes twinkled. "I actually couldn't imagine you doing either one."

A smile spread across his face before he could stop it. "I can dance."

"Ha, you're totally lying."

"I can dance," he repeated. "Just not to music."

He fell into her rich, dark eyes and he reached out to snag a lock of her hair, fingering the silky softness before he fully realized that he'd given in to the impulse. The moment grew tense. Aware. So thick, he couldn't have cut it with a laser.

"I should...go," she murmured and blinked, unwinding the spell. "I didn't mean to interrupt."

The lock of hair fell from his fingers as the mood shattered. Fortunately her exodus was quick enough that she didn't get to witness how well she'd bobbled his composure.

He'd have sworn there was an answering echo of attraction and heat in her gaze.

He wasn't any closer to unraveling the mysteries lurking inside her, but he did know one thing. McKenna Moore had taken his seed into her womb and created a miracle through artificial insemination.

What had once felt practical now felt like a mistake. One he couldn't rectify.

But how could he have known he'd take one look at her and wish he'd impregnated her by making love over and over and over until she'd conceived?

Madness. *Build something and forget all of this fatalistic nonsense.*

Women were treacherous under the best of circumstances and McKenna Moore was no different. She just had a unique wrapper that rendered Des stupid, apparently.

Of course the most expedient way to nip this attraction in the bud would be to tell her how badly he'd wanted to thread all of his fingers through her hair and kiss her until her clothes melted off. She'd be mortified and finally figure out that she should be running away from Desmond Pierce. That would be that.

McKenna fled Desmond's workshop, her pulse still pounding in her throat.

What the hell had just happened? One minute she was trying to forge a friendship with the world's most reclusive billionaire and the next he had her hair draped across his hand.

She could still feel the tug as his fingers lifted the strands. The look on his face had been enthralled, as if he'd unexpectedly found gold. She hadn't been around the block very many times, a testament to how long she'd been with James, her high school boyfriend, not to mention the years of difficult undergraduate course work that hadn't allowed for much time to date. But she knew when a man was thinking about kissing her, and that's exactly what had been on Desmond's mind.

That would be a huge mistake.

She needed to walk out of this house in three months unencumbered, emotionally and physically, and Desmond was dangerous. He held all the cards in this scenario and if she wanted to dedicate her life to medicine, she had to be careful. What would happen if she accidentally got pregnant again? More delays. More agonizing decisions and, frankly, she didn't have enough willpower left to deal with those kinds of consequences.

And what made her near mistake even worse was that she'd almost forgotten why she was there. She'd fallen into borderline flirting that was nothing like how she usually was with men. But Desmond was darkly mysterious and intriguing in a way she found sexy, totally

against her will. They shared an almost mystical connection, one she'd never felt before, and it was as scary
as it was fascinating.

Okay. Seeking him out had been an error in judgment. Obviously. But they never crossed paths and she
was starting to wonder if she'd imagined that she'd come
home from the hospital with a man. It only made sense
that she should be on friendly terms with her baby's father.

Why that made sense, she couldn't remember all at
once. Desmond didn't want a mother for his son. Just a
chuck wagon. Once she helped Conner wean, she'd finally be on track to get her medical degree after six arduous years as an undergrad and one grueling year spent
prepping her body to get pregnant, being pregnant and
then giving birth.

In a house this size, there was literally no reason she
ever had to see Desmond again. She'd managed to settle in and live here for over a week without so much as
a glimpse until she'd sought him out in his workshop.

Her days fell into a rhythm that didn't suck. Mrs. Elliot
fed her and provided companionable but neutral conversation when McKenna prompted her. Clothes magically
appeared cleaned and pressed in McKenna's closet. Twice
a week, her beautifully decorated bedroom and the ad-
joining bathroom were unobtrusively cleaned. All in all,
she was drowning in luxury. And she wouldn't apologize
for enjoying it.

To shed the baby weight that had settled around her
hips and stomach, she'd started swimming in the pool a
couple of hours a day. Before she'd gotten pregnant, she'd
jogged. But there were no trails through the heavy forest of hemlocks and maples that surrounded this gothic
mansion perched at the edge of the Columbia River. Even

if she found a place to run, her enormous breasts hurt when she did something overly taxing, like breathing and thinking. She could only imagine how painful it would be to jog three miles.

The pool was amazing, huge and landscaped with all sorts of indoor plants that made her feel like she was at a tropical oasis on another continent instead of in northwest Oregon where she'd spent the whole of her life. A glass ceiling let in light but there were no windows to break the illusion. She could swim uninterrupted for as long as she liked. It was heavenly.

Until she emerged from the water one day and wiped her face to see Desmond sitting on one of the lounge chairs, quietly watching her. She hadn't seen him since the workshop incident a week ago that might have been an almost kiss.

"Hey," she called, mystified why her pulse leaped into overdrive the second her senses registered his presence. "Been here long?"

"Long enough," he said cryptically, his smooth voice echoing in the cavernous pool area. "Am I disturbing you?"

He'd sought her out, clearly, since he wasn't dressed for swimming and wore an expectant expression.

So she lied. "Of course not."

In reality he did disturb her. A lot. His eyes matched his name, piercing her to the bone when he looked at her, and she didn't like how shivery and goose-pimply he turned her mostly bare skin. There was something about him she couldn't put her finger on, but the man had more shadows than a graveyard. She could see them flitting around in his expression, in his demeanor, as if they weighed him down.

Until he smiled. And thank God he didn't do that more

often, because he went from sexy in an abstract way to holy-crap hot.

So she'd do everything in her power to not make him smile for however long he planned to grace her with his presence. Hopefully that would only be a few minutes. If she'd known he was going to make an appearance, she'd have brought something to cover her wet swimsuit, like a full suit of armor made of inch-thick chain mail.

The way he was looking at her made her feel exposed.

She settled for a towel, draping it around her torso like a makeshift toga, which at least covered her pointy nipples, and sat on the next lounge chair, facing him.

Desmond was wearing a white button-down shirt today, with the sleeves rolled to his forearms and, despite teasing him the other day about his fashion sense, he had such a strange, magnetic aura that she scarcely noticed anything extraneous like clothes. All she saw was him.

"Are you settling in okay?" he asked.

She had the sense the question wasn't small talk. "Sure. What's not to like?"

His eyebrows quirked. "The fact that you're here in the first place."

"You're making it worth my while, remember?"

That shouldn't have come out so sarcastically. After all, she'd been the one to shake her head at monetary compensation, which he'd likely have readily ponied up.

But he was making her twitchy with his shadowy gaze. After visiting his workshop, she'd looked up the things he'd invented and his mind was definitely not like other people's. Innovation after innovation in the areas of robotics and machinery had spilled onto her screen along with published papers full of his endless theoretical ideas.

She was not a stupid person by any stretch, having graduated with a bachelor's degree in biology and a 3.5

grade point average, but Desmond Pierce existed on another plane. And that made him thoroughly out of reach to mere mortals like her.

But he was still oh, so intriguing. And they were married. Funny how that had become front and center in her mind all at once.

He nodded. "I'm sorry my request has delayed your own plans."

Clearly he didn't get offended by her jokes that weren't funny. That was a good thing.

"I have my whole life to be a doctor. Conner will only be a newborn for this small stretch of time."

It was a huge concession, and she had her own reasons for being there, none of which she planned to share with Conner's father. But her pathetic gratefulness for this time with her son wouldn't go away, no matter how hard she tried to think of breast-feeding as a task instead of the bonding experience it was proving to be.

Conner would not be her son legally once Desmond filed the divorce decree that spelled out the custody arrangement—she'd give up all rights. Period. End of story. She hated how often she had to remind herself of that. She was already dreading the inevitable goodbye that would be here long before she wished.

"That's true. I do appreciate your willingness, regardless."

"Is that the only reason you popped in here? To thank me?" She flashed a grin before thinking better of it. They weren't friends hanging out, even though it seemed too easy to forget that. "I would have taken a text message."

"I despise text messages."

"Really?" Curiously, she eyed him. "Electronic communication seems like it would be right up your alley."

He shifted uncomfortably, breaking eye contact. "Why, because I'm not as verbally equipped as others?"

"Please." She snorted before realizing he was serious. "There's nothing about you that's ill equipped. I meant because you're the Frankenstein of electronics."

Thoughtfully, he absorbed that comment and she could see it pinging around in his brain, looking for a place to land. Then he shrugged. "I don't like text messages because they're intrusive and distracting, forcing me to respond."

"You can ignore them if you want," she advised and bit back another smile. Sometimes he was so cute. "There's no rule."

"There is. It's like a social contract I have to fulfill. The message sits there and blinks and blinks until I read it. And then I know exactly who is sitting on the other end waiting on me to complete the transaction. I can't just let that go." His brows came together. "That's why I don't give people my cell phone number."

"I have your cell phone number."

"You're not people."

She couldn't help it. She laughed. And that apparently gave him permission to smile, which was so gorgeous she had a purely physical reaction to it. Somehow he must have picked up on the sharp tug through her insides because the vibe between them got very heavy, very fast.

Mesmerized, she stared at him as the smiles slipped off both their faces.

Why was she so attracted to him? He wasn't her type. Actually she didn't have a type because she'd spent the last six years working her ass off to earn a four-year degree, putting herself through college with as many flexible retail and restaurant jobs as she could score. She couldn't do the same for medical school, not unless she wanted to be fifty when she graduated.

She had to remember that this man held the keys to her future and to keep her wits about her.

Desmond cleared his throat and the moment faded. "I didn't seek you out to talk about text messages. I wanted to let you know that Larissa has resigned her position. Effective immediately."

"The nanny quit?" That sucked. She'd liked Larissa and had thoroughly approved of Desmond's choice. "And with no notice? Nice. Did she at least give you a reason?"

"Her mother had a stroke. She felt compelled to be the one managing her mother's care."

"Well, okay. That gets a pass."

Unexpectedly, McKenna's eyelids pricked in sympathy as she imagined her own mother in a similar circumstance, lifeless and hooked up to machines as the doctors performed analysis to determine the extent of the brain damage the stroke had caused. Of course, her mother would have refused to be cared for in a real hospital, stubborn to the end, even if it led to her own grave. Like it had for Grandfather, who had shared the beliefs of their community.

McKenna was the outcast who put her faith in science and technology.

"She did the right thing," McKenna said. "Have you started the process of hiring a replacement?"

"I have. I contacted the service I used to find Larissa and they're sending me the résumés of some candidates. I'd hoped you'd review them with me."

"Me?" Oh, God. He wanted her to help him pick the woman who would essentially raise her child? How could she do that?

A thousand emotions flew through her at once as Desmond nodded.

"It would be helpful if you would, yes," he said, oblivious to her shock and disquiet.

"You did fine the first time without me," she squawked and cleared her throat. "You don't need my help."

"The first time I had nine months to select the right person for the job," he countered. "I have one day this time. And I trust your judgment."

"You do?" That set her back so much that she sagged against the weave of the lounge chair.

"Of course. You're intelligent, or you wouldn't have been accepted into medical school, and you have a unique ability to understand people."

She frowned. "I do not. Mostly I piss people off."

Her mouth was far too fast to express exactly what was on her mind, and she did not suffer fools easily. Neither made her very popular with men, which was fine by her. Men were just roadblocks she did not have time for.

Desmond cocked his head in the way she'd come to realize meant he was processing what she'd just said. "You don't make me mad."

"That's because I like you," she muttered before thinking through how that might come across. Case in point. Her mouth often operated independently of her brain.

His expression closed in, dropping shadows between them again. "That will change soon enough. I'm not easy to get along with, nor should you try. There's a reason I asked you to be my son's surrogate."

She should let it go. The shadows weren't her business and he'd pretty much just told her to back off. But the mystery of Desmond Pierce had caught her by the throat and she couldn't stop herself from asking since he'd brought up the subject.

"Why *did* you ask me?"

Surely a rich, good-looking guy could have women crawling out of the woodwork to be his baby mama with the snap of his fingers. Obviously that wasn't what he'd wanted.

Coolly, he surveyed her. "Because I dislike not having control. Our agreement means you have no rights and no ability to affect what happens to Conner."

"But I do," she countered quietly. "You put me in exactly that position by asking me to breast-feed him. I could walk away tomorrow and it would be devastating for you both."

"Yes. It is an unfortunate paradox. But it should give you an idea how greatly I care about my son that I am willing to make such a concession. I didn't do it lightly."

Geez. His jaw was like granite and she had an inkling why he considered himself difficult to get along with. Desmond didn't want a mother for his son because he wasn't much of a sharer.

Good to know. Domineering geniuses weren't her cup of tea. "Well, we have no problems, then. I'm not interested in pulling the parental rug out from under you. I'm helping you out because I'm the only one who can, but I'm really looking forward to medical school."

This time with Conner and Desmond was just a detour. It had to be, no matter how deep her son might sink his emotional hooks.

Desmond nodded. "That is why I picked you. Mr. Lively did a thorough screening of all the potential surrogates and your drive to help people put you head and shoulders above the rest. Your principles are your most attractive quality."

Um…what? She blinked, but the sincerity in his expression didn't change. Had he just called her attractive because of her stubborn need to do things her own way? That was a first. And it warmed her dangerously fast.

Her parents had lambasted those same principles for as long as she could recall, begging her to date one of the men who lived in their community and have a lot of babies, never mind that she had less than no interest in either concept. The men bored her to tears, not to mention they embraced her parents' love of alternative medicine, which meant she had nothing in common with them.

How great was it that the man she'd ultimately married appreciated her desire to become a medical doctor instead of a homeopathic healer?

And how terrible to realize that Desmond Pierce had chosen her strictly because he expected she'd easily leave her child without a backward glance.

He was right—she would do it because she'd given her word. But there wasn't going to be anything easy about it.

Three

Since the nanny had left him high and dry, Desmond was the one stuck sorting out his son's 3:00 a.m. meltdown. Conner woke yowling for God knew what reason. Larissa had always taken care of that in the past, leaving Des blessedly ignorant to his son's needs.

Unfortunately, after twenty minutes of rocking, soothing, toys and terse commands, nothing had worked to stop the crying. If he'd known Conner would pull this kind of stunt, Des would have gone to bed before 1:00 a.m. Two hours of sleep did not make this easier, that was for sure.

Desmond finally conceded that he no longer had the luxury of pretending McKenna didn't exist just to keep his growing attraction to her under wraps. Larissa's printed instructions clearly said the baby nursed at night. He'd been hoping for a miracle that would prevent him from having to disturb Conner's mother. That did not happen.

So that's how he found himself knocking on her door in the dead of night with a crying baby in his arms. Definitely not the way he'd envisioned seeing McKenna Moore in a bedroom. And he'd had more than a few fantasies about McKenna and a bed.

She answered a minute later, dressed in a conservative white robe that shouldn't have been the slightest bit alluring. It absolutely was, flashing elegant bits of leg as she leaned into the puddle of light from the hall.

"Woke up hungry, did he?" she said with more humor than Des expected at three in the morning. "Give him here," she instructed and, when he handed over the baby, cradled him to her bosom, murmuring as she floated to an overstuffed recliner in the corner of her room.

Funny. He hadn't realized until this moment that she sat in it to feed Conner. He'd envisioned her snuggling deep into the crevices to read a book or to chat on the phone with her legs draped over the sides. McKenna seemed like the type to lounge in a chair instead of sitting in it properly.

The lamp on the small end table cast a circle of warmth over the chair as she settled into it and worked open her robe to feed the baby. Instantly, Conner latched on and grew quiet.

"You can come in if you want," McKenna called to Desmond as he stood like an idiot at the door, completely extraneous and completely unable to walk away.

"I would…like to come in," he clarified and cleared his throat because his voice sounded like a hundred frogs had crawled down his windpipe. Gingerly, he sat on the bed because the love seat that matched the recliner was too close to mother and child.

Similar to the other times he'd watched McKenna breast-feed, he couldn't quite get over the initial shock of the mechanics. It was one thing to have an academic understanding of lactation, but quite another to see it in action.

Especially when he had such a strong reaction, like he was witnessing something divine.

The beauty of it filled him and he couldn't look away, even as she repositioned the baby and her dark nipple flashed. God, that shouldn't be so affecting. This woman was feeding his son in the most sacrificial of ways. But neither could he deny the purely physical reaction he had to her naked breast.

He couldn't stop being unnaturally attracted to her any more than he could stop the sun from rising. Seeing her with Conner only heightened that attraction.

Mother and child together created a package he liked. He shouldn't have stayed. But he couldn't have left.

This quandary he was in had to stop. McKenna would be out of his life in two months and he'd insist that she not contact him again. Hell, he probably wouldn't have to insist. She was resolute in her goal of becoming a doctor, as they'd discussed at the pool yesterday.

In the meantime he'd drive himself insane if he didn't get their relationship, such as it was, on better footing. There was absolutely no reason they couldn't have a working rapport as they took care of the baby together. At least until he hired a new nanny.

"Is it okay that I brought him to you?" he asked gruffly. "I don't know what you worked out with Larissa."

He felt like he should be doing more to care for his son. But all he could do was make sure the woman who could feed him was happy.

"Perfectly fine. She's been trying a bottle at night with different types of formula to see if she can get his stomach to accept it when he's good and hungry. Hasn't worked so far." McKenna shrugged one shoulder, far too chipper for having been woken unceremoniously in the middle of the night. "So I take over when she gets frustrated."

"She didn't mention that in her instructions." Probably distracted with trying to pack and deal with travel arrangements on such short notice. So he reeled back his annoyance that he hadn't followed the routine his son was probably used to. It wasn't anyone's fault.

Clearly he needed to take a more active role in caring for Conner. This was the perfect opportunity to get clued in on whatever Larissa and McKenna had been doing thus far.

"Taking care of a baby is kind of a moving target," she said.

"Speaking from your years of experience?" He hadn't meant for that to come out sarcastically.

But she just laughed, which he appreciated far more than he should.

"I come from a very tight-knit community. We raise our babies together. I've been taking care of other people's children for as long as I can remember."

Mr. Lively had briefed him thoroughly on the cooperative community tucked into the outskirts of the Clatsop Forest where McKenna had grown up. Her unusual upbringing had been one of the reasons she'd stood out among the women he'd considered for his surrogate. "Surprising, then, that you'd be willing to give one up."

She contemplated him for a moment. "But that's why I was willing. I've seen firsthand what having a child does to a mother's time and energy. You become its everything and there's little left over for anything else, like your husband, let alone medical school, a grueling residency and then setting up a practice."

"It's not like that for you here, is it?"

"No, of course not." She flashed him a smile. "For one, we're not involved."

He couldn't resist pulling that thread. "What if we were?"

The concept hung there, writhing between them like a live thing, begging to be explored. And he wasn't going to take it back. He wanted to know more about her, what made her tick.

"What? Involved?"

The idea intrigued her. He could read it in her expressive eyes. But then she banked it.

"That's the whole point, Desmond. We never would have had a child together under any other circumstances. You wanted to be a single father for your own reasons, but whatever they are, the reality is that neither of us has room in our lives for getting *involved*."

A timely reminder, one he shouldn't have needed.

Even so, he couldn't help thinking he was going about this process wrong. Instead of hiding out in his lab until he'd fully analyzed his attraction to McKenna, he should create an environment to explore it. That was the only way he could understand it well enough to make it stop. What better conditions could he ask for than plenty of time together and an impending divorce?

"As long as you're happy while you're here," he said as his mind instantly turned that over. "That's all that matters to me."

He was nothing if not imaginative, and when he wanted something, there was little that could stop him from devising a way to get it. One of the many benefits of being a genius.

She glanced up at him after repositioning the baby. "You know what would make me happy? Finding a nanny with an expertise in weaning when the baby has formula allergies."

"Then, tomorrow, that's what we'll do," he promised her.

And if that endeavor included getting to know his child's mother in a much more intimate way, then *everyone* would be happy.

The next morning, McKenna woke to a beep that signaled an incoming text message.

She sat up and reached for her phone, instantly awake despite having rolled around restlessly for an hour after Desmond had left her room with the baby.

Definitely not the way she'd envisioned him visiting her bedroom in the middle of the night, though she shouldn't be having such vivid fantasies about her husband. Hard not to when she'd developed a weird habit of dreaming about him—especially when she was awake—and fantasies weren't so easy to shut off when she had little to occupy her time other than feeding the baby.

Desmond's name leaped out at her from the screen. He'd sent her a text message.

That shouldn't make her smile. But she couldn't help picturing him phone in hand as he fat-fingered his way through what should be simple communication.

Come to my workshop when you're free.

God, he was so adorable. Why that made her mushy inside, she had no clue. But, obviously, he didn't realize she was bored out of her mind pretty much all the time.

She was definitely free. Especially if it meant she got to visit Frankenstein's wonderland again.

She brushed her hair and washed her face. Rarely did she bother with cosmetics as she'd been blessed with really great skin that needed little to stay supple and blemish free. Why mess with it?

In less than five minutes, she was ready to go downstairs. Desmond glanced up from his computer nearly the moment she walked through the glass door of his workshop. "That was fast."

She shrugged casually, or as casually as she could when faced with a man she'd last seen in the middle of the night while she'd been half-naked. "I'm at your beck and call, right?"

Something flashed through his expression that added a few degrees to the temperature. "Are you? I thought you were here for Conner."

"That's what I meant," she corrected hastily, lest he get the wrong idea.

Though judging by the way he was looking at her, it was already too late. He was such a strange mix of personality, sometimes warm and inviting, other times prickly. But always fascinating. And she liked pushing his buttons.

She *shouldn't* be pushing any buttons.

Desmond was not her type. There were far too many complications at play here to indulge in the rising heat between them. "But apparently I can be persuaded to make myself available to his father, as well. Pending the subject of discussion, of course."

Desmond crossed his arms and leaned back in his chair, his expression decidedly warmer. "What would you like to talk about?"

She shrugged and bit back the flirtatious comment

on the tip of her tongue. She was pretty sure he hadn't summoned her to pick up where they'd left off the last time she'd made the mistake of cornering him in his workshop—when she'd been convinced he was about to kiss her.

"I figured you had something specific you wanted. Since you crawled out of the Dark Ages to send me a text."

The corners of his mouth lifted in a small smile that shouldn't have tingled her spine the way it did.

"Isn't that your preferred method of communication? I can adapt."

The ambience in the workshop was definitely different than the normal vibe between them. If she didn't know better, she'd think he was flirting with her. "You don't strike me as overly flexible. Maybe I should be adapting to you."

His gaze narrowed, sharpening, making her feel very much like a small, tasty rabbit. Never one to let a man make her feel hunted, she breached the space between them, skirting the long end of the worktable to put herself on the same side as Desmond.

Apparently she was going to let him push *her* buttons instead.

Last time she'd cornered him, he'd been guarded. Not this time. His crossed arms unknotted and fell to his sides, opening him to her perusal, and that was so interesting, she looked her fill. The man was beautifully built, with a long, lean torso and a classically handsome face made all the more dashing by a sparse beard. It was a perfect complement to his high cheekbones, allowing his gorgeous eyes to be the focal point.

"What would that look like?" he murmured. "If you adapted to me?"

"Oh, um...I don't know. How do you like to communicate?"

He jerked his head toward the back of the workshop without taking his eyes off of her. "I build things. Shape them, put the pieces where they go based on the images I have in my head. I communicate through my hands."

Oh, God. That was the sexiest thing she'd ever heard and her body didn't hesitate to flood her with the evidence of it, heating every millimeter of her skin as she imagined the things he'd say to her via his fingertips.

"That sounds very effective." They weren't talking about communication anymore and they both knew it.

He was definitely flirting with her. The question was whether or not she wanted him to stop. This heat roiling between them surely wasn't a good thing to encourage but, for the life of her, she couldn't remember why.

Oh, who was she kidding? The man intrigued the hell out of her and she should just stop pretending otherwise.

"Sometimes," he said, his voice lowering a touch, "more often than not, I'm misinterpreted."

"Maybe because whoever you're communicating with isn't listening hard enough."

She'd definitely listen, if for no other reason than to unlock some of his secrets. His mind fascinated her and... Coupled with the body? He could definitely talk to her all night long—with his hands, his mouth, whatever he wanted to use—and she'd be okay with that.

No. That was a bad idea. This mystical draw between them would not end well. She had goals. He was a controlling, difficult-to-get-along-with recluse. They had nothing between them but a son.

"Perhaps. But, generally speaking, people find me hard to understand."

"I'm not people," she murmured instead of *see you*

later. "Why don't you tell me something and I'll let you know if I'm having trouble translating."

Delicious anticipation unfolded in her abdomen, the likes of which she hadn't felt in a long time. They shouldn't get involved. There were probably a hundred reasons their agreement would be altered if they did. Loopholes she'd never considered would bind her to this house simply because she lacked the will to step back from her husband.

He was so hypnotic she couldn't tear herself away from what was happening. She wanted to be right here in this moment, as long as it lasted.

Slowly he reached out and slid his fingers through her hair, examining it. Giving her time to hear what he was saying without uttering a word. He caught her in the crosshairs of his gaze as he fingered the lock and his expression told her he liked the dark, heavy mass that fell down her back.

She watched as he looped a wider hank around his palm, winding it up until his hand was near her face.

Desmond feathered a thumb across her cheek that drove a spike of need through her that was answered in the heat radiating from his eyes.

His other hand slid to her waist, slowly drawing her closer until their bodies brushed.

Oh, yes, she liked what he was saying.

Then he released her hair in favor of cupping her jaw with both hands and guiding her lips to his. The kiss instantly caught fire and she moaned as he tilted her head to take it deeper, levering open her lips with his. His tongue worked its way into her mouth, tasting her with intent, and she liked that, too, meeting him with her own taste test.

She wanted to touch. Resting her fingertips on his

chest, she indulged herself in the sensations of the crisp cotton and strong male torso underneath. His wild heartbeat thumped under her fingers as his lips shaped hers into new heights of pleasure.

God, yes, he was a hot kisser, communicating with his hands as promised. The heat of his palms on her flesh radiated through her whole body. The worktable bit into her back as he levered her against it, his granite-hard erection digging into her pelvis deliciously.

The unnatural attraction she'd felt for him from the start exploded. If she didn't stop this madness, they'd be naked in half a heartbeat. Not a smart move for a woman who wanted to walk out the door unencumbered in a few weeks.

That thought was enough to spur her brain into functioning.

She pulled back, but not very far since he still had her trapped between his body and the table. Her pulse thundered in her ears as they stared at each other.

"That was…"

"Amazing?" he supplied, his gaze still hot and clearly interested in diving in again. But he didn't, which she appreciated. "Yeah. But I'm sensing we're going to stop now."

"See, we communicate just fine." She gulped. "I'm just…not sure this is a good idea."

They were not two people who had the luxury of an uncomplicated fling. He'd expressed in no uncertain terms exactly how much control he liked having over a situation. They were married with a divorce agreement already hammered out. That was not a recipe for experimentation, and she wasn't much of an experimenter anyway.

Where could this possibly go?

"Oh, it's a good idea." His piercing gaze tore her open inside as he promised her exactly how good it would be without saying a word. "But we both have to think so."

With that, he stepped back, releasing her.

She took the first deep breath she'd taken since he'd told her he communicated with his hands and nodded. "I agree. And I don't think that right now."

Four

The kiss experiment hadn't worked out like Des had hoped in any way, shape or form. Instead of providing data on how he could stop the unholy allure of his wife, kissing her had opened an exponential number of dimensions to his attraction.

Worse, he wanted to do it again for purely unscientific reasons.

The feel of her mouth against his haunted him. He recalled it at the most inopportune times, like when he should be focusing on the metal pieces in front of him as he attempted to solder them to the titanium skeleton he was creating. So far, he'd had to start over three times. If he kept this up, the end result would look more like a grotesque spider hybrid than a human.

The problem his mind wanted to resolve didn't involve robotic humanoids. It involved how to kiss McKenna again. She'd backed off and then backed away. As he'd fully expected. Women in his world fell into two camps:

those who didn't think he was worth the trouble and those who did solely due to their own agenda.

His wife clearly fell into the first group.

Either way, *all* women considered him difficult. And McKenna was no exception. This was just the first time in memory that he cared. How could he get her to the point where she thought kissing was a good idea if she avoided him? As she surely had been; he hadn't seen her in two days.

He turned the dilemma over in his mind, getting nowhere with it. And nowhere with his prototype, which should be at least half finished by now. Salvation came via an email from the nanny-placement service.

Excellent. The list of candidates scrolled onto the screen. There was nothing he liked better than data unless it was even more data. The only way to make a reasonable decision was to weigh variables and risks, then chart all of that into potential outcomes. What a great distraction from his unfinished work.

Better than that, the nanny candidates were an *excuse.* He'd asked McKenna for her help in weeding out the potentials for a number of reasons, not the least of which was that she had a vested interest in ensuring the nanny had lactation and weaning experience. And he did appreciate the way McKenna's mind worked. Handy that he'd have to spend time with her to discuss the résumés. Maybe at the same time, he could get closer to that next kiss. The pluses of this task were legion.

Except when he sought her out, he found her in the solarium feeding the baby. God, why did the sight of her with Conner at her breast whack him so hard every time? He should be used to it after the handful of occasions he'd been present for the event.

Nope.

"Sorry," he offered gruffly when she glanced up and caught him skulking at the entrance to the solarium at the west end of the house, positioned just so to catch the late-afternoon sun. "I can come back."

"This is your house. *You're* free to come and go at will," she reminded him as if he needed the reminder that she was here under duress.

"You should feel as if you can move about at will, as well." At a loss as to why this whole scene was making him uncomfortable, he ran a palm over his beard, but it didn't jog his rusty people skills. "Do you need something from me to solidify that for you?"

"No." She sighed and focused on Conner for a long moment. "I'm sorry, I'm being weird."

Biting back a laugh because that shouldn't be so funny, he shook his head. "That's usually my line. You are far from weird."

She made a face. "You're not weird either. And I meant since, you know...the other day happened, we're in a strange place."

The other day. When he'd kissed her. As he worked through several responses to that in his head, he contemplated her. She flushed and fiddled with the baby's placement, shifting him around until he was precisely in the same spot he had been before she'd started.

Interesting. She was as uncomfortable as he was. Why?

Fascinated, he crossed his arms, instantly more interested in staying than in fleeing for the safety of his lab where everything worked the way he willed it to. "Not so strange of a place. We're still married, the baby still needs breast milk and I still need a nanny. What's weird about that?"

"You know what I mean," she muttered.

"Maybe I don't." Social norms escaped him on a regular basis. But he was starting to enjoy the rush of endorphins his body produced when around her. As long as he kept a tight rein on it.

"Then never mind," she said with a frown. "Obviously the weirdness is all on my side. I guess you just go around kissing people randomly whenever you feel like it and it never costs you a wink of sleep."

Well, now that *was* interesting information. "You're having trouble sleeping? Because I kissed you? Why?"

He definitely would not have guessed they'd have that in common. And now he was curious if she'd lain awake fantasizing about what might have happened. He sure the hell had.

A blush stained her cheeks. "Shut up and stop reading into everything I'm saying."

"Is that what I'm doing?"

The concept shouldn't have made him smile, but she seemed so flustered. He liked knowing that she'd been affected by what had happened in his workshop, especially since he'd have sworn she'd backed off because she had little interest in exploring the attraction between them.

Maybe she was more interested than he'd assumed.

She groaned. "Please tell me you didn't really seek me out to issue the third degree."

"No. My apologies if that's how it came across." He could circle back to their attraction and the potential for more kissing experiments later. "I have a list of candidates from the nanny service. I wanted to see when you might be available to discuss them."

"Now," she shot back. "No time like the present. The baby has about ten more minutes on this side and then I have to switch, so I'm stuck for the duration."

"Stuck?"

"Yeah, it's not like I can drive to the store in my current state," she explained wryly. "It's a necessary part of the job that you have to stay pretty much parked in one spot. I had to learn the hard way to always go to the bathroom first. It's not a big deal. You get used to it and, honestly, I use the downtime to kind of Zen out."

He'd never considered that she was essentially trapped while breast-feeding. But it wasn't as if she could move around, get a glass of water if she grew thirsty. The realization sat uncomfortably behind his rib cage. While he'd been obsessing over how to get her into his arms again, she'd been quietly taking care of his son without any thought to her own comfort. "What can I get for you? Some tea? A pillow?"

What else did nursing women need? He'd have to do a Google search, watch some videos.

She smiled; the first one he'd gotten out of her since he'd interrupted her Zen. "Thanks, I'm okay. I learned to get all that stuff before starting, too."

It was a conviction of his gender that he'd never even contemplated any of this. Maybe even a conviction of his parenting skills. There was no excuse for him having left her to her own devices as she did something as sacred and necessary as feeding his son. "From now on, I want to be in the room when you feed Conner."

"What? Why?" Suspiciously, she eyed him.

"I simply wish to support you in the one aspect of Conner's care I can't control. If you're stuck, then I should be, too."

"Oh. That's…unexpected."

"I'm not a beast all the time." Only when it mattered.

She actually laughed at that. "I never said you were. Thank you. It's really not necessary for you to hang out with me. It'll probably be pretty boring."

"Conner is my son. You're my wife. I'm nothing if not avidly interested in both of you."

That seemed to set her back and she stared at him for a long moment. "I'm definitely not used to a man who's so forthcoming."

What kind of men did she normally surround herself with? Discomfort ruffled the hairs on the back of his neck. That was a subject best left unexplored.

"Find better people to associate with," he advised her brusquely. *Now* it was time to move on. "I've reviewed the list of nannies. There are four that stand out. I'd like your opinion on them."

"Sure."

She casually popped Conner's mouth from her nipple with a finger and rolled him back on the nursing pillow to adjust her bra cup. Then she unhooked the other side, peeling it away from her breast without seeming to notice that a man was in the room avidly attempting to pretend she hadn't just bared herself.

Perhaps demanding to be present every time she fed Conner wasn't such a bright idea. He shifted, but there was no comfortable spot when sporting an erection that never should have happened. He hated that he couldn't control it, hated how wrong it felt and hated that he couldn't enjoy the sight of his wife's body like a normal husband.

But he couldn't, not without infringing on her insistence that getting involved was a bad idea. And neither could he take back his insistence on supporting her, especially given that he hadn't hired a nanny yet. Until then, he'd suffer in the trap of his own making.

"Why don't you read me the résumés?" she suggested.

He blinked. Yes. Good plan. "Be right back."

He dashed to his room and grabbed his tablet from

the bedside table, booting up the device on his way back to the solarium. By the time he hit the west wing of the house, he had his email client up and the list on the screen.

McKenna hadn't moved from her spot in the chair by the window. Sunlight spilled in through the glass, highlighting her dark hair like a corona. With Conner tucked in close, she was absolutely the most beautiful woman he'd ever seen.

There came the *thwack* to his chest, true to form.

He had to fix that. It was a problem he couldn't deconstruct and then rebuild. All he could think about was kissing her again and not stopping. He liked this attraction between them. When had he lost all his brain cells?

"I, um, have the list," he announced unnecessarily, but she just nodded and didn't call him on his idiocy.

Clearing his throat, he read through the credentials of the four candidates he'd selected from the list of twenty. She interrupted every so often to clarify a point, ask him to repeat a section or remind her of a detail from a previous candidate. When he finished, he lowered the tablet and cocked his head. "What do you think?"

"I like number three the best," she announced immediately. "Shelly. Her phrasing gave me a comfort level that she wasn't trying to pad her experience with a lot of flowery words. She's the only one who's cared for two different infants with formula allergies. And I'll admit an age prejudice. She's two years older than the others. When it comes to caring for my—your—son, that's no small thing."

The slip hung in the air, daring him to comment on it. He should. Conner was her son in only one sense of the word. Des had ironclad documents stating such. The odds were good she hadn't forgotten that, not when Des was holding back the divorce as a guarantee she'd stay.

McKenna wasn't confused about her role here. Not at all. She'd been the one to back off in his workshop, citing her belief that getting involved wasn't a good plan.

Maybe *Desmond* needed the reminder about her role.

He chose to let the slip go by without comment and she didn't miss it. Her brows drew together. "I want the best for Conner, too, of course. I assume you know that or you wouldn't have asked my opinion."

Actually he hadn't considered that. At all. Wanting the best for the baby implied emotional attachment, which was the opposite of what he'd expected to happen here. She'd completely misinterpreted his request for her help and he'd completely missed that she'd developed a bond with the baby.

Taking a seat on the long leather couch facing the window, he laid the tablet to the side as he processed.

"I asked you to help select the nanny because I assumed you would want to ensure I picked someone suited to helping you wean. So you could leave with a clean slate."

Something akin to pain flashed across her face. "Yes, I have an interest in that, too. But that's the point. This woman is my replacement. I want it to be the right person to raise Connor."

"I will raise Conner," he corrected somewhat ferociously. He had a fierce need for his son and he wasn't shy about it.

"Well, of course, but he needs a female influence. Someone who can be nurturing and kiss his boo-boos when he falls down." She swept him with a once-over that she probably didn't mean to be provocative but was nonetheless. "Somehow I don't see you filling that role."

"Because I'm male?"

Sexist, definitely. But even worse, he wasn't sure she

was wrong. He didn't see himself as nurturing in the slightest. The relationship he envisioned with Conner would be of the mind as they discussed the philosophy of physics and argued theories or studied ancient history together. He'd never once thought he'd be the one sticking Band-Aids on his son's knees, though all of his research showed Conner would need that.

"No, because you're you," she countered without heat. "It has nothing to do with being male. I've seen lots of men be single fathers for one reason or another, but they were more…adaptable to the requirements. You're outsourcing the job of mom and I want to get the right person for that, so you can go back to hiding in your workshop."

"I don't—" *Hide.* Except he did and the fact that she'd clued in to that bothered him. How did she read him so well? Better still, she'd noticed a gap in Desmond's parenting experience and brought it to the forefront. "Tell me more about child rearing in your community."

"Really?" She glanced up, her confusion evident. "That doesn't seem like your cup of tea."

On that, she *was* wrong. "On the contrary. I have an interest in ensuring Conner grows into a happy, healthy adult. I have a job, too, albeit not the bandager of knees apparently."

She stuck her tongue out at him and the sight of it shouldn't have been as suggestive as it was, but instantly he recalled the feel of it, exploratory and hot, against his. She'd kissed him eagerly, as if she'd been waiting for him to breech that wall between them. He couldn't stop himself from wanting her hands on him again.

Crossing his legs, he tried to hide the worst of the tenting in his pants but he was pretty sure that was impossible when he'd just created a mountain in his lap. What was he supposed to do to tamp down this visceral reaction he always had to McKenna?

"I'm not saying you can't," she said, thankfully oblivious to Des's inability to stop reacting like a horny teenager whenever she breathed too hard. "Just that you're not going to be the first person he thinks of running to when he's bleeding and hurt. That's what I notice when thinking about how the families at home raise babies. Mothers and fathers alike read to their kids at night before bed. Get up with them when they have nightmares and soothe them back to sleep. Feeding, changing wet sheets, looking for lost stuffed animals. The person who demonstrates the most love, tolerance and patience will be who he comes to in crisis. And there are a lot of crises for children."

As she'd talked, her hand drifted over Conner's head, absently stroking his fine baby hair. Des doubted she'd even noticed that her fingers hadn't stopped moving, even after her voice stopped. McKenna was natural at nurturing, did it without thought. Did she realize that?

"And you assume the nanny will be that person." All at once, he couldn't imagine anyone other than McKenna being that person. He tried transposing one of the women on his list into his wife's spot on the chair, bottle in hand, and it refused to materialize.

That was…disturbing. And unexpected.

She shrugged. "Maybe I'm wrong. In that case, you tell me which nanny candidate you like the best and your criteria for choosing."

No. He was done with this discussion. She'd challenged a lot of his assumptions and brought up things he'd not examined. He needed time to acclimate to all of this new information.

But he couldn't leave. McKenna was still breast-feeding. And trapped. That meant he was, too, because he'd given his word. Suddenly his skin felt too tight as the first wave of what might be a panic attack stole over him. God, he hadn't had one of those in years, usually because he avoided all of his triggers.

"Desmond." McKenna's strong voice washed over him, filtering through the anxiety in a flash.

He pried open his eyelids, which he hadn't even realized he'd closed, to see her watching him with concern flitting across her expression. She'd tucked her clothes back into place and cradled Conner in her arms as he waved a hand in a circle, content after his feeding.

"Would you like to hold him?" she offered casually, as if she hadn't noticed he'd slid into his own head. But he didn't believe for a second she'd missed it. Neither did he mistake her offer as anything other than an intervention. She'd noticed he was troubled and sought to help him.

It worked. Somehow. As she set the nursing pillow aside and crossed the room, his body cooled and settled. Conner nestled into Des's arms and he definitely didn't need any more information to know that he loved his son. The emotion bled through him, a balm to his frazzled nerves.

Yes. This part wasn't in question. He'd wanted a baby because he'd needed this connection. From the first moment Lacey had announced that she was pregnant, his heart had instantly been engaged with the idea of a child. A baby wouldn't know that Des stumbled over things normal people did without question. His son would love him even after realizing his father hated crowds and preferred to be alone.

"I want you to come to me for bandages," he murmured softly, but McKenna heard him anyway. Her hand drifted to his shoulder, gentle and warm, and that felt right, too.

"Then he will," she promised. "I didn't mean to speak out of turn."

"No. You just caused me to think about aspects of being a single father that I previously hadn't." Maybe he didn't want a nanny. It wasn't like he needed to work to provide for his son. If Des took off a year, even two, who would care?

Well, he would. His brain did not stop creating, whether he wished it to or not. Putting the pieces together of what he saw was merely a defense mechanism designed to empty his mind. But he didn't have to be a full-time inventor or even sell anything he created, which meant no business trips to the manufacturer's locations. Nothing to distract him from being a father.

It could just be Des and Conner. Father and son. No nanny needed.

McKenna smiled. "I'm glad. The secret to being a great father is that there is no secret. All you have to do is love them. And there's nothing wrong with picking a nanny who's more in the background. As long as she can work with Conner's formula allergy, I think that's the most important thing."

All at once the reality of the situation crashed through his bubble of contentment. If he didn't hire a nanny, what did that mean for McKenna and weaning? Could *he* be the one who helped her through that? Would she even accept that?

He'd never failed to master a concept in his life. If he studied up on it, surely he could fare as well as a nanny. And then, as a bonus, working together would give him more of an opportunity to be around her. Feel out what was happening between them and his odd, disconcerting urge to bury himself inside her and never emerge.

Hiring a nanny would only impede that process.

But he couldn't tell McKenna. Not yet. First he had to figure out how to convince her it was the right decision.

While Des had already done a good bit of research on Conner's formula allergy, he hadn't spent any effort on how to transition from breast-feeding to something else because it hadn't mattered yet. Now it did.

From the moment he woke up the next day until well after lunch, he studied. With way too many videos starring breast-feeding women on a continual loop in his head, he let it go for the day and took a shower.

Des's bedroom resembled a small fortress. By design. When he'd bought the house, he'd cared mostly about its proximity to other people. Namely that they were as far away as they could be. The two-hundred-acre property guaranteed that, and the forest of trees and wild undergrowth surrounding the main house shielded him from unwanted trespassers. But just to make sure, he'd installed a twelve-foot concrete wall around the grounds.

He'd stopped short at a pack of Dobermans to roam the property. Overkill. And thus far McKenna had been his only guest, so he'd accomplished his goal of cutting himself off from those who didn't tolerate his eccentricities. For an additional escape, he'd created a bedroom retreat that rivaled the poshest resorts complete with a pop-up TV, a large, oval spa tub in the cavernous bathroom and a small sitting area in the garden outside a set of French doors.

Shame he rarely spent time here, often napping in his workshop on the single bed he'd eventually had delivered when he'd fallen asleep at his desk for the tenth time. The suite was a place to hold his clothes and store his shampoo, but that was it. The workshop was his home.

Maybe not so much anymore if he didn't hire a nanny.

The concept of losing his sanctuary filled him with a black soup of nerves. But, as he continually told himself, he wasn't losing his workshop. Just committing to spend less time hiding and more time with the family he was creating with his son.

To that end, he had to actually do that. Throwing on some clothes, he went in search of his son. He found both the baby and McKenna in the nursery. She held Conner upright in her lap as she read him a chunky board book.

He cleared his throat. "Thanks for watching him while I was busy."

"You're welcome." Her slightly cocked eyebrow had a saucy bent to it, like she questioned why he was being pleasant.

McKenna wore a dress today. A rarity. Usually she had on capri pants and a short-sleeved shirt or yoga pants and a tunic. The dress showed off her feminine curves in a way he fully appreciated.

Then she smiled at Conner as he waved a chubby fist in a circle, and the desire Des had no ability to keep in check roared through his chest like a freight train. Coupled with everything else, it was nearly enough to put him over the edge.

"Did you need something?" she asked before he'd regained his sanity.

"Do I have to need something to spend time with my son?"

To her credit, she didn't flinch at his less than civil tone. "Wanting to spend time with your son is a need. There's nothing wrong with claiming it as such, especially if I'm in the way."

She levered herself out of the chair and plopped Conner into his arms, then turned, clearly about to leave the room, which had not been his intent at all.

"Wait," he called out awkwardly as Conner started fussing.

McKenna glanced back over her shoulder. "You'll be fine. He just ate not too long ago, so he might be ready for a diaper change."

"I want you to stay," he ground out. This was not one of his more stellar examples of communicating with other people.

"Why?" She seemed genuinely perplexed, like she had no concept of how she made the room brighter by being in it. Why *wouldn't* he want her to stay? "I'm just the buffet."

"That's so far from the truth," he shot back and then registered that he'd meant it.

She was more than just a means to an end. McKenna was his wife. Against everything he'd expected when he'd convinced her to come home with him from the hospital, she'd begun to matter.

"I like you," he said, marking the first time he could recall saying anything resembling that out loud to anyone. Not even Lacey.

It was an event.

McKenna was no longer just his son's surrogate mother, and Des didn't have a good foundation for managing that.

"Yes, I got that impression the other day in your workshop," she replied blithely with an ironic smile. "I hope you aren't angling for a repeat."

Of the kiss? What if he was?

No better way to take control than to lay out exactly what was on his mind. Besides, she'd seemed rather impressed with his tendency to be forthcoming. Sometimes he had no filter owing to his lack of social niceties and other times because he genuinely didn't see the point in filtering. People could take him or leave him and usually he preferred the latter.

Except with McKenna.

And she was still edging toward the door.

"McKenna." She froze. He pressed the advantage. "Stay. We live in the same house and share a son. I like your company. Unless the reverse isn't true?"

"What, are you asking me if I like hanging around with you?" She leaned against the open door as she surveyed him. "I basically spend my days feeding your son. Adult conversation is high on my list of things I look forward to."

Obviously she viewed herself as the milk supply and he'd done nothing to counter that. Perhaps it was time to change their association in her mind. In both their minds. She was a person with her own interests, dreams and opinions, some of which he'd already glimpsed, but not nearly enough.

"Then there's no reason for you to leave." Satisfied that he'd navigated this small blip, he nodded to the chair she'd recently vacated. "Sit while I change Conner's diaper. Tell me something about you that I don't know."

"You want me to provide entertainment for you?" The quirk of her mouth said she found the concept amusing but she sat in the chair as he'd asked.

"No. Insight." The more he knew about her, the more information he had at his disposal to figure out how to exorcise her from his consciousness. But even that excuse was starting to fall short.

He just wanted to know her. Period.

"I like cotton candy, thunderstorms and books about dogs. That kind of thing?" At his nod, she laughed. "I feel like I'm on a date."

Instantly a dozen different scenarios sprang to his

mind, scenes where he romanced what he wanted out of McKenna, held her hand as he led her along a rain-soaked trail through the woods. Pressed her against a tree as he fed her cotton candy from his fingers, then kissed her to treat them both to the taste of sweetness mixed with the fire that laced their electric attraction.

He was going about his problem solving in the wrong way. If he wanted insight, a next kiss, to spend time with McKenna, "hanging out" wasn't going to cut it. He needed to ask her on a date.

Five

McKenna did not like the look on Desmond's face. Or rather, she liked it a whole hell of a lot and shouldn't.

The second the word *date* had come out of her stupid mouth, something heated and thoroughly intrigued popped into his gaze and hadn't fled in over a minute.

It was a long minute, too, as he watched her without apology, contemplating. She could almost see the gears turning in his head and one of Desmond's sexiest qualities was his mind. She'd gone to college with a lot of smart people, but Desmond's brain was wired so differently, evidenced by the fascinating way he presented thoughts and concepts, drew conclusions. Threw out unexpected comments such as *I like you.*

Sometimes she wondered if he did stuff like that as a test. To see what she'd do. But she had no rubric for the grading system and therefore no way of knowing if she'd passed or not. Or whether she wanted to pass.

She and Desmond weren't supposed to become friends. Or anything else.

"We never finished our nanny discussion," she blurted out lamely, but they needed to get on to an innocuous topic. Now.

She'd grown uncomfortably aware that Desmond's hair was wet, probably because he'd come straight from the shower. It was slicked back from his forehead as it always was and hung down around his collar in solid, dark chunks. Wet, it was darker, almost black, and gave his devastating looks a wicked edge she couldn't ignore. Neither could she stop thinking about Desmond wet. And naked.

"We didn't," he allowed. "I'd like to. Another time. I have another subject of importance. Have dinner with me tonight."

She nearly choked on her gasp of surprise and the sound upset Conner, who started to cry. Desmond rocked him back and forth but his gaze never left hers.

"As in a date?" she managed to ask.

Stupid mouth. Why had she even mentioned that word? Because she'd never quite gotten that kiss out of her head, of course. She fantasized about a repeat pretty much 24/7, so no wonder she'd slipped. A smart guy like him had no problem picking up on the fact that she'd *said* it wasn't a good idea to get involved, but that didn't mean she had the ability to turn off her fascination with him.

"As in dinner. I'd like to thank you for what you've done for Conner. And for me." His gentle rocking soothed Conner into a doze, his sweet face nestled against Desmond's chest. "You're a guest. I haven't welcomed you as one."

Oh. That was a different story. Slightly. It still sounded like all the trappings of a date without slapping the label on it. "Would it just be me and you? What about Conner? Right now, we're it as far as a caregiver goes."

"Mrs. Elliot will fill in for a few hours."

He had an answer to everything, didn't he? Desperately, she cast about for a plausible reason to refuse. Except, she wanted to have dinner with Desmond. Fiercely. And have it be every bit a date, with all the long, delicious glances over dessert as anticipation coiled in her belly...

Bad, bad idea.

"I don't have anything to wear."

The protest died in her throat as he swept her with a look that could have melted the habit off of a nun. "I have yet to see you in clothing that I did not think looked spectacular on you. Wear anything. Or nothing. I'm not particular."

The shiver his suggestion unleashed shouldn't have gone so deep into her skin. It was the most flirtatious thing he'd ever said. That any man had dared to say to her. She shouldn't like it so much, but all at once, the muddle he was making of her request to stay uninvolved put her in a dangerous mood.

"I'd love to see the look on your face if I took that dare."

One eyebrow cocked at a quizzical angle. "It wasn't a dare. I merely sought to make you more comfortable about the circumstances. If you want to see my expression once you grant me the privilege of seeing you naked, my calendar is completely clear for the evening."

Somehow that got a laugh out of her. Mostly because she had a feeling he wasn't kidding. There was something so affecting about knowing exactly where she stood with him. He liked her. He wanted to see her naked. No guessing.

But he also wanted to divorce her. The contradictions were dizzying.

"What if I say yes? Are you expecting sex as payback for dinner?"

"No. I'm expecting you to eat as payback for putting food in front of you. Though, again…if you want sex to be a part of the evening, my calendar is still open."

She shut her eyes for a beat. Why was she so surprised he'd be gentlemanly about it, putting all the balls in her court? "I don't."

She did.

Oh, God, did she want sex to be a part of her relationship with Desmond. The way he communicated with his hands during a simple kiss had kept her awake and feverish far longer than it should have. But she couldn't help imaging how much hotter those hands could be with no barriers between them.

What was wrong with her? She and Desmond had the most dysfunctional marriage on the planet and sex would only complicate everything. And then what would happen? She'd end up divorced and in medical school. Exactly as she'd planned.

She blinked. "I'll have dinner with you."

And maybe sex would be on the menu, after all. What did she have to lose besides this achy, vibrating tension between her and the man with the keys to her future?

McKenna pulled out her best dress from the back of the giant closet. Everything at Desmond's house was huge, including him. His presence dominated every inch of his realm. There was literally nowhere she could go to escape his effect on her, particularly not her bedroom.

He'd become a permanent fixture when she breast-fed, which she appreciated more than she'd have expected.

But the middle-of-the-night visits were hard to take, when she was semiconscious and Desmond wore drawstring lounge pants and a white T-shirt that showcased surprisingly broad shoulders.

It seemed natural for him to be in her bedroom. It was almost hard to watch him leave when she had to go back to her cold bed alone. That had never bothered her before. But she'd never experienced such a magnetic draw to a man before either.

And in ten minutes they were going to have dinner in what she definitely considered a date. As long as everyone understood that getting involved only worked for the short term. Surely that was Desmond's thought, too.

Nervous all at once, McKenna twirled in front of the oval cheval glass in the corner of her room. She'd never had a full-length mirror before and loved it. When she left, she'd miss that, plus a lot of the other luxuries strewed throughout the mansion, especially the indoor pool.

Of course she had to actually leave before she could miss them.

The mirror reflected a woman who looked the best she could. Her hair was low maintenance, wash and go as soon as it was dry, but she'd given it extra help with a blow-dryer a few minutes ago. No makeup, thank God, because who wanted to sit around with goop on their face? The dress fit her angular body well, except for her bust line. The fabric hugged her cleavage, smooshing it prominently high and out. Only her maternity clothes accommodated her enormous boobs, but without the baby bump, she might as well wear a potato sack on her date with Desmond. Not happening. Besides, he'd seen her breasts lots of times. No reason to hide them.

When she descended the main staircase to the ground

floor, Desmond was waiting for her at the bottom. His gaze locked onto her, hot and appreciative, sending little quakes through her core that put a whole new spin on the concept of long, delicious glances.

"Conner is settled with Mrs. Elliot and a bottle of breast milk," he informed her casually, as if he hadn't just undressed her with his eyes. "Shall we?"

He gestured with his hand toward the dining room, signaling her to walk with him. Nerves and a whole lot of zingy sparks shot around under her skin, making her jumpy. The dining room conformed to the rest of the house: cavernous, a little formal and thoroughly drenched with Desmond.

During the first course of garden salad, served by the invisible staff Mrs. Elliot managed, Desmond said, "Tell me about being part of a cooperative community."

"What? All of it?"

"Sure. Whatever you want to tell me. I imagine it shaped you in many invisible ways. I'm curious."

She swallowed. This was definitely not first-date material. It was far deeper, opening aspects of her soul she wasn't sure she wanted on display. "I don't know. I don't sit around and think about my upbringing."

Except she did sometimes. Being part of a closed, united community had a lot of pluses, but losing her grandfather hadn't been one of them. It *had* shaped her. And, based on his comment, Desmond had already figured that out.

"But it matters," he said quietly, and it wasn't a question.

His insight bothered her. She forked up a bite of lettuce and tomato to stall but his piercing gaze penetrated her anyway. "Well, yeah. Of course."

"Did it contribute to your decision to be my surrogate?"

"My background has everything to do with why I'm Conner's mother," she told him firmly. "I was raised to believe that we each have a purpose in life. I discovered early on that mine is to help people when they're hurting. You wanted a baby really badly and I had the power to give you the family you wished for. It was a no-brainer."

"Thank you," he said simply. "Conner means more to me than anything else I've ever created. I would not have him without you."

The sincerity in his voice choked her up. Why, she couldn't say. She shouldn't be privy to any of this.

McKenna blinked back the sudden moisture in her eyes, mystified why it meant so much to her that she shared something so deeply personal with Desmond.

He fell silent, watching her as the staff cleared the salad plates and replaced them with the main course of locally fished salmon and asparagus. But instead of picking up his fork to dig in, he cocked his head. "Perhaps you'd be interested in taking a role in Conner's life on a longer term basis."

"What?" Her own fork clattered to her plate. "What are you talking about? That's not the deal."

It couldn't be the deal. What did he mean? Like, picking Conner up from school or taking him to the zoo occasionally? She couldn't do that. Didn't Desmond know how hard it already was to contemplate leaving? It was easier to not have contact. That's what she'd been counting on.

"No, it's not." Steadily, he measured his words as he spoke. "But you care about Conner already. I can see it in your face when you hold him. There's no reason we can't discuss a different arrangement."

Still reeling, she gaped at him. Was he insane? "I can't

do that. You shouldn't want me to do that. What about when he starts asking questions about who I am? I won't lie. And then he'll wonder why I don't live with you and be a real mother."

It would be a disaster. And, of course, Conner might still have those same questions, but she'd much rather let Desmond answer them than be put on the hot seat herself. As a surrogate, none of this should have ever been presented to her and the unfairness of it hammered at her heart.

She wasn't mother material. The first criterion was wanting to be one and she didn't. Or rather, she didn't have the luxury of wanting to be one, which wasn't the same thing, as she'd only just come to realize. It was be a doctor or be a mother. Period. And she'd made her choice so long ago that she'd reconciled it in her mind.

Until now.

The salmon dried up in her mouth as she wrestled with the impossibility of Desmond's suggestion. With the fact that her decisions weren't as cut-and-dried as she'd have once claimed.

She did care for Conner. So much so that Desmond had noticed.

Well, it didn't matter. She cared about the baby for the same reasons she wanted to be a doctor; she genuinely wanted to help Conner. The soul-deep need to fix what was wrong came so naturally that she couldn't remember a time when she hadn't wanted to be a doctor.

Besides, as soon as Desmond signed the divorce papers, the custody agreement would go into effect and all of this would be a moot point. She was here to say a long goodbye, nothing more.

"There is a reason we can't discuss this," she reminded him, but her throat was so tight it was a miracle any sound came out. "You've been really clear about the fact that you don't want me involved in Conner's life."

"I didn't, no. But obviously circumstances have shifted."

"You don't like to share," she blurted, confused about the direction of the conversation. What happened to the delicious, sensual undertones she'd anticipated for their date? "Unless you've changed your mind about being the one to make all the decisions?"

"I haven't." His tone cooled considerably. "And you're right. I'm not being fair. There isn't a way to alter our agreement to permit you a role in Conner's life past the one you have currently."

A prickle walked down her spine as she watched Desmond shut down. Their date disintegrated into a long, uncomfortable silence as she grappled to understand what had just happened. They both ate but the stilted vibe turned everything unpleasant.

"I take it your calendar isn't so clear anymore," she muttered as the staff unobtrusively removed the dinner dishes. Hers was embarrassingly unfinished, with half the salmon lying forlornly near the edge of the plate, but she'd lost her appetite.

He glanced up. "My interest in you hasn't changed, if that's what you mean. But I sense the timing is not the best."

"Yeah. That."

It had seemed so easy to imagine that they'd have some hot sex and then she'd get her divorce at some point in the future so she could leave.

But Desmond had just dropped a whole lot of reality in her lap. He had all the control and would never give up any. The thought of getting involved with someone who refused to allow her choices didn't sit well.

Rubbing at his beard, Desmond frowned. "I've angered you."

"No." Not really. He had been completely transparent from the first and she'd ignored all the warning signs that had been screaming at her to stay far away from the father of her baby. "I...just need some air."

She excused herself and went to her room to get some sleep before the sole source of her uneasiness visited her room for Conner's midnight feeding. The sooner he hired a nanny, the better.

Once again, McKenna had run away from him. Desmond stared out the window in Conner's nursery as he sat in the rocking chair holding his son later that night.

It was far from the first time a woman had edged for the door while in the midst of a date. But this marked a rarity in that it still bothered him hours later. How had things disintegrated so quickly? First they'd been talking about McKenna's upbringing and the conversation had shifted to Conner. Why not? The baby was one of the things they had in common.

But then she'd grown upset when he'd mentioned that she might extend her role, maybe spending time with their son on a regular basis. It seemed a simple enough concept, but clearly McKenna wished to keep their agreement as it was. Nor did she want to explore their attraction.

Which was the root of the problem—he did and apparently she'd clued in far too fast that he didn't have a charming personality at his disposal to woo a woman into his bed. So he'd have to be a little more inventive than the average Joe, clearly.

He dissected their dialogue, trying to pinpoint where he'd messed up.

This had been a problem his whole life. Nothing ever unfolded the way he'd constructed it in his mind, not when people were involved. Metal parts and computer programs always came together exactly as he intended. The final creation resembled the one he'd imagined. Always. His relationship with McKenna? Not even close.

Conner circled his fist and whacked Desmond in the chest. All at once, Des had the unsettling realization that his son was a person. Unless he figured out how to relate to people, he might very well have the same issues with his child once Conner grew old enough to talk. Of course, Desmond had envisioned that the baby would love him. But years of evidence indicated otherwise.

A wash of emotion tightened his chest as he captured Conner's little fist and held it in his. When McKenna had said his son wouldn't come to him with a scraped knee, she'd meant because Desmond was difficult to relate to. Conner wouldn't naturally seek out his father.

Des had to fix his people skills if he ever hoped to forge the connections he craved.

Once Conner fell asleep, Des settled him into his crib with a silent vow that he'd never give his son a reason to run away from him. That meant he had to figure out how to entice his mother to stay, since they likely shared similarities. The problem wheeled through his mind constantly, keeping Des from fully relaxing.

The hour of sleep he got before Conner woke him for his midnight feeding didn't put him in any better frame of mind. McKenna was always so much more beautiful in the semidarkness, too.

She answered her door wearing her virginal white robe that left everything to the imagination and an expression that could have frozen lava.

Usually her naturally friendly personality was in place

no matter the time or circumstance. Was she still upset about dinner? She'd said she wasn't angry. Had that been one of those times when a woman was less than forthcoming and Des should have figured out that she meant the opposite of what she'd said?

He hated being forced to read between the lines. "Conner is ready for you."

That could have come out with less of a growl. But when uncertain, he tended to retreat behind his walls. He couldn't afford to do so tonight, and cursed himself for being such a brute.

"I assumed so."

She reached out and took the baby from his arms, brushing her fingers across Desmond's chest. The T-shirt he wore provided little barrier from the thrill of her touch, which seemed constant regardless of whether things were prickly between them.

The familiar rush of awareness didn't diminish just because McKenna wasn't speaking to him. His conscience poked at him. If he wanted to change the status quo, this was a great opportunity for him to take the initiative.

"I'm, uh, sorry about earlier," he offered cautiously as she settled into the recliner with Conner. "I did not intend for dinner to end on such a bad note."

"I know." The barest hint of a smile turned up the edges of her mouth. It wasn't much, but it felt like a lot.

Instead of letting her handle her own logistics, he picked up the nursing pillow from the floor and arranged it in her lap the way he'd seen her do a dozen times. Then he helped her get Conner situated, a trick and a half since the baby already knew what was coming and had squirmed into place against McKenna's covered bosom. There wasn't enough room for two sets of hands, a baby and the enormous sensual pull that seemed constantly coiled between Desmond and McKenna. But he stuck it out and ignored the ache that sprang up at the sight of his son and wife together in the most elemental scene a man could have the privilege to witness.

And therein lay part of his confusion and consternation. His attraction to McKenna had a thread running through it that was inexorably due to the fact that she was Conner's mother. It was unexpected. Powerful. Impossible to mistake. What was he supposed to do with that?

"I'm sorry, too," she said after the longest pause.

His gaze flew to hers. "For what? I'm the one who overstepped at dinner."

"No, you didn't. It was very generous of you to offer to reexamine the agreement. I know your heart was in the right place. I…freaked out and made it weird."

That set him back for a moment. Emotional decisions weren't in his wheelhouse. Or were they? "Only because I suggested something that had no logical possibility. It was a mistake."

One borne out of his visceral need to connect and he'd bungled it.

"On that we agree." She tipped her head back against the recliner, letting her eyes flutter closed. "It would be too hard, Desmond. I hope you understand that."

All at once, he had an inkling of what she meant. McKenna cared for Conner. He hadn't gotten that part wrong, though he'd questioned what he'd seen after their discussion, assuming he'd completely misinterpreted the expression that always stole over her face when she held him. "Hard because you're giving up a relationship with your son?"

Her misty smile was a little wider this time. "It shouldn't be. I never would have thought twice about it if you hadn't asked me to breast-feed. Or, at least, I don't think I would have. Who can say at this point?"

Her pain convicted him, winnowing through his pores as easily as if he'd poured it down his throat. He'd changed the dynamic and forced her to help, with no thought to the resulting emotional turmoil he'd be causing her. Or himself.

The empathy he'd always felt for other people's strongest emotions amplified under his own unease. *Why* did he have to experience feelings so strongly? It was exactly why he stayed away from people. But he couldn't have stayed away from McKenna short of being chained in the basement.

"I didn't realize," he finally ground out through clenched teeth as he battled to get the clash of emotion gripping his chest to ease. She hurt. Therefore, he did, too. "I'm sorry."

"I made the choice." She shrugged. "And it was the right one. What would have happened to Conner if I wasn't here to feed him? It's ghastly to even consider. So it's a done deal. The only thing we can do at this point is move forward. Hire a nanny who can help us figure out the options so I can leave."

If he hadn't been paying such close attention to her, he might have missed the desolate note in her voice. But all at once he had the distinct impression she wasn't in such a hurry to leave as she had been.

Also a benefit of being so closely tuned in to one another. He could tell what she was feeling as clearly as if she'd hung a sign around her neck.

And he had to admit that he wasn't in such a hurry for her to go either. He should be. She stirred him in ways that made him uncomfortable. But she stirred him in ways that thrilled him, too. The wonder of that kept him engaged. If he was this attuned to her now, he could only image how much more strongly they might connect in the throes of pleasure.

"I've been doing some research into formula allergies," he said casually. "It's very difficult to say how Conner will stack up against the data. He may not wean for six months."

"I know." She glanced up at Des, her expression indecipherable. "I've looked into it, as well. I may be here until he's on solid food."

"Would that be so bad?" It was a bold question and, judging by the long, heavy silence, she didn't miss the significance of it. They were talking about further alterations to the agreement.

She heaved a deep breath. "Only because it puts my goals on hold even longer."

Not because she'd be stuck here with him. Not because she didn't like taking care of Conner. More had changed than just the circumstances. But how much? Enough that she might reevaluate the complications standing between them?

He couldn't barrel ahead as he'd half planned. As his body screamed for him to. If he didn't want to ruin things between them, he had to take his time. Romance her until she was hot and breathless.

He chewed on the idea until the next morning. During Conner's midmorning nap, Des considered how to court his wife. The techniques felt fake and disingenuous, like he'd have to become someone else to simply hold a conversation with a normal person.

But his wife and son weren't normal people. He loved Conner, and McKenna... Well, he couldn't say for sure how he felt about her, but it wasn't lukewarm by any stretch. She did matter, as he'd told her. The only piece of advice that he'd gleaned from all of his research on talking to people was to engage McKenna at her level of interest.

McKenna wanted to go to medical school and he'd held her back thus far. It was time to rectify that to the best of his ability.

Six

When McKenna had too much rattling around in her brain, she liked to swim. Lately she'd been spending several hours a day at the pool as she tried to get her mind off the constant turmoil under her skin.

Not only had she let herself start to care about Conner, Desmond had noticed. Noticed and commented. That made it real.

She hated the quandary. Conner couldn't be her son and she'd walked into this agreement willingly. Sure she'd known it would be difficult to give up the baby at the hospital, but she'd done it, even though it had been harder than she'd ever imagined. She'd reconciled the loss by envisioning the family Desmond would create for himself, believing that as time went on, the regret would fade.

None of that had happened. Desmond had taken her life over by storm and, instead of moving on, she'd chosen to be in the position of caring for her son day in, day out…only to have to eventually give him up again. Each additional day she stayed in this house meant one more chink in her heart. And she'd known for a while that Desmond would eventually bring up the fact that his original three-month proposal was likely dead in the water.

Being stuck in this nebulous role of mother and not mother was killing her.

How was she going to manage the mess she was making of this?

Swimming helped. But not much. Especially when she broke the surface of the water to see Desmond sitting on one of the lounge chairs, gorgeous and intense and untouchable. Her pulse stumbled and the perfect temperature of the pool rose a few degrees.

She hadn't seen him since last night. Conner had thankfully dropped one of the nighttime feedings, but showed no signs of forgetting about the remaining one, which meant a tension-filled encounter with Desmond lay in store for her like clockwork. She wished she could say she'd shut down his advances and then dismissed him from her mind.

Not so much. As if the thought of leaving Conner behind wasn't difficult enough, she couldn't get his father out from under her skin either. Late at night there were fewer barriers somehow. The dark created an oasis where anything was possible and nothing bad could touch the three of them.

Then when the sun rose she remembered all the reasons she couldn't indulge in the sizzle that sprang up anytime Desmond entered a room.

The echoing pool area amplified the undercurrents between them in spades.

"Conner is down for his nap," he announced—unnecessarily since McKenna knew the baby's schedule well.

"And that seemed like a good opportunity to tell me you hired a nanny?" she suggested hopefully.

"Not yet."

Of course not. What fun would that be? His highness liked to have control and wield his power as he saw fit.

And now she felt petulant and ungrateful. The man was treating *her* like royalty, not acting like he expected everyone to kowtow to his bidding. Desmond wished to keep an iron fist around all of the decisions regarding his son. It wasn't a crime and it was certainly his right. Some people might simply call it being protective.

"You could have flagged me down if you needed to talk," she murmured.

Like the last time he'd cornered her here, he wasn't dressed for swimming. In fact, she'd never seen him in anything but pants and a shirt.

The long look he shot her shouldn't have put so much heat in her blood. She was suddenly very aware that the swimsuit she wore might have been considered modest on most women, but on the body of one who was breast-feeding, it became more of a boob showcase starring pointy, chilled nipples.

Some of that might be the fault of Desmond and his hot-eyed gaze that never failed to make her feel both sexy and appreciated.

"I didn't want to bother you," he said with a shake of his head far past the time when it would have been appropriate to respond.

Too late for that. "But now that I know you're here, it's okay?"

He blinked. "I can come back."

God, sometimes he was so adorable. Why was that such a thing? She'd never met anyone quite like Desmond Pierce and she was pretty sure that was the reason she couldn't stop thinking about him, despite the surety that getting involved would be the worst idea ever.

"I'm just kidding." She kicked to the edge of the pool and rested her arms on the flagstone lip surrounding the water, mostly so the whole of her body was hidden from his too sharp gaze. "You should swim sometime."

"Is that an invitation?" he asked with raised eyebrows…and there came more of the heat that turned the whole exchange into a double entendre. Everything he said lately seemed centered on sex, probably because it was on both their minds constantly.

Cursing her stupid mouth, she shut her eyes for a beat. What was wrong with her that she hadn't seen that coming?

"I thought we covered that. We have too many complications to get involved."

"I am referring to swimming. Only."

Yeah, right. All sorts of non-swimming-related things that could happen in a private area when two people were already nearly undressed shimmered in the atmosphere between them.

"You and I both know you aren't. So save it," she advised.

His head cocked to the side in the way she'd come to understand meant he was about to throw her into a tailspin. "This may surprise you, but I genuinely want to spend time with you."

Yep. Tailspin. "I don't know what to do with that."

"Spend time with me," he suggested wryly. "To that end, I have a surprise for you. I registered you for a couple of online classes that will count toward your medical degree."

"You did what?"

"I thought you might enjoy having something adult

to do since you mentioned that you're bored frequently. It's a gift."

This was definitely one of those times when she couldn't remember why it was a bad idea to get involved with him. No one had ever done something like that for her and it speared her right where it counted. Dumbstruck, she stared at him.

How dare he do something so generous and kindhearted when she had nothing she could do in return to thank him? "I can't accept."

"Why not?"

Argh. Because…of some reason that she couldn't put her finger on. But it felt like she should refuse. "I can't take classes that count toward my course work online. Medical school is about hands-on experience and labs. Working toward residency."

"I am aware. I reviewed the requirements and then called the dean at Oregon Health and Science University to ensure that the courses would transfer."

God, would he just stop shocking the hell out of her for a minute? "Why would you go to all that trouble, Desmond?"

"It was no trouble. You're sacrificing so much for my son. I wished to honor your goal of becoming a doctor, which I have not done a very good job of doing so far."

He'd been listening to her. And then gone out of his way to do something special for her. As gifts went, it was the best one she'd ever received.

She blew out a breath. And then another, fighting for all she was worth not to cry. It was so unexpected, so genuinely unselfish and… "Wait a minute. What's the catch?"

"McKenna, stop. There's no catch."

The raspy note in his voice flashed down her spine

and she was suddenly very glad she'd never levered herself out of the pool. He was too close as it was, too intense, too beautiful with his gaze that missed nothing, and she was very much afraid he'd just turned the tide with his imaginative present. She didn't want to find out just how deep he could take her when he finally sucked her into his orbit.

But then he rendered that point moot by crossing the few feet separating them and kneeling on the flagstone to catch her gaze as he spoke to her.

"It's a gift," he repeated and she couldn't look away. "Because I can be...hard to take. You didn't want to put off medical school, but I gave you no choice. I'm offering you a workable solution to compensate for the difficult circumstances."

That was probably the most shocking part of all.

"I'm here because I chose to be," she corrected him. *Because I continue to choose this.* It was so critical he understand he couldn't force her to do *anything*. But the rest wasn't off base. How could she say no? She couldn't. "It's a lovely thought. Thank you."

"Does that mean you're going to take the classes?"

"Yes. Of course."

Relief rushed over his expression, tripping her radar again. What was he getting out of this? "I'm cold and I'd like to go take a shower. Did you have anything else you needed to discuss? Like hiring a nanny?"

Desmond smiled. "You'll be the first to know when the nanny situation is resolved."

In addition to registering McKenna for the classes he'd selected, Desmond had also ordered her a desk, a leather chair and a top-of-the-line laptop. When they were delivered the next day, he set up everything himself, rolling back the sleeves of his button-down shirt to the forearms and geeking out over the equipment.

Almost none of the words he used to describe what he'd bought made any sense, but the smile he wore when he talked drove it all from her consciousness anyway.

She stood back and let him do his thing because… *oh, my God*, was he sexy when he got his hands dirty in his realm of expertise. This was Desmond at his finest, building something from the ground up, and he nearly glowed with some kind of inner fire she couldn't explain and couldn't stop basking in.

Once he got the mysterious settings of the computer's brain the way he wanted, he showed her how it worked, settling her into the chair and leaning over her shoulder. Something wholly masculine wafted from him as he pointed at the something-or-other on the screen, explaining that he'd done some kind of magic mojo to hook her computer into the private network housed in his workshop.

"It'll be fast," he promised. His tone indicated this was a desirable state, so she nodded. "And I have access to all of the top academic institutions and think tanks in the world. There is literally not one scrap of information discovered in the history of mankind that is not available to you via this portal."

Not one scrap? She bit her lip before asking if his computer could explain why she wanted him to kiss her so badly that her teeth ached. It was unfathomable to her how this small act of kindness and understanding had put so much of a deeper awareness of him under her skin. But it had. And what had been there before was bad enough.

This was different. Encompassing. Inevitable in some ways.

"I installed an instant messaging client, too," he continued, tapping a little blue icon on the screen. "I'll keep mine open and if you need anything while I'm working, you can let me know."

"Isn't that the equivalent of a text message?" She couldn't help but ask because… Come on. What was she going to need to say to him that she couldn't get up and walk the two flights of stairs to his workshop? Besides, she couldn't imagine bothering him with something he viewed as an uncomfortable social contract.

Unperturbed, he shrugged. "Probably. I've never used instant messaging. But schoolwork can be lonely and isolating, especially at this level. I didn't want you to feel cut off."

That turned her heart over in a completely different way because he could only know that from personal experience. And his solution to prevent her from feeling that way? Grant her special backstage access to the genius himself. It was touching, sending little fingers of warmth into her soul.

Because she couldn't stop herself, she reached out and covered his forearm with her palm. "Thank you for this."

He glanced down at her hand and then at her, seemingly just now noticing their close proximity, which only dialed up the awareness about a billion degrees. Prickles walked across her cheeks, her neck. Across her cleavage as he stared at her. They were so close she could see dark flecks in his irises.

"You're welcome."

What did it say that she'd started loving that gruff note in his voice? That she was insane, clearly. She snatched her hand back, chastising herself for falling prey to the intimacy he'd unwittingly created. It instantly disintegrated the moment she stopped touching him. He backed away quickly, heading for the door of her bedroom.

He turned before exiting, running a hand across his beard, which was holy-cow sexy all at once. "Let me know if you're missing anything."

Like her marbles? "I can't imagine what I'd need that you haven't already thought of."

Once Desmond had taken himself and his disturbing presence out of her room, she began the long, arduous process of downloading software, updating her preferences and finally logging on to the university website to figure out how online classes worked.

As the first syllabus spilled onto her screen, she had a total moment of bliss. She didn't love the pressure of academics by any stretch, but she did like a feeling of purpose and accomplishment. This was step one toward her medical degree and she longed to immerse herself in the wonders of the human body. Biology had been her favorite subject since ninth grade when she'd dissected a frog and realized the working parts were similar to other animals but not identical. How amazing was that? She'd yearned to learn more, and had in her undergraduate classes.

Now came the really good stuff.

Thanks to the husband she'd never expected to meet let alone like, she was finally on her way.

At some point Desmond returned with Conner for his next round of feeding. Des apologized for interrupting her, but she waved it off and settled into her recliner, glad for the excuse to get up from her hunched position at the desk. Once the baby was full and happy, she started to hand him back to his father when she realized there was something she could do for Desmond to thank him for his thoughtfulness.

"You know what?" McKenna pulled a fast one, shifting the baby's trajectory, and resettled Conner in her lap. "Let me play nanny for the afternoon."

Desmond quirked a brow. "That's my job."

"I know, but even you can benefit from a break occasionally. Go build something."

His smile was far too brief. "You have class work. Conner is my responsibility."

How many men would complain about being relieved of baby duty for the afternoon? Just one in her experience. "Don't be difficult. Let me do something nice for you."

"All right." He didn't sound like it was all right. He sounded like he didn't quite know what had hit him. "If you're sure."

She hefted Conner higher against her chest, supporting his downy head with her palm. "Off you go."

Actually she looked forward to spending time with Conner. She'd tried to limit her exposure to him as much as possible and, thus far, Desmond had been pretty on board with that. But diving into medical school had brought home the fact that she would not live in this house forever with easy access to her baby. Eventually she'd have to leave and as much as she'd been telling herself she couldn't wait and moaning about how Desmond's deal was too Machiavellian for words, she'd secretly started dreading the future.

"Two hours," Desmond finally agreed with a nod. "But only because you called me difficult."

So that was a sensitive subject apparently, judging by his indignant tone. She stuck her tongue out to lighten the mood. "Is that the magic button? I'll keep that in my back pocket then."

His mouth curved and he rubbed Conner's head in farewell. Desmond faded from the room but his presence lingered, made all the more strong by virtue of the new desk standing in the corner.

She'd probably never sit at it without reliving him leaning over her with the brush of his arm against hers.

"Just you and me, sport," she murmured to Conner, who picked that moment to wail in her ear. "Oh, none of that, now. Your daddy will come running, wondering what I'm doing to torture you."

McKenna rose from the chair and paced with Conner on her shoulder. Sometimes he needed extra burping after feeding. But a few rounds of gently massaging his tummy didn't get her anywhere. Diaper change, then.

She hurried to the nursery, which was down the hall between her bedroom and Desmond's. He'd decorated the room with rocket ships and stars, with a complete solar system tethered to the ceiling with thin fishing line. It was an odd choice for a baby but she'd never questioned it because it was easy to envision the man responsible for the décor lovingly placing each item exactly where he wanted it. The theme made sense to Desmond and she appreciated that he'd taken such care with the room his son would live in.

McKenna changed Conner's diaper in no time and that did the trick. No more wailing. Smiling at her little bundle of joy, she found his favorite stuffed animal—an elephant Desmond called Peter, for God knew what reason—and played peekaboo with it while Conner kicked happily from his bouncy seat.

What an amazing little person. He was gorgeous, with dark fuzzy hair and chubby cheeks. Her allotted two hours flew by and, before she'd blinked, Desmond peeked into the room with no-nonsense purpose on his face.

"I'm done building something," he informed her, his

voice smoothed out now that he was back in control. "You can do your own thing now."

"Like biochemistry?" She frowned. That had sounded so exciting earlier, before she'd had a couple of peaceful hours with her son.

"Yes, exactly like that." Desmond swooped in and effectively kicked her out with a nonchalant wave.

With far more regret than she'd like, she left father and baby to go back to her room, but she couldn't concentrate on anything. The first lesson of her biochemistry class blurred, turning into a giant mess on the screen. Looked like a swim was in order.

But as she splashed through the water, even the normally hypnotic activity didn't help. She kept craning her neck, looking for Desmond, though he'd only sought her out in the pool room twice in the six weeks she'd been living there.

Something was wrong with her. The melancholy she'd slipped into had all the hallmarks of mild depression, but she'd never been one to mope around. Of course, she'd been busy for years. This was the first real break she'd had from life since forever. Maybe that was part of her problem; she wasn't busy enough.

What more of a distraction did she need than new graduate-level courses? Desmond had provided her with the best prescription possible for her ennui and she wasn't even taking advantage of it. Maybe she should check out the other class Desmond had registered her for.

She dried off and got dressed, then resettled at her computer to access the second class. Embryology. Huh. She had a better than average understanding of that subject. The syllabus pretty much outlined the forty weeks she'd just experienced in real life: the stages from human conception through birth, with an emphasis on cellular development as the fetus grew.

Except, in her case, it wasn't a generic fetus, as she'd told herself for the entire length of her pregnancy. Neither had it turned out to be *just* an experiment to help her understand what her pregnant patients would be going through.

She'd carried Desmond's baby. Conner. He was a sweet, darling little angel who rarely cried and made her smile whenever she gazed at his face. Conner was her son, too.

A tear splashed down on the keyboard and then another. Finally she had to admit she'd thoroughly messed up in her quest to stay removed from the maternal instincts that surged to the surface on a continual basis.

Instead of a long goodbye, she'd started loving her son.

What was she going to do?

Go back to biochemistry. What else? Maybe she was just tired and could handle the embryonic course better tomorrow, when she hadn't just spent two hours in the company of the baby.

The first lesson scrolled onto the screen again. The concepts should have been easy, a review of the things she'd learned in undergraduate chemistry classes. But she couldn't get her brain to wrap around what she was reading.

A little message popped up to inform her that Desmond H. Pierce was online.

The smile his name pulled out of her went a long way toward drying up the waterworks. How freaking adorable was that man? He had one contact in his chat program—his wife—yet he found it necessary to spell out his full name?

She couldn't help herself. She clicked on the little blue icon and opened a chat window.

McKenna: *Desmond H. Pierce? Were you worried I'd confuse you with all the other Desmonds in my contact list?* Send.

She gave it fifty-fifty odds that he'd actually respond. He might even ignore her since she was essentially being a smart aleck. But the baby was obviously taking his afternoon nap. Maybe she'd get lucky.

Wonder of wonders. A message appeared under the blank window: *Desmond H. Pierce is typing.*

Desmond H. Pierce: *It asked for my name. That's what I entered.*

She actually laughed out loud at that.

McKenna: *You're so literal.*

Desmond: *Yes.*

McKenna: *Did you change your name in your settings? Just because I said something about it?*

Desmond: *Maybe.*

For some reason that pinged around her heart. She didn't take his sensitivity into account nearly often enough when she was bulldozing through aspects of his personality she actually found really great.

McKenna: *I like that you're so literal. I never have to question what you mean when you say something.*

Desmond: *You'll be very lonely in that group of one.*

McKenna: *I didn't join so I could hang out with throngs of Desmond H. Pierce admirers. I'm your wife, not a groupie.*

The chat window stayed maddeningly blank for the longest time. So long, that she started to wonder if she should apologize for something or clarify that she'd been messing around. One bad thing about virtual communication—Desmond couldn't see her face or hear her tone, so he didn't know she was kidding.

Finally the status bar told her Desmond was typing.

Desmond: *And as my wife, you're in the position to know that I have very few admirers.*

McKenna: *Because you spend all your time building fake people instead of communicating with real ones?*

Desmond: *Because the list of those who like literal people is very short.*

McKenna: *You say stuff like that all the time. I like you. You act as if there's something wrong with me because I don't see you as difficult.*

Desmond: *You don't?*

She shook her head and typed: *Duh.*

This time the pause was longer and she waited with baited breath to see what he might come back with.

Desmond: *Then I would expect it to be easier to get you on a second date.*

Her breath gasped out in a half laugh, half exhale of shock. *That* was why he thought she'd been so adamantly resistant to his perfectly chiseled mouth?

Actually she couldn't remember why resistance had been so set in her mind as a necessity. Because she didn't like the idea of getting involved with a self-confessed control addict? Yeah, Desmond liked to keep a tight fist on his son's life and held the cards of her future, as well. But he was also kind. Full of love for his son. Beyond intelligent. And a little dorky. For some reason, she liked that about him the best.

McKenna: *I would have expected you to try harder then.*

Desmond: *Is that the magic button?*

Her eyelids fluttered closed as she laughed again. What was she supposed to do with him?

McKenna: *I have lots of magic buttons.*

Probably she shouldn't be flirting with him. But it was fun. And she definitely didn't hate the long twinge that curled through her midsection as she pictured Desmond going on an exploratory mission to see how each button worked. And how many times he could press them to get her to come.

Desmond: *Aren't you supposed to be doing school-work?*

She'd flustered him. What did it mean that she could understand him so easily despite the two floors that separated them?

McKenna: *Biochemistry is hard. It's been over a year since I was in school.*

The chat window went completely still. She waited for some kind of pep talk or maybe a condemnation for her ungratefulness. After all, he'd been the one to register her. Was he mad that she'd complained?

The atmosphere shifted and she whirled to see Desmond standing in her open doorway. Her throat went tight as she took in the look on his face. Hungry. Gorgeous. Watchful. Not safe behind a virtual chat window but here, in the flesh. In her bedroom.

"Um...hi," she blurted out as her pulse triple-timed. "I wasn't expecting you."

"Let me help you with your homework."

Oh, God. That was the sweetest thing. Almost better than what she'd assumed he'd come for. "You don't have to."

"I want to." He sauntered over to the desk, his long, lean body fluid and mouthwatering as he perched on the edge, his attention on her. Not the laptop. "Show me what you're having trouble with."

Somehow she didn't think it would be prudent to point out the real trouble was with her lungs and the whole breathing thing when he got this close. She shouldn't let him affect her this way. "The first lesson covers the kinetics of catalyzed versus uncatalyzed reactions."

He didn't as much as blink. "You're studying analytic chemistry in a biochemistry class?"

His knee brushed her hand. She should move it. But it was resting so comfortably on the arm of the chair and the zing of his touch had gone clear to her shoulder. Moving suddenly seemed impossible.

"Apparently." But given that he'd clued in on the distinction immediately, odds were good he knew both pretty well. Her genius husband was a resource she hadn't fully appreciated when embarking on a medical degree. "The reaction formulas the professor covers are a little different than how I learned it in undergrad."

He shifted to view the screen, his thigh snugging up next to her arm. Fireworks exploded in her core as his presence overwhelmed her system.

"Wow. That is a really roundabout way to demonstrate the transition. I have some diagrams that are far more useful than this garbage."

Leaning closer, he tapped on her keyboard, apparently oblivious to the fact that her shoulder was buried in his chest. She sucked in a breath and tried to ignore the way her muscles tensed, ready to reach out and touch him at a moment's notice. Because if she started, she feared she might not stop.

"See?" He pointed at the two-color graph on the screen that had materialized from his mystical gateway to the depths of human knowledge. "Quantify the energy transfer using this and tell me what you get."

No question in that statement because he didn't even stop to consider she might not be smart enough to follow him. He just believed she was. That wrung a whole hell of lot of something out of her heart that should not be there.

He glanced at her, his expression expectant. So she indulged them both and studied his graph. The answer popped into her head instantly.

"Gibbs free energy. 20 percent." How she squeezed that out of her mouth when her tongue had gone numb, she'd never know.

Nodding, he grinned. "Told you my stuff is better than what the professor is trying to make you use. Don't hesitate to borrow my database anytime. Or me."

That had all sorts of loaded connotations she really couldn't help but consider. Her skin flushed hot as she contemplated him and his eyes darkened as he seemed to finally pick up on the less than studious energy swirling between them.

The air fairly crackled with it as they stared at each other. How was it possible that Desmond had become that much sexier just by showing off his intelligence?

But it was an inescapable fact. Her husband's brain turned her on.

She wanted Desmond H. Pierce more than she wanted to breathe and she'd spent far too much energy denying them both something that might be spectacular, solely because she didn't want to give him any more control than he already had.

There was one surefire way to deal with that—make her own choices. If she didn't like where things were going, they signed divorce papers and went on. Easy out.

"Chemistry wasn't really part of the deal," she murmured.

His body swiveled until he was facing her instead of the computer. "I don't mind helping with your homework."

That wasn't the chemistry she was concerned about at the moment. She wanted Desmond's hands on her body and his mouth following shortly behind, but she'd put up so many roadblocks it was no wonder he was practicing what she'd preached, namely that getting involved was a bad idea.

There were probably a host of things she should carefully consider before throwing caution to the wind. But right this minute, she didn't care. There was nothing separating them but her own unfounded fears.

Seven

Biochemistry. That was the chemistry Des should be focusing on, but he'd frankly lost all interest in McKenna's class work in favor of drowning in her expressive gaze. Her eyes held a whole world inside them and he couldn't stop drinking it in.

The draw between him and his wife was a whole other kind of chemistry, the kind he'd like to learn about because he had the distinct feeling there'd be a lot to absorb.

"My homework will be there later," McKenna informed him throatily. The slight rasp in her voice hooked him instantly. It meant she was as affected by his nearness as he was hers.

The desk had been an altruistic gift, solely designed to get her started on her degree. He hadn't considered that it would become a method of seduction. But the object of his affection sat within arm's length in the chair he'd selected for her. His leg had been in firm contact with her hand for the better part of five minutes but she hadn't rolled away.

"When is your first lesson due?" he asked. The last thing he wanted to do was distract her when she'd just started what looked to be a difficult class given how backward the instructor planned to teach something as straightforward as chemical reactions.

"I don't know." She didn't take her gaze from his and he couldn't look away, not when she had so many interesting nonverbal things she was saying. "But it's not right this minute. We have plenty of time to worry about that later."

College classes had definitely shifted his advantage and he was nothing if not prepared to press it.

Awareness saturated the atmosphere. So maybe she was looking for a distraction. One that had a much more explosive reaction than those detailed on her screen.

"McKenna," he murmured, and her face tipped up to the perfect angle for him to take her mouth with his, which he planned to do as soon as he was clear on whether he'd been reading her signals correctly.

Once he kissed her, he didn't plan to stop. Therefore, it would be prudent to make sure that's what she wanted.

"Desmond," she murmured back.

The way she caressed his name with her raspy voice settled low in his gut, flaring out with sensual heat that would take little to stoke higher. The virtual chat had gotten him good and primed already, especially with all the talk of magic buttons.

He should have installed a chat tool weeks ago. Who knew that would be the mechanism to get his wife to flirt with him?

But virtual chatting only went so far. Being in her presence heightened the reactions her sexy talk had started and he craved the experience of connecting with her in the flesh. There was so much to discover between them, nuances of emotion and heights of pleasure to catalog. He couldn't wait to start exploring.

"I'm going to kiss you," he informed her. "If that's not what you want, you should tell me to leave. Immediately."

Her dark eyes speared him to the core, blazing with unmistakable heat. "My mouth is one of my buttons."

As invitations went, that couldn't be much clearer. But they'd been at this spot before and she'd backed off. Twice. He wasn't going to make that mistake again. "And I definitely plan to push it. Along with several others. If that's not okay, I need to know that now."

"I want you to kiss me, Desmond."

Her exasperation came through loud and clear but he'd been exasperated for nearly a week. She could deal with it until he had the answers he needed.

"What about the complications?" he asked.

She stood so fast that the chair shot backward and tipped over, but he could hardly focus on anything other than the beautiful woman who'd stepped into the gap of his thighs. He widened his legs to give her plenty of room, aching to slip his hands around her waist and yank her closer to his center. Her heat was exactly what his throbbing erection needed.

"The only complication I'm dealing with right now is the one between your ears," she said with a half laugh as her hands slid over his shoulders. "I'm starting to see how you could be described as difficult."

Apparently impatient with waiting, she wound her fist in his shirt and pulled. He let her because… *Hell, yes*, this was the chemistry he'd come for. If she wanted to move things forward at her own pace, he wasn't going to argue.

And then their mouths aligned, both rough and tender at the same time. It was such a rush of sensation that his entire body jolted. The kiss deepened without any effort on his part as she inhaled him, drawing him into her spirit and essence with nothing more than the conduit of her mouth.

She was molten and fluid, eager. Best of all, she'd granted him permission to drop down the rabbit hole with her.

Now he could touch. With the threat of losing this moment eliminated, he smoothed his palms down her back, reveling in the firmness of her body against his fingertips. *His wife.* The mother of his child. She felt unbelievable and that was saying something considering how often he'd fantasized about having her this close, this available for his investigation.

And the kiss deepened even further, destroying him from the inside out as she nestled against the planes of his torso, thigh to thigh.

Her hot tongue slid forward, seeking and… Oh, yes, he craved more of that, already anticipating the way she filled him with her taste. He took each thrust, felt it in his bones, his blood, his groin. She crawled inside him easily and he didn't try to stop the flood of McKenna. She was right where he wanted her.

He let her have her fun for four seconds. *My turn.*

Nearly drunk on her, he wrested control of the kiss away from her in one fell swoop, spinning to capture her against the desk. His thigh spread hers and she gasped, but opened to him beautifully, accepting his hard length at her center with surprising willingness. Stars exploded across his vision as he absorbed her heat through his clothes.

She was so ready for him. Probably slick with it and swollen. He could feel her desire under his skin, where the empathy was always strongest, and it built his own need to a fevered pitch.

More. Now. He gripped her jaw and slanted it, plunging into her mouth with a ferocity he had no idea he possessed. But she met him halfway, seemingly as impatient for it as he was. Desperate little moans vibrated from her throat and it thrilled him to incite such sounds of abandon from her.

She wanted him. Wanted the connection he'd felt from the first. The sense of isolation and loneliness he'd carried for most of his life vanished in a snap as he opened his soul to what she was offering him.

Warm hands branded his back as she explored under his shirt. He returned the favor, yanking the fabric of her T-shirt from her pants and letting his fingers do the talking. Beautiful. Velvety. He couldn't get enough of her skin. Too many clothes in the way.

"Desmond," she breathed against his mouth.

He scarcely had enough of his senses left to recognize his own name. "Hmm." Her throat had the tenderest little area that his lips fit into perfectly and he got busy acquainting himself with it as he slipped the T-shirt off her shoulder to give him better access.

"I hate to mention it, but I'm, um…not on any kind of birth control. I wasn't expecting this."

That heavy dose of reality put a pall over the wonders of her skin against his tongue. He lifted his head, his mind clicking through all the possible scenarios as the critical pieces of information fell into their buckets. She didn't want to get pregnant again. Of course she didn't. And, idiot that he was, he hadn't been expecting her to remove all the obstacles between them so quickly either. Why hadn't he had an entire truckload of condoms delivered? Some genius he was.

But surely he was smart enough to salvage the situation.

"No problem," he murmured and slid a hand under her shirt to toy with her bra strap. "We're just getting started. There's a lot of you I haven't seen yet and a lot of ways I can make love to you that don't require birth control."

Her eyes darkened. "I'm thoroughly intrigued by that statement."

"Let me demonstrate."

He lifted the hem of her shirt and whipped it off. The catch on her bra came apart in his fingers with a small snick and her lush, full breasts spilled out before he could fully peel the fabric from them.

Groaning as he tossed her clothes to the floor, he packed both palms with her engorged flesh. Erect nipples chafed his hands and the heat of her zinged through his erection. There was no way he could have been more turned on in that moment.

"I need to see the rest of you," he said hoarsely, and she nodded, pulling off her pants and underwear in one motion.

Naked, she perched on the desk without an ounce of embarrassment. Slowly he settled into her desk chair and caressed her thighs, trailing down to her knees. Then pushed, opening her until she was spread wide. She didn't protest, just shoved the computer aside so she could lean back on her elbows, letting him look his fill. It was the most humbling experience of his life, except for the first moment he'd held his son. This woman had given him both.

"McKenna," he murmured and it fell from his lips like a prayer. "I can't believe how gorgeous you are."

Laying his lips on her thigh, he worked his way toward

her center. She squirmed restlessly, gasping as he abraded her tender flesh with his beard, which he'd thankfully trimmed not too long ago. It was about to come in very handy as he pleasured his wife.

The first lick in her slick center pulled a cry from her that thickened his erection past the point of all reason. *How* was she so sexy, so disturbing, in all the best ways? He'd barely started and her taste exploded against his lips as she rolled her hips, shimmying closer to his mouth.

Obviously she wanted him to go deeper. That worked for him. He gave it to her, grasping her hips to hold her still as she couldn't seem to manage that on her own. Excellent. He loved that she got so into it, crying and panting with little feminine noises as he licked her harder.

He twisted two fingers into her slick channel, gently because he was nothing if not overly sensitive to the fact that she'd recently given birth to the miracle that lay sleeping down the hall.

She bucked, her muscles clamping down beautifully on his fingers in a release that tensed her whole body. Throbbing with his own desire, he nibbled at her core until she came again, crying his name and rocking against his tongue.

The most amazing feeling washed over him and it was so engulfing, so beautiful. He couldn't sort whether he'd sensed it from her or it had bloomed from his depths. Didn't matter. They were so entwined, so connected, they'd probably generated it together. Simultaneously. It was nearly spiritual. He needed more.

"Again," he murmured and started all over.

She shook her head and tried to move out of reach, but he clamped down on her hips.

"I want to return the favor," she insisted weakly, levering higher on her elbows to capture his gaze and, without looking away or letting her do so either, he took a long, slow lick at that precise moment.

She shuddered, banked embers in her depths flaring to life in a raging fire that stoked his own.

"That can wait," he informed her. "This can't. I've dreamed about having you at my mercy, exactly in this position. You took biology. You know the tongue is the strongest muscle in the body. I can do this all night."

Her eyelids fluttered closed as he spread her again with his thumbs and proved his point by giving her the flat of his tongue. Her swollen folds welled again as she orgasmed a third time in mere seconds.

"Stop, it's too much," she gasped and then cursed as he ignored her, wholly unsatisfied with how little he'd done for her. How could a few orgasms possibly compare with what he owed her? She'd sacrificed a year of her life in pursuit of his plan for a family and delayed medical school to nourish his son.

"It's not enough," he corrected, his lips still buried inside her. "I'm only just beginning to learn which buttons to push. I need a lot more research between your thighs before I can possibly stop. For example, what does this button do?"

He rubbed his beard right in the center of the bundle of sensitized nerves. She cried out as she came again, her back lifting off the desk in an arch that thrust her breasts skyward. It was such an erotic pose that he nearly lost the iron grip he had on his own release. The need to fill her, to finally empty himself inside her, overwhelmed him and he almost couldn't stand it.

"Please, Desmond," she nearly sobbed. "I want…need. Something. More. You."

Maybe they'd both had enough. It was all he could do

to keep from stripping down and giving her what she'd asked for. No condom, just flesh on flesh for an eternity.

Reluctantly he pulled back and kissed her inner thigh. This interlude had merely been the precursor and he wasn't opposed to giving her time to recover. "We'll have it your way. More of that later tonight."

"I don't think I'll be recovered by then," she muttered and then shot him a sly smile. "And don't think I've forgotten how merciless you are. I will definitely be returning that part of the favor, as well."

We'll see about that. He had several hours to get condoms into this house and maybe a few other surprises that would guarantee she wouldn't back off again.

That was the most important thing. The less time he gave her to second-guess what was happening here, the better. He wasn't nearly finished exploring how deep this unbelievable coupling between them went.

Funny how he'd once been so determined to deconstruct their attraction solely with the intent of making it stop. Now that he'd started, he never wanted it to end.

Desmond finally left her alone after promising he had something special in mind for later that night. McKenna ate dinner in the kitchen with Mrs. Elliot and a couple of the groundskeepers, which was fairly typical, but she couldn't seem to swallow.

Anticipation kept her whole body keyed up. Throwing caution to the wind had allowed for an amazing experience at the hands—and mouth—of her husband. Frankly she couldn't imagine what else he might come up with that could top earlier. But she was totally game to find out.

After dinner, McKenna fed the baby and put him down for the night. If true to form, Conner would sleep until midnight. Four hours away.

As she hurried to her room to get dressed for her date with Desmond, she didn't pretend to have anything on her mind other than what might be considered "special." The things he'd done to her body… She hadn't realized she could come that hard or that many times in a row. Or that she'd married a man who wasn't done after giving her one orgasm. He should teach a class—in her experience, that wasn't the typical philosophy of the male gender as a whole. So far, she was a huge fan of Desmond's brand of lovemaking.

And if all the stars aligned, she'd get to learn a lot more about his philosophies. She shuddered as her body got in on the anticipation in its own way, soaking the tiny scrap of silk underwear she'd slipped on. So much for wearing sexy lingerie for her husband. Maybe he'd like it if she went commando.

Why was she so *nervous*? It wasn't like she'd never had sex before. And, for all intents and purposes, she'd *already* had sex with Desmond. The big difference, of course, being that this time he'd be participating.

The knock on her door nearly separated her skin from her bones. She smoothed the skirt of the dress she'd painstakingly picked, though it probably didn't matter. It would likely be on the floor shortly.

She opened the door and her breath caught as Desmond's gaze devoured her whole.

"Come with me," he said simply and held out his hand.

Her palm in his, she let him lead her down the hall to his bedroom. All righty then. No preamble apparently. This wasn't a date in the traditional sense, with wine and flowers. They were just going to hop into bed? Of course, given her abandon earlier, she couldn't exactly claim a sense of modesty or that she needed romance to get her motor going. Desmond pretty much just had to look at her and her panties melted.

But then he ushered her through the double doors, clicking them closed behind him as the darkness of the room surrounded her. Her pulse leaped, hammering in her throat as her pupils fought to adjust to the black.

"I hope you meant what you said about liking thunderstorms." His voice slid across her skin like silk a moment before a rumble sounded from the far wall.

A bolt of lightning forked across the ceiling in a brief flash of light. Awestruck, she watched as another one streaked across the wall. "You made me a thunderstorm?"

"I did." Another rumble of thunder interrupted him, louder this time, as if the storm was growing closer. "Surprise."

"It's brilliant." Lightning lit up the room for another brief second, revealing the four-poster. Somehow, the faux storm swirled around it, beckoning her straight into the center.

But Desmond didn't give her a chance to take one step. Sweeping her up into his arms, he carried her to the bed, laying her out on the comforter. "It took some doing. I think it turned out well."

The patter of rain echoed behind her head, coming faster now as more thunder crashed through the bedframe, shaking it with shocking realism. "I don't think you could have made it more real."

"Let's just see about that, shall we?" Lightning illuminated half his face, revealing a wicked smile that put a tingle in her breasts.

Faint music danced between the crashes of thunder, something electronic and fast with no lyrics that kept time with the storm perfectly, as if one fed the other. The divine maestro himself rolled onto the mattress, sweeping her into his arms and into the maelstrom with a hot, hungry kiss.

Instantly her body electrified. With her eyes closed, she could scarcely credit how real the storm seemed. Desmond's tongue circled hers, demanding and insistent. White-hot desire split her core, flooding her with the thick, achy need that only he could satisfy.

In the space of one peal of thunder, he pulled off her dress and crouched over her. The next time the room lit up, his gaze traveled over her, hot and heavy.

"I, um, thought it was going to be my turn to be merciless," she squeaked as he bent to mouth her throat. Her head tipped back involuntarily to give him better access. When his fingers slipped under the cups of the bra to lightly play with her nipples, her back bowed off the bed, grinding her pelvis into his.

Every erogenous zone on her body was far more sensitive than she was used to but her breasts were the worst. Best. His touch penetrated her to the marrow, swept a volcanic wave through her blood until she was writhing under the press of his hips, silently begging him for what she'd only gotten a taste of earlier.

"Please," she rasped. "I want your mouth on me again."

His lips were nearly poetic, strong, full, talented. And she wanted his French kiss between her legs immediately. She'd get busy pleasuring him very, very soon, but she couldn't help how much the earlier session on the desk had prepped her for a repeat.

"Absolutely in the plan," he murmured. "We have hours and I intend to use every last second to worship your body."

His fingers tangled in her bra straps, pulling them down off her shoulders until both breasts burst free of their confines. The first scratch of his beard against a nipple raced down her spine, unleashing a shiver. But he didn't draw the aching tip into his mouth like she'd expected, somehow cluing in that she'd had enough stimulation in that area lately.

Instead he laved at the underside, finding new places to nibble that she'd have never called sensitive, but he lit her up with nothing more than carefully placed teeth.

Gasping, she twisted against the onslaught, nearly weeping to get more of him against her flesh. He complied, inching his way down her stomach with his fiery mouth, leaving trails of sensation as he went until he hit the juncture of her thighs, where she ached for him most.

"You're not wearing any panties," he announced, a thread of pure lust lacing his voice. "It's almost as if you're asking for me to spend a lot of time down here."

Breathless, she choked out a laugh. "You read my mind."

By way of answer, his slightly rough and wholly talented hands slid up her thighs and pressed, opening her wide until her knees hit the comforter on either side. His hands—she couldn't get enough of them on her. They spoke a language all their own as his thumbs explored her center, rubbing, dipping, whirling her into an oblivion of sensation heightened by simultaneous booms of thunder and the drumming of rain.

The heat and pressure of his mouth at her core as he finally added his lips and tongue tensed her whole body, and the gush of wetness was almost embarrassing, except he groaned, lapping it up.

"So gorgeous. So responsive. I love how I can do this to you," he said and swirled his tongue with exactly the right motion to send a shower of heat through her as she slid to the edge and over, rippling through the first of what would likely be many spectacular climaxes.

"Again," she commanded, instantly addicted to his talents, delirious with the pleasure of his hands. "But this time with you."

She'd waited long enough. She wanted to see him, to touch. To bring him to climax and hear him cry out because the release was too big to keep inside. Rolling away from him before he could clamp down on her thighs again, because she knew his tricks now, she knelt on the bed and pushed at his shoulders, insisting he sit up from his position on all fours.

It clearly amused him to do as she directed since he did it. Otherwise she'd probably never have moved him. Honestly, it was a crapshoot on whether she'd have rolled back under his mouth if he hadn't. Her core still quivered from the climax and she well knew the second one would be even better. Her body craved it, demanded it, sought it with little circles of her hips even as she fingered her way down his shirt in the dark, unbuttoning as she went.

He was lucky she didn't tear the thing from his body, shedding buttons like flower petals ripped from their stems. Finally she drew off the shirt and couldn't resist her first taste of Desmond's body.

Without hesitation, she bent her head and kissed his shoulder, then dragged her tongue across his clavicle. His hands gripped her waist, holding her in place as he sucked in a breath. Bolder now, she nipped at his throat, nibbled her way up the column to his ear and laved at his lobe, eliciting a groan deep in his chest that thrilled her.

This was her turn and she suddenly wanted to lavish him with as much care as he'd showed her. She pushed him back onto the mattress and rid him of his pants and underwear. She wished she could have done a slow reveal but she wanted to touch.

Warm flesh pulsed under her palms as she covered

him and, in that moment, the thunder and lightning crashed simultaneously, lighting up the bed well enough for her to see the gorgeous length. Tongue to the tip, she licked, her eyes on him, his eyes on her.

Darkness fell again but the half-lidded expression of pure pleasure on his face had burned into her mind. She sucked the whole of him into her mouth, rolling her tongue around his shaft until he groaned out her name, hips pistoning under her palms.

"Enough," he growled and she almost ignored him as he'd done to her earlier, but he easily lifted her off him and set her back against the pillow, thumb sliding across her face in an apologetic caress. "You can have many orgasms but my physiology isn't as evolved and your mouth is amazing."

Fair enough. A rustle indicated he'd likely donned a condom and delicious anticipation filled her. This was it. The consummation of all of this foreplay.

Thunder cracked again and again, heightening the low throb in her core. He didn't make her wait. Before she could blink, he'd gathered her up and laid her down, covering her with his hot, firm body. But instead of gearing up to plunge in, he captured her lips in a long, tender kiss.

Slowly his tongue explored hers. The rush swept outward, languorously stealing over her skin as he made love to her mouth. This kiss wasn't about the mechanics of sex, which he'd proved again and again he had down pat. It was the basest form of communication and she absorbed all of what he was saying, grasping it eagerly with every fiber of her body.

"I want you," he said over and over, and it was a delicious kick to be the object of his desire. His hand drifted down her arm, caressing, lingering, then eventually working south to her waist, her thigh. The gorgeous,

heavy press of his body on hers grew more insistent. He shifted, hips rolling suggestively against hers. The kiss deepened, grew urgent, and she answered with her own suggestive shimmy and slid her thigh along his, opening herself up into a wide cradle.

"McKenna."

He murmured her name so reverently it curled through her senses. Her head tipped back against the pillow as she felt him slide into place at her core. Then he pushed and his thick length filled her, and it was so right, she gasped. Urgency overtook them both and they came together in perfect tempo with the music and the rain and the fevered ecstasy he was building in every pore of her body.

Soaring, she gave up all thought, reason, let him fill her to the brim with the pretty phrases he drizzled down on her as they wound each other higher and higher. At the crescendo of the next round of thunder, his gifted fingers danced across the button at her center, firm, hot, and it shattered her. Boneless, she came, rippling around his length in a powerful release that eclipsed anything she'd ever known. Wave after wave of something divine swamped her, spiraling her into a near out-of-body experience.

But she didn't want to be out of her body, not when Desmond was still powering through the finale of his own release. Hands on his back, she urged him on, whispering encouragement until he tensed against her thighs with a hoarse cry.

It was so beautiful, tears slid down her face.

Collapsing to the mattress, he rolled her into his arms, holding her tight against his body, wordless. No matter. The nonverbal spoke loudly enough in the darkness. *Wow.*

After a long, delicious eternity of nothing but naked

skin against hers, he nuzzled her ear. "Tell me that was fantastic for you."

She nodded far less enthusiastically than she'd have liked but her muscles were still recovering. "Fantastic is an understatement."

"I…felt it," he murmured, sounding hesitant for the first time since he'd swept her into the room. "Your pleasure, I mean. It was like a second presence and it was unbelievably amazing. It's hard to explain and now I'm sure you think I'm as weird as everyone else does."

He trailed off with a half laugh but she sat up, scowling, even though he couldn't see her until lightning forked across the ceiling on the next wave.

"Stop it. I do not think you're weird." *Different*, sure. But in a good way. "You're brilliant and kind and you made me a thunderstorm. If that's weird, then weird should be considered the new sexy."

"You think I'm sexy?"

Her eye roll was so loud, it was a wonder he hadn't heard it. "Duh. I can't even count all of my orgasms today."

"Six. So far."

Dear God. "No. Not *so far*. Absolutely no more. For me anyway. It's your turn."

He'd stopped her before she could finish the job she'd started earlier and if any more orgasms happened tonight, they'd be all his.

"I'm afraid that's not going to work for me." His hand found hers, clasped it. Twined their fingers together. "I like it when you come and I like having my mouth on you when it happens. It's so much better than anything I've ever imagined."

He yanked on their clasped hands, pulling her off balance. She fell to the mattress and he covered her immediately. She squirmed and only succeeded in grinding against his semi-erection.

"That was dirty," she snapped as he trapped her against the pillow, arms above her head.

"Not sorry. By the way, if you think you've experienced the full extent of my imagination, you'd be wrong."

She shuddered as he slid down the length of her body to nip at the juncture between her legs. There was a half second when she considered clamping her thighs together to prove a point. But then her knees fell open almost without any help on her part as he pushed on them. Who the hell was she kidding? As if she had the power to deny him access to whatever he wanted to lick, touch or bite on her body.

Delirious instantly, she thrashed under his hot mouth, so many emotions bleeding through her chest. His teeth scraped across her nub and she nearly screamed as white-hot pleasure crashed against the realization that her feelings for him went far deeper than she'd guessed.

The flood of everything crested up and over as he increased the pressure exactly as he'd learned—so quickly—would splinter her into a million pieces. The wave of her release spread like molten lava, eating up all her cold, empty places and filling them with Desmond.

This was not supposed to be happening.

Furious with herself for letting things get so out of hand, she clenched against her release, cutting it short through sheer will.

"McKenna," he murmured. "Let go. Don't deny yourself because I wished to pleasure you instead of letting you have your way."

She nearly laughed and then choked on it as he did something new against her core. The sensation gripped her in steely claws, coaxing her back to the edge. And then he pushed her over with a shattering climax that put the other six to shame.

Her husband commanded her body as easily as he'd commanded her to wait for the divorce. She'd given him that power by choosing intimacy and it scared her all at once. She didn't know if she *could* deny this draw between them.

"That was so beautiful," he said and curled her against his side. "You're my wife and you deserve to be treated like a queen. Think of me as your vassal. Sleep here. I'll bring Conner to you and put him back to bed. You do nothing more strenuous than lay here until morning. Sleep if you want. Or tell me to pleasure you again."

She blinked and settled her palm on his chest, content to lay half on top of him because he felt delicious against her overused muscles. That was the problem with Desmond. He made it sound like she'd gotten it all wrong, that he was the most selfless human on the planet. She didn't have to do anything but lounge around and wait for the next time she felt like ordering her husband to make her body sing?

If there was a downside to that, she couldn't find it.

Eight

Carefully, Desmond eased back into the bed after checking on the baby for the second time. Conner had started waking up at 6:00 a.m. two nights ago, but both times Des had been able to get him to go back to sleep without nursing.

The material he'd read suggested that if he let the baby eat, he would eat. If his father talked him back into bed without giving him what he wanted, Conner learned that he didn't have to eat just because his eyes were open. So far, so good.

McKenna lay in Desmond's bed, eyes closed and face tranquil. He'd kept her awake far past when he should have but once he'd started exploring the wonders of her, he couldn't stop. She hadn't complained. And he intended to ensure that continued to be the case.

Des had turned off the storm machine before the baby's midnight feeding, which was a necessary shame. That had been inspired and McKenna had loved it. Conner wouldn't have. Last night was the first time his wife had breast-fed his son in Desmond's bed. That unprecedented event deserved respect, as did the fact that she was still in his bed.

The first of many nights if he had anything to say about it.

He had no practice at sliding between the covers without waking another person. Somehow he levered himself onto the mattress without rocking it, then got most of his body into position, a feat considering McKenna slept with abandon, flinging an arm across his pillow and curling her legs up onto his side. He didn't mind. She had gorgeous legs.

But when he pulled the covers up, they caught on something. He yanked before realizing she'd balled up a good bit in her fist.

Her dark eyes blinked open and she smirked. "Don't tell me you're an early riser. That's grounds for divorce."

He smiled because he couldn't help himself. When he looked at her, it was like seeing the sun peek through the clouds after three days of gray. "I was checking on Conner. I didn't mean to wake you up. If you weren't hogging the covers, you never would have known I'd moved."

Long, dark hair spilled over his pillow and he resisted the urge to gather it in his hands. Barely.

"Oh, I see. This is all my fault. The fact that you handcuffed me to the bed and wouldn't let me leave doesn't have anything to do with it."

His brows shot up involuntarily as he eyed her. "Even without an eidetic memory, I would have remembered if handcuffs had been involved at any point."

Had she felt like he'd forced her to sleep here last night? That was so far from his intent.

He ran through the events again, calculating, reevaluating. She'd been so into everything, eager, enthusiastic. Nearly crippling him with her desire at times as his empathy soared along with her.

There was no way he'd misread her pleasure. Or that she'd been more than willing to sleep in his bed. When he was this in tune with her, he'd know if she'd been unhappy.

"Seven orgasms," she said, holding up the requisite number of fingers in case he wasn't clear on the count. "What woman in her right mind would sleep alone after that?"

"I see. You're a slave to my attention, is that it? I've shackled you with my orgasms."

She sighed lustily. "Yeah, I guess that's true."

Something eased in his chest and he didn't hesitate to gather her up against his body so he could say good morning in a much more hands-on fashion. "In that case, we have a couple of hours until breakfast."

She groaned. "Seriously? I'm not used to this much, uh…stimulation. I haven't used some of those muscles in years."

That pleased him to no end. They'd had little to no communication about their respective love lives, but he'd envisioned that she'd been in school long enough to have avoided personal attachments. Of course, last night had been confirmation that she didn't have a boyfriend waiting in the wings.

He frowned. That was a huge assumption on his part. Women had multiple sexual partners all the time.

A growl nearly erupted from his throat but he bit it back. McKenna was his wife and after last night, he wanted to keep it that way. "Seriously. Was I not clear enough that you don't have to move? I do all the work. You have no other job than to issue instructions as you see fit. 'Harder, Des' works. 'Put your mouth on me.' These are not strenuous sentences to utter."

She laughed and flipped over to curl up in his arms spoon style. "You were clear. But the only thing I want right now is a massage."

Her shoulder nudged his chin and he didn't hesitate to put his hands on her. Cradling her firm rear with his hips, he nestled her closer and rubbed her arms with long, slow strokes. Her lengthy sigh had all the hallmarks of a woman relaxing and it settled the beastly possession that had welled up a moment ago. Mostly. He needed to get a lot more of her under his fingertips before he'd fully unwind.

McKenna. He got serious about her request and moved into a better position to take care of the one need his wife had at this moment. They'd both shed their nightclothes after the midnight feeding, which meant there was nothing in his way. He touched her at will, reveling in the soft silkiness of her skin, kneading her shoulders, curling his thumbs around the base of her skull to press along the meridians his one foray into Shiatsu had taught him would relieve her soreness.

The strongest sense of peace radiated from her flesh as he touched her and he absorbed it like a sponge. She moaned as he shifted his fingers to the top of her head, but he didn't need the additional verification that he'd also soothed her as he soothed himself.

As his fingers drifted down to caress her neck and shoulders, she arched her back, intensifying the rub of her very fine backside against the beginning of an arousal that was about to get out of hand if she didn't quit with the sensual contact. She'd asked for a massage. That's what he was giving her, as ordered.

The second time she circled her bottom to brush his

erection, fire shot through his groin. A groan rumbled from his chest. If that was an accident, he'd apologize profusely for the mistake. Later. He slid a hand down her stomach to hold her still as he ground his hips against her gorgeous, firm rear, sliding straight along the crevice. Hot. Tight.

She gasped, desire drenching her aura. And her center, as he discovered the moment he dipped his fingers into the valley between her legs. Nudging his knee between hers, he created a gap that gave him just enough access to explore.

"Desmond," she muttered breathlessly. "What happened to my massage?"

"Still going on." To prove it, he rubbed her nub with two fingers and kneaded her buttocks with the other hand, separating the twin globes enough to slide between them much more deeply than the first time.

His eyelids shuttered closed as the pressure built. He needed to be inside her, to let her take him under, to experience all of her glorious emotion in tandem with his as he built her toward release.

"That feels…i-incredible," she stuttered. "I didn't know that was one of my buttons."

"Now we both know." The heat engulfed him as he teased her backside and he couldn't hold on. Yesterday his restraint had been…well, not easy, but *easier*, solely because he hadn't yet coupled with her. Now that he had, his body had a mind of its own, desperate for her, for the sensation of being one with this woman.

Just as he was about to notch himself in the center of her slick heat for the long, slow slide to perfection, she half rolled away.

"Where are the condoms?" she asked. "You're going to need one after all."

Uh, that was a minor detail he'd conveniently forgotten. Blindly he felt around for the dresser behind him until his fingers closed over the knob and then the packets inside. Thankfully he managed to hang on to the one he grabbed and get it on before he lost his mind.

In moments, his wife's core enveloped him fully and he paused to let the scorching, flawless, rightness of her wash over him. She squirmed restlessly, not on board with slow, apparently. The decision was taken from him as his body began to crave the sweet burn of movement. As she urged him on with small hip rolls that drove him deeper inside, he rode the wave, spiraling higher and higher toward bliss.

But the real bliss lay in her reactions, every cry, all the nuance of her pleasure that heightened his own. It was everything he wanted and nothing he'd ever experienced.

Before his brain could engage, she guided his hand back to her center and he willingly started all over with the massage, but with laser focus on her erogenous zones until she rippled and squeezed through a release that shot fireworks through his gut.

Imagine if she hadn't insisted on condoms. This dazzling experience could include so much more than just an orgasm. He could impregnate her. Today. If she conceived, he could watch her grow round with his child. He'd missed that the first time and it was an injustice he ached to rectify.

His own release exploded from his depths without any warning. As he cried out through the tense burst that left him emptied, he held her close in case she had a mind to roll away. He didn't want to miss a moment of being inside her. Not one moment of making love to his wife.

She was far more than the mother of his child. She was a crucial part of the fabric of the family he'd been trying to create. How had he missed that a family of two was nice but three was so much better, especially when they were so tightly knit together already?

McKenna resettled his arm across her stomach more closely, burrowing against his chest to let him hold her as snugly as he wanted. The problem was that she'd eventually leave the bed. And his life. For all the talk about handcuffs, he had few mechanisms at his disposal to convince a woman that she should wish to stay exactly where she was.

"I need a bath," she murmured. "And maybe a nap. By *myself.*"

The stress on that part came with a playful smack to his hand, which had apparently gotten too friendly with the curve of her breast. "That's the exact opposite of what I need."

"Well, I can't lie. This has been amazing. But maybe it's best if it's a one-time thing."

Something cold and sad crowded into his chest. Of course that was her thought. She'd been backing away from him since the beginning. Except now he had a stake in convincing her she didn't want to do that.

"Best for what?" he growled. "Did I dissatisfy you in some way?"

"What? No." She laughed and half rolled toward him, which pulled her from his arms. "This was just a... I don't know, a fling. An affair. I have no idea what kids call it these days. But it's not the kind of thing you keep doing, no matter how great it is."

That literally made zero sense. "Why not?"

"Because. We're getting a divorce." Exasperation laced her tone, inciting his own frustration. "This is a temporary situation until we can sort something out to get the baby weaned."

"Which we've already established may not happen for several months. Why put an arbitrary end date on something we're both happy with?" he countered far less smoothly than he'd have liked. But she was growing upset and empathy bled through him in a wholly unpleasant internal storm.

The blackness crowding his chest wasn't just his own reaction to the subject, though he had plenty of gloom vying for space. His was because he didn't know how to let her go. Hers was because she wanted him to.

"I'm just not the type to sleep with a man solely because he's generous in bed." She'd moved back to her pillow, clutching the sheet around her breasts in an ineffective cover that did nothing but heighten her sexiness. "This was maybe a blip in judgment at best. You're very difficult to say no to."

By design. He left nothing to chance, not when it was something he wanted. That meant he still had work to do if he wished to create the family he saw in his head. Everyone else in his life spent a great deal of energy trying to get away from him. McKenna was no different.

She was just the first one he wanted to stop from leaving.

The connection he craved, the one that had driven him to create a son with this woman, had flourished with McKenna in ways he'd never have imagined—and he had a great imagination. He couldn't cut it off, didn't have any desire to.

He nodded as if he agreed, his mind sifting through a hundred different scenarios that might work to change the tide of his future. If his wife wasn't the type to sleep with a man solely because he was generous in bed, then maybe she was the type to do so if he was generous out of bed.

Divorcing McKenna was not what he wanted any longer. He liked being married. To her. If she hadn't come to the realization that her future lay with him, then he would have to help her along. Provide incentives.

Orgasms were only one of many things he could offer that might convince her she'd found a permanent home in his bed and his life.

McKenna took her newfound sense of propriety and left Desmond's bed, determined not to repeat the mistake of yesterday. And last night. And again this morning. Twice.

While she'd been fumbling around for the proper terminology to describe the act of sleeping with one's husband—besides the obvious one called *marriage*—he'd been quietly campaigning to prove her completely incapable of resisting him.

As if the first time hadn't been enough of a clue. *Massage.* Leave it to Desmond to redefine that word into "explosive sexual encounter." And then follow it up with a second round that had somehow ended up with her on top, riding him with fluid, delicious motion that put the most sensually hot expression on his face. She could have watched him get lost in pleasure for an hour.

It was high time for a break from the maestro of the storm who'd lured her into sleeping with him all night long and confused her with his insistence that he was at her command instead of the other way around. She'd already been confused enough, what with her chest hurting at the thought of leaving the baby behind when the divorce was finalized.

Schoolwork beckoned. It was no easier to concentrate at her brand-new desk than it had been yesterday. Harder actually. The little blue icon in her system tray beckoned her to open it and connect with the man on the other side.

The chat tool had kindly alerted her that Desmond was online about halfway through her attempt at the second conversion exercise in her biochemistry class.

She ignored it and focused. The concepts were supposed to be a review of what she'd already mastered. So far, all she'd proved was that she could only get through this with the help of someone much smarter.

No. She wasn't too dim-witted to figure this out. She was just…preoccupied. Slowly she fought through the web of Desmond and Conner spinning through her mind and found a rhythm to the chaos. This was medical science. Her wheelhouse. A man and a baby would not—could not—distract her from getting her degree. Being a wife and mother was nothing more than a temporary glitch in her life. Nothing she'd ever wanted or seen for herself.

Her concentration improved drastically when she finally accessed Desmond's magic portal. It wasn't just a flippant label; the thing really was magic, producing results easily from her search terms. Why had she resisted this so long? He'd offered it to her and she'd pretended it didn't exist, just like she was pretending the man didn't exist. Both to her detriment.

She found some great papers online at Johns Hopkins University that walked her through the concepts in a whole different way that suddenly clicked everything together in her brain. The rest of the exercises were easy once she had the foundation straight.

Or they would have been if she'd had a chance to finish. A knock on her open door interrupted her near the end. *Desmond.* Here for the next round of nursing. Total and complete awareness of his presence invaded her very pores, skimming along her skin, raising the hair on her arms.

"Sorry to bother you," he said.

He definitely needed to find a different greeting. "I'm pretty sure I've told you it's no bother."

Conner's little baby noises finished killing her concentration where Desmond had left off. She stood from the desk to get comfortable in the rocker, already familiar and content with the routine Desmond had instituted where he took care of everything and fetched whatever she needed.

At her command. What a kick that was to have such a sensual, intelligent man wallowing at her feet.

Something far deeper than mere awareness of said man with the baby in his arms walloped her out of nowhere. He'd always drawn her eye with his energy, his classic cheekbones and dark swept-back hair. But now she knew every contour under that powder blue buttondown, both visually and by touch.

Her tongue dried up as he gathered her hair gently to waft it down her back, instinctively moving it out of the way without her having to tell him, then settled the baby against her bosom. It was so…domestic and tranquil and a host of other things she shouldn't be wishing could continue.

This fairy-tale land Desmond had dropped her into was temporary. It couldn't be anything else, especially when he wasn't offering her more than his home and his bed. Especially when she was already having such a difficult time focusing on biology, the first love of her life. At best, she might have another few weeks of having her body worshipped in Desmond's bed, but he'd never unbend enough to want a permanent third person in his son's life.

That wasn't what she wanted either, never mind that she could easily get carried away with a fantasy about what that looked like. Fantasy—hell, it looked a lot like this, with Conner in her arms and Desmond doting on her because he'd fallen madly in love.

Lunacy. She'd never dreamed of a man falling in love with her and handing her the moon. Not once.

Until now.

After father and baby left, McKenna lost the ability to do anything other than stare off into space and replay the memory of this morning in bed, when she'd finally had the opportunity to burn images of Desmond's body into her mind. She couldn't decide if the dark was better because she had to feel her way around him or if light was better because she could watch him in the throes of passion.

If Desmond could be believed, he would give her the opportunity to do both. Every night. For how long? Until he kicked her out of his life and the baby's?

The idea of sleeping with him until then was ridiculous, a ripe situation for her to mess up and start caring for him far more deeply than she already did. The little hooks in her heart were going to hurt like hell when he finally ripped them out. She'd already been ten kinds of a fool for letting things go as far as they had.

Best thing would be to get some healthy distance. She was way overdue to visit her parents, who'd come by the hospital briefly to check on her after the birth but otherwise had stayed out of her decision to breast-feed the baby she'd given up. Who better to provide solace than the people who cared about her most?

Before she could change her mind, she slipped her phone from her bedside table and texted Desmond that she was going out, shoving back the guilt that welled higher with each letter under her thumbs. Yeah, she was intruding and forcing him to respond to an electronic communiqué he would likely hate. But seeing him in person would just give him an opportunity to ensnare her more firmly in his web of pleasure.

Desmond immediately texted her back.

I'll have the limo driver waiting for you in the roundabout at the front steps in five minutes.

She nearly groaned. So not necessary. And so ostentatious to arrive like the lady of the manor, wheeling through the middle of the place she'd grown up, especially given that a lot of the residents in the community shunned cars. But she didn't want to seem petty so she sent him back a thank-you and changed clothes, scurrying out of the house before Desmond said he could easily pack up the baby and accompany her.

She was afraid she'd agree. And allowing tagalongs wouldn't give her the distance she sorely needed.

Her pretend family dominated her thoughts as the limo cut through the swath of trees surrounding Desmond's property. This marked the first occasion she'd left the house since moving in with Desmond, which could well be the whole problem. Regular outings into the real world *should* have been a daily part of her regime. At the very least, it would have created more of a delineation between her and the Pierce males.

Desmond and Conner were the real family, no moms need apply. She'd married the man solely for convenience. It was an easy way to avoid the legal tangle of receiving a fully paid medical degree via a divorce settlement, yet, so far, nothing about their relationship felt convenient or easy. It felt like a slippery precipice with nothing to grab on to once she inevitably lost her footing.

Oddly enough, it had only just occurred to her that

she could legally adopt Desmond's last name, too, if she so chose. There was literally nothing stopping her other than the paperwork hassle times two, because she'd surely end up back at whatever office did that sort of thing to change it again when Desmond whipped out his pen to make the divorce final.

Though no one could force her to give it up, if she did do something as crazy as change it in the first place. Desmond didn't have all the power, whether he liked that reality or not.

The limo was plush, with leather seats that smelled divine and a small bar built into the sidewall that held glasses and a tub of ice with bottles of water stuck deep down in the cubes. Nice touch. She still couldn't drink alcohol while breast-feeding, a sacrifice she didn't mind since she wasn't much of a drinker anyway. Desmond's attention to detail warmed her far more than it should have.

Once the driver left Astoria, he veered inland and the forest swallowed the car. Long, dark shadows kept the limo in partial sunlight for the rest of the drive to Harmony Gardens on the other side of the Clatsop Forest where her parents lived.

Yes, she definitely should have done this much earlier. The quiet hush of the trees bled through her soul, calming her, filling her with peace. The forest had been here long before she was born. It persevered, growing and thriving despite all the forces working against it.

She would, too.

Her mother waited for her in the small yard of the clapboard house near the center of Harmony Gardens. It had been McKenna's grandfather's house before he passed and her parents had moved in to care for him a month before her twelfth birthday. Grandfather's long battle with cancer had kept him in and out of different healing centers until he'd taken his final breath in the back bedroom. While a terrible ordeal for everyone, it had sparked the kernel of McKenna's dream to be a doctor.

The care Grandfather had received had been loving, patient. But ultimately ineffective. She'd begged him to see a medical doctor, to try radiation. *Not for me*, he'd insisted as McKenna's mother took him to yet another shaman or crystologist. Would the cancer have killed him even with western medicine? No way to know.

But McKenna could surely replicate the kindness the alternative medicine practitioners had demonstrated as she sought to heal people with the methods *she* trusted. No one else had her unique mix of drive, determination and a husband with deep pockets.

The plan would have been flawless if Conner hadn't developed formula allergies. If she hadn't started to feel things for Desmond that she shouldn't.

The driver parked near the house and swept open the back door of the limo, holding out his hand to help McKenna from the seat. She smiled her thanks, stepping back in time as she turned to follow the trail of worn brick pavers leading to her mother.

"My sweet darling," her mother crooned as she embraced McKenna.

Love enveloped her instantly, soothing her raw nerves and drawing her into a place where everything in her world made sense.

"You didn't have to hang around outside," she chided her mother gently. "I know how to knock."

"I couldn't sit still. I haven't seen you in months, except for thirty minutes in that dreadful hospital." Her mother's long, dark braid danced as she shook her head.

It was a rare occasion that the braid, now shot with a few silver strands, wasn't hanging down her back.

A tinge of grief gripped McKenna's stomach as she realized her mother was aging. Of course she was. Though in her early fifties, Rebecca Moore still looked forty, with beautiful skin that had started to sport small crinkles at the eyes and thin lines around her mouth. She looked exactly the same as she had the last time McKenna had seen her barely two months ago, after Conner had been born.

This was just the first time McKenna had a benchmark. Giving birth had done that somehow, where six years of school had not. One year had blended into the next and, finally, she'd graduated. A baby, on the other hand, grew and aged alongside you—or at least that was how it was supposed to work. McKenna's baby wouldn't come visit her when she was in her early fifties and carry along with him all of the memories of watching him grow up, of raising him, loving him. Seeing his first steps, first lost tooth, first date.

A tear slipped down McKenna's cheek before she could catch it.

"Oh, honey." Her mother clucked. "Come inside and let me get you a drink so you can tell me what's bothering you so badly that you came all the way down here to see me."

So much for trying to keep her inner turmoil in check. But gaining some clarity was the whole reason she was there. Why not tell her mom everything?

McKenna followed her mother into the small, ancient house. Her parents had done their best to preserve the interior in a snapshot of the way Grandfather had kept it. His old chair still sat by the fireplace where he'd spent many hours warding off the chill that had constantly haunted him in his last days. Photographs of her mom and dad as kids playing together lined the walls. They'd known each other their whole lives, just like many of the couples who comprised the community. Growing up, McKenna had always understood that the beliefs of many of those who resided in Harmony Gardens didn't reflect societal norms, thus they tended to stay insulated.

She'd rocked the boat by leaving. Embracing her dream of being a doctor. Moving to Portland. Having a baby and giving him up.

"I know you don't approve of my choices..." she began, but already her mother shook her head, braid bouncing against her shoulders.

"That's not what's bothering you." Her mother handed her a glass of water and pulled McKenna onto the couch that had seen many years of wear, most of it happy, and some tears. Like now. How did her mother see through her so easily?

"But I need you to hear this," McKenna said as the next tear slipped down her cheek. "You don't seem to understand how important being a doctor is to me."

Her mother slipped an arm around McKenna's shoulders, holding on tight like she used to when warding off the boogeymen when McKenna had a nightmare about creatures creeping out from the surrounding forest and standing outside her window.

"I've never questioned your commitment to following your dreams," she said. "What I've tried to do is help you see that there are other factors to consider."

"Like having lots of babies is a factor I should consider?" Frustrated all at once, McKenna shoved off the couch and out of her mother's reach.

"No," her mother countered calmly. "Like the fact that sometimes one is all you get. You know your father and

I weren't able to have more children. We wanted more, desperately. Not because you weren't enough. You're amazing and special. We wanted to give you brothers and sisters."

"And do your part to populate the community." It wasn't a secret that her parents had long held that belief. Children were not only a happy gift from God, according to them, but Harmony Gardens sustained itself by every member pitching in. The more members, the better.

But McKenna felt crappy bringing it up when the sole reason was to detract from the aching hole that had just opened up in her chest.

Sometimes one is all you get.

Was that her fate, too? Conner could be her only child. The endometriosis that had rendered her mother infertile could very well be in McKenna's DNA, too, waiting to strike after she'd birthed her first baby. That would be now.

She shook her head, shoving back the wave of emotion. "It doesn't matter. I don't want children."

The sentiment rang so much hollower than it had in the past. While she didn't want the nebulous term that encompassed "children," she couldn't include Conner in that statement. He was a baby that already existed, one she never should have come to care for.

Her mother's eyes softened. "Sit with me. Let's talk about that for a minute."

Warily, McKenna complied. "You can't talk me into wanting children. I made a deal."

"Yes, let's not dwell on that, shall we? You've made your choice and I understand that you've signed agreements that you'll never have contact with the baby, which by default means we'll never know our grandchild. What's done is done." Folding her hand around McKenna's, her mother squeezed, gracing her with compassion she didn't feel she deserved all at once.

"I..." She'd never considered that she was punishing her parents as well as herself by giving up Conner.

"Not dwelling on it," her mother reminded her. "Instead let's talk about why you don't want to have children."

"Because women don't have the same choices as men," she burst out. "Especially not in a place like Harmony. They have their first baby at eighteen or nineteen and, before you know it, they have nothing more defining them than being a mother. They're sucked dry with no time or energy left over to make a difference."

Quietly her mother stroked her hand. "The point is that having children is making a difference in their minds, and that's *their* choice. You never saw that. Nor have you recognized that some people do have careers and children. With you, it's always been either-or."

"Having children while going to medical school is not an option," McKenna countered. She could barely take two classes and maintain her sanity with a baby and a sexy man in the house. Not to mention that online classes that counted toward a medical degree were few and far between. "Besides, it doesn't matter. That's not an option."

"And that's the problem." Her mother nodded sagely as two more tears slipped down McKenna's cheek. "I was worried this might happen. You're so matter-of-fact about your decisions and you don't honor your feelings enough."

"Emotions are not a good thing to base decisions on." So easy to say. Thus far, it had been easy to do. She'd always had a practical nature, which was part of the reason being a doctor appealed to her.

How could she have predicted that she'd ever have so many impossible dreams racing through her chest, ones that hurt when she contemplated them?

"You're right." McKenna shut her eyes for a moment, willing back the next flood of tears. They were right there, threatening to well up as she forced herself to reconcile what her mother was telling her. "The problem isn't that I feel a certain way about anything. It's that I don't have a choice."

"You don't like not having choices."

This was not a new conversation. They'd had this argument many times, especially when she'd first sprung the concept of being a surrogate on her parents and they'd accused her of picking this option deliberately to thumb her nose at the concepts they'd long held dear. "That's n—"

It was true.

She knew it was true. She liked having control over her own life. Why was she about to argue that fact? Because she'd just realized she had more in common with Desmond than she'd credited?

It was the whole reason she didn't appreciate his attempts at manipulation. Perceived attempts, she reminded herself. She didn't know his motivation for being so helpful when it came to breast-feeding or in being so greedy for her pleasure in bed either, for that matter.

But it smacked of control and that she would not tolerate. Especially when he'd already made it so clear that he insisted on absolute control when it came to Conner. Fine. That was set in stone and she couldn't change it now. But she did not have to let him control anything else.

She should demand that Desmond hire a nanny. Today. She'd avoided that subject because of all the waffling going on in her heart about leaving. No more. Not only did she need a nanny in the house as soon as possible, she wanted a date on the calendar for the divorce. That was how she could maintain control over her choices.

"I see your wheels turning," her mother said with a small smile. "Keep in mind that I love you as I say this. The world is not black-and-white. You tend to think of your choices that way, when in reality, things are not so easily put into your either-or buckets. Especially not when you start to have feelings for someone."

She scowled. "I don't have feelings for anyone. What are you talking about?"

"That you want to feel like you have control over your emotions and, sweetie, it just doesn't work that way. When you meet the one, you don't have a choice. You just…fall."

"In love?" she squawked. That wasn't what was happening to her. It couldn't be. "I'm not—I mean, okay, Desmond is kind and unexpectedly…"

Hot. Wickedly talented in bed. His mouth alone should have a warning label. None of that seemed to be the kind of thing you said to your mother. Neither could she actually admit that her mother was right.

The knowing look on her mother's face said she'd already figured it out. "Go home to your husband, McKenna, and give the unexpected a chance. You might find that you have more choices than you originally thought."

But the one choice she desperately needed wasn't open to her. She could not choose to stop falling in love with Desmond. That was a done deal.

Nine

Despite promising himself he wouldn't listen for the crunch of gravel under the limo tires, Desmond did it anyway. So he knew the instant McKenna had returned from wherever she'd gone. Finally.

He'd missed her. The house had felt empty without her in it, as if it had been drained of something vital. She'd been gone for four hours and it had felt like a lifetime. He was in serious trouble here, with little to no idea how to put the final threads in the fabric of the family he wanted. But nothing would stop him from trying.

She came inside and stopped short when she saw him hanging around like an idiot in the foyer, pretending to play with Conner, as if the kid didn't have a nursery, a recreation room and maybe five other places more hospitable to a baby than a drafty open area near the front door.

Her smile lit on the son they shared and Desmond soaked it in, enchanted by the way she filled his space with her presence and still mystified why the invasion didn't bother him. It should. Not one but two people were in his sanctuary. He liked them here. And she'd been responsible for both.

"Hi," he said and it sounded as lame out loud as it had in his head. The other stuff he'd practiced dried up as her gaze skittered away from him.

Something wasn't right. His senses picked up on it instantly.

"Hey," she said.

A dark shadow moved through his consciousness as he internalized her response. He tried to ignore it. "Did you have a good time?"

"Sure."

That was supposed to be an opening for her to tell him about her day, mention where she'd gone.

"I—"

"I'm tired, Desmond." She wouldn't look at him. "I'm going to take a nap before dinner."

He let her go and tried not to stress about her mood. After all the amazing things they'd shared, it was frustrating that she didn't want to open up to him. He did *alone* better than anyone, but he'd found a reason not to be and would stake his life on the fact that she'd felt something binding them together just as strongly as he had.

For some reason, she wasn't engaging.

Without any more answers, he retreated to his workshop after dinner—which McKenna did not eat with him—and played with Conner. He put the boy to bed and fiddled around with one of the analog switches in his robotic humanoid, but his mind refused to participate in what was largely a distraction anyway.

The computer dinged to alert him that McKenna had

come online. It didn't take but a quarter of a second for him to envision her sitting at her desk studying, brow furrowed in concentration as she swept that gorgeous fall of hair behind her back. He'd like to visit her again, offer to help with her homework, but given her earlier reticence he had a feeling it would be a short conversation.

Of course there was only one way to find out.

His footfalls outside her open door must have alerted her to his presence because she'd already turned the chair a half twist as he drew even with the threshold. Maybe she'd been anticipating his arrival, remembering the last time he'd come to her room to help with her chemistry problems.

They'd resolved all of them, one way or another. But his favorite was still that first orgasm, when she'd come so fast he couldn't wait to do it again.

"I'm glad you're here," she said with a tentative smile and motioned him inside. "I think we should talk."

That was probably the last thing on his mind. And should be the last thing on hers. Lots of work to do here if talking was the first thing she wanted to do. Casually, he leaned on the edge of the desk to disguise how tense his body had grown with the effort to not sweep her into his arms. "About your homework?"

Seeing her in the flesh still kicked him in the gut, but the feeling had so many more teeth now, slicing open nerve endings and fanning through his blood with sensual heat that only she could tame.

Her gaze locked with his and she swallowed. But didn't look away, like she had earlier. "No, um... Let's start with Conner. That nanny-finding service is really falling down on the job. Maybe you should hire another one?"

"I can take care of my son," he said gruffly, still reeling from her nearness.

He'd made love to her twice just that morning. How many times would be enough to still this raging need inside?

"I know." She bit her lip, eyeing him as he moved a few centimeters closer. He couldn't help it. She smelled so good. "But the nanny will do more than just care for Conner. I feel like we've had this conversation a hundred times. I need to start figuring out how to wean so I can move back to Portland."

Well, that put things in perspective. If he'd wondered whether she'd ever thought about sticking around, he didn't have to wonder any longer. Even after last night, she still couldn't wait to be rid of him.

He needed to put some more icing on the cake.

"It's barely been two months," he countered and somehow kept the hitch out of his voice. "We agreed the baby would likely need you for a few more months yet. Are you feeling restless? I'll have a car delivered tomorrow so you can come and go at will."

She blew out a breath. "That's very generous but—"

"I seem to recall a few other ways you've enjoyed my generosity recently." He picked up her hand and held it to his lips, inhaling her scent. "I'm thinking of expanding on that. Right now."

"Oh, um…" Her eyes widened as he sucked one of her fingers into his mouth. "That wasn't what I wanted to talk about."

"So talk," he said around her finger and laved at the tip. "Don't mind me."

Her eyelids fluttered closed as he mouthed his way across her palm and nibbled at her wrist. "It's hard to think when you're doing that."

"Hint. That means you like it," he whispered and concentrated on her elbow where his tongue got a groan out of her that hardened him instantly.

"That's the problem. I don't want to like it. I want to talk about how we're going to get the baby to a point where I can leave—"

"McKenna." It was a wonder he got that out around the vise that had clamped around his throat. "Stop talking about leaving. Let the future take care of itself. In the meantime, if you're unhappy, say so. That's the only way I can fix it."

Her hesitation bled through him, ruffling the pit of fire near his groin. "I'm not unhappy. Don't be ridiculous. I'm just…concerned. I don't see any kind of exit plan and—"

"No exit plan. We can come up with one later." *Or never.* "Right now, I want to enjoy you. And help you enjoy yourself. Let me."

"I don't know what you're asking me to do." She shook her head, gripping his hand tighter instead of slipping free like he'd have expected.

Crap, he was botching this. He needed more time to figure out how to persuade her. Except she'd been so quiet all afternoon. There was no telling how long he had before she'd shut down again and, besides, he wasn't much of a verbal dancer.

"McKenna." He pulled her into his arms with a growl, determined to get her over whatever was going through her head that was keeping them apart. "I want you in my bed. I want to watch you care for my son. The shape of what I want is already there. What it's called is a question for another day."

He already knew what to call it—his family. The vision in his head would shatter without the integral third she represented. Somehow he had to communicate what was in his mind and his heart whether he had all the right words or not. There was only one surefire way to do that in his experience.

Before McKenna could blink, Des swept her up in his arms and carried her out of her room. Her gorgeous hair draped over his shoulder and he couldn't wait to get his hands on it.

Breathlessly, she sputtered, "Wh-what are you doing?"

"Taking you to my room," he growled. "Where you belong. You sleep there from now on, where I can properly take care of you."

"Or what?" she challenged as her pulse picked up, beating hard against his fingertips. It was a clear indication he'd gotten her attention.

But because he wasn't a complete beast, he laid her out gently on the bed and stepped back, giving her plenty of room to breathe, bolt or bare herself to him, pending how well he'd gauged the swing in her mood. "There's no 'or what.' Give me two minutes to convince you this is what you want."

Arms crossed, she contemplated him, her eyelids at half-mast. But that wasn't enough to conceal the intrigue and excitement his challenge had stimulated. "While I'm dressed?"

"Hell, no, you won't be dressed," he shot back. "The point is that I want you in my bed *naked*. I want you to be here when I go to sleep, when I wake up. When it's time to nurse the baby and all the times in between. I—"

As he choked on his own emotion, her gaze softened and she held out her hand. "Come here. Instead of slinging ultimatums and deals around, lie down. *Dressed*. Talk to me."

That, he could do. He stretched out next to her and laid his head on his bent arm as she caressed his temple, threading his hair through her fingers soothingly. It wasn't sexual. It was…nice.

"I don't know how to do this," he confessed. This was barely *his* room, let alone hers. But he knew he wanted to be in it. With her. She brought his entire house to life just by being there.

"I know. This isn't what I expected either." Tenderness bled through him as she let her hand trail down his jaw to rest against his neck. "Just cool your jets for a minute and stop trying to manipulate me with sex."

"That's not what…" Yeah. It was exactly what he'd been trying to do. Give-a-woman-enough-orgasms-and-she-stopped-looking-for-the-door kind of philosophy. That clearly wasn't working. "What can I do to convince you that I genuinely want to spend time with you?"

"Tell me." Her expression warmed. "I like to hear the truth. I also like to have choices."

As insights went, that was a big one. "I'm sensing you don't mean a choice between making you come with my fingers or my mouth."

She arched a brow. "Well, I can't lie. That's not really a choice because my answer is always both. No, I mean the fact that you don't like to give me any control when it comes to things like hiring a nanny. I worry that sex will cloud the issues."

Nodding, he filtered through what she was saying, her nonverbal cues and how to reconcile all of that with the aching need to keep her by his side. She clearly wasn't balking at his desire to sleep with her, just the fact that he'd been grasping the strings of his life too tightly.

Control was his default. It shielded his vulnerabilities. But she was saying he had to give or she'd walk.

"So hiring a nanny will help you feel like you've got choices?"

"Well, sure. Because it means you're not so stuck in your control-freak land." She smiled to soften the sting of her terminology but, honestly, she wasn't off base. The thought of losing her hurt far worse than being told the truth about himself.

"I don't want to hire a nanny." He held up a finger as her expression darkened. "But not because I'm trying to control you. Because I should be the one taking care of my son. I have a problem connecting with people. I don't want that to affect our relationship. If I'm all he knows, he'll come to me for a Band-Aid."

Her warm hands came up to cup his jaw as she re-settled on her pillow much closer to him than she had been. "Oh, honey. I didn't mean for that to be such a defining moment in your decisions as a father when I pointed that out."

"But it was. And it should have been." Because it felt natural and right, he tucked an arm around her waist, drawing her body up against his. They were still fully clothed but their position was by far the most intimate thing he'd ever done with anyone. "I needed to hear that. I've been reading up on how to wean a baby with formula allergies. I'm going to help you."

He should have started long before now but, as always, she saw him more clearly than he saw himself.

Something raw and tender exploded in the depths of her eyes. "Really? You'd do that for me?"

"Well, yes. Of course."

The gruff note in his voice wasn't due to uncertainty like usual. It was pure emotion. She was softening; he could feel it. Feel them binding together in this quiet moment that had nothing to do with sex. All because he'd loosened his grip. That was as much of a defining moment as anything else.

He needed McKenna to push him like this, to help him see that giving a woman choices didn't mean she'd immediately stomp on his emotions.

The sweet kiss she laid on his lips was just as raw and tender, sweeping through him with the force of a tidal wave, clear-cutting a path through his body straight to his heart.

"McKenna," he murmured against her lips, and she burrowed closer with a soft sigh, wedging a thigh between his as she deepened the kiss.

Everything shifted in the space of a moment. Urgency built, a yearning to touch, to revel, to feel.

To experience. Not to claim.

Reverently he took great handfuls of her hair. She moaned as he levered her head back to allow him access to taste her throat, the hollow behind her ear, her lobe, anything he could put his mouth on. Then he ran out of skin.

Stripping her became an act of adoration. Each button slipped free of its housing, revealing another slice of her, and he christened what he'd uncovered with a kiss. She shifted restlessly, her desire mounting so fast his head spun.

When he spread the fabric of her shirt wide, she arched her back, pushing closer to his mouth, so he indulged them both, laving at her exposed flesh and dipping under the fabric of her bra as he worked at getting her pants off. It was a much bigger trick when she was lying on the bed and he was facedown in her breasts, a problem he didn't mind solving the old-fashioned way—brute strength. He picked her up by the hips and tore off the offending garments until she was fully bared.

He took a moment to let his gaze sweep over her, lingering at her breasts, hard nipples taut and gorgeous.

Her lungs audibly hitched as he reached out to stroke. Looked like she wasn't of a mind to bolt or breathe. That worked for him.

Ripping out of his clothes in record time, he resettled next to her on the bed, stroking whatever he could reach and murmuring nonsense about how beautiful she was. His brain was a tangle of wants, needs and absolutes, all of which began and ended with McKenna. The more he stroked, the higher the urgency climbed until he was nearly writhing as much as she was.

Because he couldn't hold out much longer, he knelt to take her over the crest the first time, gratified that he could sense exactly where to put his tongue to wring the tightest, strongest orgasm from her. What a total high to discover he could use his empathy in such a pleasurable way.

She gasped and moaned her way down from the peak, eagerly collapsing against his body as he pulled her into his arms.

"More," she croaked, and he couldn't hear that enough.

But this time he needed to be with her, soaring alongside. In a flash, he had himself sheathed and pushing inside to bathe in the bliss of her body as she accepted him to the hilt, so hot and ready for him that it took his breath.

"Yes," she cried and wound her hips in a slow circle, drawing him deeper still until he was lost in the sensation. "You feel amazing."

That didn't begin to describe the way they mated spiritually as well as physically. But he wanted more and wasn't going to stop until he got it.

"Imagine how much better this would feel if we didn't have to use condoms," he risked saying aloud.

He wanted to spill his seed in her, to see if he could sense the moment when she conceived. They'd hold hands as they took a pregnancy test together, waiting with breathless anticipation to confirm what he already knew in his soul would be a plus sign.

The ghosts that had haunted him since Lacey would finally vanish.

McKenna half laughed and let her head tip back as he nuzzled her neck. "Yeah, if this is how the next few months are going to be, I should definitely see about a more permanent form of birth control."

Cold invaded his chest and he willed it back. He had months to convince her of what was happening here but, for the first time, everything seemed to be falling into place. No longer would he live in fear of his family being ripped apart by forces beyond his control.

He changed the subject by hefting her thigh higher on his hip and driving her into the heavens a second time before following her into the white light of release.

McKenna was his and he was not letting her go.

Days bled into a week and Desmond waited for McKenna to come up with another argument against living as husband and wife. But she didn't mention leaving again. At night she slept in his bed and during Conner's naps she sat in the corner of his workshop with her laptop, blazing through her online classes brilliantly.

It helped that he was right there to help, cheerfully stopping whatever he was doing—usually watching her out of the corner of his eye—to answer a question or to call up a resource from his knowledge bank.

By the middle of the second week Des didn't know what to call this euphoria. The only term he could think of was *happiness*. That had never been a goal of his and he'd never have thought it would be the result of getting what he'd asked for. But what else could this be?

True to his word, Desmond bought McKenna a breast pump and they worked together to get Conner used to taking his meals from a bottle. The baby's pediatrician proved a great help, suggesting they alternate a hypoallergenic formula with breast milk and gauge how he responded.

They kept careful watch, took notes, switched formulas as Conner reacted to the elements found in one or the other. McKenna hated the process, sometimes crying at night in Desmond's arms as the formula caused hives to break out on the baby's skin or he constantly spit up.

"I'm the most selfish person on the planet," she wailed, her distress eating through Des as he held her, stroking her hair, forehead, whatever he could get his hands on, though nothing stemmed the tide of her bleakness.

"No. This is an important step for him," he told her, quoting the doctor. "This is not just something we're doing so you can stop breast-feeding. We have to know what he's allergic to as he may have sensitivity to milk and soy his whole life."

Her tears soaked his shoulder, running down into the mattress below. "But I'm making him deal with this while he's still so tiny. I could breast-feed for a year. Two. People do it all the time."

"Sure you could. But at what cost?"

What kind of hell was this where he was forced into the role of convincing her that weaning was the right thing for everyone? Once she didn't have to feed the baby any longer, she could leave whenever she wanted. But he was slowly conceding that she needed options. He had to believe that when push came to shove, she'd choose Desmond and Conner. The concessions he'd made internally to get himself to this point were enormous. And so worth it.

"Sweetheart, listen to me." He levered up her chin with one finger until she met his gaze. "We're going to get through this. Together. I promised you."

She nodded and sighed, wiping at her leaking eyes. "Take my mind off it. Right now."

Her busy hands made short work of removing the drawstring pants he wore at night, leaving no room for him to misinterpret what she intended for him to do to grant her oblivion.

That was one thing he never minded letting her control. "Gladly."

In the morning they started all over again with the baby. Finally they settled on a rice-based formula that proved the least problematic.

After the third time feeding him without a reaction, McKenna glanced up at Desmond, her eyes bright as she held Conner to her shoulder, his little head listing against hers as she burped him. "I think this is it."

He nodded, afraid to upset the status quo with something as irreverent as speech. What would he say that could mark such a momentous, emotionally difficult occasion?

"It's kind of hard to believe I'm done," she said with a catch in her voice.

Conner made one of his baby noises and Des retrieved him from his mother in the same manner as he had almost since the moment of his son's birth. Only this time he did it to cover his own melancholy reaction to the passage of a ritual he'd grown to love.

Watching her breast-feed had been holy and beautiful. He'd never imagined he'd mourn the loss of it and regret that the last time he'd get to experience it had already happened. He'd have commemorated the occasion, or savored it longer, if he'd realized.

It was too late now. They'd reached the goal they'd set for themselves. Now McKenna could make a choice to stay with a clear head and no sense of obligation. He couldn't contemplate another scenario.

He cleared his throat. "You were fantastic. The whole time. So amazing. You sacrificed so much for our son. I—"

"Your son," she corrected. "Now that he's weaned, he can be totally your son again. I wasn't going to bring it up so soon, but while we're on the subject…let's talk about the divorce."

A roaring sound in Desmond's ears cut off the rest of her speech. "What are you talking about?"

She recoiled, her mouth still open. "Our agreement. The baby is weaned. The new semester starts in a couple of weeks. The timing is perfect for me to register. But I can't until I get the settlement money."

The baby squeaked as Desmond hefted him higher on his shoulder. Before he could have this conversation, Conner came first. He settled the baby into the bouncy seat that served as his primary residence when he wasn't asleep or being held. The stuffed giraffe hanging from the center bar caught the baby's attention and he kicked at it, his eyes tracking the trajectory of his foot.

When Des thought he could be a touch more civil, he turned back to McKenna who was still sitting in the rocker that she'd moved from her former bedroom to the one she now shared with him. He'd practiced how to approach the subject of her tuition but, honestly, he'd talked himself out of believing she'd bring it up.

The shock of her decision still hadn't faded. He swallowed as he absorbed her taciturn expression. Had the last few months meant nothing to her? He'd been falling into her, falling into the possibilities and he'd have sworn she was too. He couldn't be so out of touch that he'd mistaken that. No way was he alone in feeling these big, bright emotions.

"We have an agreement, Desmond." Her quiet voice cut through him.

"I'm aware," he said more curtly than he'd have liked, but his entire body had frozen. "I had hoped you'd reconsider."

"Reconsider what?" Her mouth dropped open as understanding dawned. "You thought I'd reconsider becoming a doctor?"

"No, of course not. I meant reconsider the divorce."

"You're not making any sense. Our agreement was that you'd file for the divorce once I gave birth. Then the formula allergy happened, but I always expected you to come through with your part of the promise." The tight cross of her arms over her still ample bosom drew his attention and that's when he noticed her hands were shaking. "Conner doesn't need me anymore. I have to go."

"I need you!" he burst out before thinking better of how such a statement gave her power to cut him open. "What do you think we've been doing here but building something permanent?"

Her eyelids fluttered closed. "No," she whispered. "We can't. That's not the deal."

"Screw the deal. I want you to stay." *I want you to feel the things I feel.*

"Forever? That's impossible!" She leaped to her feet as Conner started crying. "Now the baby is upset. I can't stand it when he's upset."

She couldn't stand it? The twin streams of black distress—Conner's and McKenna's—sank barbed hooks into Desmond's consciousness, wringing him out like a wet rag. Conflict was not his forte, especially when he hadn't been expecting it, and he did not handle it well.

McKenna hurried to the bouncy seat and scooped up the baby, cradling him as if she never meant to let him go. Didn't she see that she belonged here, holding Conner, caring for him? Didn't she see how much control Desmond had conceded to her, laying himself bare?

"I'm going to take Conner to Mrs. Elliot," she said firmly. "And then we're going to finish this conversation once and for all."

She wasn't gone long enough for his empathy to settle or his temper. The words in his head refused to gel into coherent sentences. He was losing her and he couldn't grab on any tighter.

"You can't leave," he told her grimly as she stopped a half foot over the threshold of his bedroom.

"Or what? You'll tie me to the bed?"

She let her head drop into her hands and her shoulders quaked for a beat. But then she lifted her face to reveal the deepest agony he'd ever seen. It bled through him, nearly crippling him with her grief.

"You can't keep me here. Don't you see how it's killing me to leave Conner? Sometimes I think everyone would be happier if I gave up my dreams. Everyone except me. I can't be a mother and a doctor. It's not in my makeup. I have to choose. And you have to give me that choice."

"I've given you choices," he growled even as he sensed that what she was saying was the rawest form of truth. These were things she felt deeply. Just as clearly, he got the sense she did care about him. Not enough to stay, though, and it was killing him. "Lots of them. This is not the same situation as before, when you needed to feel like you had some measure of control—"

"Yes it is!" Clearly bewildered, she shook her head. "Yes, you gave me choices with Conner and I appreciate them. But you were the one who held me when I cried and said it was important that I wean. That if I kept breast-feeding, it would have too high a cost. The cost would have been my medical degree. I thought you knew that. Agreed."

"The cost was to Conner," he stormed as the barb she'd sank into his heart cleaved through it with so much pain that it was too hard to sort out whether it was hers or his. "There was never a point where I thought we were weaning so you could leave us. I thought—" *You were happy here.*

That she was falling for him as he was falling for her. Hell, there was no falling left to do. He'd opened himself emotionally, sometimes against his will. Though, to be honest, the dominoes had started lining up the moment he'd spied her for the first time in that hospital bed.

"I gave birth to Conner for *you*. I wanted to give you a family. But that's all I can give." Wide-eyed, she surveyed him, her expression so stricken he nearly yanked her into his arms so he could soothe her. "I didn't expect you to be kind and amazing. It's hard for me to leave you, too. But this is what I have to do, Des."

She'd never called him that before. It was almost an endearment. In the final hour she'd conceded that she did have feelings for him. But her feelings didn't seem to matter.

"What do you want?" he whispered and bit back the flood of words he wished he could say. *I love you* being first and foremost. But he couldn't stand the thought of stripping himself even more emotionally bare.

"The choice," she answered simply. "File for divorce."

No. His soul cried out the word but he couldn't force it out of his throat.

"Don't you get it?" she continued when he didn't immediately agree. "You've supported me for over a year with a golden handcuff. I have nothing on my own. If you don't grant me the divorce, you've simply transferred your need to control things from one area to another. It's so hard for me to make this choice. I don't need the additional complexity of not being given one."

He nodded once. How ironic that his greatest life lesson would come at his own hands. He'd structured the agreement expressly so she had no control and, thus, no ability to hurt him. Instead she was following the agreement to the letter—and tearing him apart at the same time.

"You will still choose to become a doctor."

It was inevitable. Final. Incentives, orgasms, choices—his heart—none of this had been enough. If only he could lie to himself, he might be able to salvage the situation. But in the end, he knew the truth: he had to give her what she'd requested.

She nodded. "I have an obligation to myself. I've been working on saying goodbye this whole time. You have to let me do that."

Once again McKenna was pushing him out of his comfort zone, forcing him to look in the mirror. The family, the connections he'd been building, weren't a beautiful creation but a mirage. And if he didn't let her go, he'd be the monster instead of Dr. Frankenstein.

Ten

The university had walking paths, one of which ran right behind the little house Desmond had bought for McKenna. She'd expected to live in the dorm but he'd insisted she'd want the peace and quiet, so she'd accepted the key from the Realtor and kept her mouth shut when furniture arrived via a large van with the name of an exclusive store stenciled on the side.

This was what she'd asked for. Maybe not the part where the contents of the small house were worth more than her parents made in a year. But she did like the French country style that took shape around her, especially the functional desk she'd directed the movers to put in the dining room that would act as her office, where she'd study.

She had zero plans to entertain. Medical school was as demanding and difficult as she'd envisioned. Desmond had prepaid for her entire degree, citing the divorce might take too long to be finalized, thus he might as well pay for everything now.

One nice benefit to the house being off campus: she didn't feel compelled to take part in any of the campus activities and instead could focus on her class work, which she did, every night.

After three or four days she forced herself to drive to the grocery store in the practical Honda that Desmond had given her with express instructions to take it somewhere to have maintenance done every five thousand miles. Since she drove it less than ten miles a week, it would take about ninety years to reach that first milestone.

Of course, every time she got behind the wheel, she thought about driving it to Astoria and straight up the drive to the remote mansion along the Columbia River. What she'd do when she got there, she had no idea. This was her life now. The one she'd planned, envisioned, fought for.

The life she'd left behind at Desmond's was not hers, not real, not possible. How dare he act like that was a choice, like she could just stay there in the lap of luxury and let him take care of her while she gave up her dreams? While she ached to understand how he really felt about her without all the fantastic sex to muddle things?

The complications that had always been there had gotten worse. Mostly because Desmond had climbed into her heart and taken up residence when she wasn't looking. She had no idea what to do with that big, frightening reality.

What if she stuck around and the way she felt about him got bigger, scarier, more painful? Then she'd have no choices and a broken heart when he got bored with her and *then* filed the divorce papers. They were already signed, had been since before she'd conceived. The only thing he had to do was to take them to the court and it would be done. All part and parcel of their agreement. He had always had all of the power and no apparent qualms about throwing it around.

She'd demanded the choice and when he'd given it to her, she'd taken the opportunity to leave. It was the only way she could stay sane. After all, she ached to be with both Desmond and Conner past the point of reason, and it was killing her to be apart from them both, regardless of how necessary it was.

McKenna walked to her 9:00 a.m. pain management course on Monday, marking the first time in several days rain wasn't falling in a continual downpour. She'd tucked an umbrella into her bag because it was still Portland. Rain was predictable.

When she got to the building, one of the many guys in her class stood by the door. She started to brush past him but he stopped her with a nice smile.

"McKenna, right?"

Uh-oh. Was she being hit on? With Desmond, it was always completely obvious what had been on his mind, probably because it had been on hers, too. She missed that, missed his straightforwardness and wicked way with his hands. The ever-present ache in her chest got a whole lot worse as she drowned in memories.

And the guy was still smiling at her.

"Yes. I'm McKenna." She scouted her memory for his name but came up blank. There was a sea of faces on campus and none of them stuck out.

"It's Mark," he supplied easily with another nice smile, and she really wished she could smile back but she didn't want to encourage him.

"So, listen…" he continued. "I was wondering if you had some time this afternoon to go over the notes from last week. I missed a lecture because my daughter had an appointment."

"Oh. Um. Sure." Then what he'd said registered. "You have a daughter?"

"Yeah, she's great. My wife is a champ, taking care of her and working at the same time while I go to school. Do you have kids?"

She shook her head automatically. Conner wasn't hers and for all of Desmond's talk about keeping her around, there'd never really been any give on his part regarding that. He wasn't asking her to be his wife and his son's mother. Just the woman in his bed.

"So, about the notes?" Mark asked again, obviously interested in school not flirting. "I know it's an imposition, but I couldn't miss my daughter's appointment. It's a balance, but worth it, you know?"

No, she had no clue how someone could balance medical school and being a parent, let alone being married. "Sure, no problem."

They exchanged phone numbers and she sat through the class, half listening to the professor's long-winded lecture about chronic pain. Actually she had a pretty good idea how someone balanced medical school and life. She'd done it with Conner and her online class, with Desmond's help. And once she started thinking about how often the man she'd married had stepped up to assist her in all aspects of motherhood, classes—orgasms—she couldn't stop.

Somehow she got through the day, met up with Mark in the library to let him copy her notes, and wandered back home at the end of her last class. It had started to rain, no shock. But she didn't put up her umbrella, letting the light drizzle soak through her hair and clothes before she'd even noticed.

The phantoms she sometimes heard late at night were growing more active during the day. When she walked into the small house she could have sworn she heard Conner's baby noises wafting from the ceiling. Impossible. She shut the door and tried to care that she was dripping water all over the new throw rug covering the hardwood floor.

Her chest was on fire, aching to hold her baby, aching to be with her baby's father. But how could she stay under Desmond's thumb and never go to medical school? People who got sick like her grandfather needed an advocate in their corner. Someone to convince them that medical care in a hospital wasn't the evil they thought it was.

What choice did she really have?

Instead of sitting at her beautiful desk and working on her exhaustive list of assignments, she stripped out of her wet clothes and fell into bed, pulling the covers up to warm her chilled body. It didn't help. The cold penetrated straight to her core.

Choices. They haunted her. The ones she'd demanded. The ones she'd made.

It was the ultimate act of selfishness, wishing she could somehow have everything—the man she'd fallen in love with, the baby she'd never dreamed she'd want to keep *and* earn the medical degree she'd long believed was her path.

She slept fitfully only to wake at midnight, hot and uncomfortable under the pile of blankets. Throwing them off, she lay there naked, welcoming the cool air. No way would she go back to sleep now. And she had an assignment due in ten hours that she hadn't touched. Homework was the last thing she wanted to do. But this was the lot she'd chosen and she had to persevere.

When she booted up her laptop, the little blue icon popped up to let her know Desmond was online. Shocked, she stared at the message until it faded. He hadn't uninstalled the chat program? Had he found someone else to chat with? Also, geez. It was midnight. Was he up because he couldn't sleep? Maybe he'd been lying awake aching to hear someone else's heartbeat next to him in the bed. Doubtful. That was probably just her.

More likely Conner had woken up looking for a bottle. Oh, God. What if he was crying because he wanted his mother and was confused and frightened because she wasn't there? She had to check.

She'd clicked open the chat window and typed *hi* before fully thinking it through. If Desmond was in his workshop online, the odds were good that he wasn't taking care of Conner.

Too late now. He'd know instantly that she was messed up.

The message sat there blinking with no response and she nearly shut the program down. But then came the very cryptic return comment.

Desmond: *hi.*

Not capitalized, no punctuation. What the hell? Aliens had surely possessed the body of the man she'd married. And what was she supposed to say back? *Don't mind me, I'm just sitting here regretting everything I've ever done up to and including typing hi.*

McKenna: *Sorry to bother you.*

She nearly groaned. That had always been his line. For the first time she had the opposing perspective as the one doing the bothering. Except she'd never felt like it was a bother when he'd sought her out and, secretly, she'd always reveled in Desmond's attention.

Desmond: *Is everything okay?*

McKenna: *Peachy. Why do you ask?*

Desmond: *It's midnight.*

McKenna: *Yes, I noticed that. I was worried about you.*

She swore and tried to click on the message to recall it so she could correct that to *Conner* but he was already typing.

Desmond: *Don't do this. The adjustment is hard enough.*

She blinked. Don't do what? Be concerned? Talk to him via the chat tool he'd installed? The list of things he might be asking her to refrain from doing was long, but the better question was why he'd even say something like that.

McKenna: *What adjusting do you have to do? I'm the one in a new place.*

Desmond: *That was your choice. I have plenty to adjust to. I haven't ever been a father by myself. I miss you.*

Oh, God. She missed him, too. More than she could stand sometimes. Before she could react to that—unfreeze her fingers, breathe, *something*—he sent another message.

Desmond: *I can't do this with you.*

And then his status immediately flipped to offline. Stunned, she stared at the screen, her mind racing through that pseudo conversation, trying to pinpoint how she'd upset him. And it was very clear that she was indeed the problem. *I can't do this with you* sat there as a silent accusation, as cryptic as his initial unpunctuated and uncapitalized "hi."

Desmond missed her. It was right there in black surrounded by a blue bubble. She couldn't stop staring at it as she internalized that he might have a much bigger emotional stake in their relationship than she'd supposed. And if that was true, their conversation was far from over.

Oh, God. He missed her. He wasn't sleeping.

Everything but Desmond drained away.

She'd made a huge mistake.

Medical school could wait. Her family couldn't.

She yanked out her phone and texted him. Can't do what?

Let's see how you deal with that, Desmond H. Pierce. She'd entered him into an unbreakable social contract that required him to communicate back.

Except he didn't.

McKenna texted him again. Talk to me.

Thirty minutes later he hadn't complied. Furious with herself for caring whether or not she'd made a choice without all the facts, she stalked to the car and did the one thing she'd sworn never to do. She drove to Desmond's house. Ridiculous, stupid plan. But the panicky feeling in her stomach wouldn't stop and her brain kept turning over the fact that she hadn't really asked Desmond what her choices were when it came to what he was proposing.

The gate admitted her car without any trouble, a telling sign since it was automated to scan the license plate. Desmond had added her Honda to the list. Why?

At the front door she sent another text message: I'm outside. Come tell me to go away. She was going to get him to talk to her one way or another.

The front door cracked open less than thirty seconds later. Light spilled from the foyer, casting the man who'd opened it in shadow.

"It's late," Desmond rumbled into the darkness. "What are you doing here?"

His voice washed over her and her knees went a little weak. What *was* she doing here? She'd left this house because she hadn't seen any way to stay that wouldn't make her insane. Apparently sanity wasn't the goal because here she was again, begging for this man to talk to her, to change the tide, to force her to choose happiness instead of duty.

"Do you know what my favorite quality of yours is?" she asked instead of answering his question. Mostly because she didn't know how to answer it. Her mind was a riot of illogical, fragmented thoughts.

He sighed. "I must not have been clear. I don't want to talk to you. You made your choice to walk away. But I can make a choice to not let you back into my life."

Yes. She'd walked away. Toward a medical degree, which had long been her goal, but she'd also left something precious behind.

"That's my favorite quality of yours." She poked him in the chest because she couldn't stand not touching him a second longer. "You tell me exactly what's on your mind. Except when you don't. And that's what got me into the car, Desmond. Our conversation wasn't finished."

"Yes, it was, McKenna. There's nothing left to say."

The pain lacing his voice nearly stole her breath. She'd *hurt* him. *That* was why he kept shutting her down. While she'd been determined to get his attention strictly for her own peace of mind, he was trying to push her off because she'd hurt him.

She'd had no idea he cared that much.

What else didn't she know?

"I beg to differ," she countered softly and curled her hand around the open neckline of his button-down, holding tight and totally unsure if it was to keep him from fleeing or to keep her from dissolving into a little puddle at his feet. He wasn't dressed for bed, which might be the most telling of all. "I think there's a lot left to say. Like why you let me leave."

"Why I *let* you leave?" His short laugh raked through her. "I don't recall being given the choice. You demanded all the choices and then made your decision. What else could you possibly expect me to say other than I simply stepped out of your way."

It wasn't a question. It was a statement. A conviction. He'd done exactly as she'd told him to. Instead of having a conversation, she'd slung her own need for control around, forcing him to step back. What else might he have said if she'd shut her mouth?

She stared at him as he let her glimpse the anguish her choices had caused. Or maybe the things he felt were too strong to keep inside. "I expect you to tell me I'm selfish and I messed up. That I walked away from my family because of stupid pride and a need to do things my own way. As a result, I lost the two most important things that ever happened to me."

"That's not true." His gaze turned indignant as he argued with her. "Medical school was always important. You're incredibly intelligent, personable. Driven. You'll make an excellent doctor."

That curled up in her chest in tight, warm ball. "That's the nicest thing anyone's ever said to me."

He shrugged. "That's why I stepped out of the way and smoothed your path. I owed it to you, as you pointed out time and time again. I let you leave because it was never my right to force you to stay."

Her heart cracked open, spilling out love and pain and adoration and regret. He really did get it, displaying a wealth of understanding and willingness to change, which she'd failed to value. She did now.

"You couldn't have forced me to stay. Instead you set me free. That one act allowed me the time and distance to see where I wanted to land. It's here. With you. And

Conner. I made a mistake." Desperate to make him un-derstand, she gripped his shirt tighter. "Please tell me it's not too late to pick up the pieces of our marriage."

He shook his head. "It's too late, McKenna. I can't let you go again."

"But that's not what I'm asking you to do," she whis-pered. "I'm not going anywhere. I choose to stay this time."

The short, simple phrase bled through Desmond's chest, slicing open new wounds as it burrowed toward his heart seeking asylum. "You can't say things like that."

Not now. Not after he'd already reconciled that his family had been torn apart. He'd cataloged all the emo-tion, analyzed everything that had gone wrong and ar-rived at the conclusion that he wasn't cut out for this madness.

Some people were natural artists, others were gifted musicians. Desmond's talent was trusting a woman with life-altering power. And when the woman exercised that power, she dug big, gaping holes in his soul that would never be filled. Loneliness and isolation plagued him and he lacked the ability to resolve either.

"Why?" she asked. "Is the invitation to stay rescinded? I didn't hear a time limit attached."

"Please don't do this." It was too much for him to breathe her in and let his senses get that one long taste of her. "You're enrolled in medical school. The die is cast."

"Then why haven't you filed for the divorce yet?" she countered quietly.

That nearly broke him. She wanted truth?

"Because you're still my wife, no matter what," he admitted.

Her expression veered wildly between extremes and finally settled on tenderness. "Yes. I am. And I want a chance to see what that looks like when we both give up our need for control."

"I've already done that once, McKenna. Never again." Harsh. Although still just the plain truth. If nothing else, he'd learned that life did not go as planned simply because he willed it to be so, but he could certainly curtail the damage by never opening himself up again. He'd spent years hiding, which suited him fine. Nothing had changed.

"I hurt you." At his curt nod, both of her hands slid up his arms to squeeze his shoulders and her touch almost knocked his composure away like a cat amused by a ball of yarn. "I'm sorry. I didn't honor how difficult that was for you, to give me the choice to leave. I made the wrong decision because I couldn't see myself as anything other than a doctor. I'm not good at failing and I didn't handle the dynamic between us well."

"What dynamic?" he couldn't help but ask and then wished to bite off his tongue. He might as well come out and ask if she'd developed feelings for him that she'd yet to share. Pathetic. Hadn't he learned his lesson? Women were treacherous.

"The one where I wanted to stay but couldn't see how that would work."

Her warm hands hadn't moved from his shoulders and he leaned into her touch, craving it and cursing himself for the craving at the same time. But he'd long ceased looking for a way to resist her because that was the very definition of insanity—doing the same thing over and over again without better results. Resisting her was impossible.

"The one where I fell into your world and couldn't

break free," she whispered. "You opened your door and eventually your body, your mind, your heart, and I... loved all of it. Especially your mind."

"Again, very short list of people in that category," he countered, not at all shocked that the gruff note in his voice perfectly matched the insurrection of emotion exploding through his chest. "If you wanted to stay, why didn't you?"

"I'm selfish and stubborn, or didn't you get the memo?" she asked wryly, and he refused to smile, though it was clear she'd meant for him to.

"You're the least selfish person I know. Everything you've done since I've met you has been for someone else. You'll be a great doctor," he repeated because the point couldn't be made clearly enough. He couldn't stand the thought of her resenting him for standing in her way. "You're also an amazing mother and the only wife I could imagine letting into my world."

Her eyelids fluttered closed as she processed that and, when she opened them, the clearest sense of hope radiated from her eyes. "You've always seen me as more than I do. I didn't believe in myself nearly as much as you did. I never thought I could be more than a doctor. It was too hard to concentrate when I had Conner and you right down the hall."

That was definitely something they had in common. He'd been unable to focus on anything other than her since that first moment she'd invaded his workshop without invitation, barging into his consciousness without fear, and he'd never been able to let her go in all the days since.

Even this one. Case in point. They were having a conversation at one in the morning instead of sleeping. Nothing worked to exorcise her from his mind, her scent from his head and the ghost of her in his bed.

"Then I have to ask. Did it get easier when you left?" If it had, he'd move in an instant to somewhere he could concentrate without her invading his everything.

"No." She smiled and it grabbed hold of his lungs, heart—hell, all of his internal organs at once. "I'm afraid it only got worse. So the problem is that I can't be a doctor without you. I can't be a mother without Conner. So here I am. Now what?"

Oh, no. She wasn't throwing that ball back in his court. "That's not my choice. It can't be."

"Then that makes it mine by default. So you're stuck with me," she informed him loftily. "The only thing is that you have to forgive me for wasting your tuition money. It's too late in the semester to get a refund."

"You're quitting school?" Incredulous, he stared at her. "You can't do that. *Why* would you do that? That's the worst possible choice you could make."

"Please, Desmond. Don't lock yourself away from me. I'm begging you for another chance." She shook him fiercely as if trying to knock that chance loose by sheer force. "Are you listening to what I'm saying? I'm not leaving again. I can't. I love you too much."

So many wondrous emotions radiated from her skin and burrowed under his, winnowing toward his soul too fast for him to catch it all or block it somehow. Too late. She swept away the shadows that had crawled inside him since she'd left.

"You shouldn't," he countered as his heart knit back together so fast he went light-headed. "I'm difficult to love—"

"Shut up. Stop saying stuff like that. What's difficult is when I try to stop loving you." She laughed and one tear slipped down her face as she shared what was inside her. "I don't know how to be in love. It's scary. It has no way for me to control it. Instead of telling you this, I left."

"To be a doctor. You had a dream that I wasn't a part of. I respected that even as it tore me apart."

"I know." Her head bowed for a brief moment. "That's what finally broke me, I think. That you were willing to sacrifice for me in spite of everything."

"I still am," he admitted gruffly. "It's the least I can do for what you sacrificed to give me Conner. Please don't give up medical school."

"It's okay, I have something better. A family."

That was the part that broke *him*. He swept her into his embrace and clung, scarcely able to believe he was holding her again.

"I love you," he murmured, unable to stop the flow of words. "So much. Too much to let you make such an ir-revocable choice. There's absolutely no reason you can't keep going to school. I'll move to the house near cam-pus. Tomorrow. Conner and I will take care of you while you become a doctor."

"You'd do that?" His shoulder muffled her broken whisper but he heard the question inside the question regardless.

"Of course I would. I'm already the nanny. Why not the househusband? I would live in a shack on the side of the road if that's what you wanted. As long as you were in it." He tipped up her chin to lay his lips on hers in what was only the first of many kisses to come. "This is just a house where I build things. If I have a family, I've al-ready built the most important creation of my life. Any-thing else is just icing on the cake."

She smiled through her tears. "That sounds like an easy choice then."

"None of this is supposed to be hard. I told you, all you have to do is lie there and command me to do your will."

"I don't understand why you would do all of this for me."

Because to her he wasn't a beast. He wasn't the weird, awkward kid no one wanted to sit by. She'd chosen *him*. That was awe inspiring. And probably the only thing that could have enticed him out of his reclusive fortress designed to keep out the world.

But it turned out he didn't have to. McKenna had brought the world to him.

"Also not hard. I love you and you gave me Conner. The real question is what I could possibly do to repay you for the miracle of our son. I still don't know. But I'm going to spend a very long time trying to answer that. If you'll allow me to rip up the divorce papers."

She nodded furiously. "I'd like to burn them. In the fireplace. So I know for sure they're gone forever."

"Done. Except you'll have to wait until morning because I plan to be very busy between now and then." He couldn't stand to let her go as he led her toward the stairs and the bedroom upstairs that had been cold and empty without her.

"Oh, what did you have in mind?" she asked saucily with an intrigued expression that wasn't difficult to interpret. She was game for whatever he could envision, which excited him to no end. He had a great imagination.

"Sleep," he said with a laugh. "I haven't done that since you left and I'm looking forward to many nights of recovery."

She scowled without any real heat. "Sleep? I drove all the way from Portland to tell you my life is meaningless without you and you want to go to bed to *sleep*?"

"Maybe in a little while. I have some lost time to make up for first." And then he claimed his wife's lips in a kiss that was the second miracle he'd experienced in his life. He couldn't wait to find out what the next one would be.

Epilogue

McKenna swept Conner up for a hug, kissing him soundly on the cheek, but the precocious, dark-haired three-year-old was having none of that. He squirmed out of his mother's grip and ran off to play with Mark Hudson's daughter, the only other little person at the university's graduation ceremony.

Desmond smiled at his wife as she paused to exchange hugs with Mark's wife, Roberta. They'd socialized with the couple occasionally as Mark and McKenna worked through residency, but more often than not, Roberta and Desmond traded babysitting duty to give the other household a break during the grueling three years of medical school their respective spouses had endured.

It was over now. They'd both graduated with honors and earned their medical degrees.

"Dr. Pierce," Des murmured in his wife's ear as she paused at the reception table for a bottle of water. Happiness radiated from her, nearly dripping from her skin. "I've been waiting a long time to call you that."

She grinned and leaned into his embrace, which worked for him because that was where he wanted her. Always.

"Only because you're tired of being the only Dr. Pierce in our house."

Home. Not a house. They lived in a home, barely twelve hundred square feet worth, but he loved it. Had watched Conner take his first steps in the living room. Kissed McKenna at the dining room table as she'd applied for her second year of medical school, her residency, her name change.

"Perhaps," he conceded with a nod.

But more to the point, they'd agreed that once she'd earned her diploma, they'd throw caution to the wind and see what happened when McKenna stopped taking her birth control pills. For three years he'd been patient, letting her focus on medical school as promised.

She'd graduated. Tonight was his turn.

"Come with me, Dr. Pierce," he growled as the festivities wound down. "The Hudsons are taking Conner home with them for the night. You're all mine."

"Why, Dr. Pierce, whatever do you have in mind?" McKenna shifted her long dark hair off one shoulder as she contemplated him with a saucy smile. "A little graduation party for two?"

"Yes."

She laughed and the clear sound trilled through him. "Glad I'm not a big fan of suspense. You're as transparent as glass."

Still her favorite quality of his, as she told him often. Good thing. Saved him a lot of trouble explaining things.

"Then it should be no surprise what I've got planned. Kiss your son and let's go."

He waited impatiently as she gave Roberta a few instructions, including the one about making sure Conner had his elephant, Peter, to sleep with. And then, finally, he got her snuggled into his embrace for the five-minute walk to their little clapboard house that had not one robotic humanoid inside its walls.

The remote mansion on the river sat untouched, a monument to the man he'd once been and never would be again. But he couldn't bear to sell it because it was still the place where he'd fallen in love with his wife, where he'd first made love to her. One day, Conner might want to live there and have access to all the luxuries. But for now, all they needed was each other.

Once she cleared the door, McKenna turned in his arms, trapping him against the wood. There was no place on earth he'd rather be. His arms were full of light, desire, happiness. So many emotions raced through her, he could hardly sense one before another took over.

"Tonight's the night," he told her. "If this isn't what you want, you should tell me now."

He really didn't have to clarify. But it was always nice to hear her voice.

"Which part?" she murmured against his throat as she nibbled his skin. "Where I command you to strip me naked and have your wicked way with me?"

"The part where I get you pregnant," he corrected, his voice so rough with need it was a wonder she understood him. "Finally."

But then, she'd never had a problem understanding him.

"I've been waiting three long years for this, Des." She smiled, her hands busy unbuckling his belt. "I want to conceive your baby and, alongside you, watch it grow in my tummy. I want a brother or sister for Conner. A legacy that has everything to do with love."

That sounded perfect to Desmond. "Then come here and let me love you."

He swept his wife into his arms and took her to bed where the only thing that stood between them was skin. He did his best to savor each moment, to pay attention to the subtle cues so he could pinpoint the exact moment of conception. But in the end there was too much going on and he let the sheer pleasure of her reign supreme because what else mattered?

"You know it might take more than one try to conceive," she murmured later as they lay content in each other's arms.

"I'm nothing if not ready, willing and able to try as many times as I need to."

Smiling so wide it hurt his face, he stroked her arm. A baby would be amazing. A fantastic addition to the family he'd built, that they continued to build every day. McKenna had drawn him out from behind his curtain into the real world. And they had lots of opportunities to perfect the art of baby making. They should probably start over right now.

* * * * *

LET'S TALK
Romance

For exclusive extracts, competitions and special offers, find us online:

 MillsandBoon

 @MillsandBoon

 @MillsandBoonUK

 @MillsandBoonUK

Get in touch on 01413 063 232

MILLS & BOON

THE HEART OF ROMANCE

A ROMANCE FOR EVERY READER

MODERN — Prepare to be swept off your feet by sophisticated, sexy and seductive heroes, in some of the world's most glamourous and romantic locations, where power and passion collide.

HISTORICAL — Escape with historical heroes from time gone by. Whether your passion is for wicked Regency Rakes, muscled Vikings or rugged Highlanders, awaken the romance of the past.

MEDICAL — Set your pulse racing with dedicated, delectable doctors in the high-pressure world of medicine, where emotions run high and passion, comfort and love are the best medicine.

True Love — Celebrate true love with tender stories of heartfelt romance, from the rush of falling in love to the joy a new baby can bring, and a focus on the emotional heart of a relationship.

Desire — Indulge in secrets and scandal, intense drama and sizzling hot action with heroes who have it all: wealth, status, good looks…everything but the right woman.

HEROES — The excitement of a gripping thriller, with intense romance at its heart. Resourceful, true-to-life women and strong, fearless men face danger and desire - a killer combination!

To see which titles are coming soon, please visit

millsandboon.co.uk/nextmonth

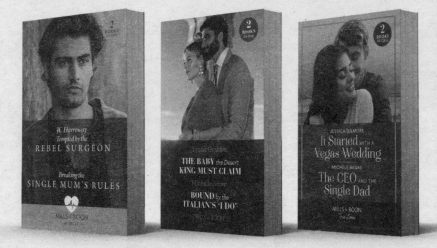

MILLS & BOON
MEDICAL
Pulse-Racing Passion

Set your pulse racing with dedicated, delectable doctors in the high-pressure world of medicine, where emotions run high and passion, comfort and love are the best medicine.

MILLS & BOON

HEROES

At Your Service

Experience all the excitement of a
gripping thriller, with an intense romance
at its heart. Resourceful, true-to-life
women and strong, fearless men face
danger and desire – a killer combination!

MILLS & BOON

HISTORICAL

Awaken the romance of the past

Escape with historical heroes from time gone by.
Whether your passion is for wicked Regency Rakes,
muscled Viking warriors or rugged Highlanders,
indulge your fantasies and awaken the
romance of the past.

JOIN US ON SOCIAL MEDIA!

Stay up to date with our latest releases, author news and gossip, special offers and discounts, and all the behind-the-scenes action from Mills & Boon...

 @millsandboon

 @millsandboonuk

 facebook.com/millsandboon

 @millsandboonuk

It might just be true love...

GET YOUR ROMANCE FIX!

Get the latest romance news, exclusive author interviews, story extracts and much more!